PRAISE FOR *ESCAPING EXODUS*

"Don't be alarmed—that dizzy pleasurable sensation you're experiencing is just your brain slowly exploding from all the wild magnificent world-building in Nicky Drayden's *Escaping Exodus*. I loved these characters and this story, and so will you."

—Sam J. Miller, Nebula Award–winning author of
The Art of Starving and *Blackfish City*

"A sweeping, smart, stunning story that dazzles brighter than a star system . . . making *Escaping Exodus* a true gem to be treasured."

—*Booklist* (starred review)

"Drayden's new novel builds on the amazing strengths she's shown before. If you can imagine a feminist, Afrocentric, queer Heinlein juvenile, with a strong discussion of class politics, then you might get close to what she's doing here. I don't think I could have imagined such a book before reading this one. This is something I've been missing."

—*Locus*

"Everything about the Afrofuturistic world-building is exquisitely imaginative, and the characters are three-dimensional, occasionally offering flashes of dark humor. The spacefaring beast is a marvel, containing a whole ecosystem with microclimates and other organisms living within it alongside humans. Although the relationship between the two young women is perpetually hampered by circumstance, as most good love stories are, it's palpable and vibrant."

—*Kirkus Reviews*

"*Escaping Exodus* is another fine entry from a clearly talented writer. Read if you ever wondered what it would be like if the *Millennium Falcon* decided to live inside that asteroid worm."

—*Lightspeed*

PRAISE FOR *THE PREY OF GODS*

**Winner of the Compton Crook Award and the
RT Reviewers' Choice Award (Science Fiction)**

"Fans of Nnedi Okorafor, Lauren Beukes, and Neil Gaiman better add *The Prey of Gods* to their reading lists! This addicting new novel combines all the best elements of science fiction and fantasy."

—*RT Book Reviews* (June 2017 Seal of Excellence—Best of the Month)

"This dense and imaginative debut is . . . a book like no other, with a diverse cast that crosses the spectrum of genders and races, and a new idea (or four) in every chapter."

—*B&N Sci-Fi & Fantasy Blog*
(The Best Science Fiction & Fantasy Books of 2017 So Far)

"Drayden's delivery of all this is subtly poignant and slap-in-the-face deadpan—perfect for this novel-length thought exercise about what kinds of gods a cynical, self-absorbed postmodern society really deserves. Lots of fun."

—*New York Times Book Review*

"Thanks to a rip-roaring story and Drayden's expansive imagination, it all coheres into the most fun you can have in 2017."

—Book Riot (Best Books of 2017)

"One of the biggest pleasures of this book is the plurality of its voices and story lines, and the way Nicky Drayden skips and weaves between them. . . . It's a book full of energy and momentum, strange wit and sensitivity. It is a LOT. And it is wonderful."

—Vulture (The 10 Best Fantasy Books of 2017)

PRAISE FOR *TEMPER*

ESCAPING EXODUS: SYMBIOSIS

ESCAPING EXODUS: SYMBIOSIS

A NOVEL

NICKY DRAYDEN

HARPER Voyager

An Imprint of HarperCollins Publishers

ESCAPING EXODUS: SYMBIOSIS. Copyright © 2021 by Nicole Duson. All rights reserved. Printed in the United States of America. No part of this book may be used or reproduced in any manner whatsoever without written permission except in the case of brief quotations embodied in critical articles and reviews. For information, address HarperCollins Publishers, 195 Broadway, New York, NY 10007.

HarperCollins books may be purchased for educational, business, or sales promotional use. For information, please email the Special Markets Department at SPsales@harpercollins.com.

Harper Voyager and design are trademarks of HarperCollins Publishers LLC.

FIRST EDITION

Designed by Paula Russell Szafranski

Frontispiece and interior art © Fernando Cortes / Shutterstock

Library of Congress Cataloging-in-Publication Data has been applied for.

ISBN 978-0-06-286775-9

21 22 23 24 25   LSC   10 9 8 7 6 5 4 3 2 1

To Dana,
Eternally faithful,
Lover of belly scratches

CONTENT NOTES

This story contains depictions of body horror and pregnancy horror (thematic).

contents

ESCAPING EXODUS: SYMBIOSIS

interlude

DOKA

Of Catching Fish and Releasing Feelings

My hands throb, pricked with dozens of splinters of my own doing. I am familiar with neither woodworking nor boat making, so I'm counting on a major favor from my ancestors that this vessel I've carved won't sink as soon as I'm on board. I bite back the pain and push the boat out onto the loamy river. The shore is littered with old, half-buried lamps, casting a warm red light that fails to pierce the dense fog lingering along the walls of the cavern. Thoughts echo in my mind as I draw upon non-existent instincts from a single fishing trip my will-mother had taken me on when I was a young boy.

The throttle fish had been plentiful back then, and it took us only twenty silence-filled minutes to catch one—me tossing fistfuls of chum over the side while Mother waited for one of them to swim up a little too close to the boat. She'd reached down and grabbed it with her own two hands but hadn't smiled when she'd caught it. I'd imagined she'd be proud, but instead, she wiped away a lone tear. It was odd seeing my will-mother lost in her emotions like that. Later that day, when I'd worked up the nerve to question her about her reaction, she claimed the tear to be backsplash from the river.

But reports now indicate that there hasn't been a throttle fish found in weeks. Nets have been cast, over and over, pulling back nothing but thorny clumps of river weeds. My constituents are breathing down my back, urging me that something needs to be done about it, though they dodge my questions as to why the fish are so important. We've got hundreds of them, probably thousands living in the bogs all around our homestead. *Won't those do?* I ask them, but they just stare at me, mouths pinched, eyes wide and expectant, acting as though I'm capable of performing miracles just because I've poured enough resources into getting the void leaks patched up and have stopped the flooding that was drowning our crops. Well, I don't have any miracles to offer them, only stubbornness, courage, and hope.

This easily accessible cavern is likely devoid of fish, so I steer my craft toward one of the ducts, getting caught up by the river's current. I'd made the boat from a piece of discarded gall husk, smooth and rounded on the bottom, just large enough to accommodate me and my fishing equipment. It's fibrous and rough on the inside, and sharp edges poke through my clothes though I'd done my best to file them down. Of course, I could have taken one of the boats reserved for me, our clan's matriarch. They're sleek, comfortable, and probably most important, watertight—but the entire fleet is carved from bone, and I couldn't stand to look at them, much less navigate one. Nor had I been able to wear the leather gloves that would have protected my hands from getting all chewed up and full of splinters. I'd gone most of my life without wondering where that bone and leather had come from, or at what cost. Now that we know this vast creature in which we've built our home has feelings, wants, needs . . . it's impossible to ignore. I guess some part of me feels that I deserve to suffer in kind.

The boat shifts, tugged along by the flow of the river. I carefully lean to one side and let my arm hang over, drawing a meandering trail in the foam. The black grit sticks to the tips of my fingers, and I roll it back and forth until I've got a little ball of putty, shaping it into the likeness of a small worm. I slip it onto my hook and weighted string, and then let it drag behind me, dredging along the bottom of the river, hoping that there's something swimming down there in the hidden depths, as eager and desperate as I am.

I relax and keep an eye on the bright red buoy tied to my line, trying not to think about the fate of my people resting in these nicked-up hands. In these few short months since our near exodus, I've already turned our people's lives upside-down, taking away their creature comforts, their livelihoods, and much of their way of life in order to stabilize our deteriorating Zenzee. And it's working. Our efforts are paying off.

But to Seske, my wife—at least for the next few hours—I haven't gone nearly far enough. I'd given in to her demands at first, stopping the gravitational spin for a while so that our Zenzee could heal, despite the toll null gravity would take on our people. I agreed to tear down homes and businesses to return the bone we'd used as construction material to where we'd stolen it from. But it was never enough for Seske. She wanted to see the whole system burn. After all the hurt she went through, I can't say I blame her. But still, I walk upon a knife's edge, knowing if I take a step too far, even my biggest supporters will turn on me, and we could lose everything. So maybe I turn my cheek sometimes, letting our people cling to questionable rituals and outdated traditions in these trying times.

And I think Seske hates me for that.

She'll be on her way to the Senate chambers soon. Technically, that's where I should be headed as well, so we can hear the Senate's decision on whether or not we can annul our marriage without interfering with my title of matriarch. And I *would* be there right now, if it weren't for the importance of hunting for throttle fish deep in these eerily quiet bile ducts, all alone and determined to do the impossible for our people.

Maybe it sounds as if I'm running away from my problems, but I'm not.

I swear to the ancestors, I'm not.

Previously explored territory edges into something else as I move downstream. Ley lights strung up from the ceiling of the duct become more spread out, and then they're gone altogether. The only light now comes from the lamp mounted at the stern of the boat, casting menacing shadows along the walls of the duct.

The fog thickens as I venture deeper. If there's a chance of there being throttle fish, it's here in these unexplored branches of the duct. Something knocks against the side of the boat. My heart jumps up into my throat. That was too big of a thump to have been caused by a throttle fish. At least I hope so. Even the small ones back home creep me out—those dour faces with too-human eyes, needle-sharp teeth, and insatiable hunger . . .

Suddenly, this idea of mine seems foolhardy. I shouldn't have snuck off like this. It was selfish of me. Our people couldn't tolerate another change in power right now, another matriarch lost, just as we're starting to make headway.

I need to get back home. So I tie my fishing string on the boat, then grab my oars to press back against the current, which is steadily picking up speed.

Just then, my buoy starts dancing. Something has caught the line. It tugs hard, moving the boat with it. My too-shallow bow dips down and is close to taking on water. Maybe I have some instincts after all, because before I know it, I've got a knife in my hand and I cut the line before it can pull me down, too. The whole length of string disappears into the murk below, buoy and all, and the bow pops back up.

I start paddling back in earnest now, but my right oar is yanked from my grip. I barely can process what's happened before I look over the edge, seeing nothing but a ripple left on the water's surface.

The boat rocks.

Rocks again.

And again.

Like something is knocking and wants in.

"Hello?" I call out, my warbling voice absorbed by the fleshy walls surrounding me. My ley light starts to flicker. It needs another shake to remix the chemicals inside, but I dare not move toward it. The last thing I need is to offset the balance of this boat.

There is silence. The waters calm. My buoy pops back up from the murky depths, bobbing gleefully as if there's still something on the line. Not ominous at all, I tell myself. Tales of the deadly creatures that lurk in the bile ducts are just stories told to frighten children into behaving, after all.

Still, I wish I had never come here. I even find myself wishing I were standing before the Senate this very moment, shoulder to shoulder with Seske, ready to hear our fate. It scares me imagining what will come next between us if the annulment goes through, but right now, what's at the end of that fishing line scares me a little bit more.

And yet, it beckons me.

What if it's not a hideous monster out to slash my throat and drain me of my life? What if it *is* a throttle fish? What if this is my chance to prove to my doubters that I am capable of so much more than they expect of me?

I bite my lip, steel my nerves, then use my remaining oar to row the boat slowly toward the buoy. When I'm close enough, I pull it back in. Dangling from the hook is indeed a throttle fish, small . . . not much more than a juvenile. Probably not yet fertile, but it will have to do. A wave of delight washes over me. This proves that they are not all gone. I place it into a jar filled with river water and screw the lid on tight. We will revitalize the rivers from this lone specimen. And as for whatever else is out there . . .

My lost oar floats next to the boat too, now, cracked in half. The claw marks gouged into the wood are unmistakable. What could have caused it, I have no idea. And I'm pretty sure I'd like to never find out. I paddle harder.

A noise comes from back upstream, like a throaty gargle. I raise my remaining oar up as if it's a weapon. Like it would be able to protect me from whatever lurks beneath these greasy, gritty waters.

"Weeeeeelllll . . ." The voice comes from beyond the bend, a sustained note, gruff and off-key. "As the river bends, so does my will, we sail the mighty ducts, till the waters doth still. Deep down she goes, and when the waters turn black, kiss your family goodbye, cause there's no turning back!"

The soft glow of a ley light comes next, and then I see her—Baradonna, my personal security guard, as she steers one of the boats from my fleet, poised and steady, as if she's been sailing the choppy waters of the bile ducts her whole entire life. The boat gleams, sickle-scaled ivory polished to a high shine, so slick that none of the water's foam sticks to it. My teeth start to ache, worrying over how our Zenzee had suffered when these sections of bone were stolen from her body. We have worked to mend and replace what we can, but the boat was carved from a solid chunk of bone, now too mutilated and manipulated to salvage and graft it back.

"There you are, my naughty little woodlouse," Baradonna coos at me, a concerned bend on her brow. She thinks herself to be more of my mother than a guard, like I need another of those. She's not much older than me, a few years at best, but she wears her hair up in a high crown of elaborate twisted knots and holds her weight like a true matron—a large, stocky build with wide hips, and perfect, pendulous breasts thinly veiled by the sheerness of her uniform. She definitely looks the part of someone formidable enough to serve such an auspicious role.

"Call me Matris Kaleigh. Or Doka, if that's too hard for you," I grate at her. We've been over this a hundred times. I honestly don't know why I bother. "And why are you still spying on me? I told you I wanted some privacy."

She aims her boat at mine, not bothering to slow down or acknowledge my words at all. Our hulls collide with a horrid smack. She latches my boat to hers, then opens her arms, as though she's expecting an embrace. I fold my arms in response and fix her with my stare.

"No warm welcome for your favorite Baradonna?" she sasses me. "The way I see it, I probably saved your life."

"Saved my life? I was already returning on my own."

"*Saved your life*," she presses, as if she's keeping a running tally of the times she's rescued me from myself. This isn't the first time. "What possessed you to venture out here all on your own?"

Sighing, I raise the jar, the throttle fish swimming around, aggravated. Little clawed fists knock against the glass. "They said they were extinct in the wild. I've proven them wrong."

"You don't have to prove anything to them. The environmental researchers should be out here scavenging in these forsaken bile ducts, not you. Why don't you let them do the work themselves? If they see you going behind them with every aim to prove them wrong, they're going to start wondering why you created the team in the first place."

"If they want my trust, then they need to do a more thorough job," I say, then bite my lip. I'm not sure how much of the blame is the team's incompetence and how much of it is them quietly rebelling against having a man sitting in the matriarch's throne. There are so many people who are itching for me to fail, which is why I can't let simple oversights like these go unchallenged. "I'll have them all strung up by their thumbs. We'll see how thorough they are next time."

"Isn't that a bit harsh?" Baradonna asks. "I know you're in a hurry to make a name for yourself, but it can take time to establish rapport. Trust is such a fragile thing. It's grown and sown, not commanded and demanded."

She's right, of course. It was my frustration talking. I take a few deep breaths to calm my nerves. "No thumb hangings," I say, trying to ignore the fact that I sound like a petulant child. "This time. But they need to know how serious this is. We need to know this Zenzee inside and out. Every crack. Every crevice."

"Do you want ol' Baradonna to sweet talk them? You know I can lay on the sap."

I shake my head. "Just let me borrow an oar." The least she

can do is spare me my dignity and let me row out of here on my own volition.

"I'll do no such thing," Baradonna says, reaching for my hand. "Please, Doka, come on over into my boat. Let me row you home."

"I don't need you to rescue me," I huff.

"I think you do," she says, pointing at my one oar.

"You think just because I'm a man, I can't figure out how to do this on my own?"

"Nobody is thinking anything like that, especially me. I'm asking to let me rescue you because your boat is taking on water," she says with one brow cocked. I look down and notice the crack in the hull, water slowly seeping in and forming a pool at the bow. A crack *she* caused by ramming her boat into mine. I've probably got ten minutes left if I'm lucky, not nearly long enough to paddle back upstream with one oar. I look at Baradonna's sleek, bone-carved craft and frown.

I swallow my misgivings and step over into Baradonna's boat. She pulls me into her bosom and nearly strangles me with her embrace. "I don't ever want you sneaking off like that again, do you hear me?"

"Yes, ma'am," I say, my voice muffled by her flesh. The Senate probably thought they were pulling a fast one on me, assigning the most junior Accountancy Guard auditor to watch over my safety, but what Baradonna lacks in experience, she makes up for in heart. And I do feel safer in her presence. Mostly.

"Good," she says, picking up her paddles, then rowing as though she was bred for it. Broad shoulders, muscled arms, and in a voice only a heart-father could love, she starts singing her rowing tune again. She's going faster and faster. I bite my lip.

"You can slow down some," I tell her. "The waters get pretty choppy around this bend. Don't want to tip us over."

"The ancestors sit firmly with us. We'll be fine."

"You could strain a muscle. Just ease up some, okay?"

"I'm beginning to think that this foolish expedition of yours wasn't about finding the throttle fish. You're intentionally trying to miss your annulment proceedings, aren't you?" Baradonna says, attempting a compassionate smile, but on her, it looks more like hunger.

I am quiet. Baradonna stops paddling. Because she's right. And she knows that I know she's right. I don't even understand *why* the throttle fish are so important. I needed to get away. The boat comes to a standstill, and silence spreads throughout the bile duct.

"You shouldn't worry," she says finally. "I am sure the Senate will decide in your favor. You've already proven your worth as Matris, ten times over. The position may have fallen on you when Seske didn't want it, but you've handled it with nothing but grace and intellect. The Senate would be foolish to dismiss you just because Seske wants to throw a tantrum and ignore her responsibilities."

"Seske's been through a lot," I say. "Her sacrifices saved our people. She needs time to think. Time to heal."

"Time to bump humble bits with that boneworker friend of hers is more like it," Baradonna mumbles under her breath.

"That boneworker saved every one of our lives too," I snap at her. I know my anger is misplaced. Baradonna has done nothing but support me, albeit in her own way.

Baradonna grunts. "Well, I don't think I'll ever forgive Seske for the embarrassment she put you through on your wedding night."

"Can we talk about something else?" I ask, trying to divert

my thoughts to avoid the retelling of that night, but it's too late. I'd shook so hard as I recounted what I remembered to the Senate and hundreds of onlookers. I couldn't recall much from that horrid moment—my wife had made sure I was drunk enough not to realize what I (or she) was doing. But the next day, I'd woken up, a groggy smile on my face despite the pounding in my head. I'd slipped my hand across Seske's clammy skin, snuggled myself into the crook of her neck, and whispered sweet nothings into her ear.

Waking up next to Seske the morning after our wedding had been the best moment of my life. I was the husband to the heir of the matriarchy, and even beyond the weight of that title, I was still so enamored with the idea of life with her and eager to start our journey in matrimony. I dared to gently cup my wife's breast, rubbed my thumb over her nipple ... and the nipple, it balled up and rolled away off to the side. I sat up and saw that I was not sleeping next to my wife in our wedding bed, but a life-size doll made of puppet gel. It was half-melted now, its entire face slipping off to one side.

And if the insult of me having fully and thoroughly romanced a lump of gel the night before weren't enough, I heard snoring coming from down on the floor. When I looked over, I saw Seske naked and cradled in the arms of another man— Wheytt, one of my best friends.

I'd stood there, nearly a whole hour, watching them sleep, wondering what I should do. What were my options? Confrontation? Forgiveness? Slip back into bed and pretend to sleep until they'd had time to cover up whatever plot they'd orchestrated to trick me? Then I'd just have to live forever with a sour pit in my stomach, playing the part of the perfect husband to our clan's future matriarch ...

That seemed like the best plan of action to protect the

reputation of both our Lines, but before another moment passed, my best friend's eyes cracked open, and the look . . . the look on his face wasn't of shock or remorse. It was the same look I had on my face when I'd woken. It was satisfaction, longing, and the face of a man so hopelessly in love. My fists balled, and I stumbled toward him and took my first swing.

It was hardly a fair fight. Despite his elite guard training, I wailed upon him with solid blow after solid blow. I was poised to become the victor, but then we were interrupted with news that Matris was deathly ill, and suddenly it was not only my world that was crumbling down around me, but that of our entire clan.

"You still love her, don't you?" Baradonna asks, shaking me from the bitter memory. "You can tell me. I won't say a peep to no one."

"She wants the annulment, and I intend to give it to her," I mumble. I shiver at the thought of Seske and Wheytt taking their connection even further, tied together through our Zenzee, tentacles tucked into every nook and crevice, communicating like the Zenzee do—without barriers, completely exposed. I would never be able to compete with such intimacy, even if she did give me a chance. I turn my attention back to the throttle fish, trapped in the jar. Its little fists beat futilely against the glass, eyes angry and a big frown on its pudgy, moss-pocked face. An hour from now, it will have the full attention of every member of the environmental research initiative—on display and being poked and prodded and humiliated in front of everyone.

And right about then I'll be standing in front of the Senate, going through the exact same thing.

"You didn't answer my question," Baradonna says.

"How I feel doesn't matter. Seske made it very clear. She doesn't want to be married to me, and if I don't let her go, she'll set her sights at tearing down the whole institution of marriage. We can't risk that right now. Not when everything's so tender." Not even the threat of the Senate taking away my title had been enough to convince her to stay with me. I didn't dare mention the tear in my heart. "Seske can't be contained. Resistance burns too brightly in her soul. I know we both want what's best for our people, but this is something I'll have to learn to do alone."

Baradonna purses her lips, then starts rowing again. She's been my personal guard long enough that she knows when I'm lying. "Don't you worry, you won't ever be alone. Not with me by your side. Day in. Day out. Watching over you while you eat. While you sleep. While you empty your—"

"Please, Baradonna. Can I have a moment of silence?"

Baradonna stares at me, as if she's trying to unearth something deeper than my unease of an annulment. In truth, I've lost countless nights of sleep, knowing that things are going so right, but fearing how fast they could go wrong. I hold my face tight, refusing to let her pry further at my worries. Finally, Baradonna turns away and sets her sight on the choppy water ahead.

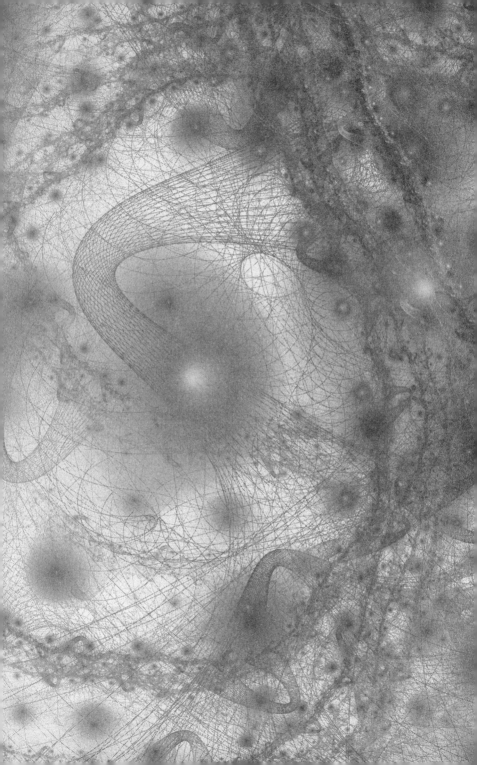

part I

· · · · · · · · · · · · · ·

parasitism

Even the most heroic among us are still parasites—
mouths always open, minds never so.
Now is the time to open your minds.

QUEEN OF THE DEAD

SESKE

Of Desolate Dreams and Fertile Grounds

Darkness creeps up behind us as Adalla and I venture farther into the abandoned heart fissure. Ichor-slickened flesh presses all around me, as if I'm sealed in a womb. Or a tomb. I keep one hand on Adalla's shoulder and keep my eyes trained on the half-dimmed light she holds out in front of her, even though it fails to illuminate anything beyond her next step.

"I'm not sure about this," I whisper to Adalla. If we get caught here, we could get into so much trouble. Adalla should know that more than anyone. Even after she'd single-handedly saved our Zenzee's massive heart from failing three years ago now, it'd taken months and months and months before she was trusted anywhere near the organ again. She's worked her way up to being indispensable now, and her knife skills are renowned . . . and I'm proud of that, I am. But really it just means that Adalla's been in such high demand at work that she's completely wiped by the time she comes home to me. Which is why I'm here, sneaking through this nauseating crawl space, hoping to steal back a little bit of her time and attention during her lunch break, despite the risks involved.

"Don't be nervous," she says, her gait sure and steady. "This section of the heart is closed off and repairs won't begin until tomorrow. It's safe, betcha. Just you and me."

I wish I shared her confidence, but the anticipation of the bone-rattling heartbeat keeps me from fully appreciating the mischief we're about to get into. I'm mindful of where I tread, stepping over the bulging capillaries threatening to trip me and avoiding the trickles of phosphorescent ooze meandering down the walls. Finally, the fissure opens into a small chamber the size of our bedroom. The warmth here is a welcome change from the chilly temperatures we pretend we've gotten used to since our near exodus. This is far from being the perfect getaway, but it's cozy and quiet, and most important, private. However, as we venture inside, I hear a panicked squeal from somewhere in the shadows—something startled by our presence.

"Oh no," Adalla says, shoving her lamp at me, as if I'm not already burdened by the load of our neatly packed lunches. She moves slowly in the direction of the noise. "The heart murmurs were supposed to be relocated. They must have missed one. Let me just—"

I sigh. Loudly. Even on her break, Adalla can't tear herself from her work.

"You know, it's fine. It's fine. I'll let someone know about it when I get back . . ." She points to the mound of dry flesh in the middle of the room—a little island that rises above the ichor-drenched floor. "This seems like as good a place as any."

The long, wavering shadows the lamp casts upon Adalla's face are both beautiful and mysterious. A wry smile plays at her lips. My defenses fall, and suddenly I'm a giddy mess, bumbling all over the place, laying out our blanket and the special feast I prepared. I can hardly keep the saliva in my mouth. There're the teal eggs I've been fermenting for over a month. Spicy cheese balls, whose secret family recipe was gifted to us by Adalla's tin uncle on our first wedding anniversary. Battered woodlice I'd spent all morning deveining, plucking away at least a thousand little legs. All her favorites. Adalla looks at me as though she's ravenous, but her eyes have yet to even flick in the direction of the food. I flush at that look and hold up the cheese, almost like a shield, intending to ask if she wants the honor of shucking the thorns off the first piece, but before I can speak a word, her mouth is upon mine.

I topple over at the force she comes at me with, kicking the plate of woodlice over too, but on the next breath, all those other cravings fade into the back of my mind. All I can taste is Adalla. The ichor splashes as we roll back down the hill into a shallow puddle. Adalla's body is tense beneath mine, a well-tuned muscle that has saved our entire people on more than one occasion: firm biceps, rippled abs, thighs that could launch a ship into space if they wanted. And yet when I trace my finger along her collarbone, then down, tugging at the neckline of her heartworker's dress, she practically becomes the puddle she's lying in. What does that make me, the sole person who knows exactly how to cause all that tension to melt away? Powerful. Confident. Adept.

Very adept.

I leave no part of her unexplored, untasted, unloved. The heart shudders as Adalla does the same, though I am unable to determine which tremor is stronger. It is an unfair comparison, anyway—the heart merely an organ and Adalla's body my whole world. I realize that maybe I am good at working to the beat, too, deepening into our connection until I find the perfect tempo. Each and every three minutes and forty-seven and a half seconds that come and go bring more quakes and shivers. And then finally, we lie in each other's arms, comforted in a nest of ichor-soaked petticoats and moss shawls, nothing of our special meal salvageable. Our hunger, however, has been more than satiated.

"Daide's bells," I say, struggling to catch my breath.

Adalla looks at me, grin so sloppy on her face it nearly sits sideways. "That was—"

"Amazing," I offer.

"Perfect, I was going to say. You've really got a bad habit of putting words in my—"

I press my mouth against hers, and in an instant, she's a puddle again. My heart knocks hard, as if it's trying to break through my ribs. Pounds hard against my eardrums, I think they're going to rupture. Today marks three years. Three years to the day since we kissed in zero gee, and unlike our wedding anniversary, it's a date that Adalla and I share alone.

I smile at that, the thought of us being *alone*. No sudden intrusions by a nosey head-wife who "forgot" to knock or the bickering of our heart-wives during dinner. No slobbery kisses shared between our head-husbands who enjoy flaunting their affection a little too much. And it's nice to escape the general annoyance of knowing that we're all breathing one another's air. Frustration curls my toes, and I tamp it back down like I usually do, but I'm left wondering if agreeing to remain in this marriage had been a mistake.

The annulment proceedings hadn't gone as we'd hoped. Or at least how Doka had hoped. The Senate had been too eager to strip away his power, salivating at the promise of annulling his position as Matris as well if we would have pressed through with dissolving the marriage. They didn't care if his policies and quick thinking had saved us from ourselves. They just saw the threat his manhood posed to the centuries-old Matriarchy, which deserved to crumble as far as I was concerned. And I was willing to let it. But something broke in Doka's eyes when they read their ruling, and I . . .

I couldn't let them take away his hopes and dreams like that.

I'd interrupted the annulment right before the decision was made final. I've never seen eyes cut so hard as those of the Senators in that room, and I can still feel that coldness arching through my spine, even years removed from it. It took time, but after hours of arguing, we came to a solution that would work for everyone . . . well, at least one that angered everyone equally: Doka and I would remain married in title alone, him retaining the position of head-husband in our family unit, and me moving to the position of will-wife, and as such, no romantic relationship could ever exist between us. He'd be free to marry according to his heart, as would I. I laugh at how naive we'd been to believe such a thing was actually possible for us, but I got to marry Adalla and Doka got to keep the crown, and in exchange, the Senate asked for a diminished capacity for his role as Matriarch, their first power grab of many. It wasn't ideal, but then again, nothing about life aboard the *Parados I* has ever been ideal since our people abandoned Earth.

But in these few short years, Doka has still managed to guide us in building a near paradise that's perfectly in tune with our Zenzee. Every organ is operating at peak performance. We've sourced renewable building materials from carefully cultivated gardens. No one among us has gone hungry or unwashed or neglected. The balance is delicate, and we still have many people locked away in stasis in order to maintain it, but we now sit upon the brink of utopia. And all I had to do to get us here was to extinguish the fire of resistance burning in my heart and allow myself to become domesticated.

"We have no right to be this happy," Adalla whispers to me as I twirl the end of one of her braids. The Lines of my ancestors' knots frame her face perfectly.

"Don't we though?" I say. "We've been working so hard. We've given up so much. Why can't we enjoy this?" I grin thinly at Adalla, but she sees through it. She knows when something is bothering me.

"What's wrong? Is it the nightmares again?"

I'm struck frozen for a moment, then I nod. It's not a complete lie. The nightmares have been back, but that's not what's bothering me right now. Adalla has plowed forward, making great strides in her career, which has left her in charge of our most precious organ. I'm proud of her for that and for pouring her whole self into healing the Zenzee's heart. Late nights. Early mornings. And for a long time, zero breaks. We've all sacrificed to get to where we are now. It's just that I feel I sacrificed all the wrong things, and I'm not sure how to tell her that.

Adalla takes me into her arms and cradles me to her chest like a babe. "I know it's hard, but you can't keep living in the past. It's going to continue to haunt you."

"I can't forget everything we went through, 'Dalla. I've tried."

"Don't forget. Just forgive."

I let loose a tight, bitter laugh. "Where would I even start? My mother for never seeing me fit to be her heir? My ancestors for getting us into this mess in the first place?" I purse my lips, still unable to get them to form anything close to Sisterkin's name. "*Her*?"

Adalla presses her hand firmly to my chest, right over my

heart. "Start here, Seske. With yourself. Life is messy. Let it be messy. And make peace with that." Adalla looks at me, and I catch something hidden deep behind her eyes. It scares me to think what it had taken to forgive me for the pain I'd inflicted upon her. My intentions have always been honorable, but like Adalla's ama had once told me, better to step in a dent pan full of shit than to be subjected to a heart full of good intentions.

I sigh, then nod. Adalla is right, but some hurts take longer to forgive than others. I catch myself wondering if the Zenzee will ever forgive us for the centuries we spent butchering them, but then Adalla's lips press against mine, and I lose track of every single thought in my head.

Not ten seconds later, I hear muttering coming from the fissure's entrance, and I flinch so hard that my teeth knock against Adalla's. Panic sets in. To be caught.

Like this.

In the heart.

Adalla's career could be in jeopardy. Our Line could be dishonored. I try not to think about the ramifications of our flippant lovemaking and instead hurriedly pick through the clothes scattered beneath us. Everything is so tangled up and matted I can't make heads or tails of any one garment. Finally, I give up and grab our blanket and pull it up to my chin.

A hand holding a lamp enters the room first, a full-on bright light that causes me to squint. Right as my eyes adjust, Doka emerges through the fissure's slit, dressed in thick leathers and a docker's cap, looking as nauseated and unsure as the first settlers to set foot inside a Zenzee.

"Oh, sorry," he says, his naxshi flushing so hard against his cheeks that they nearly become white. "I hope I haven't interrupted something."

I nudge Adalla in the ribs, her body still bare and on full

display. Even being this far removed from living with bone-workers hasn't undone the comfort of moving in her skin. She's got the scar of her pet heart murmur, Bepok, on her left breast, its tail curling around her nipple. Several other scars adorn her skin, too, like the one of the clock face on her shoulder. She's never been willing to talk about it though, so I stopped asking.

"Not at all," Addala says, rising out of our nest. She turns away from me to wring the ichor from her heartworker's dress, and I wince at the other scars—those on her back. There are five sets of raised welts from her shoulder blades down to the small of her back, forming delicate and organic patterns, almost like a tapestry. I'd think they were beautiful if I didn't know how much pain had accompanied their creation. I wonder if she really has forgiven me for putting those scars there. I know she hasn't forgotten.

Adalla slips into her dress, then rolls her eyes when she sees me still huddled up. She bends down to whisper into my ear. "He's our husband, Seske. And it's just skin."

I bite my lip. Husband, yes . . . but Adalla and I are will-wives and Doka is a head-husband, and if consorting across those intimate boundaries of our family unit is forbidden, then I certainly don't have to be okay with him seeing me naked.

"So, um, there's kind of an urgent situation with the Senate, and Charrelle—" Doka's voice cracks. He swallows the lump in his throat, then tries again. "Charrelle said she saw you two steal off in this direction."

Charrelle. Adalla and I exchange looks. Doka's head-wife. We all love her—we really do. And things are fine at home—*just lovely*—but ever since Charrelle got promoted to work the heart a few months back, Adalla has been insufferable.

She's confided in me with complaint after complaint. It was all a part of the plan to integrate members from the Contour class into doing beast work, and on paper, it all sounded great: break down the barriers between classes and share the workload. But stick two groups that come from vastly different backgrounds together, and there are bound to be issues. Charrelle was one of the best and brightest, the only Contour class citizen who'd proven herself fit enough to work the most important organ, but despite her talents, she apparently still couldn't grasp the nuances of beast work. Like privacy. Adalla had clearly been carrying a dimmed lamp that screamed "look the other way" to every other person we'd passed. To them, we were like ghosts, not even there.

But Charrelle had *seen* us, and then on top of that, blabbed about it.

It's fine, though. Everything's fine.

"Well, Seske's all yours," Adalla says. "I'm about to go report to ventricle nine, anyway. Busy day. Utopias don't build themselves."

"Actually," Doka says, "the Senators want you both in their chamber. They say there's an emergency session, and they need your expertise."

Adalla stops. "An emergency session concerning what? Can't be heart related. I know things are busy here, but we've got it all under control."

Doka shrugs. "I don't know, they wouldn't say. But I don't want to keep them waiting. They seemed really anxious."

"Well, if they're not saying, it couldn't be too important. Catch me up later, okay, love?" Adalla kisses me on my cheek then heads for the exit.

"Wait! You can't leave us here," I say. "How will we get back? What if we get lost?"

"It's a straight shot back. I'll leave the lamp for you," Adalla says, winking at me.

I shake my head. "Well, what if we do something to hurt the heart? What if I kick a capillary or get sucked through a valve?"

"Relax. The heart is resilient now, stronger than it was even before we settled here. You'd have to know exactly what you're doing to really harm it, sure is sure is sure." Adalla smiles at me once more, then disappears back into the darkness, leaving me here with Doka.

Alone.

"I'll admit I'm glad we have a moment by ourselves," Doka says. "I have a very personal favor to ask you as well." He takes a seat next to me. Adalla's warmth is already dissipating, and a chill runs through me. I pull my blanket up to my nose.

"Can it wait for me to get dressed? Last thing we need is a scandal. I'm sure Charrelle already saw Adalla leave and will be ready to tell anyone who asks." I don't bother to hide my brusqueness with him. I'd been looking forward to this time with Adalla for nearly a week, and in an instant, he'd ruined it.

Doka bristles at my tone, then his eyes go wide as if the thought of me being naked under this blanket had just occurred to him. "Of course," he says, his voice cracking again. "Meet me back at home in fifteen minutes?"

I nod and he leaves. Slowly, I get up, taking the blanket with me, draped over my shoulders as if they're regal raiment and I'm still Matris. I pick the smashed woodlice from my silks, tossing them to the side. My outer silks are completely ruined, but the inner ones are black as space, and the ichor stains don't show. I catch a whiff of Adalla's smell still on them and press them to my nose. Breathe it in. I shudder once more, a small one that fixes a smile back on my face. Leaving me here in her heart, alone—maybe that was a sign of trust. I don't want to let Adalla down, so I use our dim light to find every little scrap of food and pack them away, along with my ruined clothes.

By the time I arrive home, Doka's sitting on the front porch, twiddling his thumbs, definitely not his usually confident self. He glances up at me, almost smiles, then looks back down. Our home blends in with its surroundings, no longer the palatial bone structure I'd grown up in, but closer to a bunker made from brown-gray gall husk bricks. Paired with the glittery blues and pinks of star jewel mortar, it isn't at all displeasing to the eyes. The bricks vary in size and shape, and are piled in fanciful, meandering patterns, walls bulging out where each family-unit dwells, and a common area in the middle. It's beautiful, yet quaint—the perfect home for Adalla and me.

Too bad we have to share it with six other people.

"What?" Doka asks, standing up and stretching his legs in preparation for our journey to the Senate chambers.

"What what?" I say.

"You have to share *what* with six other people?" he glances back at our home, and I realize I must have said that last bit out loud. He sighs. "I thought you were happy with us. We've tried to give you your space."

"I am happy," I say, ducking inside and grabbing a fresh dress and plucking bits of dried ichor from my hair. Doka lurks just outside the doorway. "Everything is perfect."

"You're sure?" he asks, the skepticism in his voice obvious. "You went through a lot, Seske. It's okay if you need more time to process. No one is trying to pressure you into doing anything you don't want to."

I nod and will myself to stop from trembling. I've learned to ignore it, but the mounting pressure for us to complete our family never truly goes away. Doka's taken both of his mates already, and we've joined with three amazing heart-wives, but Adalla and I, we're still just a couple. A unit apart. "I know people are starting to talk . . . ," I mumble as I undress. I need a bath, but no time for that.

"Let them talk. You don't need to worry about finding a will-husband. Not this year. Not the next, or even the next, if you're not ready."

"Okay," I say, and I'm somewhat relieved. Living like this hasn't been easy for me, but it hasn't been a walk in the gardens for Doka, either. But he seems to understand me, and I can at least appreciate that. I finish changing clothes and change the subject as well. "What did you want to ask me, anyway?"

"It's about Charrelle, actually," he says as I rejoin him.

"Oh." I stiffen at the mention of her name. I know I shouldn't be so defensive, but I still feel guilty for practically forcing her onto Doka. Personality-wise, she hadn't been the best fit for him of all his suitors, but she had the strongest, longest matriline—one that was well-respected by many members of the Senate. It was a strategic move my own mother would have been proud of, which makes me even more ashamed to have made it.

"We should really hurry. Can we talk about it on the way?" Doka presses his hand against my back, leading me out of our home and up the path to the Senate chambers. But between here and there, all the world spreads around us. The view never fails to amaze me. We've returned as much of the Zenzee's gut to nature as we could. It took a couple years for the plants to reestablish themselves, but the blooms this year are so magnificent. The bog waters are so clear, you can see the throttle fish swim to the surface, begging for snacks. Even though we're pressed for time, we stop to feed them.

It's not my favorite custom, and as a child, I'd once protested, yelling at my will-mother that they were such frightful, ugly creatures with all those little needle teeth smiling back at me. It was the first and only time she'd clapped her hand against my cheek. *They are beautiful and perfect*; her words ring in my ear even now.

Doka and I stop at the local vendor and buy a bag of treats for a few cowries, then find a spot far enough away from all the other visitors. Together, we toss bits of boiled meat and cabbage into the water. The throttle fish swim to the surface and snatch them, stuffing the morsels into their puffy little cheeks. They blink their too-wide, too-human eyes at us before dipping back down below into their underwater caves. Doka and I go for the last morsel in the bag at the same time, and our fingers touch. We share a tension-riddled moment before he yields to me. "Take it. It's yours."

I shake my head. "It's best not to feed them so much anyway," I say, and leave the morsel where it sits. Doka folds the bag up tight.

"Maybe later, then," he says, eyes cast down.

"On our way back, for sure," I say, trying to ease the discomfort blossoming between us. "Maybe later" had become my mantra in all matters that didn't involve Adalla. I would have withered away if she hadn't been by my side, helping me to pack away all the traumas I'd endured back in that other life, when our world was dying. Avoidance isn't the best way to deal with the jumble of my still-raw feelings, but it's certainly the most convenient. "You still haven't said what you wanted to ask me."

"It's nothing. It can wait."

"You're sure?"

"Mmm-hmm."

I don't pry further. He's sensitive, this one. But I trust him. He's brought us back from the brink of extinction, after all.

Finally, we arrive at the entrance to the Senate chambers, flanked by giant gleaming columns of carved bone. These columns would have been perfect candidates to graft back into the Zenzee, but Doka proposed that we keep them here. He then ordered for the reliefs that depicted our deep histories to be sanded down and smoothed over and hired our best artists to re-carve them as monuments to our darkest moments as a people—showing the lives we'd so callously tossed away, both Zenzee and human. Histories have a tendency to rewrite themselves if you don't take certain precautions, or so Doka says. It's strange how easily forgetting comes when you're not on the receiving end of the hurt.

I open the door and let Doka pass. He stops so suddenly that I bump into him. "Go. Run now," he whispers to me. I catch a glimpse over his shoulder. The entire chamber is empty except his three senator mothers with eight young men standing behind them, clad in the most elaborate silk dressings I've seen, with thick patinas covering their faces in teals and fuchsias and golds.

Suitors for me and Adalla.

It can't be anything else. I try to turn, but fear has me frozen. I bite my lip as waves of anxiety pour through me. My heart hitting like a fist against my ribcage. So this was the "urgent matter." The "emergency session." I'm not ready for it. Not yet. Later, maybe. Much, much later.

But there is no later.

"Doka! Seske!" Doka's head-mother, Jesipha, comes to greet us, pulling me inside by the elbow. "Where's Adalla?"

"Couldn't make it," Doka says, his voice clearly irritated. "And actually, Seske is supposed to be at another very important meeting right now. We stopped by to say that we'll need to reschedule."

"Nonsense. This won't take long." Jesipha shoves me forward now, to get me closer to the men. They all smile demurely, but I don't make eye contact. "We have some friends we'd like you to meet."

"I've got plenty of friends already," I grumble.

"Seske," Jesipha says sternly. "We've been nothing but patient with you."

"Mother, don't—" Doka tries, but his words are trampled over.

"It's been almost three years since you and Adalla married. The rest of your family unit is in order—Doka, Charrelle, and Kallum. Your three heart-wives. It's time for yours to be complete, as well. Now, we don't have to make a big show of it. Just a small party with a couple hundred people, max. We'll plan everything. All you and Adalla have to do is show up."

All I have to do is show up. And marry one of these men . . . and extinguish any remaining embers of defiance that still dance in my soul. Even amid the chaos and betrayal from what seems a lifetime ago, I knew who I was and what I wanted. Now, in this time of peace and prosperity, I'm about to lose everything that I am.

I want to scream, but I don't. Not here, in front of my lawmothers. Yes, they are family, but they are also senators who would not hesitate to use my instability against me and even their own son if it suited them.

I open my eyes, force a smile onto my face. "Of course. A small party I won't object to. Next year, I promise."

"Next year cannot do!" says one of Doka's will-mothers. "We must act now."

"We have time. Don't we, Doka?" I ask, nudging him in the side for support. "It's not like there's a child on the way, right?"

Doka stares at me.

"Right?"

He bites the tip of his thumb. "That's what I wanted to talk to you about earlier. Charrelle is expecting. Not far enough along for us to talk about it openly, but she does need a mid-wife . . . someone to comfort her and see her through the whole process. We were hoping you would do it."

My womb knocks. Phantom tentacles slide against my thighs, reminding me of that Zenzee egg I had carried inside me. I shake my head. The position of midwife is for a woman who has already given birth. Who knows about labor pains and contractions and . . .

"She asked for you, Seske. Personally. She looks up to you so much," Doka says, trying to tear through my defenses.

"I don't know anything about birthing children." Not human ones anyway.

"You're resourceful and kind, Seske. Charrelle is inquisitive and patient. And you're both brilliant. You'll figure it out together," Doka says, draping his arm over my shoulder. I wither inside, but keep my chest poked out, as if I'm confident.

"Okay," I say, agreeing to that, too. What's another soul-wrenching task to stack up on top of the first?

"Excellent!" cries out Jesipha. "Now, on the matter of a will-husband . . . would you allow me to introduce you to the candidates."

"Not necessary. I choose that one." I point. The third one to the left. I've given more thought in choosing what flavor of curd I want served on top of my gall steaks.

"Seske," Doka says, "Don't you want to consider it a little more before you make a decision?"

"I don't care who I marry. It's not like I really have a choice, right?" I gesture at the suitors, well-built, dark-skinned, and handsome, so much alike that each could be a copy of the next. Faces as blank as statues. If I have embarrassed or upset them, it doesn't show. I wait for Doka to say something, but he just bites at the air. "Can I go now?" I ask, but I don't wait for a response. I walk out of the Senate chambers, and when Doka starts to follow, I fix him in place with a cold stare. I know this wasn't his fault, but I need to be alone right now.

I let my mind wander as I walk, trying to conjure up the good memories I have . . . before everything went sideways. But even my childhood is not safe. Sisterkin infiltrated our family at every turn, and even though—with her banishment—we were supposed to forget about her completely, she still haunts me in my dreams. I can't even count the number of times I've woken up, sheets drenched with sweat, Adalla hovering over me, blotting my forehead with napkins.

Even though we don't speak Sisterkin's name, Adalla knows how much that betrayal still haunts me. My own sister had tried to kill me, on several occasions, and each time with that sly smile on her face.

How does someone forget that?

"Good day to you, Seske," shouts one of the groundkeepers for the Senate chambers.

"Hello! Good to see you!" I yell back, surprised by the jovial tone I'd mustered up. My smile is sharp and practiced, though it feels as though it is made from thin glass. The slightest touch would shatter it to nothingness.

I walk faster. My legs take me to the last place I want to be right now, but it's the only place I know that will be quiet. It's cold. Dark. Silent. The equipment has all been scrapped and put to other purposes, leaving only scar tissue behind. The spot where the baby Zenzee had grown has reverted back to a small puckered fissure—ready for the next pregnancy, though there will not be another one.

I've never been in a place that felt quite this hollow, which is perfect for how I feel right now.

I lie down on my back, close my eyes, and will my heart to stop pounding. I feel like I'm spinning.

I'm having the nightmare again. I hear Sisterkin call my name, feel her cold fingers against my arm, grabbing me. I fight against it, trying to startle myself out of this wretched dreamscape.

But I realize my eyes are open, and I'm already awake.

DOKA

Of Collapsed Worlds and Expanded Populations

I stare at the charts spread out before me, bunkered in my study, ancient tomes piled high all around me. This month's report from the Environmental Research Initiative looks too good to be true. We've achieved an 80 percent reduction in energy usage, the waterways are flowing at record levels with no signs of pollution, and after accounting for the new composting program in the worm fields of the lower bowels, food waste is practically nil. In their recommendations, the ERI suggests that eight hundred more people can be awoken from stasis without a negative impact. I breathe a sigh of relief.

Which eight hundred will be the next question. I receive letters daily, dozens of them, sometimes numbering in the hundreds, begging for mothers, daughters, and loved ones to be freed from stasis. They say that life is passing them by, and if they are held any longer, they'll be strangers to their own people when they are finally freed. I wish I could deny it, but I'm afraid they are right about that.

In some ways those in stasis are the lucky ones. The first year of my reign was hard, there's no doubt about that. It had been so difficult for most people to let go of their creature comforts. I put them to work, tearing down their old lives, brick by brick. Storefronts leveled, homes too, gardens left to grow wild, nuisance fauna reintroduced despite lengthy protests. It took an emotional toll on everyone.

But even though there were challenges and hardships, it was cathartic for those who lived through it. At least they got to process it all, to see the walls of bone torn down. To see that same material being grafted back into a hurting being. To see our world healing, and a new society growing from it. They were able to come to terms with their size in this universe.

Now, each release of citizens from stasis has proven to be more difficult than the last. So much has changed in these three years, and what they wake to is foreign and difficult to comprehend. Plus, there are now whispers from the ERI that hint at negative physiological and emotional effects from spending such an extended amount of time in the sleep pods, regardless of what world the people are waking up to. They won't say anything about it outright, however. We all know how delicate this balance we have created with our Zenzee is and releasing too many people too quickly would be disastrous. Still, I feel great discomfort imagining the 2,361 souls still sleeping their lives away.

I push past the feeling and read through the rest of the recommendations.

They forecast that we will be self-sufficient within the next five years, and I'll admit, that makes me feel smug. For so long we have been like parasites—taking, always taking—

but now, we have a chance to give back to our Zenzee. To live in peace with her, in a state of mutualism. Imagine never having to leave this place. Never having to even think about culling another Zenzee or continue hunting for a habitable planet. Our descendants could live here for many generations to come.

But then I get to the last recommendation, and my mouth goes dry and tacky. I shake my head and read it again.

> viii. It is the consensus of the Environmental Research Initiative that after reviewing the studies on the effects of the One Child Policy on the population, barring any unforeseen circumstances, we recommend rescinding the policy in a phased rollout within the next decade.

My mouth stretches into a smile, but really, I don't know if I should be feeling happy or excited or scared. We are still weeks away from announcing Charrelle's pregnancy, but the thought that my unborn child could have a sibling someday intrigues me.

How would this change family dynamics? Cultural stigmas? What if there's backlash? So much of our lives have been built around this rigid family structure that our culture had become quite rigid as well. Two heart-wives and a husband, two will-wives and a husband, three heart-wives, and a child to share between them. Yes, it's efficient, but it's also stifling. Seske is still sore about my mothers forcing a will-husband upon her. I know what she gave up to remain in this family with me, and I feel as though I failed her. Saddling her with the future possibility of having to bear a child would be rubbing salt into that wound.

I will omit that last recommendation in my presentation to the Senate. For now.

Instead, I will focus on the claim of self-sufficiency. Yes. Yes. Yes.

"You okay over there?" Baradonna asks from her corner, where she's got her nose in a book, pretending she isn't watching my every move. "You look like you're about to hyperventilate."

"Just got a bit of good news. I think." I slow my breath down, concentrating on the sound of it entering and exiting my lungs. "Still trying to digest, I guess."

"Well, better digest quickly. Lover boy is on his way down."

My ears perk, listening for the footsteps that I know only her ears are keen enough to pick up. I sniff the air, though only her nose is sensitive enough to smell the traces of decontamination antiseptics on his skin under his flowery cologne. I wonder if she can feel the air he's displacing, too. If she can taste him.

I get a little jealous, thinking she can.

Half a minute later Kallum enters the room. I keep my back to the door and my eyes glued to my research because I know he delights in surprising me. His warm lips press against my cheek, and I pretend to startle.

"Guess who's back," Kallum says in a sing-song voice, still out of sight as he sets a cup of kettleworm tea on the desk next to me.

"Hmm . . . ," I say, putting my finger to my lips. "Is it Ol' Baxi Batzi, here to steal my soul?" I glance over at him, a cunning smile on my face.

"I'm here to steal something," he says, lips pursed, eyes devious. I want to roll my eyes at the over-the-top innuendo, but I also flush a little at his attention. He looks *so* good, orange patina giving his warm brown skin an enticing glow, with hints of glitter dusted around the eyes. The neckline of his purple shift hangs precariously low, exposing the tops of his well-defined pecs. He pulls a chair as close to me as feasible, then sits in it the exact wrong way. It's hard to believe someone who is trained to be so diplomatic and poised in front of foreign dignitaries loses that polish the instant he gets home.

"When did you get back?" I ask him as I help myself to the tea. I shouldn't be drinking it down here among all these price-less, irreplaceable books, but I take it into my hands anyway and allow the heat of the cup to warm me before taking a long, much-needed sip. It does nothing to calm my nerves, but see-ing Kallum here is nice.

"A couple hours ago. We debriefed the Senate on the Klang ship. The situation over there is deteriorating rapidly."

I nod. I had guessed as much. Kallum had been working closely with the Klang for months, and each time he came back home, the reports grew grimmer. Inconsistent oxygen levels, food shortages, disease, and death. We've donated what we can, but our own supplies are precarious, and about to be even more so if we release eight hundred more from stasis. I let out a long sigh and gather my thoughts. "We can loan them a few more environmental researchers. Maybe fresh eyes could help to determine the cause of all their problems?"

Kallum bites his lip. "I've already pleaded with them to consider it. Tirtha Yee thinks it might have been an option months ago, even weeks ago, but I've lost her confidence as well."

My gut sinks. Tirtha Yee was the lead environmental re-searcher for the Klang. She and Kallum work well together, and almost always see things eye-to-eye. That she was going against his recommendations now meant she'd given up hope.

I shake my head, willing Kallum not to say it, but he does so anyway.

"They want to break the embargo and commandeer another Zenzee."

"They can't break the agreement!" I say, desperation cracking my voice. "There must be some resource allocation plan they haven't tried. Rescinding feverpitch? Doldrum sails? Lessening gravity?"

"They've tried all that. Their Zenzee is still failing." Kallum manages to scoot his chair even closer. His hand brushes down my arm. "Tesaryn Wen says the Senate will be meeting on it in a few hours, so you've got time to prepare a response."

I push the work in front of me out of the way and bring up a blank screen on my tablet. Frustration runs through me, wishing I had the Matriarch's full power at my fingertips. The Senate had feared Seske's mother during her reign, and no one would dare cross her, but my influence over the Senators pales in comparison, especially when it comes to diplomatic endeavors. I try to brainstorm some ideas that could delay the Klang acting upon their decision long enough for us to generate other options, but it's nearly impossible to think with Kallum so close.

"How's everything been here, since I've been away?" he asks quietly.

I glance over at Baradonna, who's deep into the second volume of *The Histories of Gallantry* now. "Can you give us a little privacy?" I ask her.

"Oh, I don't mind if you suck face with your husband in front of me. Just ignore that I'm here." She licks her finger and flips a page. "Suck away . . ."

"We're not sucking face, Baradonna," I say, but Kallum gives me a little pout in response. Okay, so we might, but that's not why we want privacy. "We just need a moment. Maybe you can go confirm when the Senate will be meeting exactly. And ask Tesaryn Wen yourself. You know how she gets when you're around."

Baradonna perks at that. I'm not sure of the exact words that were said, or the intensity of the threats that were made, but Tesaryn Wen had once pissed herself when Baradonna had stepped in to disparage her for cutting me off in the middle of one of my speeches. It hadn't been enough to dampen her robes, but Baradonna's heightened senses had detected it immediately. Baradonna has about as much discretion as a chamber full of drunken heart-wives on All Fellows' Night, so I don't know why she hadn't told everyone in the Senate Chambers just then. Instead, she kept it a tightly guarded secret. Tesaryn Wen fears Baradonna almost as much as she hates me. Excited with the potential for another confrontation with Tesaryn Wen, Baradonna takes her leave.

I wait for the sound of her heavy footsteps to dissipate, then give Kallum a tight hug and a tepid peck on the cheek.

Kallum frowns. "You know I went through a whole hour of decontamination. No foreign parasites anywhere on this body."

"I know. It's just . . . I've got a lot on my mind right now," I mutter.

"Things didn't go so well with Adalla and the suitors? I heard."

"All the way on the Klang ship?"

"Gossip involving your mothers is impervious to the vacuum of space."

"I'm sure."

"Was Seske mad?" he asks, genuinely concerned.

I laugh at that. "What do you think? She ran off and hid

again. For an entire day this time. So yeah. And she threw away the crystal beads my head-mother got her for EE day. And you won't believe what she wore to dinner with my folks. A filament dress as bright a white as a star going nova! My mothers pretended like they didn't notice, but oh man, were they offended. White? For EE dinner? I've talked to her about it, but every time I try to smooth things over, she just gets—" I realize I'm babbling. "Sorry. Let's talk about you. And me. Us."

"It's fine. I know Seske holds the foremost spot in your heart. I'm okay with coming in a close second." He smiles and nudges me in the shoulder. "Whenever I'm feeling jealous, I take comfort that at least I'm not Charrelle."

"Kallum!" I say.

"She annoys you a little. Admit it. With the way she chews her vowels when she says your name and always scrunches her nose when she's talking, like she's just let one rip? And how she's always using the word 'moist'?"

"You're talking about the mother of our child," I whisper.

"Dowkaaah . . . come have a bite of this gall cake, it's so moist," he says, doing a spot-on impression of Charrelle, down to the pinched nose. It'd be funny if it weren't so painfully true. "Dowkaaah . . . bring me a towel. My armpits are so moi—"

I press my lips over Kallum's, and the words stop. My teacup falls from my hands and breaks against the floor. He throws me onto my desk, and for the better part of a minute, we're kissing as if our lives depend on it. Like we're both drowning, and trying to rescue the other, but we end up pulling each other down deeper. I tug him closer, and in my desperation, I knock over a tower of books. I ignore the centuries worth of our history tumbling to the floor, until I can finally take it no longer and come up for air. Kallum pulls back and wipes his sleeve across his mouth.

"Can I help you pick those books up?" he asks, a twinkle in his eyes. He starts to bend over, but I grab his arm.

"No, no. I've got them. Why don't you go and rest up? It's been a long couple weeks for you, I'm sure." If I'm supposed to be meeting with the Senate in a few hours, I need my head clear and not groggy and distracted by the joys of young matrimony. Especially when I'm going up in front of the Senate with something this important. I need a majority on my side since I can't do it by emergency decree. I'll have to sway them with my words by tapping into my pain, my fury, my vision for the future. I cannot afford to let the Klang get away with breaking the treaty.

"I'm back!" Baradonna says, hand on her chest, breathing heavily. Never have I seen her complete any task so rapidly. I start to wonder how much of her crude and plodding persona is a convenient front. She looks around, disappointed that she missed whatever she was hoping not to miss, but instead spots the mess my desk has become and the purple stain setting into the grout between the floor tiles. "What happened here?"

"Zenzee tremor," Kallum says with a smirk. "A small one. Very localized."

Baradonna raises a skeptical brow. "But there hasn't been a tremor since—"

"Just let it go, Baradonna," I say. I give Kallum a dirty look. He smiles, then makes a hasty exit before I can scold him. I sigh, looking at the mess at my feet, then up at Baradonna. "Did you speak to Tesaryn Wen?"

She nods. "Meeting is in an hour."

"An hour? That's barely time to prepare!" I start reordering the bent pages on my desk and search the volumes that have fallen to the floor for the one containing the provisions of the Zenzee treaty.

"You'll manage. You found the time to slip lover boy the old tongue. Like I always say, you're great at multitasking. Writing declarations while you're eating. Practicing speeches while you shower. Reading over Senate minutes while you're squatting on the—"

"Thank you for your service, Baradonna," I say. Interrupting Baradonna's rants has become a part-time job for me. Though she's not exactly wrong, either. Life as Matris is a balancing act, requiring more than there are hours in the day. But I manage, thanks to keeping good people around me. "You have gone above and beyond, like always, but Kallum and I were just catching up. Nothing else."

Baradonna squints at me. "You've got a little orange patina here," she says, rubbing my cheek. "You haven't worn patina since you became Matris, or is that me misremembering?"

"Help me pick up these books, will you?" I say, turning away from her so she won't see my naxshi turning all manners of colors. Baradonna wrestles the books back into a neat stack, then stands akimbo, so proud of having caught me telling a tale.

"Anything else I can help you with?" she asks.

"Not unless you're familiar with ways to counter stage four environmental degradation." I sit back down with my ledgers and notes before me. "Kallum says that the Klang ship is planning to betray the Exodus Pact and harvest another Zenzee. Theirs has gotten too sick and can no longer support them."

"Have they tried a biomolecular analysis of the spleen to determine exactly which infections are plaguing the Zenzee?" Baradonna asks.

I stare at her. Blink several times.

"What? You think I can't read books? I'm much more than a fine figure and a pretty face."

"I didn't think either of—" I shake my head. "You know what, never mind. Come sit over here. We can work through this together. Maybe a new perspective is just what I need."

"Okay, but I have to warn you, I have very sensitive reflexes when I'm focused on something that requires deep thinking. If I get startled by sudden movement, I'm liable to flip you so hard, I'll break half the bones in your body, so make sure you turn the pages slowly."

I give her a hesitant nod, not sure if she's joking or not, wondering what I've gotten myself into. "Okay, so we've got the Klang ship. Population 3,300 people, skewing slightly older than us, with an abnormally high percentage of males, nearing almost half the population."

"Ugh!" Baradonna says, and I squint at her. "No offense. A population that small suggests there was a large-scale die-out. Maybe a plague that affected women more harshly?"

"It's a possibility, but the Klang have been less than forth-coming with their history. Their leader is an elected official in service for the past twelve years. They have been aboard this Zenzee for forty-seven years. There are a few prestigious fam-ily Lines with wealth, but for the most part, all semblance of economic development and trade seems to have collapsed un-der the strain of the failing Zenzee. People are now living in squalor. Civilization is coming undone."

"If there's only 3,300 of them, why don't we invite them to live with us?" Baradonna says casually, as though she's asking a few friends over for tea.

"What?" I ask, certain I'd heard her wrong. Too many hours of staring at these pages, too many thoughts of Kallum's body running through my mind.

"Take them in. Welcome them here. Make room."

I shake my head, vehemently. "We can't take in a whole

new culture like that. It would disrupt everything! Where would they sleep? What would they eat? We don't even have the resources to take all of our own people out of stasis and provide for them!" My chest heaves at the thought. I know what it was like to have a mother stuck in stasis, body so close, yet mind so far away. I know the stress it puts on the rest of the family. To imagine us opening our arms up to strangers so readily after upturning so many of our own lives is like a slap to the face.

Baradonna holds her hands out in front of her. "Ahh, no need to yell. It was just an idea! I thought you wanted to entertain new perspectives."

"*Good* perspectives. Not ones that will collapse our society along with the Klang's. Do you know what the Senate would do to me if I came to them with an idea like that? Tesaryn Wen already has her sights aimed on ousting me from power, and there's no limit to how far she'll stoop to do it. I can't prove it, but I'm pretty sure she put a diuretic in the water pitcher that sat in front of me at last week's assembly. Nearly pissed myself before I got a chance to speak."

Baradonna nods, then steps closer. "I remember that. I'd never seen you talk so quickly," she says, her voice now smooth, deep, and quiet. "You want me to cut her? Because I will. I can make it look like an accident."

"What? No! No cutting anyone. I just need some room to think. There's a rational solution out there, one that doesn't risk everything we've worked so hard for. And we're going to find it."

"Nothing irrational about a little cutting," Baradonna grumbles.

"What was that?"

"Nothing."

SESKE

Of Fresh Fish and Rotten Eggs

Charrelle squeezes my hand so tightly, she's cutting off the circulation to my fingers. It's the first time either of us has visited the cerebral cortex. Our first Knowing Walk. Our Zenzee's brain is not a particularly handsome organ, just a large ring shape, the surface blue gray with a maze of winding grooves and deep crevices you can get lost in forever if you're not careful. Thrill seekers are driven to conquer it, daring to hike all the way around, risking shock from the electrical impulses that occasionally flicker too close to the membrane's surface. There's not a single person alive who doesn't know of Clap Ardigan, first woman to circumnavigate the ring. Took her eight whole days, and she didn't have any of that fancy equipment the hikers use now. No maps. No impulse disruptors. Just rope, intuition, and a death wish.

But no thrill seekers are present today, nor have there been since right after exodus was called and then called off. When

Doka established the ERI, their first act was to cut all unnecessary travel to vital organs. No more spelunking in the liver. No more trysts upon the great aperture, our Zenzee's ever-open maw. Survival games were eliminated across the board, but the complaints were few since life itself had become a game of survival. Doka had petitioned for the Knowing Walks to be suspended, too, but even his best arguments and logic couldn't sway the Senate to end one of our most sacred, closely guarded rituals. It is here where our ancestors first greet an unborn child, in that liminal space between birth and death. It is a rite of passage for all expectant mothers, one that was practiced by everyone—from the highest-ranking members of the Contour class to the lowest of bowel-scrubbing beastworkers. If there is one place aboard our Zenzee where everyone is treated equally, it is here.

I look down at our map, then back up at the ring. Three of the towering control nodes are visible, the devices that allow navigators to control our Zenzee's movements. I turn the map so that the nodes printed on the page are in line with the nodes standing tall in front of us. "This way," I say to Charrelle. "I think."

"You *think*?" Charrelle asks, her nose crinkling up. "If this is supposed to be some kind of trust exercise, then I'm not sure we're going to pass it."

I grit my teeth and sweeten my demeanor. She was the one who wanted me to be her midwife so badly. She could have picked someone else. Someone who's been here before and has even the slightest inkling of what to expect. I study the pattern of grooves on the map, then match them to the ones in front of us. "This way, I'm sure of it," I reply.

That's all Charrelle needs, and she smiles and nods and takes a few steps, only to promptly lose her balance. Instinct spurs me, and I rush to catch her, the cortex's surface suddenly slick under my feet. We both fall, though I shield Charrelle from direct impact, and we both go sliding down a deep dark crevice. We stop abruptly, wedged in between the folds of flesh. I cling to Charrelle. Had either of us fallen individually, we would have slipped right into these unforgiving depths, but our bodies—pressed belly to belly—are just wide enough not to sink through.

"Seske! You said you were sure!" Charrelle yells at me.

I take several deep breaths, trying to calm my nerves, trying to bite back my words, my anger, but it's useless. "Daide's bells, I'm not sure! I don't have any clue what I'm doing. Why did you even choose me to be your midwife anyway?"

Charrelle's lips purse, irritation plastered all over her face, but before she can answer me, a rope ladder falls down beside us. I look up and see Madam Wade, our soothsayer, staring at us, slowly shaking her head. "Should have stuck to the path," she says.

"Should have marked the path better," I mutter.

I help Charrelle get a good grip on the ladder, then follow up behind her. Madam Wade assists us the rest of the way, helping us to find our footing. She's bundled up tight in several layers of day moss, which I could have figured out by smell even if I hadn't seen her already. Large copper earrings dangle from her lobes, with matching sets in her nose and brows, and her braids sit simply upon her head, tied to no Line, but dyed teal, gold, and fuchsia and adorned with varying numbers of copper beads at their ends. They tell a story, I can feel that in my gut for sure; but what that story is, I have no clue.

"Thank you," I say to Madam Wade. The last time I saw her, she was reading my first rags during my coming out party.

It seems all my encounters with her are destined to be fraught with drama. "I must have strayed off course."

Charrelle sucks her teeth in disapproval.

"Mmm," Madam Wade says. Her smooth, brown skin catches a flash of bluish light. A frown lands upon her lips. "Storm's coming. We'd better get inside," she says. And in the distance, I see an arc of lightning jump from the tip of one control node tower to another. The navigators must be getting ready to adjust the Zenzee's course.

Charrelle and I don't waste time, following on Madam Wade's heels, no desire at all to get caught up in a brain storm. We enter her lair, the entrance marked by a large copper grommet inset into the cortex, revealing matte black tissue beneath. Inside, the floors and walls are covered with exposed synapses, their ends glowing faintly like distant stars. I restrain my desire to touch them. Even with impulse disruptors in place, I get the feeling that they would shock me something good.

Madam Wade lays hands upon Charrelle's still-flat stomach, then looks at me. "Seske. You're here to serve as midwife?" The surprise in her voice doesn't faze me. I'd prepared long and hard for what I'd say to her.

"I am. I have been through the birthing process, as is requisite." My words come out too mechanical, but if I can get through this inquisition, we can start focusing on uniting the ancestors with our unborn child, which I'm much more prepared to handle. "I am ready to support Charrelle as best I can."

Madam Wade is well within her right to challenge that my pregnancy wasn't valid since it involved a giant alien egg that had wrecked my womb before I'd deposited it into another Zenzee. She could also mention that my gestation had lasted mere days, and that my belly had swelled up to the size of a bog melon over the course of only a few hours. Part of me wishes she *would* reject me as midwife so I wouldn't have to deal with the memories, the hurt, the phantom pains, but I'd already promised Doka, and as much as he irritates me sometimes, I don't want to let him down. Or myself down. I know I can do this.

Madam Wade stares at me for what feels like quite a long time, and I can feel Charrelle fidgeting. Or is that me?

"Very well. Let us conjure the ancestors," she says with an exasperated sigh.

She walks to the synapse at the center of the room, the largest of them all, but also the dimmest. Around the perimeter of the divot, she lights a series of candles. Then from one of the tall shelves lining the far wall, she hems and haws over hundreds of neatly arranged burlap sacks. Finally, she chooses one and unties the drawstring. Inside are bones. Small bones that look almost like phalli. Nearly uniform in size and shape. Fifty or so if I had to guess. Madam Wade sprinkles them onto the synapse and spreads them out so none are touching, taking care that they don't tumble down the fist-sized holes in the divot.

"Shoes off," she commands Charrelle, then has her sit on a stool and thoroughly cleanses her feet with petal water, taking care to work between each toe and under all the nails. She then escorts Charrelle's to the center of the synapse divot, which is free of bones. "We will see if the ancestors sit with your child."

Charrelle trembles there, looking like not much more than a child herself. I don't know how to best comfort her, so I press closer so I can hold her hand at least, but Madam Wade swats me away.

"You'll confuse the ancestors," she whispers harshly at me. So I step back and watch.

Charrelle holds her arms straight down at her sides, staring at the small bones scattered around her bare feet. For a long time, nothing happens, but then a low hum fills the room. The floor beneath Charrelle vibrates, the synapse building up tension, as if it wants to fire but there are too many disrupters here holding it at bay. One of the bones twitches, then turns slowly, the pointy end facing away from Charrelle. Charrelle lets out an audible whimper. Another bone turns away, and another.

Madam Wade lets out an undignified harrumph as over a quarter of the bones rearrange themselves, poking out like the petals of a flower.

"What? What is it?" I ask.

Madam Wade shakes her head. "The ancestors have spoken. They will not sit with this child. They offer no protection or guidance."

Charrelle's legs tremble weakly, then she keels over, landing in the bones. She begins to heave. I run over to her and throw my arm over her back as she sobs. Madam Wade doesn't stop me. Tiny bone pieces press hard into my knees, cutting at my skin, but I don't care. I am here to comfort Charrelle, so I ignore my own pain.

"You're sure?" I say to Madam Wade. "Can't we try again? Different ancestors?"

"It is unfortunate, but not uncommon among first pregnancies," Madam Wade says with a shrug, then tugs at the length of one of her braids, coming to the beaded end and twisting them as though it's a nervous habit. "I suggest that Charrelle visit the spirit wall more often during her next. Twice a day at least. It will help build favor with the ancestors."

"Next, what?" I blurt out, but Madam Wade is already shoving a glass jar into my hands. Inside swims a small throttle fish, only slightly bigger than my thumb. It gestures rudely at me, then swims to the other side, pretending not to see me.

"This is why it is important to choose a proper midwife," Madam Wade says to Charrelle. "Someone who's already been through this. I have neither the time nor patience to explain the process to both of you."

"Please, she's scared," I say. "Don't use my own inexperience to punish her. What do we do with this fish? Offer it as sacrifice to the spirit wall?"

"It is too late for prayers. The fetus must be removed," Madam Wade says, mustering up the smallest bit of compassion.

"Charrelle is not sending our child to the wall," I say, balking at the audacity of such a suggestion. "Especially just because some old bones say to do so!"

Madam laughs. "The wall is not meant for those with whom the ancestors do not sit. But the throttle fish will smooth over your grief. It will take the fetus for you, merge with it. It will become something of the child you would have had. After you are done here, place it back in the jar and keep it in there one month. When it is done molting, you can say your goodbyes and let it free into the swamp of your choosing."

"What?" Charrelle and I say, incredulous. And then it all hits me. Is that why the throttle fish are so well cared for? Is that why they attract so many visitors? Why the throttle fish look so *human*?

I shake my head, not wanting to believe it. "You can't be serious! This is barbarous. This is not who we are as a people." But even as the words escape my mouth, I do not believe them. I know exactly what our people are capable of.

Madam has truly lost all her patience now. She pushes Charrelle onto her back and spreads her knees apart. "Open the jar," she orders me, then to Charrelle, "Don't fight it. It'll only make things worse."

Charrelle looks to me, panic in her eyes. She blinks and giant tears roll down her cheeks. "Seske," she whispers.

"Charrelle," I say, offering her my hand. She takes it and squeezes tight. I know this is scary for her, scary for both of us, but I also know that having a shunned child will bring shame upon our family. Our Line would effectively end with us. Everything we've all worked for would slowly crumble. I stare Charrelle in the eyes, realizing that even though the road ahead would be rough, so much possibility grows within her. "Do you want to do this?" I ask her.

"Doka would—"

"Forget about Doka. Forget about everyone. Do *you* want to do this?" I squeeze her hand back.

She thinks for a long moment, then shakes her head.

"Then we're not doing this. I don't care what the ancestors say. This is our child, and we will not harm it." I pull Charrelle into my arms. She buries her face into my chest.

Madam harrumphs again, then gathers her bones back up and places them into the sack. "If you need to mull on it a couple days, you may. Don't wait too long, though. The ancestors may renounce your entire womb. I've had one client who waited too long. Her next four pregnancies, the ancestors completely turned their backs to her. I've never seen the bones spin away so quickly." Then, as to emphasize the point, Madam shoos us both away.

I SPEND THE REST OF THE EVENING COMFORTING CHARRELLE. I send for my will-mother. We're not supposed to have favorite parents. We're especially not supposed to favor the mother who had carried us in her womb, but I'd always felt a deeper connection with Meme. She glances at the jar when she comes into the bedroom, then looks sadly at Charrelle.

"I didn't know who else to call," I tell my mother.

"It happens," Meme says. "It's best not to worry over it for too long. I can help. I promise to be gentle."

Charrelle seizes up against me. I feel every single muscle in her body tense. I tighten my grip around her.

"No, no. We're not doing that."

"I understand your hesitation. I had the same feelings when I went through this. And it's true that some children are born without a single favor from the ancestors. Some of them even go on to lead perfectly normal lives. But the stigma will always follow them. They have to work so, so much harder to even gain an ounce of respect, and it's always a precarious thing. So much of life comes down to our Lines."

"But all that, it doesn't matter so much anymore," I say. "Not with all the work Doka's put into making things more equal."

"I know. And while that's true for a lot of people, your family is under so much scrutiny as it is. I've heard the whispers about those trying to unseat Doka. The threats are real. You know that I am on your side, but I'm afraid another setback at such a tender moment would undo all of his work." Meme puts her hand on the jar's lid and leaves it resting there. "We'll tell Doka it was a false pregnancy. That Charrelle ate some underfermented eggs and got a bad case of intestinal lice. We've all been there." She smiles warmly, but despite her sweet and calm demeanor, I get the gut-churning feeling that my mother won't take no for an answer. Having my trust in my favorite parent turn so quickly comes as a shock, but I can't let her see it affect me.

I nod and return her wan grin. "Can Charrelle and I have a moment?" I whisper to my mother. "So I can light some candles and calm her down first?"

Meme kisses me on the forehead. "Of course, dear. I'll go get some towels and hot water ready."

And then she's gone. Charrelle is laid back on the bed, nearly despondent. "Come on, Charrelle, get up. We're getting out of here."

"What?" she mutters.

"I promised Doka I'd take care of you, and I'm going to do everything in my power to make it so. I'll pray ten times a day to the ancestors if I have to, but they are *going* to sit with this child."

I stuff Charrelle's belongings into a bag, then hook my arm around hers and help her to the window.

"Where are we going?" she asks.

I heave a sigh. "Somewhere safe."

Charrelle smiles at me, and for the first time since we left Madam Wade's lair, I see the light shining behind her eyes.

"What is it?" I ask her.

"You wanted to know why I chose you to be my midwife. This. This is why. I know we don't always get along the greatest, but I trust you with my life and with that of our child."

I smile back. Maybe choosing her to join with our family Line hadn't been such a mistake after all. And it warms me to hear "*our* child."

I want to say something kind in return, but I hear Meme's footsteps coming down the hall. No time for mushy sentiments. I push Charrelle out the window. "Move it. We've got to hurry."

DOKA

Of Bloated Chambers and Starving Thrones

The Senate chamber is packed. Every single chair on the floor is filled, and advisors and community counselors are spilling into the observation galleys up above, but the proceedings have yet to start. I press through the crowd to the front of the room, making eye contact with my allies and offering them plaintive smiles in line with this desperate situation. I'd taken heed of the words Baradonna had spoken to me, way back in the bile ducts: *Trust is such a fragile thing. It's grown and sown, not commanded and demanded.* Though my power as Matris has been impeded, I haven't let that slow me down. Instead of feeling defeated, I've entrenched myself deeper into the daily proceedings of the Senate and have logged more hours among them than any other Matris in recent history. I may not be able to make unilateral decrees, but by holding a slim majority of followers, I've been able to press through some of the most contentious policies that have made true symbiosis with our Zenzee a real possibility.

And there's a slim minority who is not happy at all about that.

I catch Tesaryn Wen scowling at me from the officer's well. The bowed table where the Senate leadership sits is stretched between us like a barrier. She's ever the politician, though, and quickly eases her face into a look of delight.

"Matris Kaleigh!" she says, arms outstretched to greet me in a hug as I round the table to take my seat. I don't want to go anywhere near her, but to shirk away from such a kind, innocent-seeming gesture would only brew more doubt in the minds of all those watching. I let her envelop me into her prickly embrace. "We were so worried you wouldn't be able to make it. I didn't realize I'd given Kallum the wrong time until after he'd left. We were about to page you, but thankfully that guard of yours showed up just in time."

"Mmm-hmm," I mumble. A few hours, my ass. It was one thing to sabotage my reign, but to do it through my own husband was particularly cruel. It didn't help that Kallum had his sights firmly set on securing a seat for himself in the Senate. He'd been born with the requisite matriline and a girl's body to match, but his heart and mind had always pulled him toward boyhood, then later, toward manhood. We were best friends through all of it, and I sat in the first row, smiling ear to ear during his bud and capping ceremony. I'd witnessed several ceremonies just like it, so I thought I knew what to expect—a celebration of life, of change, of new names, and finally, the releasing of ties to the family's matriline, since as a man, he'd no longer be allowed to retain it. And Kallum's ceremony had gone beautifully and without incident . . . right up to the point he was supposed to renounce claim to his Lines. He'd locked eyes with me, and suddenly there was something in my heart that I suppose had always been there, hidden in the shadows or buried like a seed. Kallum refused to relinquish his Line and all the rights and privileges that came with it, and instead ran back up the aisle as the ushers chased after him, bidding him to come back, as if he'd stolen something.

He had, for sure. Multiple somethings . . . my heart being one of them. I would have followed after him, had my ama's hand not been locked upon my knee like a talon.

In the end, after lengthy debates (and significant bribes, most likely) Kallum had retained his matriline. It was enough to legitimize our eventual marriage, though even that was fraught with dissent among those looking to unseat me, and even some of the general population. Two head-husbands in the same family unit? It was preposterous. There were already so few men among so many women.

You are being greedy, they told us. Reckless. Disregarding tradition.

Yes, we'd said, *but the laws around marriage only mention Lines,* so Kallum and I laughed all the way from the marriage altar to our bed linens—two greedy, reckless men.

But the loopholes weren't big enough—nor were the bribes tempting enough—to get Kallum into the Senate. They made up flimsy excuses for why a man would be unfit to serve, even one with sturdy enough of a Line behind him. *Won't he be too sensitive? Tire too easily? Get too overwhelmed?* Their feigned concern cut at Kallum's capabilities, and in turn cut at my own yet again. Were their memories that shallow? Everything they said about him they'd once said about me, and slowly I'd turned the minds of those who doubted me with my policies and leadership.

Eventually our persistence wore at their nerves, and the Senate threw a prestigious delegation job at Kallum as a distraction. Head of the ERI recognizance team, traveling between Zenzee worlds and building a set of best practices for us to share. We'd decided as a family that it would be a good tactical move. No man had ever been given that much responsibility, aside from myself. Kallum took the job at our insistence, but now I wonder if we shouldn't have pushed harder for a Senate seat. Especially when my support hinges on so few votes, thanks to those keen on undermining me, like this woman standing here with a saccharine smile smeared across her face.

"Well, it's good to see that you've made it to the proceedings on time," Tesaryn Wen says to me. "We can't wait to see what sort of insight you'll have on this very delicate situation."

I bite back my aggravation and return her fake smile. "I would have liked to have more time to prepare, but I'm sure I'll have something useful to add to the conversation." I glance at Baradonna, now standing behind Tesaryn Wen, dressed in her finest silks and leathers, hand on the hilt of her knife.

"True. You're always so articulate. Nothing at all like the men I'm used to dealing with." Tesaryn Wen lets out a flighty laugh, hand pressed to her chest, so amused with herself.

"Can I cut her now?" Baradonna mouths at me. She's kidding. I think. Baradonna looks like the old carvings of Desmona the Great when she's in her formal attire, and we all remember what happened when that legend had gotten fed up with political corruptness and unleashed her blade in a Senate meeting 260 years ago. The last major structural change to the Senate chambers had been adding four sets of emergency exit doors. Apparently, no one had considered how inconvenient it would be for 118 Senators to cram through a single set of doors while a knife-wielding mad-woman slashed at them.

I swallow the lump in my throat, subtly shake my head at Baradonna's question, then look back into Tesaryn Wen's calculating eyes. "Anyway, it's so good to see you again. And I really appreciate the three dozen gall steaks you sent to my office during the End of Exodus holiday. I'm sure they would have been delicious if they hadn't spent three days rotting while we were all off celebrating."

Tesaryn Wen tsks. "Oh, I'm sorry they didn't make it there in time for you to enjoy them! I trust the smell wasn't too horrid when you returned?" She somehow manages to say this with a straight face, though a smirk keeps threatening to curl her lip.

"On the contrary. It was beyond pungent, but it reminded me of a certain smell from my childhood. What was it again? Ah yes—when you hosted the ancestral gala at your home many years ago, and my mothers made me kiss you on the cheek. Scent memories, am I right?" I step closer, waft the air around her my way. "Yep, you've still got it. Spoiled meat and spicy licorice with undertones of bog melon rind."

Tesaryn Wen's naxshi goes a pale violet. I've never seen naxshi turn that color before. Her fists ball up, posture goes rigid.

I know I've crossed a boundary, stoking the hate already in her heart, but I can only turn my cheek to her insults so many times. Thankfully, Baradonna slams her hand down on Tesaryn Wen's shoulder, then gives it a playful jostle.

"We'd best get you seated and comfortable, Senator Wen." And with that, Baradonna is pushing my most hated rival away from me. I let loose a heavy sigh but keep my posture erect. I can't let my guard down here, especially when Baradonna isn't right by my side.

The other Senate officers are already seated. Of the eight of them, three are partial to me, three are vehemently opposed, and the other two are swing votes. Despite their feelings toward me, I offer each a deep bow of respect and flourishes bordering on ridiculous. All eyes are on me, and appearances are everything.

"Calling together all Senators for an emergency meeting," Tesaryn Wen says, reading drolly from the arbiter records, the task of the Senate officer with the lowest standing. If she'd put as much effort into improving her personality as she does plotting against me, then perhaps she would have risen in rank by now. Or maybe she's so self-absorbed that she likes hearing herself talk. "We are here to explore solutions for the Klang ship. Our resource team has confirmed that their host is no longer habitable, and the Klang leadership intends to break our treaty and secure a new one."

"Zenzee," I say loudly and out of turn.

Tesaryn Wen stares coldly at me. Wordlessly.

"We deny a part of their personhood if we continue to call the Zenzee our hosts," I explain. "We have disrespected them long enough, and the least we can do is call them by their name."

A series of claps comes from the audience—my head-mother and some of her close colleagues. I take comfort knowing that I have their support no matter what.

Tesaryn Wen's naxshi turns that pale violet color again, even if the rest of her face betrays nothing. She clears her throat and continues. "Our resource team has confirmed that their *Zenzee* is no longer habitable, and the Klang leadership intends to break our treaty to secure a new one. The other ships in the vicinity have been put on high alert to uphold the treaty at all costs."

A pit settles in my stomach. It sounds as though Tesaryn Wen is proposing that we go to battle to prevent the Klang ship from breaking the treaty. But I don't dare speak out of turn again.

The Senate tolerates my antics, but I know not to push them too far beyond their comfort zone. It is a delicate balance, and often a painful one. Marrying Kallum had nearly pushed them past their tipping point, so Seske suggested we needed to counter that reckless choice with one that was equally thoughtful and strategic. She'd chosen Charrelle to be my head-wife, daughter of two Senators as well as the Comptroller of the Accountancy Guard. We'd paid a considerable dowry for this privilege, nearly emptying the coffers of both Seske's born family and mine, but it was the only way to bring some civility and respect to our thoroughly non-traditionally structured Line. As soon as our child is born, there will be an heiress, and even my harshest opponents would think twice about crossing the Comptroller's direct lineage. Desmona the Great's wrath was nothing compared to the Comptroller's.

But until then, I remain vulnerable.

We sit beneath a bone-carved relief entitled *The Weight of Our Sins*. It depicts each of the Zenzee our people had killed or left for dead, displayed in excruciating detail. You can see the desperation in their eyes, so fearful as they reach their tentacles out for one another across the harshness of space, seeking a moment of comfort . . . and yet, that comfort never comes.

My opponents called it obscene at its unveiling. I agreed with them. It was obscene that we'd doomed eighty-seven Zenzee to the worst humanity had to offer. We should be bound by duty to remember their faces.

"The treaty must be upheld," says Farah Mosely, our lead tactician. Her expert testimony is valuable in times like these, and she knows it. She holds her head high as she addresses the Senate, eyes drilling into every single officer sitting before her. "If we let one clan break it, then the trust we've worked so hard to build between us will be ruined. We just celebrated End of

Exodus day, so it should be fresh in everyone's hearts. All the Earth clans have agreed to halt further culling of the Zenzee. We have worked together, through our differences, sharing information and strategies and resources to make sure another Zenzee life is never taken. We have sacrificed much to uphold our end of the treaty—including our Lines still in stasis. The Klang have not and must live with the consequences of their actions."

Many heads nodded in agreement.

"But what of compassion?" says Bella Roshaad, one of the few heart-wife Senators. She projects a calm aura very atypical for someone of her political status. One of the first in a growing movement to voluntarily rescind her Line, her hair stands in a spectacular white poof that claims no ancestral ties. Bella Roshaad is of the age that you'd expect her voice to shake and tremble, but it is strong and forceful. "If our sistren and brethren are in crisis, we must offer them respite from their suffering. We cannot sit perched mightily in our own arrogance, when we are but one emergency from being in their same situation. And what solutions will we advocate for then? If the Earth clans are so independent now, why do we continue to follow with the Zenzee herd instead of venturing off on our own?"

A stunned silence whips through the assembly. No one moves, and yet I feel the tension mounting. There have been talks about leaving the herd before, but the intentions had always been dependent upon finding a habitable planet to settle upon. And now Bella Roshaad is suggesting that we drift aimlessly off in space, with only the resources we currently have available. I know we are aiming for self-sufficiency, but this—

"We cannot abandon the herd!" shouts Senator Bragall,

breaking the quiet unrest. "What if—" She stops herself as she stumbles into Bella Roshaad's point. Our independence from the Zenzee herd is an illusion at best. We are all just as vulnerable as the Klang.

Bella Rashaad looks expectantly at Senator Bragall, waiting for her to finish her thought. When it doesn't come, she continues. "We must show the compassion we would expect in the same situation. There is room for the Klang here, on our Zenzee. Instead of pouring our precious resources into patching their leaks and fertilizing their dying land, we should welcome them into our homes."

If I thought the Senate hated me, it's nothing compared to how much they hate this idea. The whole chamber is in an uproar, people speaking out of turn, mostly in indignation, complaining that they still have loved ones in stasis and that we don't even have resources to completely support our own people, much less a bunch of strangers. How could such a highly respected Senator suggest such a thing?

It is my instinct to disagree with Bella Roshaad as well, and when the same idea had come from Baradonna's mouth, I had. But now I am the slightest bit intrigued by this display of selflessness.

Baradonna stares at me, her quiet glare urging me to speak out in support of Bella Roshaad. Without an assenting vote, the idea will die where it stands. However, the reports from the Klang ship worry me. How would an entire culture fare if dropped into another? What compromises would we have to make? I fear the amount of work it would take for us to get through it is more than I can ask of our people.

"Thank you, Senator Roshaad," I say. "I agree that we should focus on extending compassion, and not go around itching to destroy another clan. We have learned the value of the lives of the Zenzee, but we still often overlook the value of humanity. We must save lives, however we can."

My response is middling, I know, and the grumblings are coming from all directions now, even from my supporters. I suddenly feel like backpedaling, but I haven't really said anything to pedal back from. Maybe that's the problem. We need a new plan, yes, but an innovative one that somehow doesn't involve completely upturning our lives. What Bella Roshaad suggests is too radical, and what the tactician and Wen propose is too harsh.

I see my chance to unite the two sides, and when I look up at the relief of the Zenzee, tentacles outstretched, something clicks for me. Seske had told me about her dream with Wheytt. Maybe *dream* wasn't the best word, but it was easier for me to accept. Regardless of what it was called, she and he had forged a bond while connected to our Zenzee in the salivatory chambers—a room full of puckered orifices lined with tonguelike appendages. It was hard to fathom how deeply they'd gotten to know each other. Apparently, he'd read poetry to her spleen. She'd told fairy tales to his bile ducts. The inside of his navel was a vast desert ready for her to explore. He lounged upon the cushion of her lips as she dove into the pool of tears caught in the corner of his eye. It was dizzying to hear her describe it, and at the time, I was racked with jealousy—I'm still a little jealous thinking of it now—but it gives me an idea about how we can save the Klang's ship.

If the Zenzee communicate in a similar manner, using their tentacles to bring about absolute knowledge of one another, like a direct connection into another's brain, couldn't we use that as a tool to pinpoint what was wrong with the Klang's Zenzee and maybe shed light on a solution?

"However," I say, cutting through the noise, "offering sanctuary should be a last resort." The grumbling quiets some—now it's mostly from Roshaad's supporters—but I have everyone's full attention. "It is too soon to give up on their Zenzee. We have one last diagnostic tool that we have not yet tried..."

I explain my plan to link our Zenzee so we can better address the Klang's issues, and the Senators balk at it more violently than they had Bella Roshaad's idea. All semblance of decorum vanishes. Women leave their seats, pacing up and down the aisles, hands clenching at their braids, like they're so frustrated and unnerved, they want to tear them out.

"You would risk our entire world for the Klang!" someone shouts. I can't see where it's coming from in the ruckus, but I recognize my own mother's voice easily. My heart bucks. I thought that I could at least count on her.

"I cannot say what the risks will be for sure," I say, my voice wavering. "I am not a tactician—"

"No, you are not," Farah says, cutting me off, ready to hold her expert knowledge over me if I dare to speak again. My plan has backfired, and suddenly I am defenseless, stuck in a room full of people who hate me.

"We can run the numbers at least," says Tesaryn Wen, coming to my rescue. The cadence of her voice cuts through the commotion. Things quiet down enough for her to be heard. "If the risk is too great, we should reconsider, but Doka has put forth the first legitimate option we've heard today. Even one more Zenzee lost would be too much to bear." That Tesaryn Wen agrees with me, and is sticking her neck out for me, makes me question the validity of this option altogether.

"Thank you, Senator Wen," I say, grateful, yet still untrusting. "The Klang's Zenzee seems to be affected by a physical breakdown and not an infectious one," says Farah, the venom in her voice now replaced with that of contemplation. The reversal is unsettling. Perhaps Tesaryn Wen wields more power than I give her credit for. "If we do decide to orchestrate a ventral pairing, proper use of prophylactics on the tentacle tips should reduce the risks of cross-contamination for all parties."

"Will that dull the Zenzee's senses?" I ask, worried that a barrier would inhibit the deepness of the joining.

"A minimal loss of sensation may occur, but the connection should be strong enough for us to diagnose the problem, if there is one to find." The tactician wrings her hands. "At the least, the touch should bring the Klang's Zenzee some comfort." *In her dying days* are the words that remain unspoken.

I nod, finding some comfort of my own as I settle back into my seat. I know better than to relax in front of Tesaryn Wen, but it is so nice not to be at each other's throats for a change.

"Excellent," says Tesaryn Wen. "Time is of the essence. Every second that passes is another second the Klang's Zenzee suffers. First, we will need our pilots to perform a Rorschach maneuver, so the Zenzee's undersides are facing. Gravity suspension warnings will need to go out immediately. Then all we need is a volunteer to interface with our Zenzee so we can perform the diagnostics."

"Nandi Pharrell," Farah offers. "She's spent the past three years studying how the Serrata connect with their Zenzee via the salivatory chambers and has run hundreds of simulations involving our own Zenzee. She knows the process better than anyone else in our clan."

Tesaryn Wen smiles. "Simulations are fine, but direct practice is better, don't you think?" Then she leans over the table so that her eyes lock with mine. "And there is one person who knows *our* Zenzee better than Nandi Pharrell."

Seske, she means. And now I see how she's manipulated me. I shake my head. "Absolutely not!" I object, even before the name can be spoken aloud. "Seske's been through enough. Connecting to our Zenzee again would ruin her."

"Aren't you the one who taught us that sacrifices must be made for the greater good?" Tesaryn Wen asks. "We've given up our homes at your insistence. Our privacy. Our family members, too. Surely Seske would agree to put up with a little discomfort for the sake of saving a whole Zenzee?" Tesaryn Wen stands. There is no way for her to lose. If Seske succeeds, it will be Tesaryn Wen who comes out looking like the hero. If Seske fails, in her fragile state, she'll come undone, and our family along with her. Our Line would dissolve, I would certainly lose my seat as Matriarch, and Tesaryn Wen would be there, eager to gobble up all the pieces.

"Get Nandi Pharrell prepared to interface with the Zenzee," I command, refusing to entertain Tesaryn Wen's suggestion any further. Seske is not an option here. "I want a full risk report and as soon as we're ready, let's commence with the diagnostic."

Tesaryn Wen smirks at me. "What you want is irrelevant without the support of the Senate. Perhaps we should put it to a vote?"

I swallow, looking out at our audience of Senate members. Despite the seeds of doubt Tesaryn Wen has planted, I still have many supporters out there. My mothers nod back at me. They will vote in my favor. They must know that this is the best shot we've got. And they've seen firsthand how Seske suffers, though it's just as likely that they don't want the Klang's issues to interfere with our wedding plans. I'll take the votes however I can get them.

"Fine," I say to Tesaryn Wen. "All in favor of Nandi Pharrell leading the Zenzee coupling, raise your hand."

Hands raise, a few at first. Bella Roshaad is one of them, and I am glad to have her behind me. We don't always see eye-to-eye, but she's one of the few who took me seriously from day one. And once my mothers throw their support into the mix, many more immediately follow. But I must have crossed too many people, because we're nowhere near a firm majority.

Tesaryn Wen counts, then chimes in with fifty-three votes out of a hundred and eighteen possible. Her smile quirks. "Well, I think we have our answer. Seske is the best suited—"

"No one has cast votes for Seske yet," I say, cutting her off. "There may be some who choose to remain neutral in the decision."

"Very well," Tesaryn Wen says, pursing her lips at me. "All in favor of Seske Kaleigh leading the coupling, raise your hand."

Hands shoot up, faster this time, including Tesaryn Wen's own, but there is not a majority here either. Tesaryn Wen counts twice, then sighs in frustration. "Fifty-three votes."

All the tension I'd carried throughout the assembly slips out of my body. Breaking the tie is one bit of power they had yet to snag from me. "I guess the vote comes down to me."

"So what is your decision?" Tesaryn Wen asks. Her face is not bitter, but instead, pleading. What if I'd been reading something into her motivation that wasn't there? I thought that she wanted to use Seske to better manipulate me, but *was* Seske the more obvious choice? Wasn't it better to have someone with practical knowledge over theoretical?

About ten seconds ago, I thought I'd immediately toss my vote in Nandi Pharrell's direction, but now I am unsure. It's foolish to overlook Seske's experience in the salivatory chambers, but it's heartless not to recognize the danger it poses. I hate the idea that Tesaryn Wen might be right, but in the end, I need to protect Seske.

"Based on Farah's recommendation, Nandi Pharrell is my choice," I say, the words falling out of my mouth before I can stop them. Nandi Pharrell has never connected with our own Zenzee, but I know she'll have the skillset that we need. Still, she and our Zenzee will be like strangers working together for the first time in one of the most delicate maneuvers we've ever attempted.

The proceedings conclude and the room starts to clear, but I'm still shaking from the ordeal. Bella Roshaad smiles at me before she leaves, which calms me some. Even my middling support of her idea was more than she'd gotten from anyone else. I make a mental note to meet with her in private, to see exactly how closely our views align. It's clear that I will need to find more staunch allies.

Baradonna takes my side. "Some interesting ideas presented here today," she says to me.

I shake the nerves from my fingertips and compose myself. "I appreciate your input earlier. Maybe taking in the Klang isn't quite as far-fetched of an idea as I thought at first. It's an option we might have to consider eventually. Then and only then do you have permission to say 'I told you so.'"

Baradonna wiggles her brow at me. "Well, hopefully the Zenzee coupling will be a success. If our lead tactician thinks it might work, then there's hope."

I swallow the lump in my throat. "Do you think I made the wrong decision with Nandi?"

"I'm sure Nandi is capable," Baradonna says, suddenly serious. She puts her hand on my back to comfort me, but now I feel more on edge.

"I'm sure she is, too," I say. I wish the pit in my stomach would agree. "I've got full confidence in Nandi, but could you keep tabs on Seske for me? Just in case we need her."

WE WATCH THE PROCEDURE FROM THE TACTICAL ROOM, strapped down to our seats. We've wasted little time. Two hours have passed, and the two Zenzee are still stuck in a timid embrace, like that of distant acquaintances at a social gathering. Penetration has not been attempted, and the prophylactic-covered tentacles drift listlessly.

"This isn't working," Tesaryn Wen says pointedly, and though I am the object of her scorn, she addresses the other Senators present. "Nandi Pharrell is not the most fit candidate."

"Give it more time," I say. "This is a delicate procedure. We don't need to rush."

"On the contrary," says Farah. The lead tactician is always eager to show her support of Tesaryn Wen, especially when it means she gets to refute my ideas. "Time is of the essence and we cannot afford for our Zenzee to be vulnerable like this much longer."

I curl my lips at her. "Is that your professional opinion, or are you angling for political connections?" I boldly ask, looking from her to Tesaryn Wen and back. I've already made a lot of enemies today, so what's one more? I need the whole truth, and I need to know Farah isn't being swayed by her allegiance to Tesaryn Wen.

Farah huffs, hand on her chest and everything. "It's an unmitigated fact," she says with bite. "Our navigators are engaged in constant manipulation of the brain to hold this position. The longer and harder our Zenzee fights it, the deeper the damage being done to her cerebral cortex. Not to mention the emotional scars. We can give it another two hours, and then we will have to disengage. Perhaps we should reconsider Ses—"

"I'll go check on Nandi and the researchers," I say, looking for somewhere to channel my nervous energy and to shake off my embarrassment for doubting her. "Maybe the process needs to be spurred on from there."

"Matris Kaleigh," Farah says. "It's advisable that men do not enter the salivatory chambers."

I should trust her. She knows what she's doing, and she knows what's best for our Zenzee. And I guess I do, too, but I'm still unwilling to entertain the thought of putting Seske through yet another trauma.

"I'll bring four accountancy guards with me. They should be competent enough to keep me safe," I say with firm defiance.

Farah's warning wasn't misandry, although that might have played a part in it. No, it had merit. While women were reasonably safe to enter the salivatory orifices and connect with the Zenzee, the men who've tried it never reemerged, including Wheytt. The Serrata ship had mastered the technique we are attempting, using women they called "Queens" to interact with the Zenzee and keep her company in the absence of connecting to other Zenzee. However, it took dozens and dozens of women to even scratch the surface of the Zenzee's vast and complex mind. The Zenzee found comfort in the quaint interactions, which supposedly kept them from dwelling too much on the loneliness.

We had considered instituting a practice of using Queens

ourselves, but after careful study, the drawbacks became obvious. After months of communing with the Zenzee, the Queens become unable to relate to humans anymore. They slowly forget names. Faces. They forget how to eat on their own, and eventually how to breathe. They become completely dependent upon the Zenzee, confined to their pulsating orifices, hooked up through a series of tentacles. Thrones, the Serrata call them, as if it's a great honor. Maybe that makes it easier for them to swallow the truth behind the sacrifice.

We decided against the practice, though the Senate vote was neatly split down the middle, with me as the tiebreaker once again. Our lives would have been considerably easier if I'd gone the other way. The sacrifices we've made wouldn't have had to cut so deeply. We wouldn't have had to give up so much of our old lives. I made more enemies that day, but that was nothing new. Using the Queens would have been the easier choice, but it wasn't the better choice. Distracting our Zenzee from her misery didn't justify us causing more.

Null gravity has never been kind to me, so I allow my guards to usher me to the salivatory chamber. When the door opens, I see the small contingent of researchers consoling a very distraught Nandi, still sopping with the Zenzee's fluids and a random tentacle trailing out of the orifice and running up her nose.

"What's the status?" I ask impatiently.

The researchers balk at the sight of me. "You can't be in here!" one of them yells.

Already the orifices nearest me have started to show interest in my presence, puckering their lips in an obscene gesture. My guards dutifully swat away the tendrils that emerge from the openings. The tendrils recoil like sulking toddlers, wringing upon themselves into tight coils, before venturing out toward me once again.

"I am Matris of our people. I can be anywhere I please." I cross my arms, puff my chest. "Time is of the essence, and I've come for a status report. The sooner I have it, the sooner I can leave."

"At least move over here, then," the researcher says, pointing to the exact center of the room, the farthest away I can get from the many, many eager mouths lining the walls, yearning to lap me up with their tendrils.

"Maybe this is good," says one of the other researchers. "Maybe with more of an appetite, the Zenzee will be aroused enough to connect with Nandi."

"Please don't send me back in there," Nandi pleads. "It's nothing like the simulations." She looks as if she's seen a ghost, then starts crying again. To show such vulnerability in front of a man, in front of her Matris, means she's worse off than I'd thought.

"One more time," the researcher says. "I'll give you a sedative to relax you some. You need to relax. You know all of this! Allow her into you, as much space as she needs."

Nandi shakes her head, tears spilling down her cheeks. "I can't. Not right now. I need some time . . . to . . ." Her eyes drift off and her whole body starts trembling.

I can't help but feel like I'm doing to Nandi the exact thing I wanted to prevent Seske from experiencing. Not once had I considered that I'd be destroying one life while protecting another. But right now, we don't have time to waste on stray thoughts and regrets. There's no room for Nandi's misgivings. Or mine. "Give her the sedative," I say to the researcher, my voice even and calm, though inside, my every thought is roiling.

The shot is administered, and once Nandi's settled, she plunges headfirst into the throbbing orifice without resistance. It puckers wider, welcoming her inside. Then she's shoulder deep. Hip deep. Ankle deep. And then the glistening lips press shut, and there's nothing left of Nandi on the outside. A deep hum comes from the orifice, as though someone is masticating on a tender bit of flesh. Nandi's shrill cries peak over it for a moment before turning to whimpers, then fading to nothing.

Together, we all watch the orifice, lulled by the rhythmic motion, the sloshing, the convulsing.

"This is good," the researcher says, drawing up a virtual display in front of us. "This is much more of a response than we had before." We see the live feed of the two Zenzee again, but this time, the capped tentacles of our Zenzee are erect and purposely moving toward the Klang's. They disappear inside the Zenzee's exposed underflesh, and the Klang's behemoth lets out a massive shudder. Its limp limbs come to life and find our Zenzee's underflesh in kind. It is our turn to shudder now, but the tremor is subtle, more like a ripple. Nandi cries out inside her throne, but it sounds less like a cry of pain and more like one of pleasure.

The first images from Nandi's mind link are projected onto the screen. They're fuzzy and fleeting, like snatches of memory from a dream. We catch glimpses of the Klang's Zenzee through her connection with ours as Nandi travels from one organ to the next. While it is impossible for her to process everything, she will note where the Klang's Zenzee is failing the hardest and maybe even why. Snippets of indistinguishable data scroll across the screen, absolute nonsense from my perspective, but our finest researchers will pore over the footage, analyzing it for the source of the Klang's ills.

It's all so hypnotic.

Another scream comes from Nandi, pulling me out of my reverie. Pain this time. Intense pain. The researcher's brow cocks as she examines the screen closely, staring at a room with organically tiled flooring and a curtain of ropes hanging from the ceiling, each ending in a tear-shaped bulb that glows faintly. It's hard to get a sense of scale, but it reminds me of the inside of a ballroom. "The aliefe structure," the researcher says. "One of the several Zenzee organs with no analog to our physiology. Little is known about it. It's been almost dormant in all of the studies we've performed, but the Klang's . . . it seems to be coming alive." Nandi's screaming intensifies, but it has become like a song. Lilting and almost pleasant to listen to. Somehow arousing.

"We need more data," the head researcher says, quickly attaching nodes onto her own forehead. She hastily tests the connections, and when she's done, the virtual screens are split. Her feed on one and Nandi's on the other.

No one stops her. In another minute, she chooses the throne three over from Nandi. Or maybe it has chosen her. She barges inside and disappears. The two other researchers look at the remaining nodes sitting on the metal tray, then nod at each other, splitting them evenly between them. "More data," they say, their voices the same eerie monotone.

Then they are gone, and it is just me, surrounded by my four guards.

"Maybe we should leave," one of them suggests, but no one moves.

One of the mouths gropes for me, more so than the others. It has no eyes, but I know that it is watching me. Lusting after me. Or maybe it has sensed my arousal. A long, thick tendril erupts from its lips. Had there been gravity, it would have thumped to the floor, bridled by its ridiculous girth, but in null gee, it moves with grace. Toward me. It wants inside me, but I . . .

I—

My guards step to the side and allow it to pass. They know that this tendril is special. That it is mine.

We forget that we have made a mistake in coming to this place and wonder why we haven't been here all along. My guards each find the thrones that call to them, Queens, each and every one of them. And then I am alone.

The tendril stops inches from my face. I caress it once, like the cheek of my lover. It circles carefully around my neck, once, twice. Then tugs. The things it wishes to do to me cannot be done out here, in the open. We need the comfort and safety of a throne. I am eager, but shy to show it, and drift slowly toward the mouth that beckons me with such lustful haste.

"Ayeeeee!" comes a voice from behind me. Once upon a time, I knew who it belonged to, but it seems I have already forgotten. My thoughts are a fog between my ears, but I watch in horror as the woman raises her knife and cuts down on the tendril, separating me from my lover. I wail out in pain as thick black ichor forms droplets floating in the air.

The tendril reels back, and the mouth seals shut. Impenetrable. I feel like I've lost my home, and I fold up into a helpless ball.

"Shhh, shhh," the woman says, curling me into her bulk like a babe. She plucks thin tendrils from the corners of my eyes, my nose, nearly transparent and as thin as fishing wire. I hadn't even realized they were there. "Ol' Baradonna is here for you," she says.

I nod as my mind starts to become my own again. Gradually, I realize there is a mechanical shriek filling the room. I look back at the projection and see red warning lights showing on the feeds of the four researchers. By the timestamps, it appears they've all been there for an hour now, much too long.

"We need to decouple the ships," I tell Baradonna.

"Okay," she says. "How do we do that?"

"I don't know. All the researchers are in there," I say, pointing to the wall of mouths. Baradonna tries to pry open the rim of one the salivatory orifices a researcher is in, but it's much too tight. Doesn't even give an inch.

"Seske," I say, though I hate to have to call upon her. "She might know what to do."

Baradonna shakes her head. "I looked everywhere. I can't find her. Your will-mother-in-law says she and Charrelle came back from their outing, then ran off together. It's like they've disappeared."

"What do you mean, 'disappeared'? No one saw where they went?"

"Your will-mother said they were both quite upset. Didn't say why, though. They snuck away. I traced their scent a ways, but lost it in the second ass. Everything smells like day-old shit there."

Seske and I had been on several misadventures, and I know how good she is at not being tracked, even if she is one of the most high-profile women among our people. But if they took a turn in the second ass—

I bite my lip. "I have an idea where they've gone."

"I'm right behind you," Baradonna says.

"No," I say, "I need to go alone. Stay here, watch over the researchers. In case something changes, and they need help."

"That's seven," she says as I make a move for the door. As

soon as I pass the threshold, the mouths begin to settle back down.

"Seven what?" I ask her from relative safety.

"Times I've saved your life. Not that I'm counting."

I purse my lip, more than happy to endure her obvious gloating. And we both know that counting is what accountancy guards do best.

SESKE

Of High Times and Low Tides

I set a prayer candle on either side of Charrelle, then lay four cowrie shells at her feet, in tribute to the ancestors. Had I more time, I would have grabbed a more suitable sacrifice. My crude attempt at an altar is unworthy of a visit from the humblest of Mothers, but I cling to the hope that one will sense our desperation and come sit with us. I am already on edge, paranoid both about us being caught here, and about those other spirits who have haunted me here in our Zenzee's womb.

I check over my shoulder—for accountancy guards, for my will-mother, for anyone—but we are alone. Satisfied, I light the candles as the elevating properties begin to thin the veil between our world and that of the ancestors. I breathe in deeply. Charrelle does the same, sitting cross-legged in front of me, one hand on her non-existent baby bump.

"Will they even know where to find us?" she asks. "We are so far from the Wall."

"They will find us," I say confidently, though I possess no reasoning why I should believe such a thing.

She can sense this, I'm sure. In these past few hours, I have yet to feel confident in anything I've done. And yet, I'm also here with Charrelle now, helping her, and that must count for something, as she doesn't question my assertions.

We wait.

Several minutes pass. At first I wonder if the candles are potent enough, because I can't sense anything, but then with a smack, my mind opens up, and I am fully ready to receive spirits. I can feel every hair on my skin. I can taste a meal on my tongue that I'd eaten last week. I can smell Doka between Charrelle's legs.

Charrelle stares at me, lids heavy, head tilting to one side. "Ha! What are you thinking now?" she asks me. "Your nax-shi just brightened so brilliantly. Can I touch?" Her fingers press toward my face. I want to dodge. Though we are family, we do not share that sort of intimacy, but the candles have slowed my reaction time, and her clammy hand slaps against my cheek before I can object. "Your skin is so soft. Like the underside of a heart murmur." Her hand slides sloppily down my face, over my lips, then drops back onto her lap like a dead fish. For a moment, it looks like it is a dead fish—scales, fins, the works—but then I shake my head and it's a proper hand again.

"Maybe I shouldn't have lit both candles," I slur. I'd swiped them from our heart-wives' room. Whatever kind of praying Minique, Jesphara, and Ida were doing to the ancestors was intense. I haven't felt this out of it since Sisterkin left me for dead at the Ancestor's Wall. The thought is almost enough to sober me.

Sisterkin.

I know I'll never be high enough to entertain thoughts about her without descending into a sad, pitiful state. Her act of betrayal still cuts as sharply as it had all those years ago. She's gone now. Banished and forgotten, but with the veil this thin, who knows who might cross over. I shake my head again. Charrelle needs me to be strong right now, and I need to fill the void my sister has left inside my heart with something else. Anything else.

"Charrelle," I say, looking deeply into her eyes. "Is Doka a good husband to you?"

Okay, not that. But it is too late.

She smiles. "Of course! He is gentle and kind and patient with me. And of course, he's *so* handsome." She leans in, her lip upon my ear, even though there's no one around. "And he keeps things so moist . . . you know?"

I clear my throat, wishing I could scrub away that mental image.

"I still owe you so much for choosing me for him," Charrelle says with a warm smile. She hasn't noticed my discomfort. *Discomfort or jealousy*, I want to ask myself, but don't.

"You owe me nothing. You were the obvious choice to us all. The perfect fit for him," I bumble out.

"We do fit well together. When we kissed at our wedding, I sort of felt like there'd been this Doka-size hole in my life, and I hadn't realized it until that very moment. It was magic, Seske. And now, we've made this . . ." She rubs her belly again. "I know what we're supposed to do, but I can't. This child is ours. All of ours. And she'll be our pride and joy, no matter if the ancestors sit with her or not."

Something shifts in my gut, a gentle wave, then one of the candles starts to tip over, only it doesn't fall. Just leans. I stare at it oddly, and then when I look back up at Charrelle, she's hovering a few inches off the ground, cowrie shells floating next to her. As if gravity has decided not to be a thing anymore.

"These candles, Seske! So potent. Are you seeing this?" She flails her arms and legs, like she's swimming in a pond.

My head clears, ever so slightly. As though I'm almost, *almost* able to put my thoughts in the right order, but they flitter away. "Sooo potent," I say, watching as the candle flame goes from a pointy little thing to more of a gyrating blob. A tiny little sun. "I feel like I'm actually floating. Maybe, this is a sign from the ancestors. Maybe we were right to not give up on them. They *will* find us."

So we pray, mumbling out every favor we've ever done for anyone, hoping they will amount to enough for the ancestors to give us one in return. We sit in this meditative trance for hours it seems, and sometimes I drift off, only to be woken by Charrelle's spontaneous outbursts.

"Seske! Seske!" Charrelle is shaking my arm now, waking me again. I wonder what divine insight she has stumbled upon this time. Her conspiracy theory on the origin of humanity had sparked many thoughts in my mind—that the first family had been birthed from a string of cowrie shells on a necklace hanging around a turtle god's neck. Then there had been her treatise on colors, in which she'd described, in detail, all 814 colors that were distinguishable by the human eye. We'd gotten into a horrid argument about the true value of fuchsia and what it tasted like before I'd dozed off again.

"You smell like Doka," I tell Charrelle as my head lolls against her chest.

"Seske, wake up," she says again.

I rub my hand against her cheek, dragging my fingers through her beard stubble. "You talk like him, too. Like how he's always saying my name as if he enjoys the way it tastes on his tongue. Say something else the way he does."

She snaps her fingers in front of my face, and it startles me, alert enough that I can look at the digits. I follow fingers to arm, to chest, then to face. Funny. She kind of looks like Doka, too. They say all family units start favoring one another after they've been together for a while.

But this . . . this is something else, I think. I concentrate all my thoughts into really looking at her face, and finally realize that it's not Charrelle at all. Doka now stares down at me, with something between compassion, frustration, and desperation on his face.

"What? How?" is all I can manage.

"Ses—" He clears his throat. "I need you to snap out of this!" He extinguishes both candles with a pinch, juicy wax slipping like a wave, forward and back in the null gravity, but never meandering away from the pool. "We've got an emergency situation. We've coupled our Zenzee with the Klang's, but something's gone wrong, and now all of the researchers, my guards, and Nandi are trapped inside the Zenzee's salivatory orifices."

"That's a bad, bad thing. Where's Charrelle?" I slur, looking around, suddenly anxious.

"I've sent her home. She's safe."

"No!" I scream. "She is not safe. They want the throttle fish to take our child!"

Doka pulls me in close, his face nuzzled in the top of my hair. "She told me everything. Thank you for being there for her. I've instructed Kallum not to let a single person into our room until we get back. He will keep her safe."

I nod slightly. Kallum might not always be the kindest or gentlest person, but he loves harder than any of us and would do anything Doka asks of him. I know that Charrelle will be safe in his care.

"I knew you had it in you, Seske," Doka says to me. "That's why I didn't hesitate to ask you to be her midwife, despite what you've been through. You saved our child."

I take a few deep breaths, and my mind starts to clear ever so slightly. "I didn't think I had it in me, to be someone's hero again." I look deeply into Doka's eyes, realizing he's come to me for a reason. I've spent time with the Zenzee, connected in those very same orifices. The memories were bittersweet, and a lot of the time, I pretend it hadn't happened. But I'd had the experience, wanted or not. I know our Zenzee probably better than anyone else, and I may be the only one who can save those poor souls from suffering the same fate as Wheytt. I feel tears running down my cheeks as I remember searching and searching the orifice that had swallowed him whole, looking for traces, clues, some sort of explanation. I remember how it had wrecked me, and yet here I am now, ready to do it all again.

"I'll help," I say to Doka. "However I can."

I DRIFT NAKED IN THE CENTER OF THE ROOM, MOUTHS READY to welcome me like an old friend. Our Zenzee and I, we have a connection. I'd carried her child for a brief but crucial moment, and my sacrifice had satisfied our Zenzee enough that she's allowed us to stay with her. I guess I was foolish enough to believe a sacrifice that big would be enough to last a lifetime.

I choose the orifice Wheytt had used. The one that had devoured him whole. I don't know if this is an act of defiance, or simply a longing to be near him, or a secret wish I will endure the same fate. The mouth opens up as I near and accepts me eagerly. I bite my tongue as the tendrils enter me, then seconds later, I am one with our Zenzee and I feel *everything*.

There is so much grief. So much pain, but I can't bring myself to scream. Somehow, I know that giving it an outlet would only make things worse—releasing pressure only to be filled up again with something ten times more painful. Instead, I sit with it. Let it wash over me. And I realize it is not our Zenzee that aches so. These are the thoughts and remembrances of the Klang's poor Zenzee.

I sit in an ocean, wave after wave battering me, and in the distance, right over the horizon, a magenta sun brightens, then dulls, over and over, like a pulse. The whole of the ocean is angry and resentful, and yet only a small fraction of it affects me. For every ache and pain I experience, there are millions more. Then they roll back, receding into the dark waters beyond. I catch my breath, thinking that I have made it through the worst. I use this moment of clarity to communicate with our Zenzee . . . bidding for it to release its captives. I concentrate with every inch of my being to project these thoughts, knowing they will only register as a whisper of an echo inside the Zenzee's mind. When diplomatic pleading has no effect, I scream and scream and scream until I realize I am sitting fully on the ocean's sterile, sandy bottom, not a lick of water around me. When I look up, I see the giant wave has blotted out the sun and is about to crash down upon me.

It is only then that I realize what this connection is.

I tune back into my body, my actual body, and start to twist and squirm. One by one, the tendrils remove themselves. When enough of them are out, I press backward, kicking my heel against the inner lip of the mouth until it opens. I struggle out backward, and feel hands upon my ankles, helping to pull me free. I escape, caught by null gravity and Baradonna's rigid embrace. Doka stands right behind her, eyes wide.

"The Klang ship is dying," I wheeze, throat raw from the tendrils ripping free.

"We know that," Doka says. "We've known that for months."

I shake my head. "No, I mean something more immediate. She's transferring all her experiences to our Zenzee in some kind of death ritual. We need to get the Klang's people over here right now!"

Baradonna gives Doka a significant look I can't quite make out.

"Not now," he mutters.

I'm about to protest "Of course now!" but I see that he was talking to her. I don't have time to wonder what he means.

We leave the room in a rush, Baradonna and I helping Doka to navigate the null gravity. When we are back at tactical command, he explains the direness of the situation to the Senate officers. There is resistance, of course, and he wastes so much time trying to convince them of how imperative it is to take immediate action. I stand back, biting my tongue, feeling guilt well up inside of me. If I'd just stayed married to him properly, he'd still have the power to execute a direct mandate, and all of this convincing wouldn't be necessary. However, Doka is astute enough to smooth over most of the officers' concerns and barrels through the rest.

Shuttles are readied even as communications are a frenzy between us and the Klang. I keep my wits about me, wondering how Doka can handle such a situation with dignity and grace. I should appreciate him more. Or maybe I shouldn't. This isn't the time for my feelings to get complicated. But it does weigh on me that I was nowhere near as prepared to deal with a crisis back when I was Matris. I'd been too young, too inexperienced, and had buckled under the pressure. Me giving up the Matriarchy was the best thing that I could have done for my people.

I keep telling myself that.

And for three years, I'd detached from nearly all responsibility. Adalla and I had had the perfect life, as perfect as it could get at least. I see now that it was merely a balm, a short reprieve to allow us to soothe over the wounds we'd suffered in order to prepare us for more. As soon as those shuttles come back, our people will be in crisis mode. Nothing will be the same. I'm not sure if our utopia will ever recover, but maybe that's the problem: that we thought it a utopia in the first place. That's an argument for another time, though—for philosophers and historians to consider centuries from now. For the moment, we need to get through the next few hours, the next few days, the next few years.

And while we do, I will be there for Doka, for my people, and I will do my best to cling onto hope.

I spring into action, ordering people around, and I'm surprised by how easily it all comes back to me—and how easily people listen to me. "Call in the medics. We don't know what kind of condition these people will be in."

I catch Doka staring at me.

"What?" I ask.

"You haven't lost it, you know," he says, stars in his eyes. "The ability to lead. You would have been an amazing Matris. If that's what you'd wanted."

"You know it isn't," I say, starting to bristle.

Doka gives me a disarming smile that turns my stomach into knots. I know he's eager to be the best Matris he can be, but sometimes I get the feeling he's just biding his time, waiting for me to reclaim the throne. And as much as the thought terrifies me to no end, there's a tiny bit of a thrill lurking there, too.

He knows that. And he knows that I know he knows. We hold eye contact a moment too long, then we both get back to work.

WITH THE EVACUATION SCHEDULE MUCH MORE TRUNCATED than we could have imagined, there is not enough time to relocate everyone via shuttles, so we use the Zenzee's intimate connection to create a safe passageway. The tentacles pull so tightly against one another, a seal forms against the harshness of space. A line of accountancy guards stands on either side of the path, ready to subdue any of the creatures that lurk in this delicate underflesh, though I suspect the guards are also here to subdue any of the Klang who step out of line. Their bags are all searched, and the guards are careful to weed out any weapons or contraband technology. There were rumors that the Klang had once been accomplished scientists and inventors, but the plagues and failures they'd suffered through had driven them to desperation and barely clinging to life. Still, the precautions are necessary—if we let our empathy become complacency, we could endanger *both* peoples.

The first wave of refugees step onto the path, ribbed flesh so soft and mushy that many people stumble until they get used to the odd texture. The vegetation has been cleared and the surrounding area has been sufficiently lit, though I still catch glints of inquisitive and hungry eyes lurking in the shadows beyond—too large, too bright, and too clustered to be human. I straighten up and put on my best smile and ignore the memories of the last time I was this close to a Zenzee's ovispore.

Some of the refugees are dark-skinned, but others have skin as light as bone. They are like walking skeletons, things out of children's nightmares. Even the men aboard the Serrata hadn't scared me as much . . . mostly covered in dark beards and furs, the whites of their skins were more of a curiosity. But these people, especially the women, wear it on display. Many have their hair in braids, but only one or two. I wonder what sort of histories could be stored in such a simple pattern. Did their Lines not run so deeply? Did their ancestors not require such a tribute? Perhaps they had other ways to honor them.

As nervous and uncertain as I am about the nature of our guests, my curiosity draws me nearer. "Excuse me, can I help?" I offer to a mother carrying an infant slung around her chest as well as multiple heavy bags. She looks wary of me. "I am Seske Kaleigh, daughter of mothers—" Then I realize my Line and credentials mean nothing to her. "Just call me Seske. I am here to help."

She stops long enough to hand me one of her bundles, looking slightly relieved. She says words to me, words that don't make sense to my ears. She probably hadn't even understood me anyway. "Seske," I say, placing my hand to my chest.

"Vina," she says, doing in kind. She places a hand on her fussy babe. "Widya."

I catch a glimpse of the babe's face. Her skin is a shade of brown darker than my own, her hair thin black curls. She almost looks like she could be one of ours.

It takes hours to get everyone off the Klang Zenzee, and by then, there are no signs of life left within her. We try to get our Zenzee to let theirs go, but no matter what commands are given, no matter how hard we manipulate the control nodes sunk deep in our Zenzee's brain, they remain locked together in their caring embrace. It makes me wonder if we really have control over her at all. Eventually, we send a team to decouple them physically, with blowtorches and light saws. It is a grisly scene, but I cannot look away. Our Zenzee struggles, pulling back the severed pieces of the Klang's Zenzee and tucking them into little nooks in her underflesh. It hurts to see our Zenzee in such distress, however, we can't risk having her act out in this way. After a brief debate, Doka orders to have her sedated for everyone's safety. Though our plan is successful in the end, the look of defeat in his eyes chills me.

Twenty-eight hours later, all the Klang are accounted for after a thorough sweep of their Zenzee to make sure no one was left behind. Thankfully, they'd found someone who'd been overlooked during the exodus, a man on the verge of death, clinging on to the last traces of breathable air. With him finally aboard, it's time for us to continue our journey. It feels wrong to leave the dead Zenzee behind, a wilting corpse drifting in the cold of space without mourning her, but everyone is still in crisis mode, rationing food and water and other supplies. The ERI is busy recalculating the effects these additional souls will have long term on our environment. The Senate is busy drafting new covenants to deal with the refugees.

So I mourn the Zenzee alone from the control room, lighting a single candle and watching as the corpse grows smaller and smaller. Though I guess I'm not really alone in my grief. It surrounds me. I live within it. Breathe it. I suppose that should bring me some comfort, but it does the opposite.

The corpse is nearly completely out of sight when it flashes magenta, so bright I shield my eyes. It was the exact same shade as the star in my vision. Not crimson or pink, or mothers forbid, fuchsia. I look around to see if anyone else has noticed, but with all the chaos happening within our Zenzee, no one is paying attention to what is going on without.

I look back at the Zenzee as the flash fades back to nothingness, and soon after that, I can't distinguish her dark, dead flesh from the darkness of space. It hits me hard, and I wipe tears away. I know she is not the first Zenzee by far to die at human hands, but she is the first dead Zenzee I've seen with my own eyes, and I get the sinking feeling she won't be my last.

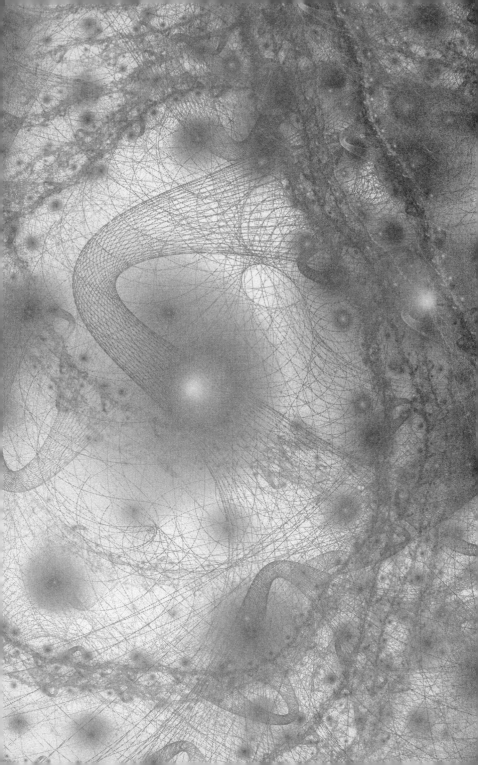

part II

. . . .

commensalism

Even if our aim was to do no harm, we would have set
ourselves up for failure. We are entwined. Entangled.
We always have been and always will be.

QUEEN OF THE DEAD

DOKA

Of Shallow Roots and Deep Conversations

Y ou've seen the camps," Tesaryn Wen says to me, the venom in her voice even more cruel and calculating than usual. I seem to have struck a particularly deep nerve with this request. "On several occasions, in fact. But if you would like me to take time out of my busy schedule to arrange another visit, then so be it."

"There is no need to arrange anything," I say, trying to mitigate her concerns of having to do extra work on my behalf. "I just want to go and look around and meet people."

"You were provided a detailed report of every single individual we've taken into our care, and a scaled map of the holding facility was also included in Appendix D."

"I was given that report, and I'm thankful for it. But nothing within those many pages told me of their happiness. Of their challenges. I'm worried that—"

"There is nothing to be worried about. Yes, we had some

incidents during the first few weeks they were here, but things have largely calmed down. Everyone is happy, and even if they're not, they're much better off than they were living on their Zenzee."

I bite my lip and let the issue die. The Senate is growing more restless with my rogue questions and far-fetched ideas. I keep insisting that we begin integrating the Klang's culture with our own, tearing down some of the boundaries we've instituted, but they say it is still too soon. I know we were thrown into this emergency situation without much time to prepare, but it's been three months, and things should have progressed by now.

"It is not your job to concern yourself with the details," says Tesaryn Wen. "Therein lies madness for a matriarch. Accept our reports and base your conclusions on those. Keep your eyes on the big picture. We need your guidance focused there. And though I hate to say it, the Klang . . . they can be confrontational. Aggressive. Dangerous."

I wince. Even Bella Roshaad, one of the biggest proponents of taking in the refugees, has turned to Tesaryn Wen's side when it comes down to the matter of integrating them. They don't like that I sit in on their meetings so often, and especially don't like it when I interrupt their proceedings to give my opinions. But how can I not be concerned with the details? How can I not wonder how 3,300 people are living in a section of the Ides that would be grossly overcrowded with half that many? And yet, each time I visit, I am greeted by a small group of smiling faces, living in a home that is crowded, yes, but not so much more than my own. They are clean and nicely clothed, with plump cheeks and friendly faces. But I do not trust their smiles. There is something hidden behind them that makes each and every visit feel like a manipulation. A carefully crafted lie. I need to see the truth for myself, and there's no way I can do so as long as Tesaryn Wen is involved.

"You are right, Senator Wen," I say. "I do have other matters that need my attention, but please, keep me updated on any changes. I want the Klang to feel at ease here—this is their home now."

The entire Senate chamber bristles at the last part of my statement. Good. They can minimize my power, but they can't minimize the truth. No matter how much they wish they could.

"Of course, Matris Kaleigh," Tesaryn Wen says to me. The tension in the room halves as soon as I take my first step toward the exit.

I rush home and find Kallum and Charrelle cuddling in bed. I snuggle up behind Charrelle and place my hand on her belly. Our baby has been kicking like mad lately, and each time it fills me with joy. Charrelle jokes that our daughter will be as great a fighter as Matris Armage who, when being ousted from power in the middle of the night, had kicked a hole clean through an accountancy guard's torso while wearing her royal slippers. Or so the story goes.

"Is this a new favor lure?" I say, tracing my finger around the symbol painted under Charrelle's navel in naxshi ink.

"From a few days ago," she says. "I'm getting another tomorrow. Here." She points to her right breast, already starting to swell in anticipation of our child coming forth into the world. "To ask a favor from our ancestors to nourish my milk."

I nod. It is not uncommon to get a few of these lures during pregnancy, but Charrelle seems obsessed with them. She's gotten twenty-four so far, and we still have three months of pregnancy left. Plus, there are so many spirit amulets in our

room that we've had to rearrange the furniture to accommodate them all.

"And has Dr. Yadilla come to visit yet?" I ask.

Charrelle turns away from me and tucks into Kallum's
arms.

"I sent her away. I already have Vonne. I don't see why I
need both." Charrelle blinks her wide eyes at me, daring me
to reply.

I know I shouldn't. I should leave it up to Charrelle, to trust
in her instincts and allow Seske to guide her toward sound
decisions, but I'm under such pressure to produce a healthy
heir, I can't bring myself to leave this unchallenged. "Vonne
just feels your stomach and paints designs on it! Dr. Yadilla has
medical devices that can look inside and make sure our daughter is growing properly."

"Vonne can feel those things as well. She says everything
is normal."

"But—"

"Doka," Kallum says. "Perhaps there is a better time that
we can discuss this. Charrelle says she feels comfortable.
That's what's most important."

I take a deep breath and try hard to tamp my feelings down
all the way to my feet. I know Kallum has Charrelle's best inter-
ests at heart, just like I do, but it's tough that everywhere in my
life, I'm constantly feeling outnumbered. "Whatever makes
you feel most comfortable," I say to Charrelle. And while I am
willing to go along with their decision a little longer, I do not
intend to sit idly by another day when it comes to other matters. "Can I borrow Kallum from you for a bit, though? I'll send
for Vonne to stay with you for a few hours this evening."

Charrelle perks up. "And I can get another favor lure? A
small one?"

"If Vonne says it's all right, sure," I say. "Kallum?"

Kallum rolls out of bed, stretches his wiry frame, finger-tips touching our not-so-high ceiling, then slips into his robes. We set off to the uncommon gardens, an out-of-the-way sanctuary for plants on the verge of extinction. Flora exchange programs have bolstered some of the species populations, but they are not yet thriving enough to reintroduce them into the other gardens.

Here we have a bit of solitude, surrounded by a thicket of awkward dill plants and carnivorous war lilies, with the shrill mating calls of blue-hatted palms drowning out our whispers. The silk cloak fungus looks pregnant with spores, their heads peaking from the mushroom cap in rows, like the buttons running down the front of a fancy coat. The spores are too big to cause humans problems, but they infect the gall worms, our primary source of meat. The worms go rogue, their minds falling under control of the fungus, causing them to burrow into the lining of the gut, right near a wash hoglet colony, and then die there. It's weird, and doesn't benefit us in any way, but we're fighting against our tendencies to place value on nature based on how it can serve us. In any case, the silk cloaks are pretty to look at, and we're far enough from the gall worm farms for them not to cause any problems.

We sit together at the edge of a pond, thighs pressing together, legs dipped into the waters. The throttle fish below tug at our toes, then swim around in the chase game they like to play when they realize we haven't brought them any food. Two of them come close to the shore to wrestle, their flipping and flopping getting Kallum and me all wet. I shoo them away, with no success. Kallum picks up a piece of shiny shell and tosses it out into the middle of the pond. That gets their attention, and they dive off to retrieve it.

"Have you gotten any more news from the Klang camp?" I ask him. "Details? Like how people are really doing?"

Kallum stares at me. "You haven't been getting the reports?"

"I've read them. Over and over. They always say the same thing. Everything is fine. The people are happy and fed and taken care of. And yet, they keep them locked up and separated from the rest of us. There has to be a better way."

Kallum raises a brow. "Ah, so you're volunteering to bring one of them into our home?"

"No! I mean, I don't know. Maybe." I frown, thinking of shoving one more person around our already cramped dining table. "It just seems wrong, keeping them cordoned off like that. And the few times I've been allowed to visit, everything seemed fine."

"That's good, right?"

"No, *too* fine. Too perfect. Like everything's been—"

"Staged," Kallum says, nodding his head. "I wouldn't put anything past Tesaryn Wen. Well, I've still got my diplomatic status. I can take you along with me for an impromptu visit."

"I'm sure Tesaryn Wen's accountancy guards would tattle to her as soon as I was within sight. They'll do anything to hide the truth. Even from me." Especially from me. They've done their best to minimize my power, but if the transgressions against our guests are egregious enough, the Senate would have no choice but to question them.

"They don't have to know it's you," Kallum says, mischief in his voice. It's the same look he'd given me when we were kids, when we'd freed a feisty gall beetle from the slaughterhouse and then rode it bareback through the central market. There was also that time we'd raided the tea bank and randomly swapped everyone's family teas around into different bins. We'd thought it would be a prank that would have the entire Contour class up in arms, complaining how their heirloom teas, the ones they took such pride in, had been thoroughly ruined. But sadly, no one had even noticed the difference. It was our first lesson in how the pretentious airs of the Contour class was a bunch of beetleshit.

The hairs on my arms stand up, thinking about the trouble we've gotten into over the years, and all the trouble we could get into now.

"What are we conspiring, dear husband?" I say to Kallum, leaning in close so that he has no choice but to whisper into my ear. I shiver as I think that maybe his lips don't *have* to brush against my earlobe the way they do, but secrecy is important.

"Security in and out is tight, but I've built up enough rapport with the Klang's environmental research team that I could propose a visit and no one would think twice of it."

"Even Tesaryn Wen?" I ask.

"If she opposes, I'll agree that it was a bad idea, and compliment her on her judiciousness. And just when she's thawed out from my kind words, I'm mention how I'd love for her to be my mentor and suggest that she keep me apprised of any upcoming vacancies in the Senate." Kallum winks at me. "Diplomacy is my secret weapon."

I laugh. "The thought of having another man in the Senate chamber would keep Tesaryn Wen up all night for sure."

Kallum laughs too, but there's a flatness to it that rubs me the wrong way. I know he loves his job, and he's damned good at it, but sometimes I wonder what it would have been like if he'd taken the unchosen path. "Do you wish we would have pressed harder for a Senate seat?" I ask him.

"I don't know. Kind of? We fought so hard for me to keep my Line, and I feel like I'm obligated to use it to further men's rights. But I can't help but feeling like no matter what I do, how much I accomplish, I'll always be an asterisk."

"An asterisk?" I ask, leaning into him.

"You know . . . like I'm living life as an exception to the rules. Two married men, and hardly no one bats an eye anymore. Flying between Zenzee and charged with bettering our worlds instead of being someone's househusband. And there are so many of our people who wish they had even a slice of what I've stolen."

I nod as if I understand, but I don't. Those all sound like good things. "I don't think you've stolen anything," I say softly. "You deserve everything you have."

"Mmm . . . ," he says, turning from me ever so slightly. It hurts to see him like this and not know what to do about it. He clears his throat, then straightens up. "So, consider us good to go. I'll put in for a short-notice visit, and of course, I'll need my own personal accountancy guard as an escort." He stares at me with his signature smirk. All traces of his melancholy whisked away.

"An accountancy guard? You want me to wear a disguise?"

"A very convincing one. It'll take me a couple days to get everything sorted. And I feel like I should mention, if we get caught, Tesaryn Wen is going to come after you with a renewed vengeance. I don't think we've seen her worst yet."

"Well, then we'd better not get caught," I say.

I KEEP LOOKING DOWN AT MY ACCOUNTANCY GUARD SILKS TO make sure I'm still fully dressed. Their uniforms are so light and sheer that it feels as though I'm wearing absolutely nothing. Oversize goggles block most of my face, my eyebrows have been thoroughly trimmed, and I've got my hair done in thin, straight plaits, pulled so tight they threaten the integrity of every single hair follicle on my head. I channel my inner Baradonna and emulate her precise gait, and the way she surveys her surroundings, head sweeping back and forth, as if she's working to the beat of a drum.

"Do you think this is too revealing?" I whisper to Kallum as we make our way to the Ides. "I think I could have used a bigger size. It's a bit . . . clingy."

"It fits fine. Just like everyone else's."

"I get that . . . it's just that, you know. We've been keeping the temperatures cold, and it doesn't help with first impressions, you know?"

Kallum stops. "Doka, are you saying you want to go back to torturing our Zenzee by tricking them into staying in a constant state of fever so we'll be nice and toasty and people won't notice you've got a little shrinkage going on in your pants?"

"No, no, no . . ."

"I swear, that's something your will-mother would come up with," Kallum teases, then looks around, making sure no one is watching before cupping my crotch. I'm so taken aback, I forget all about him insulting my mother, even though I know he's right, because in about half a minute, I'm going to have a-whole-nother problem going on in my pants.

My will-mother. I focus on thinking about how she'd looked when she'd been released from the stasis pod half a year ago—thin, pale, and slippery, like an overgrown throttle fish. I'd stalled on the approval of her release, knowing she wouldn't handle the changes well. She was particular to enjoying the spoils of the Contour class without the slightest bit of remorse for their cost. I would have put her release off another year if I could have, but I'd felt the pressure from my other mothers to free her, and in truth, I missed her, too. Eventually, we'll have to release the rest of the people still stuck in stasis, though with the added strain of the Klang on our resources, who knows when that'll be.

I breathe a sigh of relief as my arousal abates. We press through to the Ides, the area of town that traditionally was inhabited by beastworkers, though now there is some mixing of classes. A large section near the intestines was evacuated in order to accommodate the Klang's people. Warty brown domes rise up all over the place, and without interior walls, there isn't much privacy to be had. It's not the worst place we could have housed them. There were some calls to put them in the second ass, in the abandoned waif housing, but thankfully that idea was shot down without my intervention.

The natural barriers in the stomach lining mean there is only a short stretch of border that needs to be guarded, and while technically there is no wall dividing them from us, accountancy guards stand nearly within arm's length of one another, under the guise of providing security and protection *for* our new guests, rather than *from* them. The guards don't look quite so friendly when they see us coming.

"State your purpose here," says the guard. She's tall and muscular, with a brow so rigid and pronounced a wash hoglet could perch upon it. Intimidating as they come.

Kallum doesn't blink an eyelash and holds out his assignment papers.

The guard checks them over, then looks at me. "I don't know you," she says.

"Do you know every accountancy guard there is?" Kallum cuts back at her. Men have been entering the guard in record numbers lately, making it harder to keep up, and we're using that to our advantage. "This is Xendis Gills, my personal escort."

"I'm new," I say. "Been working Block 84 for the past few weeks."

She grunts, then steps to the side to let us through. "Don't be long," she calls after us.

We nod, then immerse ourselves in the chaos around us. Five steps ago, we were on familiar ground, and yet now, I feel as if I've been transported to somewhere completely foreign. The smells hit me first—some flowery and cloying, others spicy and inviting. And even through the heavy tint of my goggles, I can see the attention that's gone into turning the drab Ides homes into works of art. Mosaic paint patterns dapple the once brown structures, and beads are strung up in all the entrances, providing a hint of privacy and more than a hint of beauty. A vocalist tucked in an alleyway, just out of the path of foot traffic, belts out a warbling string of notes accompanied by a twangy stringed instrument. His people and mine are a thousand years removed from sharing the same air, and yet I still catch hints of words and phrases I know, interspersed with syllable arrangements wholly unfamiliar, ringing like chimes in my ears. His small audience claps as he finishes his song, offering him bits of food and cloth wraps in appreciation. I instantly start to doubt Tesaryn Wen's warnings of the dangers this place holds.

"Sodi sodi!" a gruff voice yells from behind us.

I turn and see a man brandishing a long, metal knife. I fumble and push Kallum behind me, though my only weapon is being able to recite all five sections and all eighteen subsections of our civil code by memory with the hope of boring our assailant to death.

"Sodi sodi nuts for you?" the man says again, nodding at the stand next to him. His words are thickly accented and I strain to understand him. "Good deal. Yours for five shell money."

I look closely at his stand. He's selling some sort of snack wrapped up in little paper packets. Roasted nuts of some sort. They smell divine.

I turn back to Kallum. "I don't know, I think I need to buy some. For cultural research. Firsthand knowledge, so that I can relay an extremely thorough account of my experiences."

He grins at me. "We should definitely gather as much data as we can."

He means five cowries, I'm assuming. A little steep for a snack, but I hastily part with the money, and in exchange, Kallum and I each get a bag overflowing with roasted nuts rolled in pine sap and sprinkled with some sort of ground spice. I bite into the nut. It's chewy, almost meaty in texture. I've been dragged to more high-society functions than I can count and have tasted the very best gourmet dishes prepared by some of our most renowned chefs, yet I've never had anything like this. It's so delicious, a curse to the ancestors crosses my lips.

Kallum's eyes go wide, but he doesn't admonish me, just nods in agreement and stuffs three more nuts in his mouth.

I grab another nut and examine it closely. Round with a little pointy end on one side and a divot where a stem had once been on the other. There's a subtle hint of striping beneath the spice layer. "Kallum," I say nudging him in the shoulder. "I think these are helm's cap. The little warts that grow on the soggy outskirts of the woodward canopies."

Kallum shakes his head. Helm's caps are good for a lot of things. Playing catch. Using their shells to trap unsuspecting hedge lice. You could even race them if you were very, very, very patient. Kallum and I had played all sorts of games with them when we were kids, but if there was one thing they weren't good for, it was eating. Kallum leans over to the vendor and says something in their tongue. He continues, and Kallum keeps nodding along, though I can tell from the subtle changes in his body posture that he's uncomfortable now.

Kallum touches his chest, then extends his hand out toward the vendor in a gesture of thanks, then places his hand on the small of my back and guides me into the flow of traffic.

"What was that all about?" I say, popping another nut into my mouth.

"Just brushing up on the language. I've gotten a little rusty since my liaison duties ended." Though Kallum is still behind me, I can hear him grimace through the words.

"Liar," I say, then turn to squint at him. "How do they make the nuts edible, Kallum?"

"It's complicated," Kallum says. "And wash hoglets are involved. But he assures me that everything is extremely sanitary. Just consider it culinary ingenuity and enjoy your nuts."

I want to pry deeper but don't have long to dwell on it with so many people pressed around us. So many couples of all sorts, hand in hand. So many men among them, it's almost dizzying. Families with two and three kids frolic. Two men hold hands in front of us, each of them holding the hand of a child. Kallum and I glance at each other.

"Imagine," he says, almost a whisper. "Imagine if it was just us."

"I thought you liked our life." I say in return, not wanting to imagine, knowing that the only place that could lead was resentment toward Charrelle and our other spouses. I get enough of that with Seske.

"I do. It's perfect. And our child, I can't wait for her to get here. But don't you ever think about it, what it would be like? Maybe Seske and Adalla are onto something. Maybe we've spent too much time marrying for Lines when we should have been marrying for love."

"*We* married for love," I say in defense.

Kallum's hand slips into mine. "Yeah, but my lineage certainly helped, didn't it? What if I had given it up? What then?" He looks at me, his eyes pleading. Without his Line, two men would have never been allowed to marry. He wants to know if I would have turned it all upside down for him. Forsaken my Line, our traditions. Torn down the whole of society for him. If Seske and Adalla's story had been ours, would I have risked everything and thrown myself across the emptiness of space for him?

I will the right words forth, but they refuse to come. Instead, I stand there, mouth hanging open, like a pitcher plant trying to catch flies.

Something in his eyes fades. The tiny sliver of a hopeful smile drops from his face. He tries to tug his hand away from mine, but I hold tight.

"Let go," he says under his voice.

"No, Kallum. I'm sorry. I should have said—"

"*Let go*," he says again, this time nodding ahead of us. Two accountancy guards stand there, watching our every move. A chill runs through me. We can't afford to get caught here. Going behind Tesaryn Wen's back was one thing, but to stoop to such trickery and deceptions—even the trust I've built up with my supporters in the Senate would be shattered.

I drop Kallum's hand and try to blend in, try to look like I belong here, but it's too late. There's no blending in. There's no belonging. Not in a place like this. They make their way toward us.

"Run!" I shout to Kallum.

We dash down an alleyway, brushing past a few vendors and hurdling over a group of kids playing billy tag with a bunch of sticks—the same game I played as a kid, though our sticks had been copper-plated and hand-etched with our family Lines. We press deeper and deeper into the maze of homes, glancing back, but the guards are still on us. We're nearly to a dead end, just a collection of pods in front of us, no way to get through, and it's too late to double back. Just when I've given up hope, a pair of hands reaches through the beaded door we're next to and drags us inside. Clammy hands clamp down onto our mouths and quilted shawls are thrown over our heads. We're pushed to a pit of burning coals, with several people excitedly chatting around it. The bead door is thrown open, and the guards peer inside. Kallum and I keep our heads down and our arms outstretched, pretending to chat with them in their animated style. I hear a woman argue with the guards briefly, and then they are gone.

I breathe a heavy sigh, then dare to peek out from under the quilt. Kallum's face brightens when our savior turns around. His whole body opens to her, and then they're caught in a deep embrace. They converse for a long moment, but I'm only able to pick up a few words here and there. Finally, Kallum turns and holds his hand out at me.

"Doka, I'd like you to meet Tirtha Yee, the Klang's lead environmental scientist. We worked very closely together. We tried so very hard." His voice cracks.

I nod. "Kallum has mentioned you. He says that you worked many miracles with your Zenzee. That you were as close as the Klang have to royalty."

Tirtha blushes. "We are all equal under the Adhosh," she says, and though I strain to parse her clipped consonants and rounded vowels, her words are clear. "But I am honored that Kallum thinks so highly of me. I must return the favor, as I hear is your custom, and say that Kallum served us as one of the most brilliant diplomats we have ever seen. He picked up our ways of speaking within two weeks, and by the time he left, you would have thought he'd been born among us." She grins at me. "You are very lucky to have a husband who is such an agile linguist!"

Then she laughs, hearty and deep—the kind of infectious laugh that you can't help but be envious of how free it is. I can see why Kallum likes her so. Even after all she's been through, Tirtha can find pleasure in making juvenile double entendres. And now it is my turn to blush.

"Quite agile," I say, and Tirtha laughs again, pulling us both into a tight hug.

"Well, I am very glad you have each other then," she says.

Finally, we peel back, and my clothes smell of her flowery sweetness. It's not in the slightest bit unpleasant. I instantly feel at home.

"Doka wishes to know more about how your accommodations are working out," Kallum says.

I nod, taking my cue. "Yes, I've gotten reports and have made visits, but I've got this feeling that somehow I'm not getting the full view."

Tirtha's smile drops, but her eyes brighten. She is eager to tell me her story, though I sense it will not be an easy one. "Firstly, we will be forever grateful for your aid. Your quick thinking saved thousands of lives, and for that, we owe a great debt. Our basic needs have been met. However, we are now many months removed from the state of chaos that brought us here, and it is time for us to reconnect with our ways. Our minds are meant to solve problems and perform experiments, yet our instruments and equipment have not been returned to us. Our hands are meant to do meaningful work and be in touch with of all the organs, yet we have not been allowed to acquaint ourselves with your Zenzee. We don't even know her name! We are used to living freely upon Adhosh where every voice mattered. Here, we have no voice. No choice. No freedom."

I bite my lip. It is now that I understand the true danger the Klang present. It is not their knives and harsh tones that pose a threat to us. It is their ideas. Not even among our own people do all voices matter equally. Some of them haven't even mattered at all. Our ways are so incongruous that they cannot coexist together, and yet here we are, shoved right up next to each other.

Because I insisted we bring them aboard.

"Can you tell me more about how things work for your people," I ask, undeterred by the danger, because even with my self-admonishment, all I can see is an opportunity to better ourselves. "I mean before your Zenzee got sick?"

Tirtha puts her hands on both my biceps, then squeezes. Kallum mentioned how friendly she was when he was aboard their ship. "Handsy," he'd said on more than one occasion. Now I was beginning to understand, feeling as though I've become her child to dote over. "Of course, iho, but first we must feed you. We can't afford for you to wither away on us. Bakti!" she calls. "Bring my sweet potato plant into the kitchen. Come, you two, we will chat there."

The man who must be Bakti jumps to his feet, and I can see from his face that Tirtha is his mother. Same features, though his skin is a much darker shade of brown, almost near mine. Handsome and well-fed, his lips press together in a wry smile. He tugs one of the large, beautifully decorated ceramic pots from its position near the entrance of the home back toward the kitchen. Kallum and I offer to help him, and he looks relieved.

We each grab a side, and the chore is done quickly and efficiently, though the leafy green and purple leaves sticking up from the gelatinous soil keep slapping me in the face as we go. We set the pot down near the cooktop and Tirtha nods in approval.

"We were on Adhosh for thirty-five years before we started having problems," Tirtha says, dipping her hands in a basin of soapy water. She rubs them together vigorously, then grabs the base of the leaves.

"Mama . . . ," Bakti whispers, but Tirtha swats him away.

"Adhosh. She is . . . was, your Zenzee?"

"More than that. She is our keeper. Our lifeline. And her life has not ended. She has merely gone on to be with her kind." She tugs and tugs, and eventually the gelatin soil crumples and cracks, releasing a knotty, purple root the size of a newborn babe. She lays it down on a cutting board, then looks at me. "Hold this for a moment," she says. "You like sweet potatoes, right?"

"Um, sure but . . . ," I begin, pressing my hand down on the tuber as Tirtha goes to sharpen a long, thick knife. "I've never—" I nearly bite my tongue when the tuber starts squirming beneath my hand. The tiny root offshoots whip futilely at my hand. Small knotty mouths all over open and close like a fish out of water. "It's moving."

"Stick your knuckle in one of its mouths. Too much stress will sour the taste."

I do what she says, looking over at Bakti for a hint that I'm doing it right. We've had sweet potato hash numerous times, but we get it from the market, already finely chopped and ready for cooking. Bakti looks at me and gives me an encouraging nod as the potato nearly sucks the skin from my finger. I grit my teeth and tap my foot to take my mind off the pain.

"Things were not perfect, of course," Tirtha continues, "but we had an egalitarian society. Every person as important as the next. Everyone had a chance to speak up on the issues that were important to them. Each year, we selected representatives at random. Everyone knew they had a duty. It was a slow process, but an effective one. We knew what the alternatives were. We'd been down that road already." Tirtha nudges me out of the way with her hip but holds my hand in place when I try to remove it. "Not yet," she whispers.

Then she raises the knife and slams it down inches above my fingers. The mouths on the sweet potato wail. The knife comes down again and again, and after a few seconds, the cries fade to nothing. The mouth with my knuckle held hostage falls open. I take my finger out and cradle it against my chest. Kallum stands behind me and wraps me up in his arms. Do I look that unsettled?

Tirtha continues until she's got a cutting board full of perfectly diced cubes. She pops one into her mouth. "Perfect," she says. "You did well."

"Thank you," I manage to squeak out.

She tosses the greens into a pot of boiling water, then oils the potato cubes, adds a thick red sauce, and sets them to roasting in an oven. She sighs. "Things started to fall apart when we suffered a doldrum breach. It was completely unexplained, but we were able to patch it, though we suffered a dozen casualties in the process. The cascade was slow enough that we were able to ignore the warning signs longer than we should have. Maybe it was pride on my part. Even through failed crops and leaky heart valves, we'd kept our Zenzee stable longer than most of the other clans through careful use of detailed metrics and environmental readings. When our leader pressed me to consider culling another Zenzee, I protested. I told her that Adhosh would not fail us. She put her trust in me, and in the end, I failed them all."

"You didn't fail us, Mama," Bakti says to her, then to us, "Don't look at her like that. Don't pity her. Who prevented the first cascading heart failure? Who diagnosed the tainted water in the idle lakes hours before it was set to be released into the main aquifers?" Bakti stands up in his chair with the confidence of an adventurer, then gestures for his mother to do the same. She steps up into her chair. "You saved us, Mama. You saved our lives more times than we could ever count."

Her lip trembles for a moment, then she pulls herself up tall and stares me straight in the eyes. "We will have to agree to let the past remain in the past. Adhosh has ascended, and we are here now. I hope that I can contribute to the success of your Zenzee and the others we have colonized." Tirtha flushes again, but this time, I know that it is not from embarrassment. Stress has taken its toll on her body. I attempt to help her down from her chair, but she swats me away and takes a seat on her own.

Bakti picks up where his mother left off, gesturing as if to distract us as she composes herself. "It is you who have saved us, but we have so much to offer you in return," he says, still standing on his chair as if he's had zero home training. I can't decide if he's grandiose or passionate or reckless. Maybe it's a mix of all three. "You must allow us to return to living our normal lives. We will help with existing peacefully with your Zenzee, turning away from our history of parasitism and working toward something beneficial to us all. It is possible if we break down the barriers between our people. Let us sit and talk further."

WE CONVERSE FOR NEARLY AN HOUR, WEAVING BETWEEN SErious issues and ridiculous anecdotes from the Klang ship.

Still, I am reluctant to share the truths of our own people. I start to understand how restrictive we've been, how limiting. How our matriarchy has shoved so many people into a false binary. Still, I am filled with hope for how things can change. But we must give the Klang a voice, and that will not be easy. My eyes keep flicking back to Bakti as he talks. He speaks so easily, so effortlessly, his words coming straight form the heart. And when he's listening, you can see his brain is churning, digesting the words, not just waiting until it's his turn to talk again. I must be staring too hard because eventually Kallum knees me under the table as we are eating. The potato morsel on the end of my fork jostles and falls onto the floor. I hold a moment of silence for the loss. Our potatoes never have compared in sweetness nor butteryness.

I look over at Kallum.

"Careful, or your eyes might tumble out and onto the floor, too," he whispers.

"Sorry," I mumble. I admit I am smitten with Bakti, but not in that way. Thoughts start churning through my mind. The Klang need a voice, but to have a voice in our society requires having a respectable Line—and it just so happens that one of our most prestigious Lines has a vacancy that needs to be filled by a suitable husband.

Bakti laughs at one of his own jokes, same infectious laugh his mother has. I smile, every single one of my teeth showing. I am brave enough to turn the world over for my family, and for the chance to give us all a better life.

Seske is going to love me for it.

Or hate me.

In the meantime, I've got a wedding to sabotage.

SESKE

Of Upheld Vows and Spilled Milk

I should have known this wouldn't be a small wedding. There are thirty-six people in the wedding party alone. We stand together, on a raised stage adorned with massive ceramic pots containing several varieties of war lilies, their feathery plumes standing erect and their fanged mouths discreetly taped shut. Banners made from our family silks drape down from the ceiling, intertwining with one another—the golds and greens and blacks shimmering under the harsh lighting. The amount of perfume my heart-mothers have doused themselves in threatens the very integrity of my sinuses, as they stand behind me, misty-eyed, locked arm-in-arm-in-arm. I guess I'd forgotten about all the pomp that surrounds the final marriage in a family unit. There would be nine of us now, and ten soon, with the way Charrelle's belly is poking out. There was no hiding that we'd started our family before wedlock was complete, so instead of trying to obscure her belly, we decided as a family that we should make it a focus, having her gown cut in a way that fully accentuated her rotund physique. She glows, standing up here with us, and I love it. At least it's a welcome distraction from the hooded man standing upon a pedestal, fifteen feet up in the air.

Remi?

Ronni?

I forget his name. Third one to the left of the line of suitors I was presented with, I remember that. I hadn't attended any of the premarital meetups. Adalla had gone to a couple at first, but when the Klang boarded, her work doubled all at once, and she barely had time for me, let alone learning to love a stranger.

All of his parents stand upon smaller pedestals surrounding his, decreasing in size—the tallest pedestal, holding his head-mother, is a mere foot lower than that of our future husband's, and the shortest, holding his will-father, is only a foot removed from the ground. Despite his status in the family, his smile is brighter than any of the rest, seeing his son become a will-husband and soon to be will-father, following in his steps.

I scoot a few feet back and a little to the left, so that I'm closer to Adalla and her heart-mothers. No one notices that I've broken rank. Every single eye in the whole of this audience is focused on the singer, belting out the history of our people in an overly dramatic fashion, hitting more than the occasional off-key note. Teary eyes nod along anyway. Charrelle is behind me, eyes closed, head shaking back and forth to the beat. Every so often a moan escapes her lips, as if she's really getting into the song. I squint harder at the singer. She looks so familiar. Then I see it's Talby Onatti, the two-bit actress who was engaged to Wheytt right before I shuttled him off to his eventual death.

Each note stabs at my heart now, with memories resurfacing that I naively thought I'd buried deep enough. Another panic attack is setting in and I need to fight it. I steel my nerves, then wedge myself farther and farther back, until I'm out of the audience's view altogether. I take a few slow breaths to settle myself, but it is not enough. I feel as though this entire wedding hall is about to collapse down onto me. I need an escape.

My eyes flick over to the corner of the room, where the buffet is set up. It will be ten more minutes before Talby finishes her song, so I slip between silk banners and duck behind the war lily planters until I've made my way to the buffet table. I stoop down and hide beneath the one with the pastries and appetizers, using my hand to probe up until it is filled with my favorite delicacies: battered woodlice, brined cheese wedges, and two jellied biscuits. The battered woodlice go down with a couple chews, that quiet popping of their segmented plating between my teeth immediately lulling me to a place of comfort. I tackle the cheese wedges next, which must have been harvested at least three Zenzee's back, judging from the pungent smell—like that time Adalla and I had gone skinny-dipping in the salt pond at the far end of the wayward canopy and happened upon the preserved corpse of a drowned wash hoglet. Daidi's bells, it's definitely not an appetizing smell, but beneath the cheese's slippery, stinky rind lies a buttery, black ooze that's so savory, it makes my toes curl in my slippers. I am extremely careful not to spill it on me as I lick the rind completely clean. I save the jellied biscuits for last. Something sweet, to wash the last bits of my sorrow away. Talby's on the last verse of the anthem now, not much time before I have to get back. I shove the entire biscuit in my mouth, but it's denser than I'd anticipated and its purple jellies dribble over my lips and down the front of my dress, leaving a dark stain upon my green silks.

Now I truly panic. Maybe it won't be noticeable. I spit on my index finger and try my best to mitigate the damage, but the stain is spreading and getting worse.

"Seske?" says a deep voice. I know it is not Wheytt's, but I am instantly transported back to the memory of my coming out party, when I was forced to choose my suitor. Wheytt had come to my rescue with a napkin then and had talked me down from my panicked state. It was his guidance that had led me to choose Doka over all the other potential husbands.

I keep my eyes clenched, because I know when I open them and turn around, it will not be Wheytt standing before me. Finally, I open my eyes and see Baradonna, Doka's personal guard. My sigh is deep and heavy. Her face scrunches up like a fist. She doesn't like me much, I can tell. Her hand goes to her knife, pulls it out. *She wouldn't*, I think to myself. Not here, not now, with so many witnesses. But she does have that look in her eye, like she's always on the verge of cutting someone.

She slashes the blade, not at me, but at the cloth covering the buffet table. Soon she's got a square patch of fabric that she offers to me. I take it, watching carefully as she sheathes her knife.

"Thanks," I whisper to her. "But you could have just offered me a napkin." I point to the pile of cloth napkins on the other side of the table.

She lets out a harrumph. "Those flimsy things aren't going to do anything but smear it in worse. Here, let me." She takes the fabric swath back, hocks up a huge wad of spit, then takes to the front of my dress. She's rough, but quick and accurate, and by the time I pull back, I look down and see the stain is completely gone. "Thanks," I say again. I appreciate it. "I am glad to know Wheytt is in such capable hands."

She looks at me coldly, and then I realize what I have said. "Doka. I meant to say Doka! I was just thinking about—"

"It's fine. Sometimes tongues slip," she says, more than a little bitterness on hers.

I start fumbling over my words, trying to explain myself, remembering the kiss Wheytt and I had come so close to sharing on my wedding night. It was not my best hour, but I was young and confused, and shouldn't have been making life decisions when I was only a few years removed from sleeping with a crib worm.

"I knew him, you know. Wheytt," Baradonna says. "We both worked the sphincter to the second ass for a time. Opposite sides. Apparently, I got assigned there because I'd taken a little too much interest in some anomalous resource allocations from the Accountancy Guard's head office and royally pissed off the Comptroller. I'm not sure what Wheytt did to pull such a shitty placement fresh out of training—he never admitted to anything. Maybe him being a man was enough. Who knows? But he worked that sphincter like a true professional. Poured his whole heart into the job like swabbing ass was his birthright. He was funny. Witty. I miss him, too."

She lays her arm around my shoulder and pulls me in for a tight, albeit awkward, side hug. "Now this new guy, Rendi." She nods at my soon-to-be husband. "He's pretty to look at, if you're into that sort of thing, but dull as dirt, I'm afraid. Though I do hear he excelled at his consort training." Baradonna arches her brow at me. "You know, I hear things . . . and notice things, better than most, and I can tell you that you and Adalla are in for some prime time cunn—"

"You know, I probably need to get back to the wedding

party," I say, fanning the spit stain away, and maybe a little of the embarrassment on my cheeks, too. "Talby is going to stop singing any moment now, and then everyone will notice I'm gone, and I don't need that kind of drama this time around. No surprises. Just a nice boring wedding with a nice boring husband, and we'll deal with any issues later, not in front of thousands of onlookers."

Baradonna steps up even closer to me and lifts her chin. "Boring? You don't seem like the type who will settle for boring. What are you really looking for in a husband?"

"I don't see how that is any of your business." I say this with my most practiced royal huff, but Baradonna isn't deterred.

"I'm serious," she says, the earnestness in her voice palpable. "If you could write your own destiny, who would you want standing by your side up there?"

I take a deep breath. *No one*, is my honest answer, but Baradonna saved my gown from biscuit jelly, so I guess the least I can do is entertain this one question. "Bright. Considerate. Passionate in everything he does. But it doesn't matter. That's"—I say, pointing at Rendi—"what I've got." I go to leave, but Baradonna pulls me back.

"Unhand me!" I say in a harsh whisper.

"You realize you've just described Doka. What was so wrong with him that you were driven to humiliate him on your wedding night? Why did you press so hard for having the marriage annulled? You undermined his power, and for what?"

My lips purse and my stare hardens. "Unhand me now, or I will be forced to have you arrested."

Baradonna squeezes my arm tightly to reassert her physical dominance, then lets go. She has so much anger for me, I can feel it, but she dares not assault a member of the royal family further. The last person who tried to hurt me in such a way got banished, and not even the fact that it was my sister had saved her from that fate.

I straighten up and flex my political dominance with a well-placed scowl, but Baradonna meets my gaze, refusing to back down. I get the feeling that maybe Doka doesn't have her as domesticated as he thinks . . . which is extremely concerning.

And with that lingering, Baradonna turns and leaves me at the table alone with my thoughts. Maybe I shouldn't have pressed to have our marriage annulled, from a politically strategic perspective at least. And it isn't as if I don't like Doka. We work well together. We have fun together. On paper, it was a perfect match, but I can't help but wonder if it could have worked off paper as well.

A chill runs through me. I look over at the wedding party. Doka is staring at me, concern on his face instead of anger or frustration or any of the other valid feelings he could have for me right now. "Are you okay?" he mouths.

I nod and conjure up a smile from the depths of my heart. At least we're still within the same family unit. I can't imagine what it'd be like if I'd pushed him out of my life completely. I hurry to rejoin the party, slipping my hand into Adalla's, her palm clammy and soft against mine. I'd married for love.

At least the once.

I stare at Rendi in his regal raiment, trying to make out the features behind his veil. I know adding a third to our will-unit will change things between Adalla and I, but maybe it'll be a positive change. A new spark to ignite the cold of our bed. Finally, three minutes later, the song comes to an end, and everyone claps and all eyes come to focus on the top pedestal. One by one, Rendi's parents dismount from their perches, each vacant one becoming a stair for those higher to dismount.

Adalla and I step forward. Rendi's parents surround us on both sides. We stand rapt as he makes his way carefully down the staircase, each step perfect and practiced, his silks flowing behind him like ripples on the water's surface. Then he stands before us. The vows are read, and we watch as his head-parents weave their burgundy family silk into the rest of our family's. Then the officiant declares us as wed. Rendi's will-parents pull back his thick veil, and I close my eyes and quickly peck him on the lips.

I wait for Adalla to do the same, but she just stands there, staring at him. I nudge her in the arm, then notice everyone is awestruck, thousands of onlookers all speechless. I look back at Rendi, but he is clearly not the third suitor from the left. From the shape of his face and the lay of his limp hair, I immediately see he's a member of the Klang. My heart sinks to my feet.

"What is the meaning of this?" yells one of the heart-mothers. "Where is our son? And who is this?"

Doka steps forward between Adalla and me. "I'd like to introduce you to your new husband," he says. "Bakti Yee, son of Tirtha Yee, the Klang's lead environmentalist."

It's hard to process the uproar swelling all around me, because my own feelings are stuck in my throat. My fists ball into tight knots and I can feel my tongue sharpening in my mouth. I know I told Doka that I didn't care who I married, but this is a total breach of trust, a flippant disregard of authority, a wanton display of recklessness . . .

And it's exactly something I would do.

I unclench my fists and turn to Doka. My scowl feels sharper than a knife, but I know Doka, and he is neither flippant nor reckless. He's got a plan in his pocket, and if it is this important to him, I need to know about it.

"What's going on?" I ask him, ignoring the world as order collapses all around us. "Why didn't you trust me with this?" If I am hurting, it is because this is exactly the kind of trouble I miss conspiring with him.

"I'm sorry, Seske. I wanted with all my heart to have you in on this, but I didn't need you implicated as well. The Klang are suffering, and they need the power of our Line to have a voice in matters that concern them."

"The Klang are well-fed and taken care of," I say, shaking my head.

"Their basic needs are met, yes, but it is a deeper need that goes unfulfilled. They are not animals that we can keep locked up and out of the way. We must integrate them into our society, fully and completely."

I must look skeptical, because Doka reaches out and places a hand on my shoulder.

"Seske, I know this is hard to process right now, but give it some time. Sit with it. I swear Bakti is a great guy. I wouldn't have considered this for a moment if I didn't believe that with all my heart."

I grit my teeth then nod.

"Good. Now, I've gone over the rites of matrimony thoroughly, and the ceremony is real and binding. There were a couple loopholes I had to jump through, so even if the Senate tries to declare this wedding null and void, they will not succeed. I just need you and Adalla to agree to it."

I turn to Adalla, who's been looking intently over my shoulder.

"You know I'm always down for bringing this system to its knees," she says with enough enthusiasm for the both of us. Her arms wrap around my waist, and in the next instant, I remember that we are one. I extend my hand to Bakti as well, and then we are a wall, a united front.

Which is crucial as a wave of Senators approaches us, looking more like a bunch of bowel-swabbing thugs than elite decision-makers. The unofficial leader among them, Tesaryn Wen, stalks up to Doka—a predator about to pounce on her prey.

"I knew you'd royally fuck this up eventually," says Tesaryn Wen to Doka. She and the Senators standing behind her make for a much bigger, much more powerful wall. "You've made this way too easy for me."

Doka shoves a piece of paper into Tesaryn Wen's face. "Everything is in order. The marriage is sound."

Tesaryn Wen doesn't spare even a glance in the document's direction. "I don't care what exploits you've found. You've gone against the intentions of our ancestors. We are in a time of crisis, and this is no time to risk turning their favors away from us. You of all people should know that." Her cheeks twitch from all the pent-up anger she's been harboring toward Doka for so long. She'd claw his eyes out this very moment if it weren't for the threat of treason against the matriarch.

Doka is not deterred by her threats. He puffs his chest in kind and takes another step closer to her. "If the ancestors chose to deny us their favor for an act of unity between our people and the Klang's, then those aren't the kinds of petty spirits I want to honor anyway." Doka pauses and stares down Tesaryn Wen. That he would denounce the ancestors publicly is full proof that he is truly without fear. It is only then that I feel comfortable enough to say we are in the right. I put my hand on Doka's in support, as do Adalla and Bakti. Charrelle walks up and joins us, with Kallum right by her side. Some of our heart-parents join us as well. Then Baradonna takes her place, standing shoulder to shoulder with Doka, her arms crossed over her wide chest. We are twenty strong. It feels like a lot, until I look beyond the Senators and see the hundreds and hundreds of faces scowling at us.

"Renounce this marriage," Tesaryn Wen demands, this time to me. "Or I will be forced to take action."

"Do your best," I say. "The marriage will stand. If you have any grievances, you can go yell them into the void."

"If that is the way you want it." She steps closer to Doka, now so close that their noses nearly touch. "This is not the first mistake you've made as Matris, but it will be your last," she whispers, so soft I have to strain to hear it. Then her lips keep moving, and I can only catch every few words, each of them pointed and sharp.

Doka's face drops for a moment, then anger wells up in his eyes. Nearly instantly, they've gone red. His fists clench, but they stay at his sides, as if he refuses to be provoked.

Baradonna, however, doesn't allow herself to be contained by political decorum. Her back stiffens, and all at once, faster than I can blink, she's reached out and caught Tesaryn Wen by the neck.

Tesaryn Wen struggles and coughs, a crooked smile beaming on her face. "Assaulting a member of the Senate is treason," she manages to choke out.

"So is threatening our Matris," Baradonna says lightly.

"I would never do such a thing, though if I had, such words wouldn't leave bruises like the ones you are surely giving me. Look at the commotion you're causing. The traditions you're ruining. Who do you think they'll believe?"

"I heard you. Doka heard you. Our word will prevail." Baradonna squeezes tighter, then lifts Tesaryn Wen up from the ground, her toes struggling to find purchase. Tesaryn Wen's smile is completely gone now. All that is left in her bulging eyes is panic. Her fingers grasp at Baradonna's grip. All around, accountancy guards converge on them.

"Baradonna," Doka says, laying a soft hand on her muscular shoulder. "Don't. She's not worth it."

"No, but you are," Baradonna says. "No one can threaten you and your family, and especially not your child. And if bruises are all the Senate is concerned with, then I might as well make it totally clear where I stand." She rips her knife from her sheath and presses the blade to Tesaryn Wen's temple.

She arcs the blade down in a quick motion, then tosses Tesaryn Wen into a heap. For a moment, Tesaryn Wen cowers there, sucking in painful gasps of air, but then the blood comes, a thin red line going from her cheek to her chin. I stand there in complete shock. I'd never been overly confident in Baradonna's ability to control her temper, but I never thought she was capable of something like this. I don't understand what's happened.

Baradonna drops her knife to the floor, then puts both hands behind her back as accountancy guards swarm her. She grins a satisfied grin as they struggle to subdue her, even though she doesn't fight back. Accusations of treason fly from Tesaryn Wen's mouth as she keeps her hand pressed against her injured cheek. The cut is neither deep nor serious, but from the delicacy of it all, we all know it so easily could have been deadly. Doka pleads for leniency as Baradonna is dragged away. But we all know that is impossible.

The trial will be immediate.

It will be short.

She will be banished.

Cold hands grip around my biceps. "Seske," comes a weak

voice. I look over and see Charrelle, a pained look on her face. I pull her into an embrace, protecting her from the chaos all around us.

"It'll be okay," I tell her. "Baradonna is strong. Doka is smart. Together, they'll figure a way out of this."

Charrelle shakes her head, taking shallow and deliberate breaths. I thought she was glowing before, but it's not that. She's glistening. Sweating. She rubs her hand over the swell of her belly. "I think I'm about to have this baby."

I nod slightly, as if she's told me that the buffet is out of fancy cheeses.

"Did you hear what I said?" Charrelle asks when she doesn't get more of a response from me.

"Yes," I say, remembering that I am her midwife and am supposed to be comforting her. "Yes. Okay. Well, obviously you can't have the baby right now. It's too early. I still have my classes to complete."

"This baby isn't going to wait for you to take more classes, Seske," she says. "She's coming. Now."

I shake my head. "Babies don't spontaneously get birthed! There are contractions and heavy breathing and broken water and . . ." I wrack my brain, trying to remember what we'd learned so far. Trying *not* to remember my own experiences giving birth to a tentacled egg. My back starts throbbing. My stomach twists up. I'm overwhelmed with the urge to take the largest shit of my life.

"Well," Charrelle says through a pained grin. She takes a couple deep breaths, then continues. "I was feeling a little odd this morning, but I thought it was pre-wedding jitters. By the time the ceremony started, I knew something was going on, but I figured I could wait it out. I didn't want to cause a scene."

"Okay, okay. Let's get you comfortable then," I say, helping her to a quiet spot near the edge of the room, then down to the floor to find a comfortable position to labor in. My phantom pains—*sympathy pains*—continue to ravage me. Everyone is so caught up with Baradonna's drama that no one notices us. I signal to my heart-mothers, and finally catch my ama's attention. She rushes over to us, hands pressed to the sides of her head.

"No, not now," she says. "It's too soon!"

"We've already established that," I say, grabbing a whole stack of cloth napkins from a nearby service table. "But the baby is coming. Right now."

"I'll run and find a midwife," Ama says, recognizing that the chances of me being any use in this situation are next to nil, and I'm not about to argue with that. "You keep her comfortable."

Charrelle pants on all fours. I rub her back, and she sways side to side, trying to deal with the pain. The Zenzee egg I carried had doped me up with alien hormones to within an inch of unconsciousness, washing away my concerns and leaving me in a state of euphoria while the thing inside me stretched my body in ways it wasn't meant for. Even after the egg had passed, long after the egg had passed, I never fully felt like the same person I was before.

"Seske," Charrelle says, thankfully snapping me away from the memory. She looks at me with tears in her eyes. "I think something is happening."

I toss up her many layers of damp, frilled skirts and help her out of her panties. Then I look and see what's between her legs. Tentacles. So many tiny little black tentacles. I fight the urge to flee, and instead, shake my head vigorously. When I look back, the baby's head is crowning, a whole mess of beautiful black hair.

I feel a hand on my shoulder. I look back and see Vonne, who's served as a midwife for countless births. She's kind, asking if I need help instead of just taking over, even though I clearly don't know what I'm doing. She somehow manages to put both Charrelle and me at ease. Charrelle pushes three more times before the baby comes.

"It's a boy," Vonne announces.

I hadn't expected those words, but I smile at Charrelle anyway, because he's so absolutely wonderful. Charrelle stares back, a mere hint of disappointment caught at the edges of her smile. "We haven't thought about any boy names," she says, exhausted.

"It's okay. We have time," I say. Boys are rare, especially in families of our status, but when they occur, they are a blessing. They are a labor of love, an investment for our whole people. It is a very honorable sacrifice, raising a child for someone else's Line, and once he is married off, our family will be able to have a girl child of our own and secure our Line for the next generation. I smile at the thought.

Vonne cleans the baby off and hands him to me, swaddled up in a large napkin with our family seal. I hold him close for a moment, smell the top of his head, then hand him carefully to Charrelle. He lets loose a cry and something within me clenches. Vonne fidgets with the top of Charrelle's gown until she's freed enough material for the baby to nurse. Mayhem still stirs all around us, people shouting and fighting, but here, at the edge of this great room, we've found a little bubble of normalcy, and I relish it.

"Seske," Vonne whispers to me, her hand on my shoulder. "You've got a little . . . stain on you." She points to my chest. I think that maybe Baradonna hadn't done such a great job of removing the jelly after all, but when I look down, I see two purple-black wet spots blooming through the fabric of my dress. My breasts suddenly feel heavy and uncomfortable.

My stomach gets queasy as I reach down inside my corset, my touch like hot needles poking at my nipples. I wince and draw my hand back quickly, and find my fingertips covered in a dark, sticky liquid.

Daide's bells, I'm lactating.

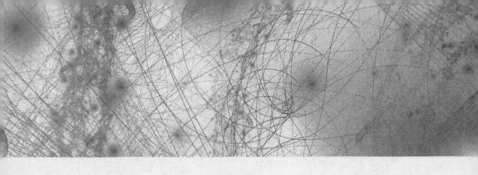

DOKA

Of Tempting Offers and Disappointing News

You're only as safe as your unborn child is. Tesaryn Wen's words strike me hard. It's impossible to not read the threat behind them. The legitimacy of my rein will continue to be tenuous until I produce an heir. After that, even Tesaryn Wen's antics would come under intense scrutiny with all the power Charrelle's family holds. No one would dare cross the father of their granddaughter.

If something happened to her before her birth . . .

I ball my fists and bid myself to keep eye contact with Tesaryn Wen, even though I'm itching to look back and make sure Charrelle is okay. My eyes start to burn at the thought of someone harming our family. But to lash out here, among so many witnesses, would be inadvisable to say the least. But as soon as I finish the thought, Baradonna's got her weighty hand wrapped around Tesaryn Wen's throat. Shock falls upon me, and by the time I gather my wits to tell her to stop, it is too late.

Blood drips from Tesaryn Wen's cheek wound in thin, dark red rivulets that continue down to her chin. They pool into a heavy drop that falls, vanishing into the sky-black floor.

I'm swept up into the resulting chaos, bodies pressing me forward as Baradonna is taken away for an inevitable conviction and sentencing. She's so close, I can almost reach out and touch her, but the accountancy guards surrounding her will have none of that. Instead, I shout to her, saying we'll find a way out of this. And we will. We have to. In the meantime, I keep my steps deliberate so I don't lose my balance and end up being trampled by this mob, thirsty for vengeance.

There is not enough room to fit the aggrieved masses inside the Senate chambers, so Tesaryn Wen has a few guards hoist her up onto one of the decorated columns outside, so that she can address the crowd. Her face has been hastily bandaged, but blood is seeping through it, making for a damning image.

"We have all witnessed the violent crimes committed against me, a long-standing and respected member of the Senate," she rasps while perched upon the hefty carved tentacle of a Zenzee, her arm grasped around another for support. "We are not a people who tolerate such vehement acts, and we cannot afford to let this offense go unpunished. Such treason and disregard for authority deserves immediate conviction and sentencing, and so it is imperative that Accountancy Guard Auditor Baradonna Resson be sentenced to banishme—"

"Stop!" I yell, my words cutting straight through the crowd's rapt silence. "Baradonna was protecting me. She only reacted that way from your threat against me and my family! She deserves a medal, not punishment."

"Did anyone else hear such a threat?" Tesaryn Wen asks

her audience. "Or are we supposed to trust the word of someone who has in one evening completely corrupted the sanctity of our institution of marriage and left us vulnerable to strangers we are yet to truly know?"

I laugh. "There is no sanctity among any of our traditions."

Tesaryn Wen sneers at me, her eyes calculating and cruel. "Be as that may, we all saw Baradonna's actions. There is nothing to defend."

"If you believe there is nothing to defend, then what is the harm in granting her a trial? Or are you afraid of the truth that might come out of it?"

"If you wish to waste everyone's time, then very well," Tesaryn Wen says with haughty airs, as if she knows I am only prolonging Baradonna's grim fate. "Who will serve as her counsel?" She looks out into the audience, but the law auditors among them all turn away, unwilling to blemish their records with such a hopeless case.

"I will be her counsel," I declare. I'd read *Misfits and Criminals* end to end, a behemoth text that chronicled the greatest trials of our history. I knew enough of the procedure that I could cobble together a defense. I look over at Baradonna. She shakes her head, warning me not to do this. Yes, it will paint a bigger target on my back, but she stood up for me and my family. I can't let her get banished to who knows where.

"You must recuse yourself from the vote, then," says Tesaryn Wen.

"I accept," I say as soon as the words are out of her mouth. My vote only matters in cases of ties anyhow, and honestly, swaying even half of the Senate to position my way will require more favors from the ancestors than they have granted me in my whole lifetime.

Tesaryn Wen gives me a sly smile. "You have one hour to

prepare your defense," she says. The crowd groans in protest. It is an awful sight—the unsated bloodlust lurking behind their eyes while they're dressed in their finest silks and their most elegant patinas, hair adorned with precious beads and shells, some of them from Earth. They came for a wedding, but are all too eager to settle for witnessing the first banishment in three years.

"One hour?" I ask. "That's hardly enough—"

"If the truth is so obvious as you claim, then it should be plenty of time." Tesaryn Wen's stance grows bolder as the audience starts chanting for justice.

Bella Roshaad stops us right before Baradonna and I are escorted away. "Do not let Tesaryn Wen intimidate you. She is loud, but she does not speak for all of us." She presses an abridged copy of the Codes in my hand. "I believe you."

Baradonna and I are taken to a private room off the side chambers where we can confer. I'm about to present her with my plan—a plea of her being in an unfit state of mind due to the confusion at the wedding, but as soon as the door shuts, it is Baradonna who does the talking.

"You shouldn't have done that," she scolds me. "You have so few allies left as it is. You are forcing them to side against you."

"They *will* see the truth."

Baradonna laughs at my naivete. "They will eat us both alive out there no matter what defense we present."

"But if we—"

"You're wasting time," Baradonna says. "When I'm gone, you'll be more vulnerable than ever, and I have no doubt that Wen will go through with her threat. A physical attack may occur at any time, and you've got to be ready. Never let your guard down. Especially when you're in public."

"I don't know how to defend myself!" I say, feeling doomed. "I'm a scholar, not a fighter."

"If you keep your eyes peeled, you can spot danger before it comes to that. Keep your ears tuned to background noise and whispered conversations. Every environment you're in will tell a story. Your senses will guide you and warn you when something is about to go awry, if you learn to pay attention to them, that is."

"That's easy for someone who's had years of training to say." Fear grips me. What's happening with Charrelle now? Are she and the rest of my family safe? How am I supposed to protect them if I don't even know how to protect myself?

"I won't be there to save you anymore, Doka. But the good news is that people are easy to read. The signs are clear if you look for them. Pay special attention to the eyes. To posture. Words are meaningless. Lies are plentiful, but the truth bleeds through the body. Now, watch me closely. Pretend I am one of your books."

Baradonna spends the remainder of our hour together teaching me to read body language, moving her own body as well as she can with her arms bound behind her. She shows me the subtleties of sloped shoulders and how they, dependent upon degree, can indicate intimidation or shame or guilt. She lies to me, then tells me the truth, and I watch how her body folds into a lie and opens up for the truth. I watch her do it again, as someone more practiced in deception, seeing the tension in her body as she overcompensates for resisting its natural urges.

Slowly, I begin to understand. It is a lesson that should last weeks, years, if it was being done properly, but we don't even have minutes left. The door opens, and through it comes an escort of accountancy guards. Baradonna stands as a hand comes down on each of her biceps to guide her away. I race toward her before they can do so and wrap her up in my embrace.

"I'm sorry," I mutter into her shoulder. "I'm sorry you ever got assigned to protect me."

"Serving you has been the highest honor of my life," Baradonna says, resting her cheek against the crown of my head. A moment later, she is being dragged away, and I am left feeling empty and hollow.

My defense takes only three minutes to lay out. It is not a very good one, just a simple plea for mercy for a blatant mistake on Baradonna's part. I relayed how sorry she was, how much remorse she had shown during our consultation, feeling how my own body folds into these lies. But lies and hope are all I have. No one would believe the truth.

"All in favor of pardoning Baradonna for her crimes, raise your hands," Tesaryn Wen calls out to the Senators.

I look out into the crowd, a motionless mass. I look to my mothers. I look to Charrelle's mothers. Not a single twitch among them.

"Then the matter of banishment shall proceed, and as of now, this person standing before you does not exist. Has never existed. To hold a single memory to the contrary is punishable by three days thumb hanging."

Baradonna is whisked away, and it is all I can do to keep my feet under me while I watch. She's saved my life so many times, and yet I've failed her.

"It's a shame," Tesaryn Wen says, suddenly standing beside me, stroking her hand up and down the length of a long copper tube. "You think you know someone . . ."

I ball my fists and keep them down at my sides, trying to ignore her obvious taunt. "Where are they taking Baradonna?" I demand in defiance of the order.

"Who now? I'm not sure I know who you're talking about." I snarl at her.

Tesaryn Wen smiles. "Well now, if everyone knew where we sent the banished, it wouldn't be much of a banishment, would it? You'd be off visiting her every day, probably. Bring her a nice cheese roll for her birthday? Decorate the place for EE day? Can't have that."

I look into her eyes, see something behind them, just like Baradonna had said. "You know where they're taking her, though?"

"All the Senate leaders do."

"Well, I'm privy to all information the Senate leaders share. I'm Matris!"

"Ah . . . well, I suppose I could let you look at the map before we lock it away . . ." She places one end of the copper tube in my hand, then yanks it back. "Oh sorry, that's right. Didn't you recuse yourself from your duties for this trial?"

"Please, Tesaryn Wen."

"It's better you forget. This trial never happened. This map doesn't even exist." Tesaryn Wen's smile grows more sinister. "But I suppose I could share what I know if you recuse yourself from all matters concerning the Senate from here on out. No one will think worse of you. You'll be busy with that little newborn of yours, after all." Tesaryn Wen smiles. "Mother and child are doing fine, I hear. You must be aching to see them."

"What?" I say, confused and untrusting of every single word that comes out of her mouth. "Charrelle isn't due for another month."

"You must have missed the news. Shame. I can't imagine what could have been so important to drag you away from your laboring wife. I suppose you want to know the child's name?"

I shake my head. Watching her posture, it doesn't seem as if she's lying. On the contrary. She's leaning totally into me, eager to use the truth as a weapon. But I don't want to hear it . . . not from Tesaryn Wen's lips. The important thing now is that I have an heir. I could meet with Charrelle's mothers to sway them individually and hope they could do the same for their allies. Maybe their numbers could grow into something significant enough to bring Baradonna home.

"Kenzah," Tesaryn Wen says. "A beautiful name."

A boy's name. She looks at me. Smile so much more vicious.

"I have a son," I whisper.

"That you do."

I nod, letting the shock roll over me. I can't hold on to it. Can't entertain the thoughts of ever-so-subtle disappointment. Don't even dare wonder if my parents had thought the same when I entered the world. "This is wonderful news," I say.

"Isn't it? Such a rarity. A true blessing." She strokes the copper tube again, almost erotically. Like she's about to fuck it. Like she's about to fuck me over. "Now, as I was saying. Recuse yourself. Go home, be a good dad. A dutiful husband. I can guarantee that no one will question the legitimacy of your marriages, particularly this last one. And of course, you'll still serve as Matris in an ornamental sense. Oversee parades, dance at the finest galas. Smile and wave."

"But I'll have no power. No deciding votes."

"You'll be free of that burden."

"And I suppose someone will have to step into that role of tiebreaker?" I squint at her.

"I suppose that before you resign, if you saw fit, you could appoint someone to act in your stead."

"You?"

"I mean, I'd be the obvious choice . . ."

I don't know what it means that I'm actually considering this plan. The whole Senate hates me now anyway. She'd be legitimizing our marriage, which means the Klang would retain their voice. Bakti could speak out about his people's needs and change could start to happen. But still, as tempting as it is, her offer still feels wrong. People *would* notice that I'd stepped down. The pressure to be more than what everyone expects of me is relentless, but there are people out there rooting for me. People who have taken the time to get to know me. People like Baradonna. I can't let her sacrifice be in vain.

"I can't," I say. I wish my words sounded as convincing as they had in my head. I clear my throat and draw up more confidence. "I won't."

Tesaryn Wen scoffs. "And here I was thinking that you actually cared about Baradonna." She takes the tube and leaves. The crowd has departed as well, and I am left alone with my guilt.

Moments pass, and I become a heaving mess. I turn and rest my head against the wall, wondering how everything had gone so spectacularly wrong. A hand comes down on my shoulder. I jump at the touch, spin around, ready to knock out Tesaryn Wen this time, but it is Bella Roshaad who stands there before me. The compassion in her eyes is almost too much to bear. Do I look deserving of so much pity?

"You tried," she says. "But the system is staunch in its ways, not matter how much we pretend otherwise."

"Senator Wen tried to bribe me to step down."

"Let me guess: she's trying to get you to appoint her to fill the vacancy?"

I nod.

"She's making a power play. I don't like to speak unkindly of my fellow Senators, but that would be very bad for the Senate leadership. She already has too much sway as it is."

"Don't worry, I turned her down." I don't mention how close I was to saying yes.

"I know you think you are without allies here, but that is far from the case. I've been looking out for you. I know you've been trying to keep abreast of all the goings on among our people, but you spread yourself too thin. You'll wear out too quickly. You've changed so much for the better. We need your leadership to last decades, not years."

"I don't know if I'll last months at this point," I mutter.

"Then take a break. Just a short one. Be with your family. _Heal . . ._" She presses her hand against my shoulder and looks me in the eyes. "I can work on getting Kallum a seat on the Senate. At least an interim one, while you're away? It would go a long way toward warming the others to the idea of having him serve in a permanent capacity."

"You shouldn't make promises you can't keep," I snap at her. I know Bella Roshaad is on my side, but dangling my husband's dream in front of me, knowing how the Senate feels about him feels like a more sinister layer of evil than Tesaryn Wen had shown me. "Kallum has petitioned to be considered at least a dozen times, and we haven't gotten anywhere. The Senate wouldn't—"

"For someone so well-versed in book knowledge, you have no idea of how politics really work, do you? You come here, trying your best to sway them, when in reality, 90 percent of the Senate's decisions happen outside the chambers. It shouldn't be that way, but it is." Bella Roshaad shrugs. "I can fill in for you while you're gone, if you'd like. At least it would chap Tesaryn Wen's hide." She laughs, and I join her. It feels good to laugh, even if it's stilted. Even if the pain behind it is still there.

"I need to go meet my son now," I tell her.

Bella Roshaad nods vigorously. "Yes, I've heard. Congratulations." She presses an envelope into my hands, then smiles at me. "You're going to make a fantastic father." And with that, she takes her leave, and I find myself alone in the Senate chambers. I look down at the envelope, then open it carefully, expecting a handwritten card and a gift of crib worm eggs to be crammed inside, but when I unfold the paper, it is a map.

SESKE

Of Loose Braids and Looser Lips

Well, the sex with Bakti has been decent. Okay, good. All right, it's great actually. But every single time we're done, Adalla immediately gets up and runs off to deal with some sort of heart emergency, leaving me and Bakti in bed alone. And I like him. I really do, but conversations with him feel so technical, as if we're two anthropologists studying each other. I wouldn't be surprised if he kept a little notebook under the covers to document all the curiosities he's observed of me and my people.

He looks at me, chest exposed, skin taut and a deep, rich brown. Twenty minutes ago, my mouth had been all over him, but now I am afraid to come too close to touching him, for fear he is some figment of my mind. A wild dream. I've had too many of those lately.

"There is a holiday coming up," he says in his lilting accent. "I've heard the heart-wives chatting about it."

"Ancestor's Day," I say with a nod. "A celebration to honor those in our Line who have come before us. We'll light candles and dance and get drunk on ales from five exoduses ago. And that reminds me, we'll have to get you properly fitted for formal silks."

"Is it an old tradition?"

"Very. But it changed a few years ago. Now we honor the fallen Zenzee as well. We are just as much of their blood. Maybe even more so."

"I will make sweet potatoes to bring to the festivities then."

I smile. The event will be catered, but I don't tell him that. He lights up so much when he's in the kitchen. It has taken me a while to appreciate his cuisine, and like Bakti, it has mostly grown on me. We were both thrown into this arrangement, but slowly we're learning more of each other. I know the situation is not ideal, but Bakti is eager to use his newfound voice to help his people, which will, in turn, help us all. I admire his unrestrained passion for creating change. I vaguely remember what such optimism felt like.

Our parents have finally thawed from the shock as well. Mostly. Bakti knows how to work a room, telling risqué jokes and musing about the differences between our peoples, and how odd our cuisine is. He even once got my stoic will-mother to crack a smile with a saucy double-entendre about the phallic nature of the crème-stuffed gall worm sausages she served at our family dinner.

His mother gifts me with flowers and interesting beads for my hair each time we go to visit the settlement. We were at a loss with what to do with Bakti's hair after the wedding. It was too sleek to hold the braids of our family Line, so we'd settled on a single braid tied up in a bun in the position of our most prominent star. Tirtha had poked little flowers and shells into it, along with small patches of red moss—the same kind his mother wore in her hair on special occasions. I liked that our cultures were blending, ever so slightly, at the edges.

His bun had fallen out during our lovemaking, and the little ornaments had become sharp hazards to bare naked skin. I hadn't much noticed in the moment, but the divot in my knee is now starting to smart.

"How are the work permits coming along?" I ask him in an attempt to make small talk.

"Thirty-three have been issued so far," he says. "Not a lot, but it's a start. My cousin Genaro has received one to work in the doldrums tending to the sails. Very exciting."

"Very exciting, indeed," I say. Then the awkward silence creeps back in.

"I enjoy wearing your silks," Bakti interjects, grabbing a robe that had been tossed to the floor. It belongs to Adalla, but he wraps himself into it anyway. "Very pleasing against the skin."

"The process for preparing the silks is very old. Longer than we've lived aboard the Zenzee."

"I would like to learn more about it," he says, a warm smile on his face, though in my mind, I see him reaching for his notebook.

"I actually don't know much more than that. We could go to the archives sometime to see what we can learn. Or even visit where they spin the silk."

"Oh really? Where would that be?" he asks.

"I actually don't know that either. But—"

A knock comes at the door. Thanks to every single heartfather there ever was for sparing me from additional awkwardness. "Come in!" I say. "*Please* come in," I mutter.

"Oh!" says Doka. "I'm interrupting. Again."

"No, no. We were just chatting. Here," I say patting the bed. "Come sit. You look tired. Got a lot on your mind? Fussy baby?"

Doka nods.

Kenzah's screams could divert a whole herd of Zenzee in the opposite direction. Not to mention the arguments we hear coming from the head-parents running late into the night. Mostly it was them shouting about whether the baby was too young to take a crib worm or not. Charrelle insisted they wait at least until six weeks, stating that the neurotoxins could cause the baby not to nurse as frequently. Doka pushed that he'd had a crib worm at this age and turned out fine. Kallum fluttered between the two, based on the amount of sleep he'd had.

I don't tell any of them that the heart-mothers have been attaching small crib worms to Kenzah's thigh since his second week of life. Not for long enough to leave a bruise ... just enough to enjoy a few quiet moments during their allotted caregiving time.

"But that's not what's bothering me. It's Baradonna," Doka says.

"Do you two need privacy?" Bakti asks. "Because I can get out of your hair ..."

"No, don't go," I plead. I would never say it out loud, but it's nice to have a third person in the room when I'm with Doka. It reminds me of the early days of our courtship, when his honor guard would eavesdrop on our conversations. I quickly shake my head, reminding myself that Bakti is my partner and Doka is the interloper.

"Yes, stay. I won't be long," Doka says. "I just feel so responsible for what happened to her."

"I'm to blame too, then," Bakti says. "We wanted to cause

a stir, and we did. We didn't fully anticipate that there'd be casualties."

"She was trying to protect me," Doka says. "Protect us."

"There's nothing we can do about it now," I say softly. "I know it's still a sore spot for you, but you really need to try to forget."

I grimace, knowing that it's so much easier to give that advice than to take it. I know Baradonna didn't like me much, but she was a good person. And she was loyal to Doka above all. She deserved better.

Doka is silent for a long time. The kind of silence that reads like mischief in a bottle that's yet to be uncorked.

"What?" I ask him.

"Maybe there is something we can do about it," Doka says. "The location of the banishment is recorded and sent to the Senate's Keep."

"Well, there's no way we can get into the Keep," I say. It's heavily guarded. High treason against Senators and governance didn't happen often, and banishment was a fate worse than getting shot into space from the Zenzee's third ass. It was worse than getting the ancestor's lace. In fact, it had only happened one other time in my life . . . to my own sister when she'd tried to kill me.

Doka unrolls a sheet of paper, with ducts branching out in all directions. A map.

"How did you—?"

"I have a few allies in the Senate yet," Doka whispers, cutting me off. He takes a deep breath, then points to the end of a branch, marked with a silver *X*. "Baradonna was banished here. It'd be a day's journey through dangerous rivers, but with provisions and protection, I think I could do it."

"You?" I shake my head. My thumbs are starting to ache

just letting the conversation move in this direction. "You're not risking your life to splash around in the bile ducts to save someone who no longer exists. We don't know what's out there, but I can promise you it's not good."

"Baradonna would do it for me. She has done it for me." Doka lets his head drop. "It's the least I can do to repay her."

"But if you do find her, then what? You can't exactly bring her back here."

"I'll find somewhere safe for her. Somehow. I don't know. I just can't leave her alone and suffering . . ."

Frustration curls my nerves. Doka isn't going to let this drop. He's not thinking straight, and someone's going to have to keep him safe. I could think of a hundred reasons why it'd be unwise to spend my evening venturing into our Zenzee's rancid bile ducts. But who needs reason? The history books are already going to have a lot of awful stuff to say about me. Might as well make it all worth it.

"Well, let me come with you. You and me, going on an adventure, just like old—" I look at Bakti. I can't just exclude him like that, right in front of his face. "You and me and Bakti, going on an adventure . . . making new memories."

"Are you asking me to be a part of your mischief?" Bakti asks.

"We're not asking," says Doka. "We're begging. You've got good reflexes, think fast on your feet."

Bakti purses up his lips and shakes his head slowly. "I'm a will-father now. Aren't I supposed to be encouraging you to make sound decisions and think things through?"

"You're Kenzah's will-father. Not ours," I say. "You don't have to encourage us to do anything."

Bakti leans over, kisses me on the lips, then pulls back. "Well, someone's got to stay here and be a father to Kenzah.

Maybe I'll read him some Uday and Ulmer fables. Mother sent over my old books. If our child takes after Doka, I'll need all the head start I can get to keep him from diving into risky situations." Bakti gets up, shakes the wrinkles out of his robe, then heads to the adjacent washroom. The soft sound of water falling into the tub follows.

"Bakti thinks this is risky," I say. "Do you think it's risky?"

Doka and I stare at each other, both knowing this is a bad idea, and not just because we're venturing off into uncharted waters with no idea of what we're doing. There's something odd welling up between us, especially now that our family dynamics have changed so quickly and so drastically.

Doka lets the question hang and says, "Let's do this."

I RUN MY HAND ALONG STIFF, SMOOTH BONE, AND A SHIVER runs through me. This feels wrong, riding in a boat made from the Zenzee's bone, but Doka assures me it is the most viable option.

"Trust me—you don't want to try the alternative," he'd said as we'd launched.

We've outfitted ourselves with nets and knives and enough food rations to last us a week, just in case we get lost in the maze of ducts. Bakti made us a fresh batch of sweet potato hash and gave us pearl pendants from the oyster farm on Adhosh to bring good luck.

I twirl the pearl beads whenever I get scared, marveling at their green glow, so much brighter than any of the pearls I've ever seen. It's been quiet so far, so they must be working. As we venture farther into the ducts, the ley lights become more and more sparse. I row and Doka navigates, guiding us into darker and narrower ducts. He sings an old sailing song about river bends and black water to ward off the fear. The song ends with kissing your family goodbye, so it really doesn't actually help much. The fog thickens, and in some patches, renders our visibility to near zero.

Small talk might help to keep our terror at bay, so I shout out the first thing that comes to mind. "How do you think the Klang came up with the name 'Adhosh'?" I ask Doka.

He thinks about it for a while, then shrugs. "Maybe it has some sort of cultural meaning. Or maybe they liked the way it sounded."

"Maybe," I say. "Well, what do you think we should call our Zenzee?"

"I don't know. She kind of seems like a Gladys to me. Or a Marian."

"Or a Sue," I say with a laugh. Maybe I laugh a little too loudly because a stiff breeze zips past us, and seconds later, the ley light mounted at the bow of our boat fades to a dull glow.

"No worries. I can shake it back up," I say, pulling my oars into the boat, though the current has picked up enough that it carries us on its own.

Doka nods. "I'll steady the boat. Be careful."

"Sure thing." I go to my knees, put one hand on the side of the boat for balance, and reach out for the lamp with the other. I can barely make out my own hand in front of me. I unhook the lamp, give it a good vigorous shake until the whole duct is aglow with its amber-golden light. Then I go to hang it again. "See, no prob—" I look out and see the drop ahead of us. "Daidi's bells!"

"What?" Doka asks.

"There's a dip coming. Hold on."

He clutches the pendant Bakti had given him in one hand and holds the side of the boat with the other. But the river twists us, turns us, and tips us over, and we both go face first into the murky waters.

"The boat!" Doka cries when he surfaces. "Our stuff!"

I swim after our overturned boat and together, we work to flip it back over. He helps me in, then starts tossing me the knife and the fishing pole and the map. "We lost the food and my pearls," he says to me as he pulls himself up. "And I don't think the smell is ever going to come out of our clothes."

I look down. It was bad before, but having the smell this close to my skin is so much worse. "I . . . Ugg. Turn around."

Doka complies, and I strip down to my panties and wring out most of the water over the edge. "Pass me my canteen," I say. Doka must not be peeking because it takes several attempts for him to find my hand. I take a swallow for myself, then rinse my dress the best I can without wasting too much water. I take another smell. Better. Barely.

I turn and see Doka, his back toward me, wringing out his shirt as well. The skin on his back is so smooth, and I catch myself staring at how his muscles flex beneath. What is this I'm feeling?

"Okay, you can turn around now," I say.

He does, then his breath catches. "You . . . you're not dressed."

"It's just skin," I say, surprised by my confidence. Maybe *boldness* would be a better word. *It's just skin, it's just skin,* I chant to myself in the awkward silence that's growing between us.

"Ummm . . . ," Doka mutters.

"And it's not like we've never seen each other naked. Plus, we're married."

"We're married," he says. "But not married like *that*."

Well, not anymore, thanks to me pushing him for the annulment. But I still remember flipping back his veil after he was pronounced mine, and the taste of his lips when we'd kissed in front of thousands of onlookers. I hadn't been in the right mind to enjoy it at the time, but it hadn't been completely unpleasant.

"Well, you can face the other way for the rest of the trip if you want to. I'm not rowing anywhere in a wet, stinky gown." I pick up my oars and start rowing again. "Which way do we go next?"

Doka stares at the map way too hard. My heart nearly stops beating. "What?"

"The ink faded. But I think I can still make it out." He comes closer, placing the map between us and pointing at it with his finger. "I think we're here." He slides his finger closer to me. "And we're trying to get here." His finger doesn't stop at the X that marks the spot, just passes right off the edge of the page and onto my skin, until he's got one hand pressed softly against my side. Neither of us moves. Neither of us breathes.

"You're much softer than puppet gel. And warmer. And I bet if I touched your nipple, it wouldn't ball up and roll off."

I laugh. Mostly from painful awkwardness, but a little of the happy kind, too. "I was a jerk. Sorry."

"You were a kid. I was too. Besides, I let go of that a long time ago." He looks up at me bashfully. "More or less."

His hand moves up, cups my right breast. I tense ever so slightly.

"What?" he asks. "Do you want me to stop?"

I shake my head quickly. "No. I'm just . . ." How in the world do I explain that up until two weeks ago, I had pads stuffed in my shirt because every time I heard Kenzah crying, I'd spontaneously produce some sort of purple sap from my nipples that was nearly impossible to remove from clothing once it dried. *You don't, Seske. You just don't.* ". . . nervous, I guess. If we get caught—"

"Who's going to catch us out here? There's no one except me and—"

Something collides with the boat, and we lurch. Doka topples, nearly falls overboard again, but I grab his hand, pull him back in. There's knocking against the hull. It doesn't sound random.

"Shhhh. Something's down there," Doka whispers, grabbing the net behind him.

"Something?" I ask, "Or someone? Because your face is saying 'someone.'"

"I don't know. But I've heard something like this before." He waits until the next collision, and not half a second later, he throws the net over, moving quickly, then he tightens the drawstring. The bucking and thrashing against the boat intensifies.

"Does this seem like a bad idea?" I ask him, panic in my voice as we haul the net back in. "Because this seems like a bad idea to me."

He nods, but keeps pulling. With a final coordinated heave, we get the net aboard. Inside, squirming and kicking, is a throttle fish, but it's huge—nearly the same size as me. Its hands pull at the netting with three-inch claws, sleek black fins on its back looking sharp as knives.

The net won't hold forever.

I quickly dress, hoping to put at least a thin layer of fabric between me and those claws. The netting starts to tear. This was definitely a bad idea.

"Help me throw it back in," Doka says, grabbing it by the tail. I can't wait to get it out of here, either.

"I'm on it," I say, but when I do, the fish stops struggling and looks right up at me. The throttle fish back in the bogs at home are almost cute—chubby cheeks, bright eyes, the works—but this one's face hold sheer malice. Mouth open, it bears silver, needle-sharp teeth. But there is the same humanlike eeriness with this one, even tucked this deep in the bile ducts, completely removed from civilization. The beast's scowl slowly works itself into a smile, and I let go of my end of the net, recognizing the face that has so long haunted my dreams.

"Sisterkin," I whisper.

"What?" Doka asks, scrambling over to my side so quickly, he nearly topples the boat over again. He stares at the hissing monstrosity. "It can't be—"

The throttle fish claws through the net and slices at Doka, barbed fins leaving a gash across his chest. He spends half a moment in shock, then throws up his arms to protect himself. I jump onto the net and hold the fish down, but it's all muscle, and before I know it, it's got its clawed hands clenched around my neck. I struggle to breathe. Darkness comes for the corners of my vision, then all I can see is the face staring back at me with so much hatred.

Then there's a whack, the sound of bone hitting flesh, and slowly, my vision returns. I sit up and see Doka standing there, holding the fishing rod in both hands, visibly shaking. He looks down at the fish, incapacitated. Maybe dead.

"Seske, sorry, I—"

"You did the right thing," I tell him. "Don't second guess yourself." I rub at my neck, feeling welts swell up beneath my fingertips.

"It looks so much like her," Doka says.

Too much like her.

"We'll take it to the scientists," I say. "Maybe they'll have some idea of what it is." Doka agrees, but right now, I'm pretty sure we're both more worried about what else is out there than how this fish came to be. I've got a sinking feeling that there's something more sinister lurking nearby. Something that can't be disabled by a bone-carved fishing pole. I look up sadly at Doka. "I'm afraid Baradonna is going to have to wait a little longer. But we'll find her. I promise."

DOKA

Of Familiar Faces and Peculiar Embraces

Seske and I slam the throttle fish down onto the floor of the research lab with enough ruckus to catch everyone's attention, but no one looks our way. They're all glued to a holoprojection of a pulsating star. Or something like a star. It glows magenta, and just beyond the depth of the light it emits, I can make out something moving along the surface, like bloat flies circling a lamp. It's mesmerizing, I'll give them that, but we've got more pressing problems right now. I clear my throat, loudly and obnoxiously. Finally, one of the researchers notices, then scrambles over to the mess we've made on her pristine floor.

"What is this?" she says, bending down to examine our catch. She backs up when she sees the size of the fangs.

"We were hoping you could tell us," I say. "We found it in the bile ducts."

"What were you doing in the bile ducts?" another researcher asks. They're all swarming around us now, hands itching to poke and prod at the specimen. Its jaw hangs slack, and its eyes have gone milky. My blow had been deadly. I'd be remorseful if the terror of seeing it clenching Seske's throat wasn't still prickling at my nerves.

Seske nudges me aside. "Um, that's restricted information. What's important is that we figure out why this fish looks so much like my sister."

All eyes suddenly go wide at the use of that word—sister, almost a vulgarity. And mentioning this particular sister made things a thousand time worse. Each and every researcher finds random things to stare at. No one dares to meet Seske's gaze.

"It's fine," Seske says, shoulders slumping forward. "I know she was banished, and that we're supposed to forget she ever existed, but clearly, that's no longer an option."

"It appears to be some sort of throttle fish," the head researcher says, tentatively lifting up one of the gills. "A different species perhaps? One that grows larger than our domesticated ones."

"Or one that's simply fed on the flesh of a human for a long period of time," says another researcher.

I flinch, remembering the story Charrelle had told me, about the throttle fish that Madam Wade had tried to force upon her. They'd tried to explain it as a kindness, that sparing a child's life without the blessing of our ancestors was a noble act. One of caring. Wouldn't it be better that they lived out their days carefree, swimming in ponds? That they were bound to live entwined within the flesh of an alien fish didn't even cross their minds as to be a cruelty.

The head researcher nods. "These parasites are masters of incorporating genetic material into their own. Mouth latching on to feed, and over time, taking on the characteristics of their host. There could be dozens more out there, just like this one."

"Dozens?" Seske asks.

I try not to imagine Sisterkin somewhere out there, being fed upon by more of these fish. It was no wonder banishment was considered a worse punishment than getting expelled into space. That death was quick. Nearly instant. Sure, you had to watch your blood vaporize and you'd bloat up like an overcooked crag egg, but then your lungs collapsed, and it was all over. Quick and dead, less than a minute. This . . . months, maybe years of losing yourself slowly to parasitic creatures.

It was horrifying.

"Maybe hundreds of them, if she lasts long enough." The researcher gives us a pitying smile, but instead of probing further, they all turn their attention back to the pulsating star. As if none of this even matters to them. A lump swells up in my throat.

"Baradonna," I say softly. I try to keep my mind focused on the here and now, but I can't stop thinking about how we've failed her. She's out there somewhere, suffering. I can't even imagine the depths of the nightmare she's living through.

Seske wraps her arms around me, and I melt into her.

"She's strong," Seske whispers into my ear. "If there's anyone who can survive this, it's her. Come on, let's get you home. I'm sure Kenzah misses you."

Maybe Seske can tell I'm about to spiral into a really bad place. Maybe a change of scenery will help. I sure don't want to spend another moment here. She takes one last look at the dead face of her sister, then we leave.

I CRADLE MY SON IN MY ARMS, KALLUM'S CHIN RESTING ON MY shoulder, as proud a father as there ever was. We've made a handsome little child with impressively strong lungs. I wonder which of Charrelle's favor lures had drawn that blessing. I flinch as his wailing raises an octave, tearing at my eardrums. Maybe it doesn't matter much if the ancestors don't sit with him, because I'm sure they'll hear his screams either way.

Seske watches us from the far corner of our sitting room, a smile on her face that might be more of a grimace. She's so close to the window that her shoulder is draped by the thick curtains meant to keep out the cold. Their embroidered leaf pattern nearly matches her dress as well. It's as if she's trying to blend in with her surroundings.

"Come closer," I tell Seske, patting the open spot on the sofa next to me. "Kenzah needs his will-mother."

Seske looks doubtful. I think something about the child scares her. It took her three weeks to even hold him.

"Please," I say. "You're the reason he's here. I want you to know this happiness." Having my family surrounding me is a balm that helps smooth over all my other worries. And despite the tension that's always stretched between us, Seske is a part of that. That tension is thicker now, since the incident on the boat. I'm not even sure a knife could cut through it.

Seske sighs, then scoots next to me. I hand the baby to her, orchestrating a careful maneuver that keeps his bobbling head supported. Her braids graze my shoulder, and our cheeks nearly touch, but Seske pulls back just in time. Kenzah fusses some, but Seske sticks a knuckle in his mouth, and he settles, sucking contently.

"He's so beautiful," she says, then sniffs the top of his head, full of black curls. Her eyes go soft, and her body slackens ever so slightly. I probably wouldn't have even noticed before, but my mind has been constantly reminding me to be on alert, even in intimate moments such as this one. It's like the confident and carefree Seske I knew from before is back for a fleeting moment.

"I think he's got Seske's smile," Kallum says, both his arms wrapped around me now.

Seske looks up, confusion on her face, but then Kallum winks at her. I know it's hard at first, getting used to the idea that he is all of ours, and that Line is thicker than blood.

"Perhaps," she says with a grin. "And if he's as smart and headstrong as his head-fathers, and as passionate and free-spirited as his head-mother . . . maybe we could find a way to extend our Line to him. Maybe he could be next in line to be the matriarch."

"Seske," I say, remembering the fear Baradonna had in her eyes after the wedding. I want none of that for my son. "We're all hoping for the kind of change that would make that even a remote possibility, but we need to be realistic. Right now, the best way to keep Kenzah safe is for us to keep attention off him. We need to be a normal family."

"What about our family resembles anything close to normalcy?" she asks, and the walled-off Seske is suddenly back. "Kallum all but stole his Line. I'm married to a beastworker and a person from another Zenzee. I think we passed 'normal' a long time ago. And we're stronger for it. Besides, we've got years to wear them down. And don't you think it's ridiculous that we should give up the protection an heir brings to our family, just because Kenzah was born a boy and not a—" Seske's eyes widen. Her arms go slack. Kallum rushes over and scoops the baby from her just in time. She looks as though she's about to pass out.

"What? What's wrong, Seske?" I ask her. I help her down to a lying position on the floor.

"Kenzah is a boy," she whispers.

"Yes, yes. We know that."

"Baby boys are rare. Especially among high ranking families."

"I know that, too."

She waves me off in annoyance. "Except the Klang have an abnormally high rate of males born . . . almost half of all births. What if they're not the odd ones? What if we are abnormal for having so few boys?" She stares up at the matte black ceiling, speckled with a dusting of star jewels that mimic the constellations of our Line. Her eyes twitch back and forth, tracing from one star to the next in the pattern she'd known since childhood and the one the rest of our family had gotten to know through marriage into it. Finally, she breaks away and locks her eyes directly into mine. "What if it's deliberate?"

Kallum's brows pinch, concern on his face. "That's not how biology works, Seske. Fewer males have been born for centuries. You're trying to say that there's been some grand conspiracy all this time to keep the numbers artificially low?"

My heart skips in my chest, remembering how easily our people had bred then slaughtered hundreds and thousands of workers, just to power through the excavation and expansion phases of culling a new Zenzee. All that death so wealthy people like me and Seske and Kallum could settle into our homes a little faster.

Seske and I exchange looks.

I know where she's going with this, and I hope upon hope that she's wrong, but I would be foolish to deny even considering it. Something prickles my gut, something I realize has been there for a long, long time. Was it really a rarity to have a son born to such a prestigious Line? It wouldn't have been if Madam Wade had gotten her way. Which leads me down another path: What if she'd known that Charrelle had been carrying a boy, and all that talk about the Ancestors sitting with our child was just a ruse masquerading as another one of our sanctified traditions?

I feel sick, thinking about the hundreds and hundreds of pregnancies Madam Wade has presided over. And the many Soothsayers that came before her . . .

"Are you okay, Doka?" Seske asks.

I nod. I can't speak aloud something so atrocious. Not before I have proof. "Kallum, you've been aboard other ships. What's the gender split among them? Are they more like us, or more evenly split, like the Klang?"

"You're not dragging me into the middle of this nonsense," Kallum says, shaking his head. "What about the Serratta? They're practically all men!"

"And we all know the reason behind that," Seske interjects. "They sacrifice their women to run the ship. Something is definitely rank here."

"Each clan is unique, and they've all got different practices and customs and taboos," Kallum says calmly. "The first thing I learned is not to compare, and you'd be wise to do the same."

Seske's nostrils flare in frustration. "Well then, we could check our Texts for historical references. Comb through the Accountancy Guard annals. They document everything. If something really is amiss, then we'll find it."

I nod and help Seske slowly to her feet. Her hands are soft in mine, but I know that her softness—in her hands and otherwise—is only superficial. There is power beneath that skin, and it feels good to see Seske slowly coming into her own again, despite the circumstances around it.

"Great idea," I say to her. "I'll have Baradonna fetch the—"

my breath catches. I'd forgotten that easily. "I'll fetch the annals and you can get started researching through the Texts. I'll
meet you in the study."

"You're wasting your time," Kallum calls after us as we de-
part. He kisses Kenzah on the cheek, then gives me a sigh of
resignation. "At least be home for dinner!"

"We will," I say, returning to give him a kiss as well. Kallum's eyes soften and his smile becomes less strained. I soak
him in, knowing that if my suspicions are correct, our entire
world will come crumbling down, and it will be a long, long
time before we can enjoy something as simple as dinner again.

HOURS LATER, SESKE AND I ARE LOST IN THE STACKS OF MY
study. She's on her fifteenth paper cut as she flips through the
Texts, finger meandering down each page, looking for evidence to jump out at her. I crunch census numbers from the
last five hundred years, punching the data into my tablet and
scrutinizing the resulting graphs. While there is no obvious
evidence of a conspiracy, the numbers are damning. Three
centuries ago, there was a nearly even split among men and
women. Then slowly, almost imperceptibly from one generation to the next, there was a shift.

The last notable shift was barely over a century ago, when
heart-husbands were dropped from family units. The justifi-
cation was there just weren't enough men to go around. People
just nodded and accepted it. No one pushed back.

"Maybe life aboard the Zenzee caused some kind of hor-
monal change," Seske says, clinging to optimism despite the
facts laid about before us. "One that made it more likely for
females to be conceived?"

"Then wouldn't the Klang have been affected in the same way? And the other clans?"

"There has to be some other reason. We can't be the kind of people who would just allow . . ." Her voice breaks.

"Every single pregnancy comes under scrutiny, to see if the ancestors sit with the child, but I don't think they're testing for that. What if they're checking if the child is a boy?"

"Doka . . ."

"I didn't want to say it. I don't even want to think it. Charrelle had gone to visit Madam Wade with grim results. How many expectant mothers had gotten the same results? How many of them were carrying boys? What if there's more to it than the conveniently obscure threat of having a child that the ancestors didn't sit with?"

Seske shudders. "Zenzee react differently to men and women in the salivatory chambers. What if they can detect those differences in pregnancies as well?"

"Exactly."

"Daide's bells." Seske fidgets roughly with the hem of her dress. I watch her body closely, almost able to see the nervous energy coursing through it. There's anger there, too. And maybe a hollowness I don't quite know how to interpret. "We have to do something. We have to tell someone!"

"We have to dig deeper," I say. "But old books and dusty records aren't going to tell us what we need to know."

Seske nods. "Then we need to go where it starts. We need to question Madam Wade."

WE MAKE OUR WAY TO THE CEREBRAL CORTEX, SESKE TAKING the lead and guiding me away from deceptively slick paths eager to send the unsuspecting travelers into one of the deep chasms of brain folds. I'd been to the cortex once, soon after I'd officially adopted the title of Matris. I'd wanted to see how it was that we could control the whims of a beast so incredibly massive. I felt like a microbe in comparison. An infection. A parasite that had bent the will of its host.

When we arrive at Madam Wade's quaint shack, she is not happy to see Seske, and is even less happy to see me; she's eyeing me suspiciously, tension in her body as if she's torn between offering me a salute of reverence or telling me to go fuck off.

"What is the meaning of this?" she asks, somewhere in between the two, voice polite yet firm. She stands fully in the doorway, intent on not letting us pass. This will take some diplomacy. I wish we'd brought Kallum with us.

"We know your whole performance is a sham," Seske says. "The Knowing Walk is fraudulent. You manipulate the bones somehow. We know the ancestors are in no way involved."

So much for tact.

"*Matris*, you need to turn away from here," Madam Wade growls at me. "You have no idea of what you're tampering with."

I grit my teeth. "I know exactly—"

While she is distracted by me, Seske pushes past her and storms inside. She pulls a bag from a shelf on the wall, then upturns it. Dozens of little white bones fall to the ground.

"How do they work?" Seske demands.

Madam Wade throws her hands to the sides of her face. "What are you doing? Why are you wrecking everything?" she says, scrambling to pick up the bones.

I take a step over the threshold, and as soon as my foot makes contact with the floor, the air within this place changes. I feel as though I'm back in the salivatory chambers, but instead of tongues licking out at me, the entire place starts to vibrate. On the selves lining the walls, dozens and dozens of bags hop like something has come alive inside them. Inching closer to me. The bones spilled on the floor do the same.

"Take off your shoes," Seske yells at me.

Madam Wade hears this and lunges at me, but she is too slow, and I brush her to the side. I slip out of my shoes and place my bare feet on the floor. It is the same process that Seske and Charrelle had described to me, only I am not pregnant, and the ancestors shouldn't care about me being here.

One by one, the bones turn to face me. Then one jumps up from the floor and smacks me in the shin. Another one comes, launching itself harder at me this time. The next thing I know, all the bags are rumbling violently. The entire room shakes beneath my feet, reminiscent of the old tremors that used to ravage our Zenzee. I duck as one of the bags flies at me. It hits Seske in the shoulder. By the look on both her and Madam Wade's faces, I can see none of this is normal.

"You need to leave," Madam Wade rasps. "Immediately. Or—"

The shelving buckles. The wall pounds outward.

"Or this whole thing will be exposed as a sham. Too late for that," Seske says, grabbing my hand. "Let's go."

She slings me toward the door, then snatches Madam Wade right before the shelf lands on her. We keep running until everything quiets.

"What is going on in there?" I ask Madam Wade in my sternest tone. She may be my elder by several decades, but I don't want her to forget who is the one in charge. "Tell me the truth. I won't hesitate to have you strung up by your thumbs if I find out you are omitting even the tiniest detail."

She stares at me, trying to determine if I'm bluffing. She then looks away. "I am sworn to secrecy," she mumbles.

"Your secrets are killing innocent people. They're harming

families," I say. I can't imagine a world without Kenzah now, and I have to keep my anger pressed down into the back of my chest to keep from lunging at her and strangling the truth out.

"It's tradition," Madam Wade says this time. "And there is no killing. The children live on."

"As fucking fish!" I say. I can't take it any longer, I grab her by the lapel and pull her close to me. "Tell me how it works!"

A weighty silence lingers between us, then she finally speaks.

"The Zenzee's synapses are sensitive to human hormones," Madam Wade stutters, refusing to meet my eyes. There is deep shame buried within her. "They can sense the changes in blood during a pregnancy, even as early as seven weeks, discerning between female and male fetuses. The disruption in synapse firings happens in a predictable pattern. I'm not exactly sure of how, but it manipulates the iron in the marrow of the bones, causing them to turn in certain ways. Of course there are natural variations in hormone levels, so it's not completely accurate, but it's close enough."

I let Madam Wade loose and she starts sobbing into her hands.

"The ritual was passed down to me by the Soothsayer before me, and the one before her, and so on. For generations. We are taught to bear the pain of this knowledge so that others won't have to."

"Will you testify to this in front of the Senate?" I ask.

Madam Wade shakes her head vehemently. "I can't. People come to me in confidence. I won't breach their trust."

"You breached their trust the moment they stepped foot in the Knowing circle," I say, my voice firm. If she is looking for compassion, she won't find it here. "You almost killed my son. Should I bring him here, so that you can look him in the face and tell him that his life was better off spent swimming in a bog?"

Madam Wade is silent, but I see the thoughts churning now. Feelings have flooded her body. Hopefully one of those is remorse. "I—" she mutters.

"This has to stop. And stopping it starts with you. *Please*."

Madam Wade is quiet for a long moment, then she nods. "I'll do it. I'll testify."

Seske and I look at each other, then sigh in relief. The proof is mounting on our side.

ARMED WITH SEVERAL BAGS OF MEAT AND CABBAGE, WE work well through the night. We visit four different bogs, me luring throttle fish with tasty morsels while Seske scoops them up with a net. She pinches their mouths shut so their screaming doesn't draw unwanted attention. Harassing throttle fish like this was something we were taught early on to be morally reprehensible. I suppose I understand now why that trip with my mother through the bile ducts had been so fraught. Maybe she hadn't known the true depths of the silent genocide, but she knew it was something shameful, and people tried to soothe that guilt through their revered treatment of the throttle fish.

We take genetic samples from every throttle fish we can wrangle. Though some come up as inconclusive, the vast majority are male. Seske and I return to our study with the weight of this new knowledge on our shoulders. Our bodies are worn, and so are our spirits.

"I don't know how much more of this I can take," I say to Seske.

Her head hits my shoulder and she utters a noncommittal grunt. "We should rest. Today has been a lot."

"I wish I could, but we need to take our evidence to the Senate first thing tomorrow, and we should spend every second we have between now and then preparing what I'm going to say to them. And I need you to be by my side, or else I'll look like a frantic man spouting conspiracy theories. I always feel more confident when you're with me."

"I always feel more confident with a full night's rest, but I guess that's shot now."

"Fine, a ten-minute break," I say. "Then we're back to work, okay? We've only got a couple hours left."

"Make it twenty minutes and I'll do anything you say."

I let out a deep sigh, then stand up to stretch. My legs ache from stooping down on the boggy shores so long. Seske stretches too, arms thrown back, standing on her tiptoes. Then she lets out a huge yawn. The fabric of her robes clings to her curves, and I have a hard time putting our time in the boat behind us. Nothing had happened. I'd touched a part of her bare skin, simple as touching an elbow or a knee. Except I hadn't touched an elbow or a knee, and Seske hadn't minded.

"What do you think's for breakfast?" I ask, trying to distract myself with something a little less tension-filled.

"Egg loaf, mostly likely. It's Adalla's turn to cook, and that's what she always makes."

I nod. "Have you mentioned to her that maybe she could use less hedge leaf? It gets stuck in my teeth. And fewer peppers? It's always so spicy."

"It's a beastworker custom, so probably no. And you can always ask me if you have hedge leaf stuck in your teeth. I'll for sure let you know if you do."

"Well, see anything now?" I ask, then give her a full glimpse of my teeth.

"No. Nothing. Wait. Maybe. Come a little closer."

I comply, but I hide my smile behind my lips, tilt my head down to hers, so close, I can feel her breath against my face. My heart pounds, knowing that the thing I desire the most is so close, and yet so far.

"Your lips are in the way," she says to me.

"Maybe my lips are in the exact right place they need to be," I say. Closer now. Shivers run through me.

Seske blinks rapidly, then pulls away, diving back into one the ancient tomes she'd had her nose buried in earlier. She's flipping the thin pages so hard and fast, I fear she might tear them. She clears her throat. "Maybe we should get back to work. Every moment we waste—"

I shut the book and turn her back toward me. "We've drowned ourselves in the atrocities of our people. We've lost sight of the surface. But we need to remind ourselves what we're fighting for. That there's something on the other side worth fighting for."

My eyes soften, and I lean in closer.

Seske raises a skeptical brow. "And let me guess . . . I'm going to find that by shoving my tongue in your mouth? That's mighty bold of you."

"No, but, on the boat—"

"Nothing happened on the boat. And even if something had, are we just supposed to forget about Adalla and Bakti and Kallum and Charrelle? Are we supposed to ignore all of our duties and obligations, just because maybe we have feelings that run so deep, we can hardly stand to be in the same room together? Are we supposed to forget about how well we fit together? To forget about how maybe we once had something great, and I was too young and naive to realize it, so I just threw it away?" Her voice trembles and so does she.

"Yes."

"Yes?"

"I do want to forget. Just for a moment," I say, dead serious, though the consequences of violating our marriage oath tap against my brain. *If you're found out, seriously dead is just what you'll be.* Apart from my head-spouses, I am forbidden from romantically consorting within our family unit structure, but those rules are all just a construct to prevent jealousy and complications and unnecessary drama. Things are different between me and Seske. We have a history. We have something special.

It's disconcerting how easily I quiet my reservations. This one moment is all I need, and it is our moment that's been owed to us. For just a while, we'll exist quietly outside of this place. Outside of this time. It is ours alone.

Seske's mouth opens, closes, opens again, gasping for words that refuse to come. Then she throws herself upon me, our lips behaving like they've grown appendages, trying to pull each other in a passionate tug-of-war. And the war within me grows. With Seske, I feel like I've got too many arms, too much skin. Too many tongues. More dicks than I can count. And I think we're fucking, but I can't even be sure, because there's just too much of me, and too much of her, and this moment won't stretch big enough to fit us both.

Seske moans and screams my name, and then my mouth is full of a tacky sweetness that runs down my throat. I swallow as much as I can, but there's too much of that too, and then I'm drowning, drowning. Her skin burns against mine. And now I'm on fire as well, but I don't care, because her mouths are putting them out, one by one.

By one.

Just the one dick now . . .

. . . spent and limp and happy, barely clinging inside her. I stay perfectly still, so that we can remain connected a little longer. But already I know that our moment has already moved into the next. We drift asleep anyway, arm in arm, sticky and sore.

I dream of her. And in that dream, we have a hundred sons, each of them loved and nurtured and cared for. They lie together in a big, snuggly pile, smiles as bright as stars. So bright, their smiles shatter.

My elbow is wet. And warm. It wakes me from my dream. I'm lying in liquid now, purple . . . pretty sure it didn't come from me. Less sure it didn't come from Seske. Smells like tea, though. I run my finger through the puddle. Taste it. Definitely tea.

Extra kettleworms. Too strong. Just the way Kallum makes it.

I tense up, close my eyes.

"I just came to let you know that breakfast is ready," Kallum says, his voice nearly lifeless.

Seske wakes at the sound of his voice, and I feel her scrambling as she fumbles for her clothes, cursing every heart-father there ever was. "Sorry," she finally whispers to me. "But you're going to have to face the Senate alone." Footsteps splash through the tea puddle, and then she's gone.

Bold of her to think I'll live to see the Senate. I open my eyes and turn to Kallum, who's holding his silver serving tray down at his side. "I'm—"

"Don't apologize," Kallum says sternly. He takes several

harsh breaths, nostrils flaring in an unsettling rhythm. "You won't mean it. This is what you wanted. This is what you've always wanted. I'm not going to tell the Senate. Not to spare you punishment, but because I won't allow you to destroy this family. I just want to know if it was worth it."

There is no answer that will quell his heart, or that will soothe his hurt, so I remain quiet. But I need to know myself: Was it worth it? It's scary to admit that some sort of sleep-deprived lack of judgment had caused us to shatter our lives and those of our spouses, and our whole family. It's even scarier to admit that, if given the chance, I'd do the same all over again. And again.

And again.

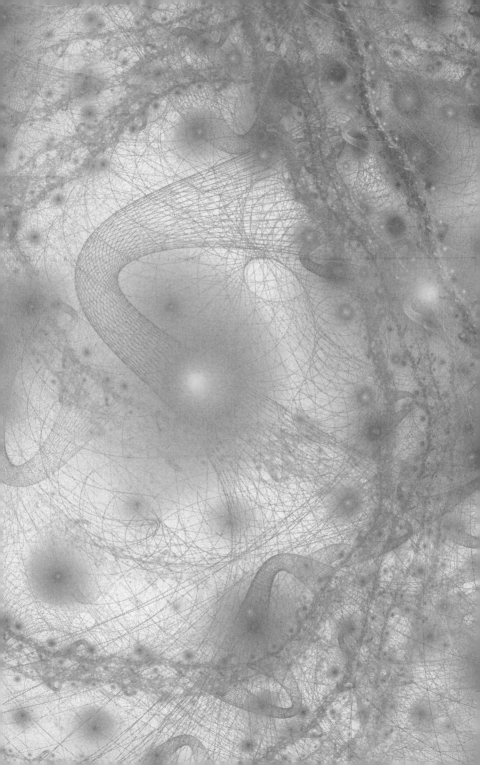

part III

. . . .

mutualism

In your desire to control and dominate, you have
forced us to better ourselves.
Now it is time to let us return the favor.

QUEEN OF THE DEAD

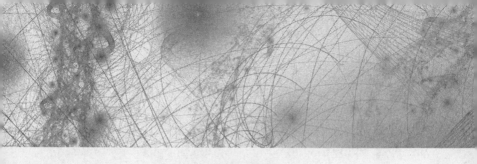

SESKE

Of Closed Hearts and Open Space

I've made a mistake. An awful, terrible mistake. And all it took was a moment.

But what else did I expect from a relationship riddled with awkward tension and guilt? Maybe we could have found a way to work through it, but now everything is gone, broken, ruined, and the rest of my life with it—and for what? Some weird, mediocre sex?

When I kissed him, it was as if his lips had become like those of a frog, prehensile and trying to pull me into him. It was like he had a dozen arms, each groping at me, none of them knowing what they were doing. Tongue all over the place, too, licking all but the right crevices. I'd yelled his name, urging him to slow down. To take his time. To allow ourselves space in that moment, but he was spent before we'd even gotten started.

I don't know if I'd even call it sex.

And then, he'd just laid there, pulling me close, still tethered together by that rope of limp flesh. I didn't want to move, because once we were free of each other, the shock would wear off and the regret would come crashing down on me. I closed my eyes, trying to ignore my poor, sore nipples, my confused humble bits, and the stick of his skin against mine.

He snored right in my ear, eye movement rapid behind his lids. Dreaming.

Then I heard footsteps, and I knew we were done for. I opened my eyes and saw Kallum staring back at me, holding a tea service for three. I'd never seen such pain in anyone's eyes before. It was like watching someone die—the light fading, the soul collapsing, the body going slack, then eventually rigid. He died there, right before me, but remained standing. Breathing. Staring.

Minutes passed, ten, maybe twenty. Maybe it had only been seconds. Not a word was spoken between us. Barely a blink. Finally, his arms went slack, the tea fell to the ground with a shatter. I flinched and pressed my face into Doka's chest. Finally, he woke.

All I could think about was getting out of there, so I grabbed my clothes and ran back upstairs. I cleaned up the best I could. I filled the wash basin with warm water, ran an entire bar of soap over my skin until nothing was left but a sliver, but no amount of washing could rid me of the stains that plagued me the most.

I find Bakti, Charrelle, and the baby, and two of our heart-wives, Jesphara and Ida, sitting around the kitchen table, with Adalla at the stove putting the finishing touches on a pan of egg loaf. I greet them with a hearty, over-the-top good morning, then sneak up behind Adalla and wrap my arms around her, press my nose to the back of her neck. Breathe her in.

We're so close, I can feel the raised scars on her back through the layers of fabric that separate us. I cringe, thinking of the pain I have inflicted upon her in the distant past.

And the not-so-distant past.

"Good morning, love," she says. She lays her knife down and turns to me, looks me over. I hold my breath, wondering if she can smell Doka on me. Or sense it somehow. But she pulls my chin close to her and kisses me. Pure. Simple. I nearly cry with how beautiful it is. "Are you okay?" she asks. Rubbing a tear from the corner of my eye.

I nod. "Just the peppers," I say, pointing at her cutting board. "They're a little strong."

"Oh! Should I use less next time?"

"No. I like the way you make them. Don't change. Anything."

Adalla smiles, kisses me again, deeper this time. A length of saliva links us when we're done, then snaps. My whole heart snaps as well. I muster a smile, then kiss Bakti on the cheek, and he leans his head on my shoulder, resting there for a few seconds, before he turns back to Charrelle, who he's caught in conversation with.

Feeling like an interloper, a ghost, I take my seat.

They all talk, they all laugh. They take turns with a very fussy baby. But it all washes past me, as if I'm not really here at all. Minique, our other heart-wife, joins us too.

"What's taking Doka and Kallum so long?" Adalla asks—me presumably, since I was the last to see them. I shrug and pull a string loose from the frayed end of a cloth napkin as she sets the loaf in the center of the table.

"You know them. Probably fucking in a pile of ancient papers," says Minique.

"Language!" cries Charrelle, putting her hands over Kenzah's ears. "If there's one thing this baby knows, it's how much his fathers love each other. Some of you could probably learn from their example."

Minique gets flustered and grabs the serving spoon, then digs out a chunk of the egg loaf and plops it into her bowl. She doesn't wait for us to acknowledge the favors that went into preparing this meal, and starts shoving egg loaf into her mouth, not even bothering to cut around the gristle. Minique and her wives are the most intelligent people I know, and their unrivaled beauty makes for a very nice family portrait. They came to our family as a bonded unit, as heart-wives often do. They'd been married ten years already, and it was clear from what we'd observed that Minique was often on the outs with the Jesphara and Ida.

"'Dalla," I say gently as soon as she's taken a seat next to me. "Take me with you to the heart today. Maybe I can help out? I've been practicing my slicing skills." I take an imaginary swing in front of me, nearly knocking over my cup of beetle milk.

"Not today," Adalla says grimly. "We've had a few slight arrhythmias spread over the last couple days. Nothing major, hopefully nothing to worry about. But we need everyone on their best game, betcha, and that means no distractions. Even if they're very cute distractions." She nudges me in the shoulder, then kisses me on the cheek. "In fact, I probably should be on duty now, but I wanted to squeeze in breakfast with you at least. It's going to be a long day. Don't stay up waiting for me, okay?"

"Maybe I can bring you a lunch, then?" I say, knowing how important it is that she keeps up her energy. Besides, if I keep my mouth moving, my mind moving, I can keep my guilt at bay. "Something fast and nutritious?"

"It's the dessert I'm worried about," Adalla says with a

saucy grin. She cranes her neck, peeking out into the hallway. "Where are those boys?"

"Maybe we should eat without them," I suggest, a knot in my throat.

Minique stops chewing long enough for us to acknowledge the favors from our ancestors. It is Kallum's turn to lead the prayer, but in his absence, it falls on Charrelle.

She stretches one hand out toward the middle of the table, balancing Kenzah with the other as he perches on her knee. "Ancestors across the great divide, we give thanks for your favor in providing us with this bounty. May it fill our bellies. May it nourish our bodies. May it clear our sinuses . . ."

Adalla laughs, a delicate flutter that echoes in my heart. It spurs my denial into anger. She's been gone so much lately, pouring herself into her job. Was it any wonder my heart had started to wander?

"Let us all come together," Charrelle continues. "The bond of our family forever strengthening, the ties between us, honorable and true. Please do us this favor."

On this cue, we are to link hands, but mine stay buried in my lap. Adalla nudges me, already locking fingers with Bakti on her other side. Charrelle reaches to me with her free hand. Normally, it would be Doka who I'd locked with, but we'd done quite enough of that for the day, hadn't we? My stomach roils. Vomit kicks at the back of my throat, and I run out into the hall, spewing thin, acidic vomit all over the wall.

"Sweetie," comes Adalla's voice. "Are you okay?" Her hand strokes my back. I can't look anywhere in her direction.

"I don't know," I choke out.

"Do you need me to stay—?"

"No. I'm fine," I say.

"I can take care of her," Bakti says, on my other side now.

He's easier to look at. The betrayal doesn't run nearly as deeply. "Why don't you finish eating and get to work."

"Mmmm," Adalla says. I can tell from her voice that the thought of food right now isn't at all appetizing. "I'll pick up a snack on shift," she says. "Promise you'll take good care of her."

Bakti nods, then Adalla kisses us both on the cheek and is off. I want to shrivel up into a ball. I want to dive headfirst into the Wall and let it digest me alive. I push the thoughts away. What good would that do for my family? For my people? I know what's done is done, but maybe if I can be the perfect wife from here on out, maybe that will absolve me? Some at least.

I look to Bakti, now the distraction falls upon him. I drink his body in with my eyes, desiring for nothing more than to have him wash away the aftertaste of Doka from my mouth. From everywhere.

"Bakti, have you ever been to the aperture?" I ask.

"No! That's not something that was allowed on Adhosh. But I've heard the view is spectacular."

"We should go," I say.

We haven't been together for long, but the hesitation on his face is easy to read. He fusses with the trim on the deep V cut on his blouse, then finally mutters, "Isn't it dangerous? Especially if you're feeling—"

"I'm fine. We should go now. It think the war lilies are still in bloom. You have to see it."

"Um, okay. If you're sure."

I tug his arm and he follows behind me reluctantly. "Shouldn't I get properly dressed first?"

"Oh, we won't be needing clothes."

We travel the whole length of the gut, then hike through

the rugged terrain of an inactive esophagus, getting as far away from civilization as you can upon our Zenzee without being banished. It takes us nearly two hours walking at a brisk pace, but the sights and smells offer a welcome distraction. To our left and right, the walls are covered with overgrown patches of lichen and slick mucous spots, and glow lice the size of my hand skitter around, burring into the flesh of the wall when we get too near. The brush ivy gets so thick, we get pricked by the bristles as we squeeze through, leaving tiny scratches across my arms. I barely feel them.

We must be getting close.

Finally, we arrive at the airlock. It's attended by three dour-looking guards who act as if they haven't seen another human besides themselves in weeks. Even with our pedigrees, they protest letting us through. They know the reputation of the couples who tend to come here, and frivolous travel to vital environments such as this have been banned. But after offering a very generous donation of cowries and a promise that I will have Doka suggest longer shift breaks for outpost workers, they allow us to pass, escorting Bakti and I to a room with a large barrel of protective gel.

"We'll have to cover our skin with a heavy coating," I tell him. "It'll dry and provide protection against the void of space." I strip down in front of him, then take a handful of the golden gel, guiding it sensually around my breasts. I hold intimate eye contact with Bakti as I do so, waiting for signs of his arousal.

"What are you doing?" he asks, trying and failing to hide his concern.

"Putting on the gel."

"Yeah, but why are you being all weird about it?"

"I'm not being weird," I say, tilting my chin up and rubbing my neck, up and down. Up and down. "Just thorough. You know, I can help you, if you want. Don't want to miss any spots."

"Aren't there suits we could use?"

"Yes, but what's the fun in that? You can't really know space until you've felt it all over your body. Maybe we could venture toward the mouth tentacles. Press your back down against one of the suction cups so it holds you in place, and you know . . ."

"No, what?"

"Fuck," I whisper into his ear, then nibble his lobe. "You know, Jesphara and Ida have done it. Wouldn't stop talking about it for a year. It could be our moment, just the two of us. Do you know what they call it? 'Riding the Deep Silence.'" I rub a handful of gel down his chest. Down farther, rake my fingers through his pubis, hold the bulk of his manhood in my gelled fist, then slide right over the tip. "Don't want to miss a spot," I say again.

There's still concern on his face, all right, but at least now he's a little intrigued. "Maybe," he squeaks out. "Just for a bit."

I smile. He smiles back, then relaxes some and we cover each other in gel. We grab our re-breathers when we're done, and meet at the airlock, where we're given brief instructions, including a warning to stay away from the forward section of the aperture. That's where the tentacles begin. That's where things can get dangerous. We both nod, grinning, then head through the airlock.

Dark surrounds us, so thick at first it's nearly impossible to tell where the mouth ends and space begins, but then our eyes adjust to the low light. Only a few bare patches of war lilies remain, but the aperture is still amazing, boasting blue streaks that lead from each throat to the tentacles, like hundreds of cobblestone paths spread all around this immense open maw. Each path is bordered by fields of knee-high pink nodules. Some of them shudder and squirm, others pucker open at the top taking a deep gasp, then closing again. Still others jiggle violently, then go flat, expelling their contents into a throat. Slowly, very slowly, nebula dust and gasses are collected to nourish the parasites living within the Zenzee's gut. It is a harsh reminder of all the work that goes into the garden that our Zenzee has cultivated within herself. It is balance she has maintained for centuries. It is deliberate, not the random placement of plants we'd assumed. She benefits from the nutrients the parasites release in a beautiful act of symbiosis.

Then we came along, the invasive and toxic weeds in her garden.

"Seske, look," Bakti says, pointing outside the mouth. I can just make it out now, the nebula we're in. Roiling, puffy clouds of blue and pink with a crown of golden yellow. I feel as though we are among interstellar royalty.

"Daide's bells," I mutter.

His hand slips into mine. Neither of us find the courage to venture out toward the tentacles, but we fuck anyway, off in the field, mostly hidden among the curious nodules that nibble at us, wibbling, wobbling, then deflating in exasperation. Bakti works diligently—vigorous and fitful at first, but then he falls into a steady rhythm, our re-breathers rubbing against each other. Pressed against each other, the cold of space cannot wick away the heat of the gel on our skin, and we become like a furnace, the awkward smolder that had always existed between us now fully aflame. I let my mind clear, head tilted slightly back so I can see the stars.

I feel insignificant. A small blip in this universe. And as someone so insignificant, not even my biggest, most monumental fuckup would cause a noteworthy ripple within the great unknown. One of the stars flickers, seeming to hang closer than all the others. I blink, then it's even closer still. I blink again and start to panic as the star takes up more and more of the sky. I'm hallucinating, I know it. Or maybe my re-breather has run out of oxygen, and now I'm dying. Upon my next blink, I realize that it's the same sun from my vision.

Seske . . .

It calls out to me, and a shiver runs down my spine. That voice.

Seske . . .

Come for me . . .

It's nothing more than a whisper in my mind, but it screams out to my very soul. It disconnects me from my body, and the rhythm of Bakti's thrusting fades away to nothingness. It's as if I'm floating, out there in space, a primal urge to reach that sun. To reach that voice, even though it has hurt and betrayed me so many times.

Sisterkin's voice.

She'd been banished and forgotten, but I still feel her. Her siren song is sweet, tempting . . . and most of all, dangerous.

I shake my head, until I'm back in Bakti's embrace. I concentrate on the heat of the gel between us, on the feeling of the Zenzee's mouth flesh pressing upon my skin. I concentrate on the medicinal taste of my re-breather and the rasp of my own breath moving in and out until the hallucination fades completely.

I've spent the last four years trying to forget Sisterkin. She needs to learn how to stay forgotten.

DOKA

Of Sharp Knives and Dull Testimony

I feel like a giant. Massive. As if I'm larger than life. In my arms, I clench my evidence to my chest, a binder filled with genetic reports and family trees and citations directly pointing to the genocide of over ten thousand children. Finally, I have hard evidence and the confidence I need to face these women. The Senate will listen to what I have to say. I cannot fail another child.

I may not have Seske at my side, but maybe that's for the best. She'd be a bigger distraction. I'm having a hard enough time not thinking about her. About us. Kallum's beyond mad. I've never seen him like this. Won't even talk to me. But if I'm successful at tearing a hole in the legitimacy of the Senate and all their years spent complicit in this cover-up, maybe I can start to tear into other institutions as well. We'll have to rethink everything, including how we love.

I'm ready, standing out here, right next to the entrance of

the Senate chamber, but my star witness has yet to show. I'm not nervous. Not yet. Madam Wade is only a few minutes late. I want to go over her testimony one more time before she takes the stand. Another ten minutes pass, though, and I decide to go to her house and fetch her myself.

I knock at the door. Her house is quiet. Just she and her will-wife are all that remain of her family. Their pet wash hoglet greets me at the door, snout trembling in anticipation of a treat. Madam Wade's wife gently knocks the hoglet away from the door with her foot.

"Oh, Matris!" she says with a hefty round of flourishes, though she doesn't open her body fully. There is some anger hidden in there, frustration. Fear. We both know that Madam Wade is risking everything to testify about a corrupt practice. "What a favor you bestow upon us in visiting our home." From her tone, it's clear she doesn't think this is a favor at all.

I return a half bow. "I am more grateful for the favor Madam Wade is doing for me. I know this is a hard time for you both."

"She is willing to go through with it. I will support her." Yet there is venom behind those words for sure.

"Can you tell her to hurry? We're due to meet with the Senate in less than an hour."

"Oh, I thought she would have been there by now. She got called to an emergency Knowing Walk this morning. It shouldn't have lasted long."

"What? She promised to stop practicing," I say, my worry for all the little boys like Kenzah starting all over again.

"She has. She's been telling people the results are inconclusive and to come back in a couple weeks. She can't stop altogether, though. People would get suspicious."

"Well, they should be suspicious," I growl. "Thank you for your time."

I head to the cerebral cortex, frustrated that the twenty-minute journey will severely cut into our prep time, but I suppose we can talk quickly on the walk back. The control nodes come into view first, allowing me to get my bearing. Each node is made from copper, thick poles jutting twenty feet out of the surface, and reportedly they go down much farther deep below. I am at Madam Wade's hovel and I'm careful not to cross the threshold so we can avoid another incident like the last time I visited, but then I notice the room is already subtly trembling.

"Madam Wade," I call. "Please come. We're going to be late."

"Mmmmm . . . ," comes a muffled voice. "Matris," says a pained whisper.

I venture farther in, stepping carefully around the exposed synapses. The trembling intensifies, but not so much that it brings the threat of flying objects. I see Madam Wade laying in the middle of the Knowing circle, in a pool of her own blood. My heart drops, my arm hair stands on end. I still my breath. I hear her raspy breathing as well as coarse breath coming from someone else close by. The attacker is still in the room. My whole body goes cold, and I stand there, frozen. All I can do is be thankful that Kenzah has two head-fathers, because I'm nearly certain he's about to lose one of them.

A man jumps out from the shadows, knife pointed in my direction. My vision falters for a moment, but then I compose myself and open up my senses. I need Baradonna's guidance now more than ever. I observe his appearance, his actions. He's burly and hastily dressed, a deep shadow on his face as though he hasn't shaved in several days. I wonder at the wives who would let him out of the house so unkempt. I wonder if they're okay.

"You've heard?" he says. "You've heard what they do to little boys before they can be born?"

"Yes," I say. "And that's why I'm here. To make sure it stops."

He shakes his head. "It's too late. You've seen what they've done to us. They have all the power. Our numbers continue to shrink. I hear they're going to phase out will-fathers soon. There aren't enough men to go around, and they like it that way."

"Nobody is planning on phasing out will-fathers," I say. "Please, put the knife down, and let's get some help for Madam Wade."

He spits at her. "I bet the heart-fathers didn't think they'd get phased out either. But now look. All that's left of them is a running gag. 'Daide's bells!'" he says, grabbing his crotch. "We can't allow it. I don't want to be someone's joke."

The way his eyes are darting around, he's obviously hopped up on mad vapors, but there is real sadness painted all over his face. "You won't be a joke," I say to him calmly. "Now, please, put—"

"Don't come near me!" he screams, then lashes forward. The knife he has is big and metal and sharp—definitely belonging to a beastworker of high status. I jump back. He's unstable. If I'm going to have any chance of saving Madam Wade, I've got to think on my—

Feet.

I glance down at my shoes, then back up at the armed man. When I'd come here before, things had started getting weird as soon as I'd placed my bare feet down on the ground. Vibrations. Flying bones. This place was not fond of me stepping on it before, but now it might offer me the distraction I need to get the upper hand. I speak to the man softly, trying to keep his attention. "Hey, so you're a will-father. You've got a kid then?"

"A girl. But I guess you already knew that," he softens some. "Kimbra. She's eleven years old."

I slip out of my shoe in a single motion.

"Ah!" he says, lunging at me. "Feet in shoes. Do you think I know nothing about what goes on in here?"

"Me? I wasn't doing anything. Just an itch between my toes. So Kimbra? Named after Kimbra the Wise?"

He looks surprised that I'd know something about beast-worker lore. I guess all of those dinners with Adalla have come in handy.

He nods, moving in the opposite direction as I do. Keeping his distance, as if we're in an odd, slow-motion dance. I keep talking, mentioning all the beastworker customs I can think of—like the dimming of ley lights for privacy and mirrors kept by the bedside to ward off evil spirits and those damn too-spicy egg loafs that always leave my tongue burning. He laughs some at that, saying that his wives complain about him adding in too many peppers as well. He relaxes some, and as I get closer to Madam Wade, I make gentle eye contact with him. "Is it okay if I check on her? Shoes stay on?"

"Yeah," he mumbles, some bit of remorse filtering through his high. "Yeah, shoes stay on, though."

I turn my back to the man as I kneel at Madam Wade's side, making myself vulnerable, but allowing me to spit discreetly into my palms. It's not petal water, but it'll have to do. I rub my hands together quickly, then I place them against the floor, hoping it's just skin contact that the synapses need to get a full read on me, and not something particular about the feet.

Immediately, the ground lurches, then bags on the shelves

fly at me. I duck at the last moment, covering Madam Wade with my body as dozens of bone-filled projectiles zip by overhead. I hear a thud and a moan. When I look up, the man is covered in bags. I go to rouse Madam Wade, but she's nonresponsive. Her face already ashen, eyes glazed and staring blankly at me.

She's lost far too much blood. I'm stunned, watching the life drain from her, but by the time I come to my senses and think to fetch help, she's already gone. I cringe, looking down at her body. My evidence is deep, but all speculative. I needed her—someone with direct experience—to tie it all together. Now she's dead, and conveniently, a man is to blame for her murder. But I don't believe for a moment that he orchestrated this alone.

I HAVE NEVER SEEN SO MUCH SCORN FILL A ROOM, WHICH IS impressive, since barely half of the Senators decided to even show up to hear my grievances. What cuts worse is that it's nearly an even cross-section of the Senate. Both those who have supported me and those who haven't. Neither side cares to face these accusations.

But of course, the one person I wish would disappear stands before me in her finely pressed robes, looking as though she's waited all her life to trounce me at my lowest point.

"Genocide?" Tesaryn Wen says, a smirk on her face. "Interesting that you use such a term against those who are not yet born. Are you suggesting that all mothers who take upon using the throttle fish are murderers then?"

"No, I—" I stumble over my words. "That's not what I'm trying to say at all. It's just that the affected children—"

"Fetuses," Bella Roshaad gently corrects me. I've asked for

her help in Seske's absence. I didn't know who else to go to. She stands firmly by my side, nodding for me to continue.

"The affected fetuses, they're overwhelmingly male. We took samples from the throttle fish in five different ponds."

"Samples. Maybe sometimes they're more male. Maybe sometimes they're more female," Tesaryn Wen counters. "I'm sure the statistics balance out over time. Plus Zenzee hormones are known to shift, and since we are tied together so tightly, it can affect us as well. There are hundreds of factors that could be at play. I'll tell you what, I'll have Farah perform a full diagnostic on our Zenzee. I'm sure that'll shed some light on whatever you think is going on here."

"And I'm just supposed to accept whatever she says as fact? You have Farah and every other tactician eating out of your palm," I shout. "As well as half the Senators and who knows who—"

"Careful," Bella Roshaad says, leaning into me so that none of the other Senators can hear. "Outbursts like that will make it nearly impossible for me to talk the others into giving Kallum a seat."

I pull back. She's right. With Kallum's Senate seat on the line, I have to tread carefully. More carefully than I had before. Too much is on the line now, and it isn't just about me anymore. And yet, I can't let this atrocity go unmarked.

"If it is merely the Zenzee's changing hormones, then how do you account for the near even split between the Klang's women and men? Wouldn't they have progressed as we have, one way or the other? What about the other ships?"

"Our dearest Matris Kaleigh," Tesaryn Wen says to me, with the most over-the-top display of flourishes—both hands doing circles while taking her knee bend all the way down to the floor. "We know that you truly enjoy letting your thoughts meander down these fantastical paths, but we, the women of the Senate, have real work to do. If you have no further concrete evidence of your conspiracy, then I'm afraid we'll have to move on to the next matter of business."

I grit my teeth. I will not fall quietly by the wayside. Not on something this important.

"You fucking know I had more evidence!" I shout back at her. She's gotten under my skin, and I resent her for it now more than ever. "Madam Wade was going to testify to her part in this eugenics plot, but she was conveniently silenced before that happened. You want to talk about conspiracies? Let's talk about who had the motivation to kill her! Maybe it was one of you."

I stare directly at Tesaryn Wen, refusing to break her gaze.

The entire chamber erupts at the accusation. I have no basis for it, but I was feeling cornered. As the commotion mounts, my shock wears thin. I glance over at Bella Roshaad, and even she shakes her head at me in disapproval. I can't afford to lose her support as well, but I may just have. She says she's close to having the votes she needs to approve the legitimacy of Kallum's Line. *We're getting close. Really close. So close now . . .*

"I'm sorry," I say, holding my hands up. "Please strike that from the record. I didn't mean—"

"Yes, Madam Wade's death was unfortunate," Tesaryn Wen says, suddenly seeming mournful, as if the entire weight of our Zenzee rests on her shoulders. But her body is held too tense. It lies. "We hear she was murdered by a man who'd heard about your theory and believed it. Do you see how dangerous spewing such nonsense can be? It's best that we drop this matter for now before more damage is done."

It's as if my outburst is all she needs to sweep everything—the theory and my accusation—under the rug. "That's not what I—"

But no one is listening to me.

I stand there, angry. Stewing. Shaking. Of course, they will not take me seriously. They are the complicit ones. What reason would they have to give up that leverage? This couldn't have been the first time our gender imbalance had been questioned, not with the way the Accountancy Guard has documented every crumb of food, every drop of water, every lash upon every citizen's eyes for the past few centuries. How many times has the truth been buried deeper and deeper?

I wait for someone to speak out on my behalf. I look back at Bella Roshaad, but even she refuses to meet my gaze now. My outburst had been too much. I'd gone too far. I can't help but wonder if I would have been able to keep my composure with Seske by my side.

"Cowards!" I shout at the Senate as I pack my belongings. "May your ancestors sit in your shame with you." No use in holding back now. It is clear that I will have to find allies elsewhere, since I no longer have them aboard *Parados I*.

But again, no one is listening. They've already moved on to whatever else they think is more important.

"You tried," Bella Roshaad says, patting me on the back. "You should have come to me sooner, before you started chasing down evidence. I could have better prepared you to go up against them. Or at least I could have warned you that it was a losing battle." She lowers her voice. "Some traditions are not traditions because we want them, but because we need them."

I look up at her, puzzled.

"You have to choose your battles, Doka," she says to me. "You can't be the champion of every cause. Every injustice. You'll worry yourself sick. Last thing we need is another dead Matris."

I already feel like a husk of a person. She's been doing this so much longer than I have. Perhaps she has a point. I nod. "Did I completely ruin Kallum's chance at the Senate?"

"Their grudges run deep, but their memories are short. It will take some time, but I will try to smooth things over with the others. I suggested this before, but I think you better heed me now: take a few weeks off from your duties. Make yourself scarce around here, and give the Senators time to forget. And that means no more snooping or digging up new problems."

I look at her sharply, but there's no anger in her voice. Rather, there's sympathy in her eyes. I nod. Maybe that would be the best for everyone.

She smiles. "That's a good lad," she says, patting my cheek before heading back to her seat.

The next speaker is already presenting her case before the Senate—a tactician raising concern that the Zenzee herd has made a sudden change of course toward the anomalous star— that magenta pulse that dominates more and more of our sky. There is worry it is unstable. That it could pose a threat. Several of the other ships feel they are ready to break free from the herd, not willing to risk what we'd find at the end of the three-year journey. I stop fuming and tune my ear to the discussion.

Ideas churn in my head. I see opportunities: one, a way for me to get off this ship (and therefore away from the Senators) for a while, and two, to get us closer to self-sufficiency. Our goal should not be only to minimize the damage we do our Zenzee, but instead we should seek to actively feed back into the system, helping her to become stronger as well. And not just our Zenzee. If we establish a rapport, bring down the walls of secrecy between *all* our ships, then we can be independent and interdependent at the same time. And with those downed walls, it would be much harder to bury the secrets that haunt our history. And our present. I smile to myself.

After the assembly has adjourned, I catch Bella Roshaad as she exits the chambers.

"You said I should make myself scarce around here. Well, what if I leave our Zenzee altogether? I'd like to propose that we form an exploratory task force to gauge the interest the other clans have in breaking off from the Zenzee herd," I say to her. She's the one who suggested that I come to her with my ideas before I had time to fully hatch them, so here we are. "And I could head it. But I really need your help to bring this idea before the Senate."

Bella Roshaad sighs. "I also said that you shouldn't be snooping and prying. The point is for you to get some rest, not get fixated on inter-Zenzee relations. Besides, no one's going to support us leaving the herd. We're nowhere near ready."

"We could be ready if we make it a priority. I think I should call a meeting with all the heads of the other ships. It's time we seriously discuss striking out on our own. We'll have safety in numbers. We'll be able to share our knowledge with the other clans and form a more perfect harmony with our Zenzee, so that we benefit mutually from each other. We can't truly be independent until the temptation of the Zenzee herd is gone."

Bella Roshaad shakes her head. "It's too risky. And I told you, you need to be resting."

"But it was your idea! You're the one who suggested it at the assembly when we were dealing with the Klang's dying Zenzee!"

"I only proposed such a thing to prove a point and to make the idea of taking on refugees more palatable."

"It might have been a far-fetched idea then, but look how far we have come since. We've integrated an entire clan into ours. I know it's been slow going, but your vision of being more compassionate is growing closer by the day. We're allowing the

Klang to work among us now, and that's already paid off from their added knowledge about the Zenzee. The researchers say we've got many decades now, maybe a whole century that this Zenzee will last us, and that's if we don't continue our improvements. Soon she'll be better off than how we found her! Consider it? Please?"

Bella Roshaad's loose, don't-give-a-care demeanor is difficult to read, and none of Baradonna's lessons pay off now. There's not a hint of tension in her back, not a nervous twitch to be found anywhere on her face. But finally, a smirk winds its way onto her lips. "I'll gather up some of my supporters and see what I can do."

SESKE

Of Lively Rescues and Deadly Queens

"Get up, Seske," Adalla says, shaking my shoulder. "It's nearly noon."

I shake my head and bury myself deeper under the covers. "I'm too tired."

"Then maybe you shouldn't have stayed up all night."

I grunt. I can't sleep, because if I sleep, I dream, and if I dream, they turn into nightmares . . . Sisterkin calling me into the deep dark of space. Strangling me before I can die of suffocation and exposure. And yet, being in those dreams is better than being awake, dealing with the taint of this reality.

"Can I make you some tea, then?" Adalla offers. There is so much kindness in her voice, and I hate it.

I have to tell her.

"I fucked Doka," I say, feeling the words fall out of my mouth like a brick of shit. It sits there between me and Adalla, fouling up all the air in the room.

Her lips go tight. Her body closes up to me in a million ways, though she's barely even moved a muscle. She nods slowly. "When?"

"A few days ago. We were up all night preparing for our Senate presentation, and I don't know. I guess I was tired. Wasn't thinking right. Anyway, I regretted it the very instant it happened. Hurting you and Bakti was the last thing I ever wanted to do."

"Does Bakti know?" Adalla asks, voice flat and perfectly neutral. I've seen Adalla work out problems in the heart, able to set aside emotions to do what was necessary, and oftentimes what was necessary involved a very sharp knife.

"No," I mumble. "Just you and Kallum. He . . . walked in on us. But he promised not to tell."

"Good. Don't tell anyone else," Adalla says. "I'll talk to Kallum."

I don't know what else to say, but it doesn't matter anyway, because Adalla gets up and leaves. I feel part of my guilt leave with her, which I know isn't fair, because now that pain is sitting squarely on her shoulders. I don't realize I'm crying until the whole front of my night gown is soaked with tears, cold against my skin. I take refuge under the dark of the covers.

I feel a hand upon my biceps. I am not under here alone.

"Bakti?" I speak into the silence. I know that it is not him. He left with Charrelle and Kallum to get Doka some new robes for his trip.

It can't be Adalla, either—I could tell from the look in her eyes that it would be a long, long time before she would ever want to touch me again.

But I feel the body next to mine, pressing closer. Sharp prickly skin, like fish scales. Rotten breath runs down the ridge of my nose.

Come for me . . .

I throw the covers off, but there is no one lying in bed except me.

"Leave me be!" I yell out to my sister, wherever she is. My voice echoes off the bedroom walls as I listen closely for a response. There is nothing beyond the sound of my breath slipping in and out of my lungs. Sisterkin is quiet now, but I know that there's only one way to silence her for good.

I head for the gall harbor and commandeer one of Doka's boats, then I venture off into the bile ducts, with nothing but the ruined tatters of the map we used to search for Baradonna.

I keep my light low, my paddling minimal, and allow myself to get caught by the current. There is no room for mistakes when I'm out here all alone. The ducts fork several times, branching off into narrower passageways. This last one is so shallow I can touch the ceiling as I pass, but then the duct opens into a chamber. The walls look inflamed—red and pus-ridden, not like the slick, dark-green walls I'd followed here.

The place reeks of human manipulation. This is the place. I have arrived.

I paddle a little farther, then, through the foggy murk, I see a protrusion from the wall. As I get closer, I make out the shape of a body. The light from my lamp gleams against too many pairs of eyes though, maybe a dozen. The sound their mouths make as they pop away from feeding on flesh sends ripples through my gut. The bulbous eyes of throttle fish stare at me, considering whether to fight or flee, or simply return to feeding. They're all small, though, the largest no longer than my arm, and they err on the side of caution and disappear into the murky water.

I stare at the figure, barely recognizable as human. Head and torso and limbs are all there, but there is so much more—

tumorous growths stretching between her and the wall, and I can't tell where she ends and it begins. It's as if the wall had half devoured her, like some cruel and sinister version of the spirit wall our people use to honor our dead.

This is no honor.

The tumor on her head has extended over her forehead covering both eyes, but I can tell it is Sisterkin. She doesn't move, not even a twitch.

"Help . . . ," comes a raspy voice. At first I think it's Sisterkin in my mind again, but then I see another figure, not too far away. Baradonna. I paddle right up next to her and shine the light in her face. This is a mistake. A group of throttle fish hatchlings are feeding from her cheeks, and one has nibbled a hole all the way through. It looks at me through the fleshy gash, hisses at me, then retreats back into the cavern that is Baradonna's mouth.

The shock makes my fingers forget how to function, and I drop the lamp. Luckily, it falls into the boat and not the water.

"Baradonna," I say to her. What's left of her. I want to comfort her, to tell her that I'm here to rescue her from this nightmare, but I am at a loss for words, and—more so—for ideas on how to actually save her.

Her bulging, bloodshot eyes slowly trace their way toward mine. "Doka . . . ," she mumbles, shaking her head from side to side. The throttle fish hiss at the movement, then decide to abandon their dinner for less animated fare.

"He's . . ." I swallow hard and force a weak smile onto my face to keep my urge to vomit at bay. "He's okay. He's fine. Don't worry about him. Here, let's get you down from there." I row closer, then grab my knife. I've seen Adalla cut at tumors several times, so it couldn't be hard, right? *Cut deep, cut confidently*, she'd say. The tumors that hold Baradonna in place are few and small compared to Sisterkin's. I start low, at the ones tangling her knees. I press my knife into the wall, a few centimeters from the base of the tumor, then slice in deep, as if I'm trying to scoop the pulp out of a bog melon. The base pops free without much resistance. I do the same for the other tumors around her thighs and the largest one near her abdomen. I get a little cocky at how easy I'm making it look, but then realize my mistake as soon as the large tumor pops free from the wall. It had been the main support keeping her anchored there. Baradonna's weight drops, held now by the only the tumor surrounding her neck. She starts to choke, thrashing about. Her hands twitch, arms wanting to go to her neck, but her muscles have already started to atrophy, and she has no strength.

I try digging behind the tumor, but the flesh is hard there, very tough and it won't give. Then I notice that it's different from the other tumors. This one sinks right into her throat . . . like some kind of feeding tube? I don't have time to think. I ditch my knife and grab onto the esophagus-like protrusion and wrestle at it until it starts to pull free from her throat. It keeps coming and coming, several feet of pus-covered tubing, as though I'd pulled out the whole of Baradonna's intestines, but I know it's not that. The length of rope flesh definitely doesn't *feel* human.

Finally, Baradonna is free, and she falls into my out-stretched arms. At one point, I wouldn't have been able to handle her girth, but there's so little of her left, she's like a porous husk. I gently guide her into the boat and cover her body up in tarps to keep her safe and warm.

She's gained enough strength that she's able to paw at her mangled neck. The wound doesn't bleed though, just looks raw and angry, exactly like the hole in her cheek.

"Sorry about that," I mutter, knowing I have nothing to give her to ease her pain. "Rest now. We'll get you home soon."

I row back past Sisterkin, and my fingers probe around for my knife. There's no rescuing her. After four years, it'd be impossible to detach her without seriously wounding both her and the Zenzee. But I can put her out of her misery. No human deserves to be treated this way. Not even Sisterkin.

Knife in hand, I search for a vulnerable place to cut, but she's so covered up in tumors, it's like they've become an impenetrable shield. I consider cutting through the gristle of her feeding tube. Starvation would be a slow death, but anything has to be better than suffering like this.

The throttle fish are back, and they've brought their bigger, brawnier mates this time. I kick as they near, wave my knife at them threateningly. They back off into the shadows, but I still feel their beady eyes watching me. I step out of the boat. It's shallow here, the water only up to my shins. I walk up to Sisterkin. *Not Sisterkin*, I remind myself. *Just the husk they've left of her.*

I place my knife against the feeding tube, rubbing the serrated edge against flesh as hard as metal. I work for a minute, but only the faintest notch has formed. It's useless. The throttle fish won't stay at bay forever, and I've got to get Baradonna to a doctor. If I can find one that I can trust.

"I'm sorry," I say to Sisterkin, whispering close to her, where her ear would be if it weren't covered over with a gray scab of throbbing pus. It's then that I see it, a small section of exposed skin on her throat, close enough to the jugular vein. If I can get the right angle with my knife, she'll quickly bleed out. I press the tip of my knife there. To my surprise, the droplet of blood that forms is red, pristine. Human. I'd expected some sort of neon green sludge. "Okay, I can do this . . . ," I whisper to myself this time, my mind doing agile flips to justify why this won't be murder.

Seske . . .

The voice comes. Her voice. But her lips haven't moved. I'm so stunned, my knife flies out of my hand and falls into the water with a splash. I whip around, looking to see if the throttle fish are still backed away, but they're all gone now. Somehow that makes me feel even worse. I stoop down, feeling the bottom of the submerged floor, searching for the knife. Thankfully, I feel the blade, but a ripple forms next to me, and before I can get a grip on the weapon, it's snatched away from me, leaving me with a generous slice down the middle of my palm.

I jump up, holding my hand, blood gushing down into the black water, attracting who knows what. There's a hand on my thigh now. A half-grown throttle fish. It grins at me, then sinks its teeth into my leg, like dozens of red-hot needles. I yell out in pain. There's another hand on my shoulder, but it is not the hand of a fish. Swollen blue-black knuckles hold me firmly. Engorged, milky-white veins run all the way up the arm, disappearing into the giant mound of a tumor. Sisterkin has me. Draws me closer. Her mouth edges into a smile.

Come for me . . .

She opens her mouth, and out comes a long, thick tentacle. I beg myself to stop screaming. To close my mouth. To faint. To do anything, but it squirms inside me, slipping down my throat, coating it in pungent jelly.

My terror eases, as does the throbbing pain of the fish bite. My cut hand feels fine. I feel fine. Wonderful, even. It's as if I've crossed a threshold, letting go of everything that never really mattered. There's so much empty space between my thoughts, like all the space between stars. I see one of the stars. Flashing. Flashing. Flashing.

"Come to us," Sisterkin says to me. She struts into one of those open spaces between thoughts, looking as regal as a queen ought to. Skin a smooth deep brown with an almost pearlescent shine. Her braids are done up in the way of our Line. Only when she nears do I notice they are not braids at all, but tentacles—thin and black for the most part, intertwined with purples and blues. She is so stunning, I feel I should bow to her. And maybe I would, if I hadn't known the state of her body back in the real world.

"Why did you call me here?" I demand.

She looks me up and down. Even in the confines of my brain, I have managed to put together a poor ensemble for myself. Stained dress. Holey scarves. Robes that look as though they've been slept in for three days straight.

"I'm not calling you. I'm not calling anyone. They are." She points at the strobing star. "I'm just the messenger."

"Who are they?" I ask.

"The dead. Though, that term doesn't translate well for human sensibilities. Think of it as a Zenzee graveyard . . . but that's maybe a little haunted."

I nod, unfazed by this news that ought to frighten me. I feel the same calm I'd had when I'd delivered the Zenzee egg . . . as if I've stepped outside myself and away from my emotions. "I saw a flash like that from the Klang's Zenzee as it died. Is it like a beacon?"

"Yes, similar. When life ceases upon the Zenzee, there is a secondary life that occurs, several other organs spring to life, dedicated to helping the dead find their way to the graveyard. The light is them calling."

"But why can I hear it?" I ask.

Sisterkin points at my dress. The stains grow, as thick streaks of blue-black sludge run down the front again, and my breasts suddenly feel so heavy and full, it's as though they're about to burst. "You are a part of them, and they are a part of you. You have bettered them. They have bettered you."

I stand there in stunned silence. I'd lamented the changes carrying the Zenzee egg had brought upon my own body, but I'd never even considered that I'd contributed something of me to them by that same very act. Somewhere out there was a Zenzee still in the womb, one that would one day have children of her own, carrying bits of me across the eons. It should make me feel immortal, but instead, it makes me nauseated. My womb ripples. Phantom tentacles slap against my thighs. I vomit right there, further ruining my dress, the acidic sting tearing up my throat. I know that it is not actually vomit, but it sure tastes like the real thing.

"I am glad that you still think of me, though," Sisterkin says, extending her hand to me. "I am glad you came."

"For better and worse, you are hard to forget." I feel so many conflicting thoughts right now, but I extend my arm as well. "Mostly worse," I add with a huff and a grin.

"I am truly sorry for the pain I have caused you. And I forgive you for the pain you have caused me. Even if our aim was to do no harm, we would have set ourselves up for failure. We are entwined. Entangled. We always have been and always will be. I am hoping there is still a path for us. I have much to offer." She touches my cheek, then my shoulder. A cool breeze rattles against my skin, and the very next moment, I'm wearing a pristine gown that matches hers. She then cups her hands together in front of me, and when she opens them, a lime tart sits in her palms, covered in whipped candy creme. It was our Matris's favored dessert, one designed and prepared only for her. As small children, we had slobbered over them as we watched Matris pop one after another into her mouth, nearly reeling from delight. Sisterkin and I often conspired how we could get one of our own, each plan more outlandish than the last.

Though I can safely say that none of our plans ever came close to being this bizarre. This horrifying. But there's something about the sugar-sweet smell of lime tarts that makes you forget you're being held captive in a bile-filled swamp . . .

I take the tart in my hands and start to split it in half.

"No," Sisterkin says. "It's all for you."

I take a bite. I don't worry over it being poisoned. I am already at Sisterkin's mercy. My eyes roll back as the smooth taste of tangy custard hits my tongue. My toes curl. And a warm tingling sensation rolls through me, from head to toe. "Wow" is all I can manage, catching the drool and jelly slipping out of my mouth when I do.

"Here you can eat what you want, do what you want, fuck who you want, and no one will care. There is no pain. No fear. No regret. Stay with me, and we can rule them together." She points at the Zenzee graveyard. "We can help call them home."

I want so badly to forgive Sisterkin, if only to know that someone who has done something so awful is deserving of being forgiven. I consider it for half a moment, which is half a moment too long. Co-leader to mostly dead Zenzee with my banished sister who tried to kill me on at least two occasions?

"I can't stay. I've got a life and family to get back to."

Maybe.

She smiles. "I love how you think this was an invitation. You're already mine. All that's left is to do something with this hair . . ."

My head feels heavier all of a sudden, and when I reach up, the knots of my Line slither past one another, alive and writhing upon my scalp. I try to scream, but tentacles are falling out of my mouth now, too. I reach back to my real body to feel the pain in my thigh. My hand. My heart. But there's nothing.

"Stop fussing," she says in the way our heart-mother used to while braiding our hair. "Or I'll get the Lines all wrong."

"Let me go!" I scream.

"There's nowhere to go but home," she says. "Now sit straight, look forward, and stop fussing."

I feel the pain now. In my throat.

Sisterkin stops. "No!" she screams. She's not looking at me but staring off into one of the voids between thoughts.

The pain sharpens so much that I'd pass out if I were in my real body. And then suddenly, I am in my real body. My throat is on fire. My hand throbs, and a dozen throttle fish wounds dig into my skin. But I'm held tight in arms that have no right to be this strong after all they've been through.

"Baradonna, I—"

"Hush. You saved me. I saved you. We're even." Her voice sounds as though she swallowed a thousand knives, but it's soothing to hear anyway. She lays me down in the boat next to the spines of several throttle fish, picked clean save for the meat at the head. The shriveled faces still bear Sisterkin's dead stare.

"How long was I like that?" I asked.

"Well, it took me a while to get my strength back. Maybe a couple days."

Days?

"I'm ready to get home now," Baradonna says. "You?"

I feel dizzy with this information. Or maybe it's just a really bad hangover from having Sisterkin plugged into my very being. The violation runs deep. I feel it lurking in my core. But my family, they must be worried about me. And Doka . . . he's supposed to be leaving for the conference. "We need to tell Doka about this," I sputter out. My mouth is dry and tacky. It tastes of dead things. "He's going to meet with the other ships. He needs to know about the graveyard before he leaves."

Baradonna nods and starts rowing, raspy voice singing, "As the river bends, so does my will, we sail the mighty ducts, till the waters doth still. Deep down she goes, and when the waters turn black, kiss your family goodbye, cause there's no turning back!"

DOKA

Of Trust Falls and Suspicious Behavior

I'm strapped tightly into my seat, ready to be launched out of this shuttle bay and into the black of space with Kallum's taste lingering in my mouth. He'd made it clear that it was important that we kept up appearances, to the outside world as well as within our family. So in these last couple days we'd fucked a lot, like a couple remiss about spending some time apart. He'd laughed heartily at my jokes at the dinner table, his hand constantly on my thigh. He was so good at his act that sometimes I'd forget it was an act, but if I got too comfortable, Kallum was always quick to correct me with a sharp cut of his eyes when no one else was paying attention. This performance was for their sake, not mine.

The pilots perform the final checks, and as the doors close, I hear Seske's voice. I guess she's come to see me off after all. My heart quickens, becomes like a hammer in my chest, pounding hard in my ears. She'd run away again. I was worried, but the rest of the family seemed unbothered. Perhaps they'd finally grown tired of her impulsive escapades. But her absence had felt different to me this time. It was days instead of hours, and the culprits she usually ran off with were all accounted for. Seske is safe now, and that's all that matters.

She's shouting. I can't make out her frantic words over the hum of the engines, though. Something about the star. Something important.

I struggle against my restraints, craning my neck to see if I can see her through the cockpit window, but she's hidden from view by the bulk of the seat in front of me. A few moments later, the ship starts rumbling as it exits through bay doors that had once been intrusive metal things but are now a retractable curtain of flesh.

Then all the world drops away, and we're surrounded by the void and the vibrant colors of a cottony nebula. In the middle of it sits the blinking star the Zenzee herd now travels toward. We follow the herd. We always have, but now is time to reassess our ways. After several days of rigorous meetings with the Environmental Research Initiative, we concluded that venturing out on our own could be feasible, but only if we had the support of the other Earth clans. There is safety in numbers, in redundancy—just ask the Klang. If we continued to work together and became more open instead of keeping our secrets close to our chests, we could not only be independent of the herd, but we could thrive, taking full advantage of this system of mutualism. We could fully embrace symbiosis and live as one with our Zenzee.

There is enough fear built up around what the anomalous star holds that many Senators are willing to at least hear the opinions of the other clan leaders. They feel the pressure. With our herd thinning and now acting erratically, we must be open to all options. I've got several tactics to address the concerns of dissenting leaders as well. I'm polished. Well-spoken. Politically versed. And while it is difficult to hold myself up to the standards of our Senate, I will not be the only man present in the leadership summit.

The Renmoor ship is not far off, just beyond the range of weapon's fire. We have come here to build relationships, but trust is still much too fragile to risk that sort of vulnerability. I can make out the Zenzee of the other clans in the distance. From what I've been told, nearly half of the leaders lean toward separating from the herd, though I haven't been told a lot. Despite our treaties, the wall of secrecy has not been breached. Communication between the clans has to be cautious and calculated. This summit will hopefully change that.

As the leaders arrive aboard the Renmoor ship, we are escorted to a great hall that would map approximately to our throne room. Their Hall of Representatives is something like our Senate, but much larger in membership, and they report to no one except the people. They dress in heavy leathers, which I find out are made from the tanned hides of gall worm larvae right before their final molting. The cut of their clothing is simple, though the natural hide patterns do make for interesting design, boasting mottled browns and greens. They also wear dozens of gauzy ribbons in their hair. From quick observations on how people interact with one another, I can tell the different colors have meaning, but what that meaning is remains lost to me, just as I'm sure our braids are lost on them.

The men from the Serrata are here, too. I recognize one from the video conference we'd had so long ago—their leader, Commander Chubahl. They dress in bulky moss cloaks, the smelly stuff that grows prolifically near the ponds by the old boneworker blocks. We have a dozen people whose job it is to keep the moss trimmed back and from taking over the water supply. It is possible that somehow we've created nutrient-dense runoff that speeds its growth or have killed off one of its natural predators. I will be sure to ask the Serrata if they have any ideas on how to keep the moss under control.

The Ulaud delegation is clad in intricately layered silks that resemble the petals of a flower, and with all four of them, an obvious gender doesn't stand out. They've brought a sleek and statuesque wash hoglet with them as well—thoroughly groomed with better manners than half the people here.

Then there are the Vaz who are cloaked in all black and seem to speak only in parables; the Illiam who have pieces of copper technology embedded in their skin that they constantly stroke—perhaps communicating silently with one another; and the Cantors who spontaneously ululate when the fancy strikes and switch from one topic to the next so quickly that I get a headache if I linger in a conversation too long. And there are another five delegations that I haven't even met yet. I marvel at how different we all are, cut from the fabric of the same Mother Earth. Those differences are to be celebrated. They will give us the best chance of continuing to survive out here in this hostile environment.

The first day of the summit starts off relatively stress free, even with the fate of our species on the line. We do team-building exercises, each delegation being responsible for leading one. Our hosts, the Renmoor, go first. Their leader, Pasma Lang, passes cards out to the delegation leaders, each containing a series of numbers. We receive a bowl of marbles as well, and an empty glass jar, and whenever one of the numbers on our card is called, we are to drop a marble into the jar. Halfway through the exercise, I have twice as many marbles in my jar as the next delegation and feel as though I'm close to winning whatever it is we're playing.

Finally, after the last number is read, we are asked to call out the number of marbles in the jar. "Eleven" shout the Serratta delegation. "Six," say the Illiam. "Twenty-three," I call out proudly. Thirteen. Nine. Twelve. Eight. Six. Four. Four.

"Three" say the Renmoor, looking smug in their colorful hair ribbons. It is then that I realize this is a game where the smaller number wins.

"Each marble represents—to the best of our records, which we assure you are quite thorough—the number of Zenzee your people have harvested over the past two-hundred and ten years. These marbles represent the lives we have taken. Please let them sit in front of you for the remainder of the day as a reminder of where we are coming from, and where we want to go."

The Ulaud delegate holds up an empty jar. "We are in favor of breaking away from the herd and removing the temptation to continue down the path we've been on. It's time that we venture out on our own . . ."

I grit my teeth, feeling even more embarrassed with this too-full jar sitting in front of me, and I'm pained to know there would be many, many more marbles here if we started counting from the beginning. I feel as though maybe all these years, we haven't even been trying. While all eyes are locked on the Ulaud delegate, I swipe a handful of marbles from my jar and stick them in my pocket. It doesn't make me feel any better. In fact, it makes me feel worse. Wasn't I the one always pressing others to remember?

"It is not time to discuss that just yet," Pasma Lang says, interrupting the Ulaud's plea to separate. "We are still getting to know one another. Building trust takes time."

The Ulaud delegate looks offended by the prospect of trusting anyone else in this room and sets their jar back down on the table with an agitated huff.

The Vaz's exercise involves composing a heavily structured poem about our hopes for the future and then reading it in front of the room. Words refuse to come to me—though I am not sure if it is hope that I am lacking or poetic skill. In the end, I cheat and scribble down the fifteenth verse of the Wedding Ballad, switching up the number of syllables in the couplets to align with the assignment.

I suffer through four more exercises before the Serrata's, which is a drinking game that apparently involves a very sacred rum and honest confessions to each other that border on insults and verbal abuse. By the end of it, tempers have flared, and we decide to take a break from the presentations and stretch our legs. Some of the delegations had opted out of the rum and instead consumed spiced beetle milk, but many others are tipsy as we mingle. It seems like the perfect time to approach them to dig deeper into my hunches about the ratio of men to women in their clans. I already know about Serrata and their lack of women, plus, they appeared to have taken their game a little too seriously and are all passed out, so I approach one of the other men present.

"I'm Doka," I say, extending my hand to the head of the Tertian delegation, who's surrounded by a group of fierce-looking guards. "Doka Kaleigh, from the *Parados I*."

"Pleased to meet you. I'm Admiral Wallund Erisson," says the man. He extends his hand and gives me a hearty handshake before pulling me into a hug, as if we've known each other forever. "You're the ones that suggested that we start strategically repopulating the heart murmur colonies? The treaty has been a godsend to us. Life aboard our Zenzee has improved tenfold."

A joyous warmth runs through me. "I'm glad our ERI reports have been useful for you."

"I am surprised now that the idea came from a clan that has slaughtered so many Zenzee. Did you see how many marbles we had? Thirteen. I was sure we'd have the most, but then there you go, just showing off how good you are at culling. The initial harvesting requires such precision and so much effort. I am truly impressed."

I wince at the compliment. Is it even a compliment? "Our past with the Zenzee is not something we are proud of, but our Environmental Research Initiative has been making strides."

"You are too modest. And you've taken in the Klang. Very noble of you. We would have offered, you know, but politics can be brutal. We were already dealing with the fallout from our last revolution. Eight coups in twice as many years. Bombings. Poisonings. Stabbings. My predecessor was pushed out of an airlock on our most holy holiday, and her predecessor was killed in his sleep by his wife of seven years."

My ears perk up. "So it's not unusual for you to have male leaders?"

"Heavens, no! Seems a little boorish to determine leadership abilities based on what people have in their pants, does it not?"

I nod my head vigorously. I want to know more, but I'm anxious about asking the wrong question. I steady my nerves anyway, hoping I can arm myself with ideas to go up against the Senate. "So you would say that aboard your Zenzee, men and women are treated as equals?"

Admiral Erisson pats me on the cheek with his rough,

heavy hand. "How quaint. It's no wonder your people are chewing through Zenzee with such haste. You don't take time to think. To observe. Such limiting distinctions are wholly inadequate and have no bearing on the quality of a leader."

"I know this!" I say, practically shouting. I look around, hoping I haven't caused too much of a commotion, but all the other delegates are either too drunk or too caught up in other conversations to care about me and my outburst. I think of the needless challenges I've faced as a man. I think of how things could have been easier for Kallum—before his bud and capping ceremony and after, if he'd had the support he'd needed to navigate a world that was so suddenly against him. Maybe he wouldn't have felt like an asterisk this whole time. I don't want anyone to feel like that, but we are so entrenched in our ways, I don't even know where to start. "What can we do to be more like your people?"

Admiral Erisson serves me a knowing smile, then nods. "First, you need to stop trying to sort people into buckets, or you'll miss the beauty and strength of the variation amongst us. It is a much better strategy to indoctrinate *all* children and train them in the ways of combat. Natural leaders will rise through the ranks regardless of sex or gender. We have a series of tests . . . Sizing Battles, we call them, to weed out the weak and undeserving."

"You . . . train your children to be fighters?"

"Warriors. And more than that. Passionate about life and seizing opportunities. To always think ten steps ahead and never turn down a challenge. To be ready to fight at the drop of a hat and kill if necessary. You have children?"

"One," I say, afraid to admit it to this man. "Six months old."

"Ah, good age to start pre-tactical training. You should paint a red dot on the back of the left hand and a blue dot on the right hand to facilitate hand-eye coordination while they are crawling. It's never too early to start shaping a warrior."

I smile, teeth clenched. "That's nice," I mumble, wondering how long it will be before someone tries to kill him in his sleep.

So, theirs isn't exactly the society I am hoping to emulate, but there are plenty of other people here. Somehow, though, I manage to offend three of the other delegates with my prying questions. Thankfully, Admiral Erisson steps in, urging me back to my seat so that he can begin his exercise, something he calls "trust falls."

He walks into the middle of the room, then makes a clicking sound, and Hattie, his assistant, comes running, taking up position behind him. She's slightly built and painfully plain, with long, straight hair the yellow of powdered fungus.

"It is an easy exercise," Admiral Erisson says. "You don't have to count marbles, recall your history, or drink until you retch. All you have to do is trust." He crosses his arms over his chest, then leans back. Hattie stretches her arms out in waiting. Finally, Admiral Erisson tips, and Hattie catches him in her arms, as if they've practiced this a million times.

"Now I recognize that it is easy for me to trust Hattie. She has been by my side as my aide for eleven years, and we were friends even before that. What will take true courage is turning to your neighbor, a person you only met hours ago, and trusting that they will not let your head crack against this hard floor!" Admiral Erisson lets loose a boisterous laugh. "Are we ready? Now everybody pair off."

I make eye contact with the Ulaud leader, but they look past me and pair up with the leader of the Renmoor. The leader on my other side has already paired up with Commander Chubahl from the Serratta.

"Doka Kaleigh! Looks like you're with me," says Admiral Erisson. He waves me over to his spot at the front of the room. "Are you ready? Building trust between our people is vital. It is something I learned quickly. There are many factions among our clan, and our confidence in one another is brittle, but we are starting the process of healing."

"We are going through some similar things on the *Parados I*," I say. I suddenly feel ill-equipped to represent such a diverse range of experiences, but maybe Admiral Erisson is right, and I'll be able to take what I learn here back to our people.

"Here, then. Let me show you how this works." Admiral Erisson spreads his arms wide, waving me toward him with his fingertips.

I take a deep breath, then face away from him. I imagine Tesaryn Wen behind me. I wouldn't trust her to serve me tea, much less saving me from falling. And yet here I am, entrusting a virtual stranger who I'm pretty sure runs a baby fighting ring. "Okay, here I go," I say, putting my arms to my chest, closing my eyes, and hoping for the best. I lean back, feeling my center of gravity shift to an uncomfortable place in my gut. Next thing I know, I'm falling. Not half a second later, I'm safely cradled in Admiral Erisson's very muscular arms. He props me back up, the rush of adrenaline still coursing through me. "That was pretty amazing," I say to him. Then I hold my arms out. "Your turn."

He looks me up and down, then turns his attention back to the rest of the delegates. "It seems like everyone has already finished up and is getting back to their seats. Perhaps another time."

"Perhaps," I say with a slight bend on my brow. So much for practicing what he preaches.

My own team-building exercise doesn't go over as well as I hoped. I'd had everyone close their eyes and imagine what Zenzee organ would best represent them and describe how it'd feel to function. My intent was to forge a mental bond with our Zenzee, but it quickly devolved into laughter after Commander Chubahl chose to represent the Zenzee's sex organs and went into quite graphic detail about how they worked.

After that, I am more than ready when we retire for the night.

The next morning, we begin discussing the more pertinent matter of following the Zenzee herd to the anomalous star or venturing out on our own and becoming truly self-sufficient. To my delight, as the delegates present their cases, a slim majority are for separating from the herd. They point out the facts. That there are so few Zenzee left. That it would be genocide to cull any more. And even if they didn't object morally, it would be only a matter of generations before the Zenzee were extinct altogether. And then where would that leave our people? What if the herd becomes erratic again, and instead of heading toward a star, it leads us to a black hole?

The question and answer segments are hot and contentious, but I imagine they would've been worse if we hadn't done the bonding exercises yesterday. People seem to be actively listening and entertaining everyone's opinions with an open mind.

"I vote to stay the course," the Illiam leader says. "Like it or not, our lives have become intertwined with the Zenzee. I propose that this is a good thing for both us and them. We've had a period of adjustment, sure, but now we are entering a new phase. Our scientists are working on ways to enhance our Zenzee's functioning. We are making them stronger, as we are making us stronger. We are each the steel rod against which we sharpen our blade."

"I agree. Abandoning the herd is a mistake," the Vaz leader says, his voice slow, deep, and melodic. Almost hypnotic. "Yes, self-sufficiency is admirable, but if you think about the whole picture, we'd be harming the Zenzee further, permanently taking away loved ones."

The delegation completely engages with the Vaz leader as he speaks, and my heart sinks. He's tapped into the emotional part of our brains. He massages our guilt and kneads our internalized faults like a master baker working a ball of dough, urging us to rise to the occasion and join his side. I can see why he's found himself in a spot of leadership.

I look around the room, a frown on my face. Everyone is entirely rapt by his talk, except Admiral Erisson's aide. She's standing on the other side of the room, fidgeting. Sweaty. Nervous. Baradonna's training comes back to me. I notice how she carries herself differently than before, body like a question mark. She's about to do something, and when I notice there's a new bulk around her mid-section, I get the odd feeling that it's something we're all going to regret. She nods to herself, then starts aggressively approaching Admiral Erisson.

I have only seconds to act. I think about trying to tackle her, but with the training she's probably had since birth, there's no way I'd be able to take her out in hand-to-hand combat. Then I remember the marbles in my pocket, the ones I so embarrassingly hid from everyone. As Hattie approaches, I roll them into the path in front of her. She slips, falls back, knocks her head against the floor. Admiral Erisson sees this happening, and in an instant, he is running to her side.

I start to second guess myself. I hadn't meant for her to take that big of a spill.

"I saw what you did," Admiral Erisson says, teeth clenched, as if he's about to sink them into my throat.

"I'm sorry, I'm sorry. I thought there was something odd going on. I'm sorry."

Admiral Erisson turns his attention to Hattie, calling out her name, checking for breath. Several other people from various clans crowd around us, staring me down like I've broken the trust we were only starting to develop.

Hattie is unresponsive. Admiral Erisson pulls aside her robe to help her breathe, revealing a device strapped to her chest. Lights are blinking. Faster, faster. "Explosives! We've got to get out of here," he yells. "Everybody out now!"

And in the next moment, we're all running for the door. The blast comes before I can make it out. I'm thrown forward into the person in front of me. Shreds of shrapnel rip through my skin. Screams come from all over, sounding odd and metallic in my ears.

My vision throbs to the beat of my heart, white at the edges. I take deep breaths, gather my thoughts, looking at my surroundings as wounds are tallied. Medics rush in, dealing with the most severely wounded first. My own injuries are cleansed and bandaged. Fortunately, the cuts are not deep, but my back still feels like a raw piece of gall steak.

We are bruised and bloodied. However, the explosion was very localized, so the broken bones were few. Instead, something much more fragile has broken. Our trust in one another. Each of the delegates gathers their own, cutting glances aimed in all directions.

My plan to bring the Earth clans together has had the exact opposite effect.

"I was wrong about you," Admiral Erisson says, laying a bloodied hand on my shoulder. I wince, feeling splinters of metal move beneath my skin. "That wasn't my first assassination attempt, but it was the closest to succeeding. A lot of people would have died if you hadn't acted. Including me."

I mumble something, trying to bite through the pain to form a response, but my brain flashes bright white in response.

Admiral Erisson leans in closer to me so the medics won't overhear. "I know you have your heart set on independence and venturing out on our own, but we should stay with the Zenzee herd," he whispers, his breath hot in my ear. "Our scientists have determined that the star they are chasing isn't actually a star."

"What is it?" I ask.

"That we don't know. But what we do know is our herd isn't the only one heading toward it." He raises a brow.

The implications of this blur past me so fast, I get dizzy. Or maybe it's just a new wave of pain that's caught me off guard. The main reason half of the delegates are entertaining the idea of leaving the herd is because there just aren't that many Zenzee left. Scarcity was driving them to expand their minds and consider alternate lifestyles. If they knew there was another herd to exploit, maybe numbering in the hundreds, or even thousands, they would lose all that motivation and settle back into the status quo of culling a new Zenzee whenever the need arose. "Why are you trusting me with this?" I say.

"Our instruments are more sensitive than most, but it's only a matter of time before the others notice as well. Things are about to get complicated, and I need leaders on my side who I can trust. I can trust you, right, Doka?"

I nod, feeling as though I'm jumping out of a raging fire and into the cold mouth of the void.

Two medics carry a body bag past us, the lumps inside resembling piles of flesh and nothing remotely shaped like a human. We had been extremely lucky, but there was one death in all of this: Hattie, his assistant who'd so dutifully caught him in the trust exercise yesterday.

Admiral Erisson watches them haul the body away. I expect anger to hang on his face, but instead, he looks saddened.

"Trust seems like a very fragile thing among your people," I say.

"I didn't expect this from Hattie, but I can't say I'm exactly surprised. When you're in our position, betrayal can be around any corner."

I think about how Tesaryn Wen had worked to diminish my power, to banish my personal guard, to tear up my family. I knew she wouldn't rest until I was left completely powerless, but I've stood up to her the best I can. If the Senate really wanted to silence me, there were more effective ways available to them. I bite my tongue so hard that I yelp.

"What's wrong?" Admiral Erisson asks me.

I shake my head. I'm sure it's nothing, but I retrace the aide's steps in my memory. She'd taken the long way around to Admiral Erisson. Why hadn't she gone the other way? It was quicker. More direct. Unless Admiral Erisson wasn't actually her target.

"Hattie was with you at all times, right? Why would she have to take you out with explosives? Couldn't she have poisoned your meal? Or slit your throat while you slept? Or—"

"Okay, okay. I get it. Yes, I can't say it exactly makes any sense. She's had total access to me for over a decade. Why would she wait until now? She loves her kids more than anything. I don't know why she would possibly sacrifice their future like that." Admiral Erisson blinks a few times, then his lip curls in disgust. He pulls out a device, types into it, and then waits for a response. Seconds later, two beeps follow. He stares down at the screen for a long moment, then looks back at me. "Her two oldest children are of age to fight in the next Sizing Battle, but she has recently paid their way out of competition. It is very costly. And very shameful."

"She did this to keep her kids safe."

"They'll be laughed at. They'll be seen as cowards. She has brought great dishonor upon me and everyone who has called her a friend. I'd have more respect for her if I *had* been her target. But if it wasn't me, then who was it?"

"I could think of someone who wouldn't mind seeing me dead," I say. "And who wouldn't mind paying a large sum for it."

Admiral Erisson's eyebrows arch. "I could check for communications between our people. Even if they masked their signatures, our algorithms will be able to crack it." Admiral Erisson starts typing into his device again, chunky fingers moving fluidly over the screen. He scowls at the results. "I see a series of unlogged communications between our ships, one each of the past four days. IDs are forged, but I can dig deeper if you want specifics."

I nod, taking it all in. There's so much to process. I knew Tesaryn Wen hated me, but I never thought she would stoop this low.

"Do you want me to see if I can reconstruct the signal into a voice pattern?"

I shake my head. "Don't bother. I just need to know what I should do now."

"Is this your first assassination attempt? There's nothing like your first time." Admiral Erisson smiles wistfully. "Well, if I were in your shoes, I'd bribe the crew here to let your people know that you'd been mortally wounded. Whoever is responsible will let their guard down, allowing you to sneak in a counterattack. Act fast, while the coup is still tender. While you still have allies willing to risk everything for you."

I do as Admiral Erisson says, and after a hefty bribe, I am on my way back to *Parados I*, dressed as one of my escorts. When we arrive, the whole place is eerily quiet. No one about. I make my way to the Senate chambers, ready to confront Tesaryn Wen, but when I throw open the doors, it's completely empty.

Almost.

At the front of the room, there are three boneworkers taking their tools to the reliefs depicting our people's greatest sins against the Zenzee. They've already smoothed down a third of the bone canvas, prepped and primed, as if it's about to be carved again.

"Excuse me, where is everyone?" I call to the workers, all bare-chested and covered in decorative scars, their hair nearly white from all the bits of bone entangled in their braids.

"Doldrums," one of them barks back. She nods her head. "Big meeting. Not to be missed."

As I turn to leave, a fourth boneworker carrying several bags of tools and paper scrolls enters the door and runs right into me. Her metal tools hit the ground like a bunch of chimes, and one of her scrolls speeds across the floor, unrolling itself. I look down at the sketch of a woman dressed in matriarchal robes, hand reaching up at a star. A familiar star. A familiar face.

"Tesaryn Wen," I say, gritting my teeth. Then run as fast as I can to the doldrums.

SESKE

Of Corrupted Bodies and Just Desserts

Adalla's hand touches the back of mine. My heart flips, and I look over at her with a tentative smile, but her face is completely neutral. "Sorry," she mumbles. An accidental touch, then. We're crammed in here so tightly that it's hard to maintain space between us. I keep my smile on my face, though. If I let it drop, I might never find it again.

I used to hate coming to the doldrums, but since the ERI had implemented a whole host of environmentally friendly upgrades, they're not so bad. They've been refitted with colorful sails, like aboard the Serrata, and not only do they make the energy exchange more efficient, but they're beautiful to look at from down below, like the delicate wings of kite fish flapping in all their glory. But this cavernous space on the Zenzee barely accommodates us all, now that the Klang are here. They're segregated to their own little area of the room, in the back and out of the way, a line of accountancy guards standing between us and them.

Bakti's hand touches mine, on purpose, and we thread our fingers together. "I think I see my mum," he whispers to me, craning his neck toward the Klang. He waves with his other hand. "Yes, that's definitely her."

I turn and wave as well, big goofy smile spread across my face, then settle back into my nerves. "This has got to be a major announcement. I bet Doka and the other leaders came to a decision already." I bite my lip. I haven't told anyone about the Zenzee graveyard. Didn't tell anyone about Sisterkin. Didn't tell anyone about Baradonna either, except Bakti and his mother. She needed a place to heal and to hide. The doctors among the Klang would tend to her wounds and track her progress, undoing the damage that had been inflicted upon her. The physical damage at least. I can't even imagine the pain of being so cruelly cast aside by your own people like that.

"We should visit Mother soon," Bakti says.

"I don't think she likes me very much," I reply. I'd dumped an injured, exiled woman in her lap, after all, on top of stealing her son away. I know I wasn't even in on the plan, but the way I catch her looking sideways at me sometimes . . . I can feel the heat in her sharp glare.

"It's all in your imagination. She loves you."

"She tolerates me. Because she loves *you*," I say. "There's a difference."

"Well, it's not like you have to see her every day. Just put on a smile, rave over her cooking, laugh at her jokes."

"Even if they're at my expense? I don't feel welcome there. But you go. Brings some flowers from me."

"Seske . . ."

"Bakti...," I say, mocking him.

"She's just poking to get to know you better. Once she figures out that she can trust you, you'll see how she really is."

My fake smile is back. Trust. He makes it sound so easy. "Okay, I'll think about it."

He hugs me tight. "I'll count that as a yes. Adalla, you're coming, too? All three of us being there would make Mother so happy."

"You know I love your mum," Adalla says sweetly to Bakti. "I wouldn't miss it."

I sigh.

Finally, the proceedings start, and the awkward tension between Adalla and me gets directed at the stage. Tesaryn Wen walks out front and center, looking beyond regal.

"Today is the day we have strived so hard for. The day we have sacrificed so much for," she says, carefully annunciating as if each word she speaks holds some sacred truth. "Today is the day our lead scientists have declared that we have achieved mutualism with our Zenzee. And what does that mean? It means that as we benefit from our Zenzee, she benefits from us. Ours is a relationship that is self-sustaining. We could live upon this beast for many, many generations to come."

The crowd erupts in applause. A lump forms in my throat. We have indeed given up so much of ourselves to get here, and now Doka's vision has been fully realized. I am only sad that he is still at the leader's summit and will miss sharing this occasion with us.

"We have sacrificed our creature comforts. No longer do we live in bone castles, but huts made of renewable bricks. We are cold all the time. We work till our fingers bleed. We feast upon staple foods and at times go to bed hungry. But we have done it—we've achieved Doka Kaleigh's dream of mutualism. We have lost pieces of our culture. We've given up our luxuries. But we are living the dream, right? Utopia? Let's hear it!"

There is applause again, but less vigorous this time.

"Raise your hand if you are proud of what we've accomplished," Tesaryn Wen says.

Nearly every hand shoots up into the air.

"Good, you should be. This hasn't been easy for anyone. Some of us lived for years with our loved ones locked away in stasis. But we're all here now, aren't we? Well, minus the ones still stuck in stasis, suffering who knows what kind of permanent damage because of it. But we're happy, right? Who's happy? Really and truly happy? Let's see some hands!"

Only half of the crowd raises a hand this time.

"Who's happier now than they were before Matris Doka Kaleigh assumed his rule?"

More hands go down. Rumbling whispers and hushed tones grow within the crowd—a deep, rustling sound that turns my gut, making me queasy. I get a sinking feeling that Doka's absence from this meeting is by design.

"Our Matris, Doka Kaleigh, promised us Utopia. Balance. And on that, I can say that he has delivered. He sold us a dream. A goal. And we ran toward it, embracing him all along the way. But never did we ask if that *should* be our dream. Or if it was truly a worthy goal. That is not to say that we think this exercise in seeking mutualism has been completely useless. We have found many efficiencies and techniques to extend the amount of time we stay aboard a Zenzee. Our scientists add that we could spend as many as seventy or eighty years aboard a single Zenzee and still go back to a more comfortable way of life. Imagine balmy weather. Imagine feasting upon a wide variety of delicacies until your stomach is full, and your children's stomachs. Imagine *children*! More than a single baby to call your own."

The crowd gasps. Those words are nearly blasphemous.

"We have been told there is another Zenzee herd only a few years' travel from here. Our own scientists have now confirmed it. There are thousands of them. And with our zoonautical advances, the Zenzee will repopulate at a rate that exceeds the pace at which we will need them. We will have a sustainable society. We can expand, form additional colonies.

"There will be room for everyone," Tesaryn Wen concludes, stepping back to allow our people to process this life-altering news she's dropped in front of us. Some shameful part of me is tempted, too. Giving the Klang a Zenzee of their own would ease so much tension. And there is comfort in the idea of having our people spread around different worlds, for redundancy's sake. If we'd stumbled upon this news sooner, I wonder if Adalla wouldn't have had to work so hard, if we wouldn't have needed to give up so much. I wonder if things would have been better for us. For everyone.

The room is silent for a long while, but then clapping starts. It soon rolls into an ovation that hurts my ears.

"No!" I scream out. We'd still be killing Zenzee, albeit more slowly. "This is not what we want!" But I am drowned out. I keep yelling until, finally, the applause subsides. "Doka doesn't want this!" I scream at Tesaryn Wen. "There's no way he would approve of this."

"You're right about that, Seske," Tesaryn Wen says, taking a few purposeful steps toward me. Her lips quirk. "But I'm sure he would have come around, if he'd had all the information that we have at our fingertips now. However, we will never know for sure. I hate to be the bearer of awful news, especially at the mark of such a monumental undertaking, but it is with a heavy heart that I must tell you, there was an attempt on our leader's life during the summit. And unfortunately, Doka Kaleigh was killed."

The world around me starts spinning. Charrelle wails out in agony. I'm falling, but Bakti catches me under the arms and holds me close to his chest. "Seske . . . Seske . . . ," he whispers into my ear.

"We are at a very tender time. This assassination has fractured the little trust we had built between the other clans, and our tacticians warn that war may be on the eve," Tesaryn Wen continues. "We need a competent leader to guide us through this monumental wave of change. The throne would fall back upon Seske Kaleigh, but since she has conceded it already, and since there is no female heir or suitable women within her family to claim the title, I vote that their Line be dissolved immediately, and all powers within it be conferred to me as interim Matris until the Senate has time to fully consider a suitable replacement. With the looming threat, our immediate action is required, so unless there are any objections among the Senators, then—"

"I object," comes a voice. A voice I know so well. Doka's voice. Relief floods me, and I scramble back onto my feet, but I cannot see over the crowd.

"Pick me up!" I say to Bakti, and he hoists me up by the hips. There . . . I see him, coming up the aisle. Dressed in ill-fitting common robes, but it's Doka. It takes Tesaryn Wen a moment to recognize him, a heavy scowl forming on her face the moment she does.

"It seems the ancestors have granted me more favors than you anticipated," Doka says, strutting down the aisle toward the stage. "Care to tell our people exactly who it was that orchestrated the attempt on my life?"

Tesaryn Wen crosses her fingers, index fingers pointing up, then stands there as if she's posing for a portrait. "I'm not sure what you're talking about, and I'm afraid you have no Senate standing in this matter since it directly involves you. You must recuse yourself from all your duties, including voting on the matter."

Doka looks unbothered. "Then we will call upon the Senate. Who among you will choose not to deny what we have built together? Who will support me as we continue to stretch the bounds of our lives upon this Zenzee?"

None of the Senators raise their hand.

"Senator Kerell? Senator Baisle? Surely you, Gnasha? You've always complimented me on my policies."

Their lips remain pressed together.

"I only need one objection . . . ," Doka says, voice deflated of energy. "So it's like this then, Senator Roshaad? You've been like a mentor to me."

Bella Roshaad stares at Doka coldly. He's managed to alienate every single one of his supporters.

Tesaryn Wen smiles. I clench inside, knowing what's going to happen next. I remember seeing a family lose their Line when I was a young girl. It put a fear in me. "Put me down. Put me down," I say, patting Bakti's shoulder. As soon as my feet touch the ground, I tell him that we need to get out of here. I tug at him and gesture to the rest of my family to follow. We push through the crowd toward the exit, but then I hear a guttural scream, and when I glance back to check on everyone, a dozen accountancy guards rush after us. One of them has Kallum. He's struggling, kicking, trying to fend them off, but it's too late.

For all of us.

Twenty additional guards cut off our path, and soon we're

all being dragged back onto the stage. Doka is up there, too, breathing heavily and looking defeated. His eyes lock with mine, and there is no regret or awkwardness there, only anger and hurt.

"I hereby announce that the Kaleigh Line has been dissolved," Tesaryn Wen says. She steps up to Bakti, pulls a few pins out of his bun, and his black thick braid falls down past his shoulder. A few more touches, and his hair is all flat again, running down his back. "It is unfortunate that you had to be a part of this, but you are free to return to your people." Tesaryn Wen does a quick hand gesture, as if she were shooing a pesky cricket out of her house and back into the garden and not tearing our family apart.

Bakti turns back to me. "Seske . . . I—"

"Just go," I say. "Go and don't turn back." My voice trembles. Perhaps I am being too cold, but I do not want him to witness what is coming next. I want him to remember me how I was.

He nods, then starts the slow trek up the aisle to where the Klang are being held.

Hands come for our hair, many pairs of them twisting and pulling and unraveling our braids right out here in front of everyone. They are not gentle, and my scalp yells out in pain, my head being yanked this way and that. Hairs pop and snap. Tears fall down my face. Never again would I feel the familiar pattern of my Line's braids upon my head. No longer will my ancestors look down and see me. They will not find me, will not know what to do with all the favors I've built up over the years. They'd soon forget all about me.

Charrelle sobs as they do her hair, clutching our baby to her chest, but when they come for Kenzah, she loses it. His hair is barely long enough to hold a few tiny twists, but they too must come out. Charrelle elbows the accountancy guards coming for our son. I shake off the people still in my hair and undo my last few braids myself before running to her aid.

"It's okay," I whisper to her. "Let them take the twists out. They will be gentle."

Charrelle looks at me, her eyes bloodshot. "You. You are responsible for this. This is all your fault. You couldn't keep your hands off my husband. You were running through his mind all the time, and he couldn't concentrate on his job. Couldn't concentrate on his family."

"What? No. We didn't—" I almost deny it, but Charrelle cuts me down with a look. Did Kallum tell her? Doesn't matter. This isn't something we should talk about here. "Shhh. Calm down and let them finish."

"You want me to calm down," Charrelle snaps at me. "You fuck my husband, make us lose our Line, turn our child into a bastard, and you think I need to stay calm. I trusted you! I thought we were friends!"

The entire hall goes quiet. Tesaryn Wen slithers up between Charrelle and I, laying an arm over each of our shoulders. Charrelle stiffens. Eyes wide. Too late does she realize what she's done.

"I'm sorry. I'm sorry," Charrelle says, blustering all over the place. "I didn't mean it. I mean, I don't know for sure. It's just that there was always . . . this tension between them, and I got used to it, but then all of a sudden, there wasn't, and I asked Kallum about it and he couldn't even look me in the eye, and he started crying, and then—"

"It's fine," Tesaryn Wen says to her, rubbing her back now. "You didn't do anything wrong." She waves off the person trying to take out the baby's twists. Dissolving our Line had been an appetizer for her cruelty. Infidelity was the real meal. I could practically feel her salivating at the thought of stringing Doka and I up by our thumbs. And she had total authority on how long we would be like that. Days. Months. Years, even.

"Go ahead and ask us," Doka says, coming to my side. "We won't deny the truth. Seske and I have nothing to hide."

"We made a mistake," I say. Doka flinches at my words, then nods. "We hurt the people we love most. And we are prepared to pay." I twiddle my thumbs, remember how Adalla's tin uncle, Sonovan, had hung by his thumbs for weeks for infidelity with his heart-wife.

Tesaryn Wen smiles, then goes to confer with the Senators.

"A mistake," Doka whispers to me. "That's really the way you feel?"

"Don't you?" I ask. "Look at what we've done . . ."

He lets his head fall forward, nods slightly.

"If there is no denial of infidelity between will-wife and head-husband, then we shall hand down immediate sentencing. For the crime of infidelity between family units, I sentence eleven days of public hanging by thumbs to Doka and Seske Kaleigh."

My gut sinks. In the back of my mind, I knew there was the chance that we'd have to face this public shame, but I never thought we actually would. Eleven days, in the swamp that had once been the central market, thumbs bound and high above us. Eventually our legs would grow too tired, and our whole weight would be borne by our thumbs, which would dislocate, causing pain that would last us forever. But I don't have long to lament our fate, because then Tesaryn Wen starts talking again.

"And in the matter of inappropriate sexual conduct with a member of the crown, I sentence Doka and Seske Kaleigh to expulsion from the beast from the third anal sphincter."

The crowd gasps.

"Our crime is one of infidelities," I scream out, "not of . . . inappropriateness . . . sexual or otherwise!"

"Your wanton fornication has corrupted the throne. There is precedent with the daughter of Matris Bordal. Of course, you remember Baxi Batzi."

"But she was a beastworker!" I say. "Both Doka and I are in the ruling class. It shouldn't be treated the same!"

"Curious that you favor class distinctions now, isn't it?" Tesaryn Wen says, lips quirked in a wry smile. "You are free to raise your concerns with the Senate."

I swivel to look at them, frowns stare back at us. We still have no friends there.

"Any objections from the Senate that we punish for the greater crime first?" Tesaryn Wen asks. There are no objections. And with that, hands come down upon Doka and me.

I lock eyes with Adalla. She stands there motionless, her lip trembling, then comes running to me, looking as if she's ready to fight off every single accountancy guard surrounding me. I shake my head at her, and she slows. I reach for her, best I can, and she does the same, our fingertips just able to touch.

"I'm sorry," I say to her, the words dredging up the entirety of my heart. "I'm sorry for everything."

PER CUSTOM, WE ARE BATHED AND GIVEN NEW ROBES AND FED a final meal. It is quite the spread, though it goes untouched. Doka and I sit there, across the table from each other, staring. I barely recognize him: his naxshi scrubbed from his face, his hair out of braids altogether, held up like sunbursts in thick, chunky twists. My hair is in loose braids following no particular pattern. I smell the fragrant yonatti oils in there, reminding me of my childhood. The women who dressed my hair insisted on it despite my pleas. While it made your locks strong and shiny for a while, they would become brittle over time, but I suppose that doesn't matter anymore. By the end of this day, both our bodies would be floating in the cold dead of space.

Our untouched entrees are moved, and desserts are placed in front of us. Lime tarts, symbolizing the rebirth of the matriarchy.

I laugh. Today of all days, I am presented with the dessert I have pined after for most of my life. "Say what you want about Tesaryn Wen, but her sense of irony is flawless."

Doka nods and picks up the tuning fork. "Some poor chef must have spent hours on this. We shouldn't let her work go to waste."

I pick up my fork, and we both strike them on the metal bowl. His fork rings an octave lower than mine, and we move them closer to the lime until it begins to hatch. The hairy flesh of the lime bulges out, then nearly a dozen hatchlings erupt from the rind, tumbling down the mound of whipped candy creme and settling into a river of jelly. Doka and I stare at each other for a moment, awkward silence besides the fading ring of the forks. I turn my attention quickly to the lime tart and when all the hatchlings have drowned, I go in after the first bite, grabbing the perfect portions of flaky pastry, creme, and lime jelly.

I take a bite and close my eyes. "Amazing," I say. Doka agrees, swallowing his tart without even chewing once.

"You should take your time. Savor it," I tell him.

"You're right," he says, fetching another tart then holding

it up to his nose and staring at it. "Sometimes I get so excited, I rush through things."

"You do," I say.

He stops, looks at me. "We're talking about the tart, right?"

"Right," I say. "What else would we be talking about?"

"Right." He takes a smaller bite now. Chews. "See, I missed that the first time . . . that spice? Anise? Interesting take. And the bits of lime hatchlings, they kind of stick to the roof of your mouth. A little heat to it, but the creme balances it out."

"Ha, so you're a connoisseur of fine desserts all of a sudden?"

"Just more experienced. I messed up the first time. I knew I didn't want to do that again if I ever got the chance to take another bite."

"Do you want to know what I learned from my first taste?" I ask.

"Of course," he says.

"Sometimes you take a small bite, but it's still bigger than you can chew. Maybe you don't like the taste or the texture or there's a weird hairy patch in it, and it's too late, because it's too rude to spit it out. So you just chew. And swallow."

"Then maybe you shouldn't have been eyeing the lime tart the whole time and just stayed at home and ate your too-spicy egg loaf every day for the rest of your life."

"I should have," I say. "But the tart was parading around in front of me, looking so . . . delicious. And it was nice. And kind. And thoughtful. And beautiful. And maybe I spent so much time building it up in my head as the perfect dessert, I sort of set myself up to be disappointed."

"Ouch," Doka says, then shakes his head. "I mean, I imagine that would hurt to hear. If I was a lime tart. Because that's a hundred percent what we're still talking about."

I nod. "Definitely."

"So you don't like tarts," he says.

"Oh no, I love tarts. Almost more than anything. I'd give my life for a lime tart. I just can't enjoy it . . . sexually." I put my fork down and stare at the pile of creme sitting before me. I seem to have lost what little of my appetite that I'd had. "So maybe there will be this weird tension between me and lime tarts for the rest of my life . . . which I guess isn't all that long, so maybe I shouldn't even be worrying over it."

Doka sees me sobbing, so he pulls his chair around next to me and puts an arm over my shoulder. "So what would you rather worry over?"

Adalla? Our people? Our family. Our child? The Zenzee? There was too much worry left and not enough time. "Why do we have to worry about anything? What good would it do us? What good has it ever done us?"

The attendant comes out and politely says, "If you're done with desserts, would you like tea service?"

I shake my head. "We're done. Finished. Ready to go."

"Very well, ma'am."

We stand up and are escorted to the third ass, passing first through the other two sphincters. Doka and I walk shoulder to shoulder, slowly, as if in a wedding procession. Ruddy waters lap at our ankles, fissures erupt to form islands of undulating flesh. Four accountancy guards guide us carefully around the dangers—so we won't die prematurely, ancestors forbid. Through the second ass, we come to the sphincter, waiting as the guards pry it open for us to pass.

We step over the threshold.

The air is sour and crisp, and I lose my breath. A thin wall of flesh is all that separates us from naked space. Doka's hand finds its way into mine, and I grip it tight as the guards retreat back to the safety of the second ass. Then, we wait in silence.

And there's a whole lot of it. Here, in the third ass, nothing lives. No chirping of beetles, no hissing of petulant vines. It is all just matter the Zenzee can recycle no further, ready to be expelled into space.

The puckered, purple sphincter trembles, then begins to dilate ever so slightly. Almost immediately, pieces of dirt and clumps of clay near it get sucked through. Hissing winds fill our ears. Then a large slab of clay slams down over the opening, and the sucking stops. For a moment at least.

Doka looks at me. "I'm sorry, Seske," he says. "This is all my fault. I ruined everything."

I shake my head. "I made that decision, too. We can't go back and change the past now."

The piece of clay breaks in half and is sucked out. The sphincter continues to widen. Larger objects start to get pulled toward it. Our robes included. I catch the reflection of stars in Doka's eyes. He's looking, out there, into space, but I can't do the same.

"Do you think it'll be quick?" I ask. "Death?"

"Maybe we shouldn't think about it. Maybe we should keep our minds somewhere else." Doka says this, but still he is not able to look away. I pull his chin toward mine.

"We should keep our minds elsewhere," I say, raising my voice to speak over the squall.

"Meditation?" he asks.

"Maybe?" But I've never been much good at concentrating on such things. I lean forward, pressing my body against his. I bite my lip. "Maybe not."

"Seske . . ."

"It's not like we can get into any more trouble than we already are." I run my arm over his shoulder, down his arm. "And look how stiff and nervous you are. Like you're afraid I'm going to bite."

"I'm afraid you're about to do something that we'll both regret."

I raise a brow. "See? You're already thinking like we have a future long enough to harbor regrets." We lower ourselves down to the ground, bracing against the increasing winds. Doka has always been a distraction, and I'm even more grateful for it now, keeping my fear at bay.

He takes his time, thinking it over, as if we had hours, days, weeks left to live, and not seconds. Finally, he leans forward. Our lips press together, ever so slightly before the winds whip me away. Doka reaches out to save me, but he loses his purchase as well, flipping over and over, all the while reaching for me, futilely. We pass through the wide gap and into space. Immediately, my face starts to burn and swell. My vision turns to pinpricks, but before it blinks out altogether, I get a glimpse of the view Doka had been so stuck on. It is amazing.

Deadly amazing, yet peaceful. As far as final resting places go, this isn't so bad, I suppose.

Death must be reaching for me, because now I'm starting to hallucinate. My eyes are failing me, because it seems as if a whip slaps around Doka's waist, and then he's no longer in my view. I twist my neck, my muscles already stiffening from the penetrating cold. He's being pulled back to our Zenzee. I maneuver myself, but kick without resistance. Doesn't matter, because next thing I know, I'm being caught by the waist as well and pulled back inside.

My whole body feels as though it's on fire now, as is my

brain—whether from lack of oxygen or confusion, I don't know. I try sitting up, only to be forced back down, a cool salve going over my exposed skin. By the time I catch my breath, I see Baradonna beating against the pucker of the third ass to get it to seal back up. I still can't breathe, but as my lungs ache for air, at least I don't feel like I'm about to pop. Bakti's mom shoves a re-breather into my mouth and I suck at it like a wash hoglet at its mother's engorged teat. My thoughts start to cohere, and I look over and see I'm lying next to a puppet gel version of myself. Am I back at my wedding night again? Did I die out there in space, and this is some kind of fevered afterlife dream? I touch the puppet's face.

"So lifelike, right?" Bakti says to me over the re-breather's comm.

When I said I was having coherent thoughts . . . I lied. "What are you doing here?" I ask. "Are you dead too?"

"We're here to save you," Bakti says. "Now strip out of your clothes so we can get them on these puppets." He tosses us a couple of thin shifts. I will my hand out to catch them, but my arms don't respond, and they land in the puddle next to us.

"How did you find us?" Doka asks.

"You know I worked the second ass for a stretch," Baradonna calls back to us, still wrestling with the ass, almost sealed up now. "I know these anal fissures like I know the back of my hand." She points over to a fissure not far from us, big enough for her to pass through.

"We'll toss these puppets out the ass, and everyone will think you're dead," Bakti says. "You can come back with us, live in the camp. We have a secret room to house you both. We'll keep you safe."

"You'd do that for us?" I ask him. "Even after what we did?"
Bakti shrugs, as if he's impervious to hurt. "You made a

mistake. One moment of indiscretion isn't so insurmountable a thing to overcome."

Doka and I stare at each other, somehow managing not to make any eye contact. One moment of indiscretion had already turned into two, maybe even three, depending on when you start counting. And if I'm being honest, making sound decisions isn't exactly my forte.

"Maybe this is something we should talk about when we're somewhere that doesn't smell like rotten ass," I say.

Baradonna agrees with me wholeheartedly, and after she shoves the gelled bodies into our suits and robes, she drags the puppets toward the sphincter. She pries it open wide enough to wrestle the first puppet out without evacuating the whole ass again. "One down," she says, taking a quick breather. "One to go." But before she can continue, the sphincter leading to the second ass starts to shudder. Baradonna notices and tries to work faster, but the purple flesh has become stubborn, some sort of involuntary contraction perhaps to prevent all the asses from being open at once?

Doesn't matter. A couple seconds later, all four accountancy guards are rushing at us. It takes them a moment to put together what's happened and also to realize that they are now outnumbered. Maybe that didn't matter too much at all, because as soon as they lay a finger on Baradonna, she becomes enraged and starts swinging at them. She takes the first one out with a punch to the throat, her hands moving so quickly, I don't realize she's made contact until the guard is falling. One of the others attempts to put her into a choke hold. She rears back, using the guard for balance as she kicks the one in front of her, then shoves all her weight into backpedaling until the guard choking her gets slammed up against the ass wall. The guard gets the wind knocked out of her, and she falls to the ground, struggling to catch her breath. The remaining guard stays back a few steps, more wary than the others.

"Seal up the ass," Baradonna barks at Bakti and his mother, nodding toward the second ass, though her eyes stay locked with the guard. "Fancy meeting you, Genda," she says to the guard. "I'm pretty sure it was your antics that got me stationed here in the first place."

"It was your own fault," Genda says. "You should know when to go around prying into details and when not to. That's accountancy guard basic training."

They move together, working around the ass as though they're locked in a dance, arms out, fists locked tight. Bakti and his mother work together at the rim, tugging and pulling until it tightens back up into a perfect pucker. Hopefully, the third ass is now primed for one final expulsion. Baradonna rushes at Genda, knocking her forehead into the bridge of her nose. Blood erupts, covering them both, and Genda falls down.

Baradonna leans over our new hostages, wipes Genda's blood off her brow. "They'll be looking for two bodies out there. We've released one already. We just need one more. Now, that body can be another gel puppet, or it can be one of you . . ." Baradonna looks the guards over, one by one by one by one.

"Please . . . ," one of the guards says. "We won't tell anyone."

"Good, because if I hear a single whiff from anyone doubting that it was Doka and Seske's bodies floating out there, I will come for you."

"But what are we to say when you all show up—"

"You worry about yourself," Baradonna snaps, "and we'll all be fine."

"We weren't even here," Genda says, scrambling back onto her feet, ready to make a hasty exit. "Everything went according to procedure."

"Good, I knew I could count on you." Baradonna says, patting her on the cheek. She then reaches into the guard's pocket sash and pulls out her tablet. "I'll be taking this."

And with that, she dusts her hands, then returns to shoving the second puppet into space, and for all practical purposes, Doka and I are now dead, both for a second time.

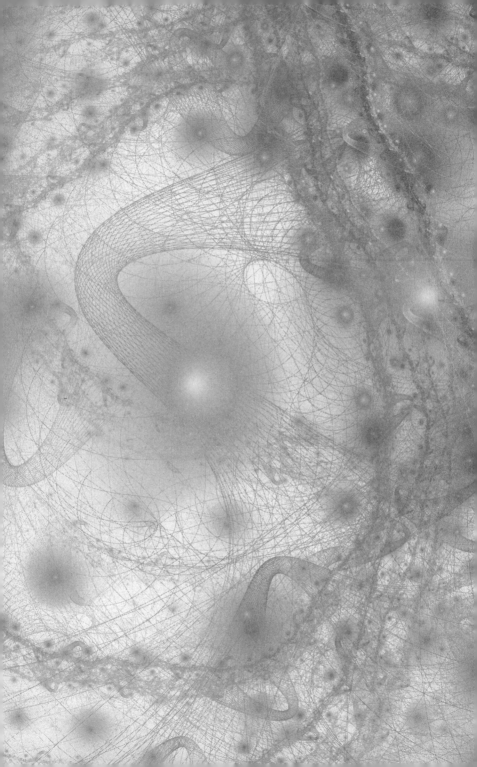

part IV

surviving symbiosis

Our lives became entangled long ago, and as our worlds grew, so did our interdependency. The ways in which we were tied together were so complex that undoing those knots seemed unfathomable. And yet, in but an instant, they've been severed. I wonder how long we would have lasted if we'd realized how simple it was to break free of this symbiotic relationship, and just like that, escape into an unknown future.

QUEEN OF THE DEAD

DOKA

Of Cold Shoulders and Hot Combs

I pull a red bean from my pile and hold it delicately between my fingers. I slowly raise it above the fourth Katsito stack from the left, twelve beans high so far, and set it down gently. When I release, I hold my breath, nervous that the stack will fall. It's staying so far. I back up quickly and bid Seske to go.

Seske picks up a black bean from her stack, choosing the obvious second stack from the right. She moves even slower than I had. Katsito is a game that requires both slowness of mind and slowness of movement—the perfect game to play when you are a refugee within a refugee camp, where time is your only asset.

"You're sure you want to go there?" I ask her.

Seske startles at my words, though they are barely above a whisper. We haven't spoken since we started the game nearly an hour ago now. "Hush, you! I almost knocked over a stack." She scowls at me.

"Sorry," I mumble. "Carry on."

She goes to set the bean, then notices the trap I'd laid for her. She grins, then choses the first stack. "You're prolonging the game," she says to me, keeping her voice low as well. Katsito is a game of quietness as well. "You don't want the satisfaction of winning?"

"Oh, I still plan on winning," I tell her. "Just looking to raise the stakes, see how high we can take this." If there's one thing I've learned in our four months of living in Bakti's mother's back room, it's patience. And while Katsito is a competitive game, there is a cooperative element to it. To create this landscape of stacks requires trust in the beginning, while you're planning strategies that won't unfold for twenty or thirty more moves. All of that concentration could be undone by one wrong play. Winning by default holds no honor. It was the titillation of the end game that made all the planning worth it.

I take another red bean and stack it upon my last.

"Oh, no you're not," Seske says to me. She must see what I'm really up to now. She examines the board from several angles, then bites her lip. "You're trying to bull square me."

"Trying to, no. About to, yes. You have no way to block me," I say smugly. Seske holds eye contact with me, a rarity these days.

"I wish Bakti had never taught us this game," she says too loudly. The beans on her end of the board start to rattle.

"Shhh . . . ," I tell her. The stacks wobble, but soon the beans calm back down. My heart's still beating hard, though. Can't ruin the game now.

Seske aims a "don't shush me" look in my direction, then places her bean in a desperate attempt to ruin my bull square.

I must be nervous, because when I go to select my next bean, it slips out of my hand and goes sailing across the board, nearly knocking into one of the stacks. It slides to a standstill. Seske picks it up and extends her hand to me, palm up. When I take the bean from her, we touch, lingering a second too long before I pull my hand back.

I don't know how, but in that moment, all my strategies drain from my head. I look back at the board and can't find where I'd intended to do my bull square, though a minute before, it was all that I could see. I search the stacks, then look pleadingly at Seske.

"You lost it, didn't you?" she whispers.

"No," I say.

"Then go ahead and place your bean."

"I will. Just give me a minute."

She stares at me. I stare back.

"Is it just me," Baradonna says from the corner, face lit a ghastly blue from the glow of her tablet, "or is there, like, a whole lot of sexual tension in this room right now?"

Both Seske and I startle. I often forget Baradonna is here; she's so quiet, always fiddling with accountancy numbers of some sort and typing her accountancy guard secrets. Her deep, rough voice spooks the beans. Seske and I try to settle them, but it's too late. Several of the beans buck and topple the beans above them. The stacks start to fall, crashing into others, until the whole board is leveled.

"Baradonna!" we both call out.

"Sorry? Did I talk too loud? I've been staring at this screen so long, I'm afraid I've lost my internal filter."

I sigh. "I hate to tell you this, Baradonna, but you've never had an internal filter."

The bells on the front door ring, and we instantly go quiet. Seske and I clean up the game pieces as quickly and quietly as we can while Baradonna stashes her stolen tech, then we move from the cramped back room into the even more cramped back room closet. We're all pressed up against one another. Usually, we stand with Baradonna separating Seske and me, but in our hurry, I'm pressed up to Seske, nose to nose. I keep my thoughts from wandering, and instead focus on the fact we're hiding for our lives. If anyone discovers that we're here, we will face horrible consequences, as will Bakti and his whole family.

The family often has visitors. Tirtha is a pillar in the community and people come to her for advice or help or just to chat. Sometimes the visits are short. Sometimes they run for hours, and by the time we get out of the closet, we're so cramped up that its painful to move.

We strain to listen to the conversation so we can guess how long this visit is going to be. Suddenly, I feel Seske's body go stiff against mine.

"What?" I ask. "What is it?"

Seske doesn't say anything. I look up at Baradonna. She's tight-lipped now, but I can tell by her expression that she knows, too. I listen harder. Then I hear it. It's Adalla.

"Move," Seske says to me. "I'm going out."

"You can't," I say, suddenly becoming like a wall between her and the outside world. "If she sees you . . ."

"She won't," Seske says, attempting to shove me aside, but I don't budge. "I just want to get closer, so I can hear better."

"You can't do that, Seske. We can't risk it."

"Don't let me by and I'll scream. How's that for a risk?" She stares me down, calculating eyes full of pain and already ten moves ahead of me. I step out of her way.

"Don't let her see you," I warn again.

Baradonna and I watch as Seske moves toward the door to the front room, staying well hidden behind the beaded curtain. She clutches herself as she listens.

"She's crying," Baradonna whispers to me.

"I know," I say.

"Kallum's doing well," Baradonna reports to me. "So is the baby. He's really close to walking."

"Baradonna, please . . . ," I say, shaking my head.

"Sorry, I thought you would want to know."

"I do, I . . . don't know if I can handle it, though. It reminds me there's a whole world out there beyond that door. A world that thinks I'm dead and probably has already forgotten about me."

"I doubt anyone's forgotten about you," Baradonna says, snuggling me close. She preens the ends of my twists, and I find myself feeling like I'm back at home. As close to home as I'm going to get at least. But deep in my heart, I know that this will never be enough. We'd escaped our punishment, but being trapped here with Seske is a whole different sort of torture.

Twenty minutes later, Seske comes rushing back into the closet, and not half a minute later, Bakti draws back the beaded curtain to tell us it's safe to come out. We venture into the back room again and are joined by Tirtha.

"I take it you heard everything," she says to Seske, knowing she'd been eavesdropping.

Seske nods.

"She brought a gift for me. I think you should have it." Tirtha presents Seske with a silk shawl. Seske breathes it in, probably hoping to catch a whiff of Adalla still on it, but she's left disappointed. It's a Klang shawl, probably bought here in the market.

"Thanks," Seske says anyway. Tirtha gets up to leave, but I reach out to her.

"Wait!" I say. "We can't stay like this forever. Can't we get out and go for a walk? See something other than these walls?

I promise we won't talk. We can cover our hair. Just for a few minutes?"

"It's too risky," Tirtha says. "What if someone asks you a question? What if your hat gets knocked off? You'd be spotted immediately."

"Well, we can learn to fit in. Teach us. Like you taught Kallum to fit in when he was aboard your Zenzee."

"Adhosh remembered," Tirtha says, placing both hands together in prayer, then to her chest. "I can teach you, if you are willing. But it will not be easy. And if you do not meet my standards, then you will not pass this door. It is my family that you risk. Do you all agree?"

"I'll do everything I can to impress you," I say, then I look at Seske. "Please. We have to do this. How many more games of Katsito are you willing to play with me? I don't want to die holding a red bean in my palm. There's no going back to our old lives, but we could make a new life here."

"I'm willing," Seske says.

I look up to Baradonna. "And you?"

Baradonna shakes her head. "I don't belong here. Best chance I'd have of fitting in is if you draped me in beads and called me a door. Best thing for a forgotten person to do is stay forgotten. But don't worry about ol' Baradonna. I'll find a nice little spot in the third ass, secluded and out of the way. And if I'm ever feeling up to it, I'll go and haunt the living on occasion. Maybe I can even get my own folk tale, be the next Baxi Batzi."

"You're sure?" I ask, shoulders slumped. "You know I'll miss you."

"We'll miss you," Seske adds. She hugs Baradonna. I join in.

"First lesson," Tirtha says. "There are no such things as goodbyes. Only, until next times."

I nod, dabbing the tears out of my eyes. Baradonna rises back up to her full height, then rushes out the door. I blink, wondering if she'd been standing here at all.

THREE MONTHS PASS, AND EVERY MOMENT THAT TIRTHA doesn't spend entertaining guests, she spends teaching us the ways of her people. We learn their language, at first being taught as if we are children: we learn the words for mother and father, siblings, and family. Basic objects and silly songs. We rush Tirtha to teach us more age-appropriate things, but she insists on teaching us in layers. Too much context is lost otherwise, or so she claims. We learn to chew our vowels differently, to hold our posture differently. I have to throw everything Baradonna taught me about reading people out the airlock, because here, everything means something else. Head tilts. Hand gestures. Mannerisms. We learn their family structures, looking something like trees when they're laid all out. Two parents usually, and two or three children typically, though there were more variations than we could count on one hand.

When I have my first dream in the Klang tongue, I am so delighted that I wake up Seske from sleep to tell her about it. She stops me and asks me to define a word, and I realize I reached for the language in my awoken state as well.

"Do you think in their language as well?" Seske asks me.

"Nearly half the time," I admit. "You?"

"Never. Not yet, anyway. You're doing well."

"You'll be ready. Don't fret."

Tirtha's final exam is only two days away. She's having a small group of trusted friends over for dinner to test our skill. We will have to truly blend in. Become near invisible. With only 3,300 people, nearly every person knows everyone else. But toward the end of the Klang's time on Adhosh, everyone was so focused on the dead and dying, it was almost possible that someone could have been overlooked. But if we are quiet, don't make waves, if we stick to our backstories, maybe we'll pull this off.

When I tell Tirtha my dream later that evening, she looks pleased. "You are ready here," she says to me, tapping my temple. "Now we must prepare the outside." She lays out clothes for me and Seske, traditional wear of a sheer blouse and slacks. There is a metal comb with a thick handle laying out with them. Seske's hand comes down on my shoulder.

"Is that what I think it is?" she asks me.

"Ama Ravi's comb," we say together. Ama Ravi's comb was equal parts prank and tradition. The comb was priceless, over three hundred years old, and had been the bane of every Contour class child since. At each Exodus, a new family was chosen to hold it, usually one that was in danger of falling out of favor with the ancestors. During the high holiday each year, the chosen family was forced to take down their braids and flatten their hair with the heated comb until it fell loosely down their backs. It was meant to signal a clean slate—a plead for forgiveness and a begging for favors from the ancestors to return them to good standing. If the family humbled themselves enough, smiled through the pain of burnt ears, then they could pass off the comb to another family. Those who kept the comb twice tended to fall out of favor altogether, and sometimes whole Lines were dissolved.

If I had a cowrie for every time my parents had threatened me with Ama Ravi's comb, I probably could have bribed at least a dozen men into the Senate.

"No no no no no no . . . ," Seske keeps muttering. "Nope. Nope. Not doing it."

"We have to, Seske," I say. "It won't be too bad. You might like it. Besides, it's not like it's permanent. And this isn't Ama Ravi's *actual* comb." It can't be, right?

Seske stares at me a long, long while, then proceeds to cuss out every single one of my ancestors.

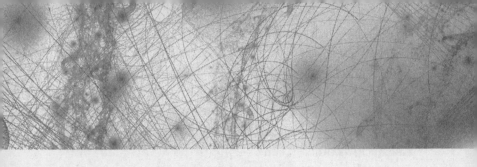

SESKE

Of Second Chances and Third Asses

I extend my hand to Macario Talan, standing tall and meeting his gaze. I keep my smile tight, my eyes soft, my words delicately pronounced as I greet him. His skin is pale, even for the Klang, face clean-shaven, hair shorn. It is like staring into a sun. My eyes hurt, but I do not turn away. Tirtha has ground his importance into us. He is one of the Klang's most prominent figures, a scientist in his former life aboard Adhosh, a baker now. No matter how we perform at dinner, we must not embarrass ourselves in front of him.

Macario Talan assesses me from top to bottom. His gaze is thorough, calculating. I worry over how I hold myself, how the lace of my baro falls to my knees. I wonder if I should have acquiesced to another pass of Ama Ravi's comb.

"You wear our clothes," he says briskly. "But you are not one of us."

In an instant, everything I've learned falls out of my ears.

I'm struggling to regain my composure when Doka comes up next to me. He introduces himself, speaking so clearly and eloquently, but I can't keep up. I catch words here and there, nodding along as Macario Talan laughs at jokes I don't understand. How can Doka be so much better at this than I am?

Our other dinner guests arrive, all dressed in thin layers of embroidered silks that straddle casual and formal. The iridescent threads shimmer, even in the dull lamp light. There's Javis, a navigational specialist aboard Adhosh. His eyes are beady and darting, as if he's used to communing with the grandness of stars and not the smallness of humanity. He's working on establishing the camp's first speculatorium—a small financial exchange that invests money in burgeoning businesses. There's Gracie, director of health aboard Adhosh, who runs both of the camp's underground health clinics. There are still trust issues between our people and the Klang, especially when it comes to medical interventions. And finally, there's Maki, former astrophysicist, who's taken up weaving. She boasts the most intricate shawl: an embroidered star map, deep black fabric with pinpoints of golden thread hanging upon her shoulders as though she's bearing the weight of the entire sky.

"Tell us of your family," Macario Talan says to me. "From what Sky Island do you hail?" His brow raises, a few silvered hairs among the black. He knows who I am, what I am, but I must still pass this test.

I swallow the lump in my throat. I'd practiced this line a million times. Their ship had originally launched from a great Earth archipelago called the Sky Islands. There were 307 of them, floating a half mile above where the many thousands of small islands their ancestors had called home had been long lost to the rising sea.

"My ancestors hail from Tabon," I say, the island of lost secrets and a technological haven. The Sky Islands were a lot like our Lines, though you picked your Sky Island based on those of your parents, or sometimes grandparents or great-grandparents if there was a better match. One of the islands would speak to your personality. So while siblings would sometimes share a Sky Island, more often than not, they didn't. "We skirt the shadows, we raise the sky."

Macario Talan nods, satisfied by my answer. I breathe a sigh of relief.

"And you, Rico, from what Sky Island do you hail?" he asks of Doka. Or Rico, I should call him now, and I do, when I remember. On the outside, I'm trying to assimilate, but my thoughts are not quite so malleable, hanging on to scraps of the past I've left behind.

Doka pokes his chest out. "Little Sahul, can't you tell? Three of four grands hailing, my choice was obvious. Eyes skyward, hearts full. It was Little Sahul that built our engines. First three of our captains, Little Sahul. A Little Sahul xenobiologist was the first human to map the entirety of a Zenzee's brain, giving us the ability to control our world and our destinies."

"You are more Klang than any of us here," Macario Talan laughs, clapping Doka on his back.

"They won't fool any of us who gives a second look," Tirtha says, proud but cautious. "But they will fool the guards around this place. If they keep their heads low, they should be safe to move around without much notice. They'll need new homes. New families."

Javis aims his darting gaze my way, though our eyes never meet. "How are you with numbers?" he asks.

"Numbers?" I reply.

"Math," he says. "You've studied it, yes?"

"Yes, of course. Addition. Subtraction. Multiplication . . ." I fish for the word *division* but come up short. ". . . The other one. Percentages. Ratios."

"Children's math, then. No calculus? Trigonometry?"

I've learned fifty-two Klang cuss words, and it takes all my might not to use them. "No. None of those things," I say quietly.

"How are you with children?" Gracie asks.

"I don't hate them," I say. I must be making a sour face, because she makes one right back at me. I reach for a less tepid response, wishing I had some anecdote about how I'd connected on some deep level with a child before, but I'd never really met any other than my own son, and I could barely stand to be in the same room with him. My cohort was now only starting to have children of their own, and obviously none of them had younger siblings, as they do here. We stuck to ourselves. The younger cohorts did the same. "Well, I appreciate them. Mostly from afar, but they are our future, right? Loud, crying, snotty little blessings, with their pudgy feet. And angry fists, and—"

"Nena and Rico are both quick learners and would both excel at meaningful work," Tirtha says before I can damage my reputation further. "Who could accommodate them?"

"Would they need separate dwellings, or are they willing to share?" Macario Talan asks.

"Separate!" Doka and I say in unison, our words perfectly matched on this matter.

"I can take Rico, then," Macario Talan says. "He's got the nimble mind of a baker."

"And who will take Nena?" Tirtha asks.

The entire table is quiet. Am I that much of a risk? Did I not impress a single one of them? Finally, Maki raises her hand. "I could use someone to work the loom in the back of my store. She would not have to talk to anyone."

I sigh in relief.

MAKI'S CHILDREN GIGGLE AT ME. I WAS TRYING TO TELL THEM about one of my adventures with Adalla, but it seems I've chosen another wrong word. I am unsure which one. I go over my sentence in my head once more, then see the problem. I used the word for *syrup* instead of *space*.

"We jumped through the cold, emptiness of *space*," I say again, and their laughter quiets down, ready for me to continue my story. I feel so far removed from those times; they feel more like fairy tales than memories.

I am a few years older than Karin, Maki's oldest. She's spirited and is in charge of running the loom, along with Farel who makes sure none of the fibers get tangled. Karin was studying to be a scientist back on Adhosh before the cascade failures, but those days are long gone. At times, she seems to long for that other life, but she's never complained once in the four months I've worked here, and I catch glimpses of her brilliance in the complex embroidery she produces.

Now we have some time off, so I harvest pineapple leaves with the younger children, pulling long iridescent fibers from the lavender leaves that are about as tall as I am. I grab the next leaf from the pile, but when I go to tear the barbs off the side, one of them gashes my palm.

Farel jumps up and has a bandage ready. "Don't worry," he says. "It happens to all of us."

"Thanks," I say. "I wish I was as good as you were, though."

"It takes practice," Farel says. "We weren't learning this too long ago. We had synthesizers make our fabrics up until about five years ago, but they wasted so much energy when our resources were thinning, so they were put to use for more critical fabrication projects."

"Your mouth wastes too much energy," says Karin. "You're supposed to be looking over the loom."

Farel jumps back up to his feet, makes a face behind his sister's back, then says sweetly, "Yes, sis. Right away."

Maki sticks her head through the beaded curtain. "Karin, I need you to run the front of the store for me for a moment."

"I'm super behind on orders," Karin says. "There's no way we're going to make the Holdover rush as it is."

"Okay, Farel, come on."

"I'm watching the thread," he says.

"Have Otis do it."

"It's a seawell pattern, Mama. Otis can't keep up with that."

Maki's eyes slowly find their way to mine. "Nena," she says. My new name still catches me by surprise. "Can you mind the store for me while I'm away?"

"I . . . I don't—"

"It's simple. The prices are all marked. Just stand behind the counter and smile and try to be helpful. I'll be gone thirty minutes at most."

"You've got this," says Karin. The younger kids nod with their big grins. I'm not sure if they really support me, or if they're eager to see what mistakes I'll make next.

"Okay," I say, then venture into the front of the store. It doesn't smell like the damp musk of pineapple up here, which is a nice change. Instead, it's flowery and sweet. The baros Maki sells are all made to order, but there are a couple sample garments hanging near the front door, thin white blouses that shimmer when they catch the light just right. Scarves take up the rest of the floor space, dyed every color.

Maki gives me a set of too-quick instructions, then leaves me alone in the store. I'm so nervous, I'm sweating. I practice my backstory in my head, recite my vowels. Fix my posture. My smile. I'm ready.

Finally, a customer walks in. She runs her hand down the front of the baro, finger tracing along the delicate lapel. She looks at another, then another.

"Can I help you?" I ask.

She looks up at me, startled. "Where's Maki?" she asks.

"Running an errand. I'm looking over the store for her." I've got my backstory primed, but before I can get out a single word, the woman has lost complete interest and has turned back to the baro that's caught her fancy.

"Do you think she could make one of these for me before Holdover?"

I pull out Maki's job list. "It looks like there are a couple spots left. Can I sign you up?"

"Yes, please." She gives me her name and I make an appointment for her to come in for measurements. She leaves happy, and I'm beyond elated as well. I'd passed. Didn't stumble on a single word. I'm so glad Doka pressed Tirtha to let us make new lives for ourselves. And now look at me: a new family, a new job. It's been hard, but I think I'm finally ready to say goodbye to the old me. Maybe it had been a fairy tale after all, the characters all figments of my imagination.

The beads in the front door rattle, and a figment steps right into the room with me. I freeze.

Adalla. She walks past me without even looking up and heads to the back where we keep our best scarves. She browses them, her back toward me.

"Do you have anything like this, except in blue?" she says, still not looking in my direction.

"Sorry, ma'am, but no." I pitch my voice an octave lower, making sure to lay my accent on thick. There are in fact a few dozen scarves finished up yesterday still in the back room, but I know if I went back there to look, I would never find the courage to come back out.

Adalla hems and haws a few moments longer, then selects a deep teal scarf and sets it on the counter in front of me. It is the same hue as our Zenzee's blood, same hue that had stained our sheets on so many occasions when Adalla had missed a spot while bathing. I keep my head down, eyes on the scarf. I flip the tag. "That'll be twenty-four shell money," I say.

As Adalla fusses with the shells in her purse, I dare to glance up at her. Her naxshi is different. The pit that's been in my stomach starts rolling so hard, I think it's going to knock straight through my ribs. She's gotten remarried. To the Admore Line. Presdah Admore, most likely, from the cohort ahead of ours. Many of her parents are physicians and scholars, and she was on the same path, from what I can remember. Studying to be a cardiologist, fixing human hearts. I'm happy for Adalla to have found such a solid Line after what she'd been through. I tell myself this over and over, hoping that soon I'll believe it.

Adalla places the cowries in my hand, her fingertips gracing my palm.

I know I should be quiet. I shouldn't risk it, but I do anyway. "So, is this purchase for a special someone?"

"My law-mother. Well, sort of. It's complicated."

I put the cowries in the till, then fold the scarf up into a neat triangle. "Well, I hope she enjoys it. And I hope you shop with us again." I hand the scarf to her, eyes still cast down, but our fingers touch this time. I hang onto the scarf a second longer than I should, waiting for some kind of spark to pass between us, then finally let it go.

"Thank you," she says, then leaves the store.

"You're welcome, Adalla," I say, barely a whisper, and not until I'm sure she's long gone.

I rush into the back, look at Karin. "I can't do it. I can't go back out there," I tell her. "You do it. Please?"

"You're doing fine, Nena. Just take a couple deep breaths. Mama will be back soon."

My breath saws in and out of my lungs. "You don't understand. I can't. I . . . I think I'm having a panic attack."

Karin stops weaving, failing to catch the dowel. It clacks against the floor. She comes over to me and squeezes me tight. "Are you okay?"

I shake my head. "There was a customer. A woman . . ."

Karin nods. "Deep brown skin, sparkly blue paint on her forehead. Bought a teal scarf?"

"Yeah, how'd you—"

"Seske," Adalla's voice comes from behind me, saddest word I've ever heard come out of anyone's mouth.

Daidi's bells.

I bite my lip and turn around. She shakes her head when she sees me. Her chest heaves. She drops the scarf on the floor.

"This is a dream. I'm dreaming," she mutters to herself. "How?"

The words spill from me in a rush. "Doka and I were rescued right after we were thrown out the third ass. We've been living here since, trying to fit in. I couldn't tell you. I couldn't tell anyone. But I wanted to tell you. I thought about you so much. And the family. And everything and everyone we've left behind. It's been hard. It's been so hard, but we're safe. We've been here," I say again, and once I realize I'm babbling, I stop myself. I stare at her, my chest heaving. My emotions spin out of control. I want her to reach for me. To tell me she's happy to see me. That she's missed me as much as I've missed her. That she's forgiven me.

But she just stares back.

My face feels so naked now without my naxshi. She'd known me practically our whole lives and had never seen my bare face. Never seen me without my braids.

"I mourned for you," she says. Anger there this time. "I mourned so hard. For you and for us."

"We couldn't risk telling anyone."

"Who rescued you?" Adalla asks.

"Baradonna," I say. "And Tirtha. And Bakti."

"They knew all this time and didn't say anything? I came to visit them."

"I know. I saw you."

"Adalla," Tirtha says, walking in from the back entrance. I turn and see Maki is with her, and behind them Baradonna.

"You had no right to keep this from me!" Adalla screams at Tirtha. "You were like a mother to me."

Tirtha shakes her head. "I'm sorry, Adalla. I didn't want to implicate you. And while I understand your pain, I'm afraid we have bigger problems now."

The room begins shaking, something like the tremors our Zenzee used to suffer from years ago, but we'd stabilized the hormones that were causing them and hadn't had a tremor since. This had to be something different.

"What is that?" I ask.

Baradonna steps forward. "It's bad, Seske. The clans have turned on one another. They're fighting each other. Hung myself halfway out the third ass, just to see it myself. Weapons firing, tearing through Zenzee flesh. Tentacles entangled. It's a mess, but I'm afraid the conflict doesn't end there." Baradonna hands me her stolen accountancy guard tablet, displaying the log screen they use for collecting data. There's a transcription of a conversation between two people designated as *Senator 1* and *Senator 2*. I scroll through the lengthy conversation until Doka's name jumps out at me:

> Staging Doka's assassination aboard another ship was a mistake. There were too many variables we couldn't control. If we can't find allies, we'll be terribly out-matched in this war.

Doka suspected it was Tesaryn Wen who'd staged the as-sassination, but he never had proof. But now, here it was. "How did you get this?" I ask Baradonna.

"You know, I was in the third ass, minding my own busi-ness, making a quiet life for myself. No one ever comes to the third ass, except for the occasional criminal going to meet her demise. I was filing down my toenails when I heard some-thing. I hid and saw a fissure open. Now, I thought I knew every single fissure in that ass, but this one comes out of no-where. Real covert-type ass polyp, clean as a whistle too, be-cause two women come out of it, not a lick of shit anywhere on them. They talked freely. I heard them conspiring and say-ing that a war was about to start. Talked about finding allies on different ships, reaching out with a form of communication that couldn't be traced. Said they'd used it to plot Doka's assas-sination."

"Tesaryn Wen," I say. "She was one of the women."

Baradonna shakes her head.

"That can't be. It had to be her!"

Baradonna just shakes her head again.

"Then who was it?"

"Bella Roshaad and one of her supporters."

This time I shake my head. She was practically Doka's mentor. "Are you sure? Couldn't you be mistaken?"

Baradonna raises a brow. Accountancy guards aren't exactly known to make mistakes.

"Who cares who it was right now?" says Karin. "We can't allow the Zenzee to war for us. In Adhosh's name, we must do whatever is in our power to prevent it."

"What can we do, trapped here in the camps?" I ask. "We barely have resources to live, much less to stop a war!"

Tirtha and Maki exchange looks.

"We should tell her," Maki says. "She's one of us now."

Tirtha nods. "Come."

Confused, I follow.

DOKA

Of Delicious Recipes and Distasteful Plans

One hundred!" I yell out, slamming the perfectly formed ball of rice dough onto a bed of leaves. I raise my hands up in victory. I've got rice flour beneath my nailbeds. Up my forearms. And there's a little wad of it sitting at the tip of my nose. I brush it off, leaving more flour smeared across my face, but I don't care. I've done it. I've beaten Macario at his own game. He's still on his eighty-sixth dough ball.

Macario inspects each line of dough, poking at a few to make sure they're all the right consistency and not damp from mixing in too much beetle milk. It'd been tough going through a couple of weird tremors, and I'd lost almost an entire row of rice balls to the floor, but I narrowed my focus and staged an amazing comeback.

"They're all to your liking?" I ask with a grin.

Macario nods in approval. "Very good, Rico. We may beat the morning bibingka rush yet."

"Well, I have a good teacher," I say. "And a foolproof recipe."

"There's no such thing as a foolproof recipe. Baking is part science, part art. A good baker knows when to stoke the oven. When to leave a bread in for an extra minute. How to improvise when needed." Yet Macario beams like a proud father. He has no children of his own. Married to his job, he always tells me, no time for distractions. No thoughts to spare for shaping the formless goop that is an infant's mind. But having a fully formed adult child, who is quite frankly a genius with handling dough, suits him nicely.

"Noted," I tell him. "What's next?"

"Well, let's get these up front to the display. You've got all the toppings prepped?"

I nod. "Diced the peppers this morning, shredded the shrimp last night. Everything else we've still got as leftovers from yesterday." I start packing up the raw rice cakes into a tray when there's a knock at the back door.

"That's Hada with the rice delivery," I say, dusting my hands on my apron. "I'll let her in."

I run to the door, but when I open it, Tirtha is standing there, with Seske and her sponsor, along with three of Seske's new siblings. And Baradonna is here, too. She grins at me. It's been months and months since I'd last seen her, and I'm ashamed that I'd forgotten how much I missed having her at my side. I'm all caught up in my feelings, and after I blink away my tears, I notice one of the siblings is not a sibling at all, but Adalla.

"Is Macario here?" Tirtha asks.

"Yes, of course. Come in," I say, nearly choking on my words. Adalla knows we're alive. Who else does? Kallum too? My heart flutters as their entire motley crew files into our cramped kitchen.

"We're in need of one of your secret recipes," Tirtha says to Macario.

Macario's eyes go wide, looking at all the people suddenly in his kitchen. "All of you?" he asks, his normally relaxed body suddenly rigid. "Seems like secret recipes can't stay secret if everybody knows about them."

"You can trust everyone here. We're all in need of knowing." Tirtha looks at me. "We can trust you, right?"

"Yes, of course. Macario has entrusted me with all of his recipes."

"Not this one," he says. Then he slides the wall-mounted spice rack to one side. It clicks, and a door appears—one I've never seen before. He pushes forward, and the door opens into a dark room. "Quickly, inside," he says. We file into the new room, twice as large as the kitchen, though it looks much the same with a countertop and ovens, and the technology here is much more advanced. Violet lights circle and buzz around inside them. Rows and rows of glass bottles containing various substances line the walls: some oozing, some glowing, some moving.

"I get the feeling these recipes call for more science than art," I say to Macario.

"You'd be surprised," he says. "There's quite a bit of overlap between being a baker and a quantum scientist."

I knew he had been a scientist, but I'd never known what kind. "Kallum never mentioned meeting any quantum scientists during his visits."

"It's something we held back. We couldn't trust your people with all our secrets. We knew that in the event of evacuation, it would be better if you weren't intimidated by our technology. Especially given how dangerous it was. You'd start sniffing around and find out that it was the reason—"

"Macario!" Tirtha calls out. She gives him a stern scold.

"What? You say we can trust them. If so, they deserve to know." Macario clears his throat, forces his head up. He gathers his nerves, fortifying himself against deep-seated guilt. "It was my fault Adhosh suffered a cascade failure. One of my discoveries broke through its containment, tunneled right through Adhosh, hitting her heart through and through. The breech lasted less than a minute, but the damage was done. We repaired what we could the best we could, but apparently, we underestimated the damage. The failures started soon after that. Everything else we told you was true. The starvation. The polluted water. The venting air. All because of this."

Macario walks up next to an orb the size of a bog melon, a bright pink line of fire winding its way around and around.

I look in awe, but Adalla pushes her way in. "The heart? You trashed your own heart with this weapon, and now you've brought it here? You could have ended us!"

"It is not a weapon," Macario says, getting defensive. "And it's fine now. There is no threat to you or your Zenzee. We had to bring it. Even with the destruction it caused. It represents four generations of research."

"How did you get all of this equipment aboard *Parados I*?" I ask. Personal belongings were limited and thoroughly checked. There's no way he could have snuck aboard with it. And yet, here it is.

"With this," he says, pointing to the orb.

"I don't understand."

"Maybe it's easiest if I show you." Macario engages the orb, and a pool of black space stands in front of it. It resolves, looking like a clear image. A mirror, showing this lab. It takes me a moment to notice that what I'm seeing is the back of my own head. Macario plucks a wad of rice dough off my shoulder and throws it through the mirror. Not half a second later, something hits me in the back. I look behind me and see another mirror. On the floor, the dough ball is sitting at my feet. "I stayed behind after everyone was on board and getting settled, then dismantled my lab and sent it through to here, piece by piece. Some of it, anyway. My old lab . . ." He looks off wistfully. "Well, I make do with what I've got now."

"Sure seems like it could be used as a weapon," I say, regaining my composure. "What if you'd fired a gun through it and not a wad of dough?"

Macario looks genuinely hurt. "I would never do something so dishonorable! We owe our lives to your generosity. Yes, we are not in ideal conditions, but things are changing. We have several dozen people doing work assignments outside of the camp. We have hope."

"What we have is war," Seske says. "It's raging as we speak."

"Those tremors from before?" I ask.

Seske nods.

I gather my thoughts. If war has started, the Senate will have called a special session to deal with all the fallout. I look at Macario. "Can this mirror of yours be cast anywhere?"

"Anywhere in the vicinity. The farther the distance, the more accurate you have to be with the calibrations. Same for the size of the mirror. Best to keep things small and local."

"Could you direct it to our Senate chambers?" I ask Macario.

He nods, then works the orb again. The mirror disappears from the room. Smaller mirrors appear for half a second at a time, his fingers tapping against their shimmering surfaces until he finds a good spot in the Senate chambers where it won't be noticed, high up and behind one of the pillars. We gather close to the opening, no bigger than my fist, listening.

"—and if the other clans insist on this aggression, we must react by laying claim to the Zenzee we need, right now and in the future," says Tesaryn Wen. "We should pick the best of the lot, strongest and most agile. If anyone has a problem with that, then we'll fight them for it."

"We should divide the herd among the clans evenly," says Bella Roshaad, offering a voice of reason, though I am dismayed by the suggestion. "It is the only fair way."

"The Serrata and Ulaud remain staunch in their plans to leave the herd. They should forfeit their right to claim any Zenzee," says Senator Gillis.

"We'll need at least ten Zenzee to start," says one of our scientists. "We can expand quickly into each, growing our populations as rapidly as we can. We should lift all reproductive restrictions as of right now and reinstitute embryo harvesting."

"We keep talking about *how* we should take on new Zenzee, but we never discussed *if* we should." I'm surprised.

It's Kallum's voice.

I push everyone else out of the way so I can see. There he is. My heart climbs into my throat. "Bella Roshaad got Kallum a Senate seat after all," I whisper to the others. "I never imagined it'd be possible, not after the stain I'd left upon our Line. At least she's always been in my corner."

"Oh, Doka . . . ," says Seske.

I turn to her. "'Oh, Doka' what?"

"The attempt on your life, back on the Renmoor ship . . ." She pauses, lips pursed in distaste.

"What about it?" I ask, my hackles raising at the mere mention.

Seske thinks for a moment then says, "Never mind. The important thing is that they didn't succeed. You're here now, and if we all work together, we can stop this war from happening."

"Tell me, Seske. I need to know."

"He needs to know," Baradonna says, echoing Tirtha from earlier and stepping up to me. "I'm sorry, I should have caught it sooner, but the control she practices is so much better than I'm used to dealing with. Pathological, nearly."

"Control?"

"Over her body language. Over her microfeatures." She places her hands on both of my shoulders. "Bella Roshaad ordered the operative to kill you during the Leaders' Summit. I heard her admit it with my own two ears. I'm sorry."

"Bella Roshaad?" I go slack, but Baradonna catches me in her arms. "Why? I—"

"Shhh . . . ," says Tirtha, still poised with her ear next to the mirror. "They're voting now."

We all rush back. A slight majority raises their hands.

"We will declare our intentions to claim Zenzee immediately," Wen says. "Anyone who opposes the deal shall be fired upon."

"What do we do now?" Macario asks.

We have little time and fewer resources, but we desperately shoot off ideas anyway.

"We need to reach out to Admiral Erisson of the Tertian ship," I say. "We built up a sort of trust with each other. They have a lot of firepower. If we get them on our side, then maybe we'll have enough leverage to stop the war before it really gets started."

Macario nods. "I could try to patch a connection through to him, but it'll be tricky with the distance between our ships. It could take twenty minutes to reach that far out."

"We have to try."

I watch carefully as Macario manipulates the orbs, just as I had watched him when I was first learning to bake. He peers into the small mirrors, and I can see that they are each tiny windows to other places. He selects the one closest to the Tertian's Zenzee, then recalibrates, drawing up another set of mirrors. With each iteration, his concentration deepens and his movements become more exact. A bead of sweat meanders down his forehead. I realize I'm watching him so intently that I've stopped breathing. I keep holding it until he calls me over. "Is that him?"

I peer into a mirror no bigger than my eye. It's him.

"Admiral Erisson!" I yell through the mirror. The admiral startles, his hand going to his weapon. He turns and sees the tiny mirror, probably my eye looking back at him.

"What in the—" He leans closer. I pull back so he can see my whole face. "Doka?"

"It's me. I don't have much time to explain. Our Senators have decided to go on the offensive so that they can have first selection from the new Zenzee herd."

"They're late to the party. The Vaz and Renmoor have already laid claim to half the herd between them. It's chaos out here." I hear their Zenzee shudder as ours had, but much more violently. Admiral Erisson barks out a series of orders to his second in command. I can just make him out over the admiral's shoulder.

"I was hoping we could join forces," I say when he's done, but he looks so distracted. I suddenly feel like I'm imposing.

"I wish we could assist you, but my hands are already full trying to keep things together over here. Nearly half of my lieutenants broke rank this morning, and that was before all hell broke loose. I'm not sure how much longer I can—" A pulse flashes behind the admiral, then he falls to the ground with a thud. Behind him, his second in command holds a laser rifle. He kicks at Erisson's unresponsive body, then fires again, the beam of light sailing right at us. Macario quickly disconnects.

"Oh no," I mutter.

The others are already regrouping, moving on as if nothing had even happened. As if we hadn't just witnessed another coup in a long line of coups. I suppose it was only a matter of time, but I'd distracted him. Caused him to let down his guard. But perhaps I'm most shaken at seeing the casual look on the new admiral's face as he made sure Erisson was dead.

"What do we do now?" Adalla asks.

"I have an idea," Seske says boldly. "It's scary, but we don't have much to lose. Adalla, I could use your help."

Adalla looks hesitant but leaves with Seske anyway.

I don't know what to do next. It's taken all my energy not to fall apart right now. Admiral Erisson had been kind to me when no one else was. Sure, he was responsible for enabling an entire baby fighting ring, but he's the main reason I'm still alive.

"You okay?" Baradonna asks, tilting my chin up so I meet her gaze.

I nod. "Yeah. I guess."

"Good. Because I've got an idea, too." Baradonna raises a brow. "I wish I could say it's a good one, but it absolutely most certainly is not."

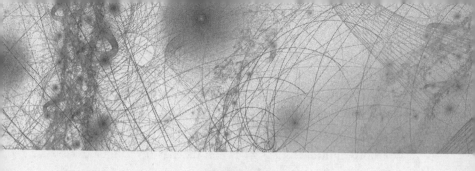

SESKE

Of Bright Lights and Dull Echoes

I paddle as fast as I can, Adalla doing the same behind me. I need no map. The route is like a scar I can trace across my own skin. Going back feels like the exact opposite of going home. It's like voluntarily walking into a nightmare. And maybe that's exactly what we're doing, but we need Sisterkin's help. She may be the only one in this world who can help.

We reach the cavern in the bile ducts where Sisterkin is bound. I angle the boat closer to the wall, swatting away the fog lingering there, but I do not see her. At first, I think that I've gone off course somehow, but then I notice the woman-shaped divot and the severed tendrils that had once been attached to her.

"I don't understand," I tell Adalla. "She was right here."

Throttle fish knock up against the sides of our boat, desperate for a meal. I shoo them away with my oar.

"You're sure you didn't dream it?" Adalla says. "The way you described your nightmares, they always felt so real."

"I couldn't make something like this up, 'Dalla," I say. I bite my tongue, realizing I've used her nickname. It feels wrong now, implying a closeness between us that no longer exists. "Besides, it couldn't have been a dream, because if it was a dream, then we're screwed."

Splashes rise up all around our boat, fish tails turning the water's surface to foamy bubbles as they slap against it. Seconds later, every single throttle fish in this cavern races for the exit. I get the feeling we should be doing the exact same thing, except our boat is facing in the wrong direction, and our bodies weren't made to navigate these ducts so quickly. Through the fog, an abomination approaches us. I know what it is—who it is—before she's totally visible. I can feel her in my bones.

Her skin is the color of lichen, a dull green gray, rough as tree bark. I'd expect that after four years of being embedded in the walls of this duct, her movements would be stiff and lurching, but she moves with the grace of a Matriarch. The spots where she'd been connected to Zenzee tissue have scabbed over. She has adorned herself in a gown made of throttle fish fins and a chunky necklace crafted from their skulls. Despite her adornments, she is not any closer to looking human. New appendages erupt from her forearms, slick, glistening tentacles, long and thin, like another set of fingers that nearly reach her toes. They move independently, one of them extending gingerly toward me.

"Sister," she purrs. "I knew you'd come back to me eventually. I've been waiting."

I shake away my fear. My contempt. "Our Zenzee is in trouble. We need to get her to fight back against the Senate's orders. We know you have a connection with her. With the others, too. Tell them all to stop fighting."

"I can tell them anything I want. It's the humans who control them that are the problem."

"There has to be a way," I plead. "Our Zenzee went against our will when we tried to decouple her from the Klang's Zenzee. It must be possible."

Sisterkin nods, her tentacle tip tracing down my cheek now. I hold back a shudder.

"Death does stoke an emotion so intense that it is capable of slipping beyond human control," she says. The way she says *human*, it's as if she no longer considers herself to be among us. "There is one way to end this war, but to do so, a Zenzee must die." Sisterkin quirks her lip. "Or must appear to have died."

"We're listening," I say. "We'll do anything."

"Good. Because what I am about to share with you has a price." Her tentacle snakes around the back of my neck, gently nudging me closer to her. "Once you are done, once the Zenzee are safe, you must return to me, Seske. I want you to rule beside me. I don't want to be lonely anymore. Even the throttle fish avoid me now." She touches her necklace of throttle fish skulls, as if she hasn't the faintest idea of why.

I swallow the lump in my throat. I said I'd do anything, but . . .

Adalla's lip trembles. Her fingers twitch, as though she wants to reach out to me, but there's still so much bad blood between us.

"You hesitate," Sisterkin says. "We don't have time for hesitation."

"You're asking her to become a monster," Adalla growls, ever my protector. Old habits. Those twitchy fingers are at the hilt of her knife now.

"I'm not *asking* anything," Sisterkin says with a nonchalance that has the ring of finality in it.

Adalla takes an aggressive step toward Sisterkin. "I won't let—"

"I promise. I am all yours," I say, before Adalla has a chance to do something we'll all regret. "Just tell me how to save our people."

Adalla stares at me, unnerved, but what choice do I have? I've disappointed her so many times. I've upturned our whole world. The least I can do is try to save it.

Sisterkin smiles, and it is both beautiful and wretched. "There is an organ . . . one you assumed had no function. It doesn't, in life. It only activates when the Zenzee has died. I will tell you how to bypass the mechanism that keeps it dormant. Once the beacon flashes, all Zenzee in the vicinity will become stricken by an incalculable grief so intense, it will override all other functions. The war will end. For now, at least. It will give your people enough time to regroup and come to your senses. You should take Adalla and that big knife of hers with you. There is no external access, so you'll have to cut your way through."

"How do we get there?" Adalla asks.

"You'll need a map," Sisterkin says. "Lucky for you, you already have it." One of her tentacles stretches out and touches the middle of my forehead. A memory surges forth—not my memory. Another person's, from another time, upon another Zenzee. But I retrace their steps, and it's like I'm there.

I know exactly where we need to go.

IT IS NOT ICHOR THAT FILLS MY MOUTH. THE BLOOD THAT flows after each of Adalla's cuts is not liquid at all, but a pungent gas that burns the lungs. Sisterkin hadn't warned us that we'd need re-breathers, and by the time we realized we should have them, it was too late to turn back. The gas is lighter than air, though, so we're able to stoop down to catch our breath near the floor every so often. After ten minutes of grueling, physical work, Adalla has yet to ask for a break. She's sweated through her dress, the fine silk clinging to her skin, and I'm able to make out each and every raised scar upon her back. Her body is like a machine. Slash, rip. Slash, rip. Dip for air. Then do it all again. And again.

"You never stop working," I say as we're catching our breath, both of us on our knees. She stares at me through the green-tinged air.

"What?"

"Since the day you got assigned to the heart, you never stopped. I always knew you were meant to be there. And I wanted you to be there more than anything, but I never imagined it would take all of you."

Adalla grunts in frustration. "We don't have time for this. I need to get back to—" She stops herself right as she raises her knife, realizing she's doing it again. Avoiding me. Losing herself in her job. It must be one or the other. Maybe it's both.

"There was always some emergency," I tell her, ready to say what's needed to be said for a long time now. "There was always a life that needed saving. You'd come home, we'd make love, then you were gone again. Our bed was always cold. Even when you were in it."

Adalla's lips purse, as if she wants to say something, but then she's back on her feet. She slashes, rips. Slashes, rips.

Dips for air.

"So that's your excuse, then, for why you strayed?" she spits. She's not concentrating on her breath, pulling up before

I can get a word in. She keeps slashing this time. Slashing and slashing and slashing, and my lungs feel like they're going to rip through me. I dip. She doesn't. I'm left alone, on my knees with my thoughts.

"It's not an excuse!" I shout out. She might be surrounded by fouled air, but she can still hear me. I stay on the ground. "What I did, I'll never forgive myself, and I don't expect you to forgive me, either. I know now is not the best time, when you're trying to save the world again, but if we die in here, I want you to know that I know I fucked up. I should have told you how lonely I was. How much you made me hurt."

The slashing stops, but Adalla doesn't dip.

"Adalla?" I say.

"I still feel them," she says. "The scars on my back. I know I told you the pain had faded over time, but it hasn't. I still feel them like the day you laid them upon me. I know why you did it, but it doesn't ease the hurt. Working focuses my mind away from it. But when I'm with you—when you touch me . . ."

"You're there on that day all over again?" I offer.

"Mmmm." Adalla grunts. Slashes, rips. I finish up my breath and try to catch up with her. She's gotten way ahead of me, still refusing to dip; whether it's superior lungs or grudge-fueled spite, I can't tell. But by the time I catch up, I'm lost for what to say to attempt to comfort her.

"You were like my star," Adalla continues, breath worryingly thin. The edges of her mouth curl down, then she stoops to catch some clean air, but when she comes back up, things are still murky between us. Literally and figuratively. "You were like a beacon of death, drawing me toward you. I couldn't turn away. I couldn't even dare to want to. Because I loved you as much as I hated you. And eventually, it got to the point I couldn't tell the difference between the two."

She looks pleadingly at me, but my heart is blank. My mind, too.

Adalla sighs. "Presdah says I need to forgive you. She thinks I won't be able to truly move on and settle into our relationship until I do. I've been working on that. Honestly, it was a lot easier when I thought you were dead."

Adalla makes a hefty slash, and the path of carved flesh opens up into a large, domed chamber lined in dull gray hexagonal plates. They clack and echo as we step upon them, flashing a violet-tinged white beneath our feet. Adalla and I make our way to the center, spinning around to take it all in. From the ceiling, hundreds of coiled vines hang down like fancy chandeliers, each ending in a large dewdrop.

"I feel like we're in a ballroom," I say. My voice echoes. No . . . more than an echo. My voice comes back distorted, pitched higher and lower, getting louder and louder.

> *I feel like we're in a ballroom.*
> *I feel like we're in a ballroom.*
> *I feel like we should be dancing.*
> *We should dance.*
> *Dance with me.*
> *Dance with me.*
> *Be with me.*

I clap my hands over my mouth as Adalla and I exchange looks. Her face sours. "We need to figure out which cord to pull," she says to me.

> *We need to figure out which cord to pull.*
> *We need to figure out which cord to pull.*
> *There's no way we can pull this off.*

We need to cut the cord.
We need to cut the cord.
Cut the cord.
Back off.

The bite in Adalla's echo gives me chills.

The main cord that Sisterkin mentioned is hidden among all the coiled vines, but Adalla's keen eye finally spots it. Now we just need to detach it from the ceiling.

I gesture to Adalla, making scissor cutting motions with my fingers, then point to the cord hanging in the center of the room, hanging just out of reach. Blacker, thicker than the others. Glistening. I point to my back and stoop down on one knee. She mounts my shoulders, and I heave myself back up. She's all muscle and heavier than I anticipated, but the pressure fades some as soon as she's got a grip on the cord. She tugs on it with all her might, but it's slick and keeps slipping. Sisterkin said that dislodging the cord from its base it will trick the organ into thinking our Zenzee is dead, at which point this death organ should spring to life, but we're not having much luck so far.

I don't want to speak again. I have no idea what truths my echo will get at this time, but we're running out of options and time. We're insulated from most of the sounds and tremblings of war, but I know it's still raging outside of this little time bubble Adalla and I are trapped in.

"Hold tight. I'll tug at your waist," I whisper, hoping the echo won't pick it up, but it seems to have made things worse. My words boom back at me.

Hold tight. I'll tug at your waist.
Hold tight. I'll tug at your waist.

Sorry, I've wasted your time.
I've wasted your time.
I'll waste your time.
What a waste.

I shake the voices away, and once Adalla has a good grip, I pull, yanking her this way and that. If this doesn't work, she's going to have to climb all the way up to cut it. Or try to. The gravity feels different here, more intimidating. A fall from that high up could mean broken bones or worse. Finally, she drops down a few feet as the cord starts to peel from the ceiling. I'm able to get my hands around the cord, and together we pull until both our feet are touching the floor again. We heave against it until our bodies ache, until my shoulders feel like they're about to pop out of their sockets. Finally, with a sickening *plop*, the cord pops free from its base, and plummets down into a neat pile.

Adalla and I tumble to the ground, slick with sweat and whatever substance the cord was drenched with. We attempt to catch our breath, waiting for something to happen. Waiting for *anything* to happen. Neither of us dares to speak a word. Finally, one of the dewdrops pulses violet light. Another joins it. And another. The flashing quickens and intensifies, and the plating around us starts to glow as well. Adalla and I jump back to our feet, looking for the exit seam, but it's too late. We're all disoriented now. And it's only getting brighter.

I close my eyelids, but they offer no reprieve. The light becomes heavy, like a blanket laying on top of us. I can taste it, both sour and sweet. I breathe it in, and it fills my lungs. I look back at Adalla and I can see through her. Her bones, her heart beating, and all the thousands of little veins and arteries leading throughout her body. Her chest rises and falls with each breath, her milk ducts like the petals of two beautiful flowers.

I'm a hundred percent certain that being exposed to whatever this is will kill us, if not now, eventually, but still, seeing Adalla like this, I wouldn't trade this moment for the world.

The light is so heavy now, I can no longer bear to stand. I lower myself down to the floor, feeling the blanket squeeze me. But when I find the strength to lift my head, I see that I'm still standing there, exactly as I was. I see inside me, the wreck of my womb. Spots within me that I wouldn't dare call human. And then I'm solid again, skin and all, and Adalla and I are tugging at the cord, once again attached to the ceiling. Then we're walking backward to the exit seam, and with a hefty reverse slash, it's sealed up again.

We're traveling back through the bile ducts now, only in reverse, exactly as it happened. The vision blurs in spots, like when Sisterkin had emerged from the fog to reveal herself. The memory tugs sideways, another sitting on top of it. This time, I hadn't intervened fast enough, and Adalla had thrown herself at Sisterkin, knife brandished, ready to protect me from the monstrous thing my sister had become. But Sisterkin is ready for her, a tentacle ripping the knife from her hands and a stiff forearm sending Adalla flying back into the boggy water. I punch Sisterkin, then strangle her with her own necklace made of skulls. I flinch as she reaches her tentacles around my neck and does the same. We are at an impasse, both of us dying, but it seems like I am dying a little bit faster. My vision fades to blackness. Death welcomes me.

But instead of leaving me feeling hopeless, I'm supercharged with power. I explore more of the paths not taken and am intrigued with what awaits me. I trace back through time, recalling various memories that branch this way and that, reliving alternate realities as if they'd actually happened. I dare to ride all the way back to that fated moment in the study with Doka. I find eight different versions of the day I'd ruined our lives. In four, I don't give in to Doka's advances. We share an awkward moment looking into each other's eyes, then continue with our research. Kallum comes down, serves us tea. We all laugh, taking a well-earned break before getting back to work. Then things diverge right before we are to meet with the Senators to present our case:

> *Madam Wade is murdered, just like before.*
> *Doka is killed by Madam Wade's murderer.*
> *Doka is assassinated in the Senate chambers.*
> *I am assassinated in my sleep.*

In the first echo, after Madam Wade is murdered, the attempt on Doka's life aboard the Renmoor ship succeeds. All four of these echoes end in war and destruction. Humanity is decimated, at least in our little pocket of space.

In the echoes in which Doka and I fuck, three times it is, frankly, amazing. We connect. I almost feel vindicated, knowing that there'd actually been something meaningful brewing between us. Instead of him dozing off and dreaming, we talk afterward, his finger tracing along my collarbone, down between my breasts, around my navel and back. I feel as though our souls have been intertwined. Two of the times, Kallum catches us in a kiss so deep, so passionate, that he turns us in immediately. There was no disguising that kind of hurt. Doka and I are jettisoned out of the third ass, locked in each other's arms. And a little way down the line, war ends humanity again.

One time, we aren't caught, escaping Kallum, but only barely. We continue our affair in quiet, and after months, we dare to Ride the Deep Silence—fucking in our Zenzee's mouth. We're brave and reckless when we're with each other, and we venture out near the tentacles. We make love there, space biting at our backs, stars in our eyes. Doka really puts the "deep" in deep silence, and he thrusts so hard and with so much desire that we lose our grip on the tentacle and go tumbling right out of the mouth.

We don't die right away. We've got our protective covering and our re-breathers. We could call for help, but we both know that being caught like this would just lead to getting tossed into space from the Zenzee's other end, this time without any gel.

We die in each other's arms.

It's not the worst way to go, but without us to stop the war, humanity still ends.

Then there is this echo, the one we're caught in, with the bad sex, and the hidden affair, and Madam Wade's murder, the failed attempt on Doka's life, the discovery of Sisterkin, and the escape from death and subsequent start of new lives in the Klang's refugee camp. I dig through hundreds, maybe thousands of echoes—all in a matter of seconds—and yet this is the only one in which humanity perseveres.

This can't be it, I think. This can't be the only way. There must be an echo where Adalla and I could have been together. Forever. One in which I hadn't hurt her so badly. I reach for another and another until the light fades. The heaviness lifts, and we're back in the death organ. It's returned to its original gray state now, except all the dewdrops look smoky, as if they've burned out.

Adalla lifts her head from the floor. "You okay?" she asks. I brace for her echo, but it doesn't come.

"Yes, you?"

She nods. "Did you have weird dreams?"

"Yes," I say, though we both know they weren't dreams. "I saw different versions of the past. I was searching for one where I hadn't hurt you, but they all ended badly. I know I messed things up. I can't even tell you how sorry I am. How much I wish we could go back to how it was before—"

"But you can't."

"You're sure?"

"Sure is sure is sure." Adalla draws in a long breath, then lets it loose between barely parted lips. "I looked for futures. In about half of them, I kiss you right now. They all ended in heartbreak."

I've got definite feelings about this. I want to argue with Adalla, that maybe it won't have to end badly. That maybe there's an echo she missed. But I bite my tongue. "What about the other half?"

Her eyes soften and a warm smile spreads over her lips. It's the same smile she'd given me as she roused me from stasis, back in that other life. Bright and full of possibilities. "Things between me and Presdah are good. Sometimes *really* good. But beyond that, I find a way to be whole again." She looks down, fiddles with the damp hem of her dress. "I forgive you. And I love you. But we need to stay friends. For my sake, and for the sake of everyone out there who needs your leadership right now."

I'm numb all over, but I manage to nod. I'd do anything to keep Adalla happy and safe. Turns out that means letting her go.

Perhaps this has always been our fate, and I was just too stubborn to realize it. Our lives became entangled long ago, and as our worlds grew, so did our interdependency. The ways in which we were tied together were so complex that undoing those knots seemed unfathomable. And yet, in but an instant, they've been severed. I wonder how long we would have lasted if we'd realized how simple it was to break free of this symbiotic relationship, and just like that, escape into an unknown future.

The silence grows between us, but in that moment, I realize our Zenzee has stopped shaking. The war has ended—or, at least, the battle has. And with that ceasefire, Sisterkin has held up her end of the bargain, so I've got no business worrying over futures anyway.

As of right now, I belong to her.

DOKA

Of Tainted Air and Bated Breath

Ready on three," I say through the mouthpiece of my re-breather. I'm standing upon the open rim of our Zenzee's third ass, preparing to launch myself at the Tertian's Zenzee that's steadily barreling toward us. She looks like a moon-size soldier, her entire hide layered over with interconnecting metal plating and weapons protruding through her flesh. Even the tips of her tentacles have been fortified with barbs that could slice through our Zenzee's thick skin, right down to the vital organs. I can't even imagine what effort and resources were expended to arm her like this.

I swallow back my reservations.

This is a solid plan, right? Make a short jaunt through naked space, then strut right onto a ship full of warriors who were trained to fight from birth? But I've seen Baradonna in action. If she thinks we can swim through the void with a smattering of protective gel and twenty-year-old re-breathers and then commandeer their ship, why should I doubt her? If we fail, we're as good as dead anyway. After watching the way they tore through the Vaz's Zenzee, we know our weapons are no match for theirs.

I've got Macario's orb packed with me, and we're hoping it's enough to help up navigate across the enemy's Zenzee without being seen. I think I can get the mirrors big enough that we can shoulder our way through from one room to the next, using the element of surprise to subdue anyone who gets in our way. Then, once we've secured the control room, we can stop the Zenzee from firing upon us there. Baradonna says that if we work strategically, it'll take five minutes, eight max.

She also warned us it wasn't a very good plan.

"One," I say. The Tertian's Zenzee is even closer now, tentacles splayed perfectly wide, ready to rip us apart. The Tertians have such precise control over every movement of their Zenzee. I have no doubt her deadly grip will pose just as much of a threat as those cannons firing at us, quaking our Zenzee with each landed shot.

"Two." My heart is racing. This is it. I glance over at Bakti, geared up in makeshift armor like the rest of us, mostly made of baking pans from Macario's shop. He smiles at me as if he's waited all his life for this moment. Not a trace of fear anywhere on his body.

"Thr—"

But before we can jump, a bright fuchsia light fills the sky. Or maybe it's more magenta. I close my eyes, but it still bleeds through. Burns so badly. It's all I can do to keep my grip on the Zenzee's ass and not get tossed into space. When it finally fades, it takes me a long while to get oriented. Back outside, the Tertian's Zenzee has stopped charging at us. Her tentacles move slowly, naturally, like they do when they're still in their herds—before we colonize them and rewire their brains. I look around and see all the Zenzee have stopped fighting, in fact. The ground no longer trembles.

"Seske and Adalla must have done it," Bakti says, daring to throw a fist into the air.

I nod, still at a loss for words. We'd taken several damaging hits, though, and I can't help but worry about Kallum. "We need to get to the Senate," I say. "We have to talk some sense into them and stop this from ever happening again."

"Two ghosts and a Klang confronting the Senate," Baradonna says. "I think we had a better shot against the Tertians." Yet she leads us through one of the fissures, navigating us through secret channels and overlooked crevices until we're back to civilization. The turmoil is mounting all around us, people screaming, babies crying, and beyond that, a weighty sadness hangs in the air. On the way, Baradonna and Bakti stop to help a woman who's been injured by fallen debris. I keep pressing forward, though, eyes set on the Senate chamber doors.

I throw open the doors. Everything is in such disarray that the guards don't even notice me. Papers and wreckage are strewn all over the room, senators helping one another up and back into their seats, as though a war hadn't just started and they're in a rush to get back to business. I spot Kallum, dusting off his robes.

"Hello, Kallum," I say, staring at him. My voice rings metallic through my re-breather. I'd forgotten to remove it, but I pop the seal now and let it hang loose around my neck. Kallum looks up, past my bare face devoid of naxshi, past my straightened hair, and sees me. Or sees a ghost is more like it.

He gasps for air once. Twice. Then he tries to scramble away. He nearly falls, but I catch him by the hand. This touch reassures him he's not hallucinating. His fear turns to something else . . . rage, anger. Whatever it is seems so foreign on his face.

"You're dead," he tells me. "I saw your body drifting through space."

I can't imagine what he's going through now. His half-healed wounds ripped right open again. I hang my head. "It was a puppet dressed up to look like me. Seske and I have been living with the Klang ever since. I wanted to contact you but—"

Kallum starts cussing out my Line, well my old Line, I guess. So loud, we're attracting attention. I drag him back to the far wall of the Senate chamber, where we can have something that approximates privacy. He is still cussing, but he doesn't resist coming with me.

"I'm sorry if I hurt you," I tell him.

His eyes widen. "*If* you hurt me? You know fucking well that you hurt me. You tore my fucking heart out, and worse, I had to go and pretend it didn't happen to try to save all of our asses."

"You shouldn't have had to do that. I would never have wanted you to shoulder that burden."

"Well maybe you should have thought about that before you decided to shove your dick in your wife, and then die without me getting a chance to—" Kallum bites his lip then crosses his arms and turns away from me. I touch his shoulder, but he shrugs me off.

"How's Charrelle?" I ask, changing the subject to something less charged. "How's the baby?"

"They're fine," Kallum says sharply. "She's remarried to Vellah Pranim, the woman who oversees the Uncommon Gardens, and her husband. We've been splitting custody of Kenzah."

Kallum stews for a minute longer, then turns back around.

His face has softened. "He's been so amazing, Doka. He's walking now. Talking some. His first word was 'pai.'" He smiles at me, a tear sitting in the corner of his eye that refuses to budge. "Well, it sounded more like 'ba,' but I know what he was saying. He was calling for you."

I shake my head. "You're his pai, too," I say. It was a conversation we'd had a dozen times. There was only one term for head-father. I'd wanted us to share it. It carried so much weight, but Kallum was as flighty as ever and wanted to come up with his own term. He lived life on his own terms, so it was fitting.

"I decided to go by Dad," Kallum says. "I know it's archaic, but it has a nice ring to it. I tell him stories of his pai all the time, though. From before, when we were kids, and everything wasn't so complicated. I wanted him to know the man I'd fallen in love with."

"I wish more than anything that I'd been here for both of you," I whisper.

"Me too," Kallum says.

The sadness in his voice nearly melts me. If we go on talking like this, it might.

"We need to put an end to this war for good, Kallum," I say, abruptly changing the subject again. "The Senate isn't going to do that without pressure. I've lived among the Klang long enough that I see how we could function. I've seen the bonds they've built. No, they're not perfect, but fuck perfect. We just need to be *better*. I'm glad you've got a seat in the Senate. I know how much that meant to you, but a seat isn't enough. We've got to flip the whole damn table. I want to do that for you and Kenzah or die trying."

Kallum's lip trembles, but his eyes remain distant. "You talk a good talk, Doka. You always have. But I don't think—"

The main doors to the chamber slam open. The screams start almost immediately. I crane my neck, and then I see it, too. Kallum pushes me behind him, like he's going to protect me. Like he's the father and I'm the child. Maybe fatherhood has changed him. Regardless, I push my way to his side, standing right next to him. Our fingers twine instinctively. Seconds later, we both notice and drop each other's hands like hot coals.

The creature steals our breath and thoughts anyway. It's like something that's walked out of a nightmare. Gray skin with black tentacles erupting from her arms, and a gown sewn from parts of throttle fish. She bares a crown upon her head, made from their fangs. A necklace of skulls hangs low around her neck, and right above the loop, a glowing mass throbs against her chest. When she looks our way, the face is immediately recognizable. She scowls in our direction. Kallum's hand is in mine again, but this time we don't let go.

"Sisterkin," Kallum and I say at the same time.

The doors slam behind her, and the walls start vibrating all around us. Spurs erupt from the bone-carved doors, sharp and thin tendrils that intertwine with one another, sealing off all the exits. Sisterkin walks gracefully down the center aisle, then takes her spot—my old spot, where the matriarch presides over the Senate proceedings.

"Greetings from the ancestors," she says, then chuckles to herself. "Not your ancestors, mind you, but those of the Zenzee. Their Line reaches back to before humanity was even a thought. And yet, in the brief time since you have encountered the Zenzee, you have managed to decimate an entire pod. The good news is that they have forgiven you. They understand you are bound by the limits of your nature. And they think you are capable of redeeming yourselves . . . with a little help."

The bulge on her chest swells even more, pulsing like a

heartbeat. Suddenly, it starts to crack, glowing red-hot along the edges, then a white cloud erupts, spilling over the first two rows of senators before dissipating. Kallum and I look at each other. I snatch my re-breather from around my neck and latch it over his face, then rip a swath of fabric from his robe. I press the thick fabric firmly over my nose and mouth.

"Doka—" he says to me.

"Don't argue," I say back. "I'll be fine."

Coughing surrounds us. She's poisoning our air, trying to destroy us.

"Breathe in, my dears," Sisterkin says, her arms thrown wide.

"You can't kill us!" Kallum yells out. I pull him out of her line of sight, toward relative safety, but he tugs against me. "It's barbaric! What kind of person would do this?"

"An evolved person," Sisterkin says with a laugh. "We are not trying to kill you. Didn't you hear that you've been forgiven?"

Banging comes from the rear doors. I hear Baradonna yelling for me from the other side.

"Doka," Kallum says, averting my attention back to Sisterkin. The lump on her chest is swelling again, ready to release more of the white mist. "We have to take her out. Who knows how far her poison might spread if we let it leave this room."

I nod. We race down the aisle, charging Sisterkin. She might have superhuman strength, but there's two of us. And we've got the tunneling orb.

Sisterkin watches as we approach her, then blinks. In one motion, five senators from the aisle seats on both sides step into our path, blocking our way.

"Move," I tell them. But they come at us like they're not thinking. Like they're being controlled. Fright washes over

304 / NICKY DRAYDEN

me. It's not a poison cloud, but one of spores. Just like the ones from the fungus that affect the gall worms, causing them to burrow against their will. Sisterkin was telling the truth. She isn't trying to kill us. She's doing something far more sinister.

The mind-controlled Senators attack us, their movements jerky, like gel puppets. Kallum kicks a Senator in the shin and she goes down, wailing a wet gurgle that barely sounds human. I punch Bella Roshaad in the jaw, nearly breaking my fist. I shake out the pain in my knuckles. She deserves worse for trying to kill me, so I guess it's too bad my hands were made for signing declarations into effect and not fighting.

The door bangs open, and I see Baradonna standing there, flanked by Seske and Bakti.

"No!" I yell, watching the spore cloud swirl toward them. They've got re-breathers on, but the people on the rest of the ship . . . "Close the doors!" I say. Baradonna sees my panic and complies.

I shake my head. That was too close. But now we've got backup to help stop the next round of spores from releasing.

"Help us get Sisterkin," I yell. Baradonna storms forward, throwing Senators off us left and right. But another group of them have stationed themselves in front of the stage, a wall between us and Sisterkin. We're blocked, until I remember something.

"I've got an idea," I say. "Keep them off me for a minute."

Senators keep rushing us, a dozen at a time, but Seske, Bakti, and Baradonna handle them efficiently. I crouch down in the aisle, gently pull the orb from my satchel. I'd only watched Macario use it a few times, but I knew his movements after four months of watching him bake. It was an art as much as it was a science. Supposedly. I take a deep breath through the slim protection of my fabric swath, then set it aside, holding on to this lungful of air. I move my hands as Macario had done, and the mirrors form, small ones at first. I peer into each, looking for a glimpse, then press the one in the Senate chambers. I reconfigure, drilling down until I'm looking at the stage. Reconfigure again, and I'm staring at the back of Sisterkin's head. I widen the mirror. A bit more. A bit more, until it's slightly wider than my fist.

Then I just . . . punch. Hard. Sisterkin pitches forward, and her link on the Senators breaks. My hand is aching worse now, and I'm so gripped by the pain that I don't notice she's looking through the mirror, staring straight at me until it's too late. Tentacles whip through the mirror and wrap around my neck, choking me. I tug back at the tentacles, trying desperately to get my fingers under them so I can break the seal.

Sisterkin's grip tightens. She leers at me through the mirror, like a voyeur who's taken an intense interest in my suffering. "Breathe in, Doka," she huffs. "Even the most heroic among us are still parasites—mouths always open, minds never so. Now is the time to open your minds. You'll be happy, I promise. You want to be happy, don't you? Under my rule, all will be equal. All will be at one with the Zenzee. Isn't that what you wanted?"

My lungs burn so badly. Sisterkin pulls my head to her chest bulge. It pokes through the mirror, and my cheek presses against it. It's hot, yet slick. The caustic substance nearly burns me. I feel the jagged seams widening, ready to release more spores.

This was exactly the distraction we needed.

Baradonna seizes the moment and surges past, knocking Sisterkin with a stiff forearm. Sisterkin goes flying across the stage, and her tentacles release me. I'm free, but my lungs can't take much more. Just as I'm about to be forced to take in a spore-ridden breath, Baradonna pops in the mirror to slap a spare re-breather onto my face. I fall back, sucking in clean air at last. I pull myself up from the aisle, close the mirror, then tuck the orb back into my satchel so I can rejoin the fight, even though my hand is pretty much useless at this point. I run up to the stage, watching as Baradonna has Sisterkin pinned down.

I start to praise Baradonna for her quick thinking, but notice she's not wearing a re-breather now. It wasn't a spare re-breather. It was hers. The spores release, right in her face. Almost instantly, her bulky frame goes slack, and her arms fall to her sides. She rises off Sisterkin in an inhuman motion, as if her center of gravity has slipped to her knees. She looms, eyes empty, leaning farther forward than her strength should allow.

"Size and might are not interchangeable," Sisterkin says, the bulge on her chest starting to regrow yet again. "I thought you'd figured that out by now. Just as humanity claimed control of a being the size of a moon, so shall these spores claim control of you."

I start shaking, trembling with rage. I keep my eyes from turning back in Baradonna's direction, because if I do, I know I'm going to lose it. I'll rip every single scrap of flesh from Sisterkin's bones. And what will that make me? A murderer? No. She's already gone to us. Banished and forgotten. You can't murder someone who never existed. I lunge for her.

"No!" Seske shouts, coming between us. "She is not the enemy."

"You're infected, too," I tell her. "It must have gotten through your re-breather filters. Out of the way, or I'll have to come through you, too."

"You wouldn't, Doka," Seske says.

I wouldn't? Wouldn't I? Sisterkin poses a threat to every person on this Zenzee. Kallum. Kenzah. Everyone who I've ever loved. My fists clench, and it's all I can do to swallow back the scream of pain I want to release. "Please move out of my way, Seske. I won't ask again."

"Look past her," Seske says. "Listen to the words. She speaks for the Zenzee. It was with her help that we were able to stop the war. We'd all be dead by now if it wasn't for her."

I shake my head. "I'd rather be dead than have that happen to us." I nod at Baradonna. She stands there like a husk. Eyes blank. Empty inside.

"So it's okay if we control the Zenzee, but suddenly you're all righteous when they start controlling us back? It's fine for us to drive towering spikes into their brain and bend them to our will, but a fungus does the same thing, and it's the Zenzee who are out of line?"

"I . . ." My mind flips back and forth, trying to justify the difference, but I'm coming up blank.

Seske steps closer to me. I bristle at her presence. "It's okay," she says calmly. "You don't need to answer. You'll understand. You just need to take the time to listen."

My chest heaves. Alerts ping in my ear. I'm hyperventilating and my decades-old re-breather is having a hard time keeping up. I attempt to control my breath, metallic tasting air flowing in and out of my lungs. "Okay, I'm listening!" I say, turning to Sisterkin, but she doesn't speak. I stare at her. Waiting. I have no idea of how to read her. No idea of what her posture means. She's too much of a threat. Too unpredictable. I shake my head again. "We can't trust her. She could say anything. We are completely vulnerable."

"I trust her," Seske says.

"But I don't trust you!" Even when our world isn't coming

to an end, Seske hasn't always made the best decisions. And, I guess, neither have I.

"I know," she says sadly. "But you should. For Kallum. And Kenzah. For everyone. We've yearned for a chance to atone for our past sins. Now it's time for us to take it." Seske moves her hands to her re-breather.

"No!" I shout, but the seal pops and Seske breathes in the spores. Thinking quickly—or not thinking at all—I rip the orb from my satchel and conjure up a mirror that leads deep into space. The wind whips, and papers go flying along with everything else in the Senate chambers that isn't nailed down. The air escapes into the void I've created, along with any remaining spores. But when I look up at Seske, she's changed already. It's too late.

I close the mirror. Sisterkin looks entirely at ease. She and Seske join hands, and the bulge on her chest stops pulsing.

"You see, we are learning again to trust," Sisterkin says. "The Zenzee do not want to see humanity dead. You have made them stronger. You upset millennia-old ecosystems and challenged them to adapt. They did, taking their inspiration from you."

"So now they're going to domesticate us," I spit back. "Turn us into mindless drones to tend their crops and do their bidding?"

"Domesticate? Perhaps. But they don't need mindless drones. Your minds are what they value most. Does this anger you?"

"Yes, it angers me! You can't take away our free will!" I shout but clap my hand over my mouth as soon as I've said it. Why can't they? Isn't this exactly what Seske accused me of? Don't we deserve the exact same thing we've done to them? Yes, we'd apologized. We'd stripped our lives down to the bare minimum, tried to live as close to nature as we could, but had we actually made amends? Had we earned their trust? Could we ever?

"You still aren't listening," Sisterkin says. "You need to listen."

"I've heard every single word you've said," I scream.

She shakes her head. "Not my words. I haven't the time to tell you all the things they want you to know." Sisterkin raises her hands and all the doors in the chamber fling wide open. I stand in awe of her power. "Follow me."

I look around at the remnants of chaos, the entire chamber littered with debris and ruined furniture, but all is completely silent. Each and every Senator stands in that odd-leaning way, jaws slack. Bella Roshaad, Tesaryn Wen. My mothers. Terror grips me hard, staring at the faces that either loved me or hated me, supported me or tried to have me killed. For the first time, they all look at me with the neutrality I craved so much, but now I'm wishing it could go back to bent brows and restrained resentment.

I have no choice than to comply with Sisterkin. Hand in hand, she and Seske walk briskly to the Uncommon Gardens. The sprawling vegetation looms over us, strange and scary and growing as if it's been holding a grudge.

"Listen," Sisterkin commands me.

I quiet my mind, maybe for the first time ever. I hear the splashing in the bog. The cry of the war lilies. The rustle of a coat. I look over and see the spores release from the silk cloak fungus. They are too far removed from their natural environment and will never reach the gall worms, their intended host. The worms will never be driven to burrow, and the wash hoglets will never feed on the infected carcass, and in turn will never perform whatever wonder they'd been doing for thousands of years. I see now that what we have created is only the facade of nature being restored. We didn't want to truly live in symbiosis with our Zenzee. We'd worked so hard to mend her broken bones but had left the control nodes in her brain. We'd reintroduced vital native species but kept them from performing their intended functions. We'd embraced peaceful living but had left the cannons we'd mounted through her hide to protect ourselves, just in case. And once we had the opportunity to become self-sufficient, we gave all that up to try to take control of more Zenzee.

"We are bound by our nature," I say to Sisterkin. "To control. To dominate."

"You don't have to be," she says.

"But we are explorers. Scientists. Bakers. Lovers."

"You can still be all those things. And more." Sisterkin steps up to me, the bulge on her chest pulsing once more. "In your desire to control and dominate, you have forced us to better ourselves. Now it is time to let us return the favor."

Let us return the favor.

I hear the voice, like an echo, but not. It is in the bugsong, in the rustle of leaves, in the creak of ancient bone. It is in my own breathing. It is a voice that's always been there, but we've refused to listen. I'm listening now, though. Humans and the Zenzee are no longer two separate things. We are all parts of a whole. Slowly, I take off my re-breather, not just for me, but for all of us.

The spores rupture from Sisterkin's chest. Air fills my lungs. I don't feel much different at first. Then my brain starts to grow heavy. Pressure builds, and a headache rages, feeling as though it's going to split me in two. Then it fades. And I feel normal. Better than normal.

Kallum looks at me, lets his re-breather drop from his face as well. Bakti follows suit.

"What is our Zenzee's name?" I ask Sisterkin.

She pronounces it for me, the sounds in her throat wet gurgle that goes on for nearly minute, like the chorus of a song. "But you can call her Annacklo."

THE ZENZEE GRAVEYARD FILLS UP HALF THE SKY, A BRIGHT beacon that outshines the stars.

We are only a few weeks from reaching it now, where Annacklo and the others will pay their respects to the dead. We've seen the scans. The graveyard is massive, ancient. Our scientists say it has already started to accumulate its own atmosphere, and speculate that if it grows massive enough, it could actually become a star. I wonder what the Zenzee will do when that happens—start another graveyard? I wonder how many of the stars out there started the exact same way.

Our pod joined with the other Zenzee pod a little over a month ago, and they've all been fondling each other since. Tentacles shoved here and there and all over the place. I suspect there are quite a few new pregnancies. I also suspect our Zenzee have inoculated the others with spores, too, just in case we humans try to branch out again, and I cannot blame them for taking the precaution.

Kallum and I have come here nearly every day over the past two years to talk. Our Zenzee's mouth has become our safe space, where we can leave the world behind and work things through. Kallum's mind was ready to take me back, nearly from the start, but his heart is taking a lot more convincing. Though if there's one thing Annacklo has taught me, it's how to listen.

We stay pressed back, near the opening of a throat. Neither of us dares to move out toward the tentacles, especially with rogue ones whipping inside every so often. Whenever I even think about venturing forward, another Zenzee's tentacles twists up with one of ours—just like one is doing right now.

Kallum and I watch, supple tentacle flesh pressing together. Rubbing. Undulating. I wonder what sound it would make if there were sound out there. Suddenly, the flesh all around us begins moving, and the aperture leading into space changes shape, narrowing from a near circle to an oval.

"Annacklo is smiling," Kallum says to me, his voice metallic and reedy over the re-breather's comm system.

"I wonder if she knows that Zenzee already," I say. "Are they reuniting, or is she excited to meet someone new?"

"Reuniting, definitely," Kallum says. "That kind of tentacle action says they're more than friends." We watch the tentacles slipping against each other. More have joined, and now we feel awkward, like we're voyeurs.

"Should we give them some privacy?" I ask. Kallum nods, and we venture back into a throat. We take off our re-breathers and peel out of our suits. We've had to cut our session short, but we'll go a little longer next time. Besides, we need to get back to work.

The spores have changed everything, and yet not much is different. They don't control us, just help us to listen. Sometimes a whisper here, suggesting that we increase the heart murmur population. A whisper there, bidding us to wait a few more days before we harvest our crops. Sometimes it's simply the feeling of euphoria when we watch the flowers of a bog melon bloom. But most of the time, our minds are our own. It was us who voted to bring an end to our harmful practices and silent genocides. It was us who chose to integrate the Klang fully into our world, to break down those barriers we'd erected—not the spores. All had become equal under Sisterkin's rule, just as she promised. And Seske's rule. They work well together. I never imagined they'd be able to heal the rift between them, but now they've become inseparable. Sometimes navigating the path to forgiveness seems insurmountable, but with enough time and patience and understanding, anything is possible.

Kallum taps me on the shoulder. I look up at him. He's got that look on his face when he wants to tell me something important. No, it's not that. I listen with my whole body. I hear the rasp of his breathing, catch the twinkle in his eyes, the slight pucker of his lips. His body leans into me, ever so slightly.

Next thing I know, his lips are upon mine. And it's as if I'm diving into my favorite watering hole again for the first time. It lasts only a few short seconds before Kallum pulls away, taking a piece of me back with him. I look at him dizzily. He smiles.

"Annacklo made me do it," he says with a mischievous grin. It is the same excuse that our son Kenzah gives us whenever he breaks a plate or gets caught shoving cheese cubes up his nose.

"Annacklo knows best," I say. We twine our fingers together. Thousands of possible futures race through my mind, but they all start right here.

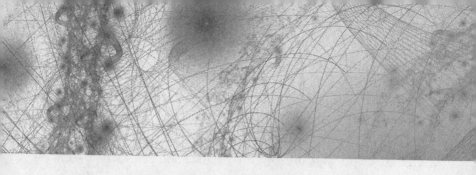

Acknowledgments

Phew.

2020.

If there were ever a year that drained my creativity, this was it. And yet, with a little (a lot of) help from my friends, I was able to pull through and finish this story. I am thankful for each and every one of my quarantine buddies, especially this bunch:

Myndi—BFF extraordinaire, sharpest wit and warmest heart—So thankful for our email chains that would probably reach the moon.

Edria—Captivating, innovating, fast talker and gentle soul—You built me back up, brick by brick, and helped me find my joy.

Elle—My partner in crime fighting and collector of misfortunate typos—our cowriting sessions kept me in stitches and (mostly) on deadline.

Ehigbor & Des—My Friday Nite Crew and bonnet pals—Our joy has been EARNED, and I'm so excited to see the greatness you'll unleash into this world.

Yuki—Positive energy personified, thoughtful and giving—Our backyard yoga brought me balance and calm when both were in short supply.

Daniel—Blast from the past and more awesome than humanly possible—We built a few chapters together, and they were the exact ones I needed.

Ronnie—Dependable, chill, and the queen of sidestepping drama—I miss our coffee shop meetups terribly, but I'm happy we took them virtual.

Matthew—Funniest guy I know and also the nicest—Glad we finally get to see what happens when two of the weirdest minds in Austin meet.

Bad Roll Models—T.R.O.Y., Bitch Witch, Katya, and our ridiculously wonderful G.M. Oh, and Mollusk Man? Mollusk Master?—Thanks for hopping off this world with me and into one where the villains are a lot less scary.

Yase—Friendship forged in the dot com days, brilliant mind and mad baking skills—Thanks for the amazing tentacle cake and backyard chat.

Andrea—Undisputed best giggle in the galaxy, closest thing I have to a sister—The years and miles melt away whenever we chat.

Richard—Last, but in no way, shape, or form, least, wise beyond his years and always caught up in the best kind of mischief—Your voice in my ear smooths out the bumpiest of bumps.

We all leaned on one another, and I'm so grateful for the light you've all brought into my life, filling my cup, and allowing me the privilege to fill yours a bit too.

About the Author

Nicky Drayden is a systems analyst living in Austin, Texas, and when she's not debugging code, she's detangling plotlines and mixing metaphors. Her award-winning debut novel, *The Prey of Gods*, is set in a futuristic South Africa brimming with demigods, robots, and hallucinogenic high jinks. Drayden's sophomore novel, *Temper*, is touted as an exciting blend of Afrofuturism and New Weird. Her travels to South Africa as a college student influenced both of these works, and she enjoys blurring the lines between mythology, science fiction, fantasy, horror, and dark humor. See more of her work at nickydrayden.com or catch her on Twitter at @nickydrayden.